Rock nodded, voice just a little gruff. "You add coffee to the mix and this'll be a perfect morning."

"All I have to do is push the on button."

Rock laughed. "Oh, you've pushed it, Alex. You've pushed it hard."

"Good to hear it. You've done a fair amount of pushing yourself." He stole one more kiss and then got up. "Come on, you head for the shower, I'll start the coffee and join you."

"Sounds like a plan."

Rock got up, apparently unconcerned at wandering through his apartment naked. No wonder, the man was well built, not an ounce of fat anywhere, nothing but skin and muscles.

"Watch out for the hot water nozzle. I had to jerry rig it closed. Oh! And the toilet flushes with the chain on the side, not the handle. I had to rig that up too."

Rock chuckled. "You're quite the rigger, aren't you? Guess those hands are good at more than just making a man come."

"Hey, emergency triage's is my specialty. I just rig stuff up until the pros show." He grinned and watched that hard ass disappear into the bathroom. He sat for a second, thinking and blinking and shaking his head, before going to start the Mr. Coffee.

Yep. Utterly, completely, and unequivocally fucked.

No question about it.

"Get that sweet ass in here, Rigger, and show me how the fuck to turn the hot water on!"

TOP SHELF
Don't Ask, Don't Tell
An imprint of Torquere Press Publishers
PO Box 2545
Round Rock, TX78680
Copyright 2005 Sean Michael
Cover illustration by Alessia Brio
Published with permission
ISBN: 1-933389-43-5
www.torquerepress.com

First Torquere Press Printing: December 2005
Second Torquere Press Printing: June 2008
Printed in the USA

The Jarheads Series
by Sean Michael

Don't Ask, Don't Tell

Personal Leave

Three Day Passes

Tempering

Out of the Closet

On the Sand

Don't Ask, Don't Tell

Don't Ask, Don't Tell
by Sean Michael

romance for the rest of us
www.torquerepress.com

Don't Ask, Don't Tell

CHAPTER ONE

Man, there was nothing like looking hot as fuck. Tight jeans, white t-shirt, hat, shiny buckle -- Alex had the whole fucking package and he knew it. He be-bopped around the pool table, beating Harrison easily -- okay, that would be more impressive if the dickhead hadn't been completely stoned and exhausted from three nights of practicals, but a win was a win.

"Go sleep it off, dork. Table's all mine now."

"That's a matter of opinion," said a low, gravelly voice and Alex turned to find the Jarhead who'd been scoping him out since he got there standing right behind him. Good lord and butter the man's eyes were *blue*.

Oh, hello. "You wantin' to play?"

Come on. Say yes. Alex hadn't had a decent fuck in *days* what with Mickey changing rotations.

He was given a once over, the look long and slow,

almost a caress in and of itself. "I am."

"Well, well. Cowboy up, mister. Loser buys the next round."

Those eyes held his now. "I don't lose."

"No?" Oh, man. He was either going to get killed or fucked. "There's a first time for everything, Blue Eyes."

Oh, that got him a laugh and the man had a smile to go with those eyes. "I have heard that said. Been a long time since I've seen a first time."

He clucked and winked. "Well then, let's give you a whirl, shall we?"

Alex racked up, bent down over the table and offered Mr. Tall, Hot and Manly a look-see. It might have been his imagination, but he swore he heard a purr come rumbling from that amazing chest.

"You want to break?" He stood, stepped away, feeling fine.

"Sure." One of those hips nudged his as Blue Eyes went by him and the ass that bent over the table as the man took his shot? Fine. Damned fine. Alex leaned back against the wall, admiring, just looking his fill. Blue Eyes broke and sunk all but two of the stripes in short order. Stepping back, that amazing smile was flashed on him again. "You're solids."

Well, fuck him raw... "Nice shot."

Those eyes checked him out again. "I got lucky."

"Mmm... Hopefully we both did."

That earned him that grin again. "I imagine we might have at that."

Oh, fucking A. Fucking -- or at least flirting, which was the fun part of fucking -- and not ass kicking. Go him. He pegged off a good couple shots, sinking three before he missed.

Blue Eyes finished the game on his next turn, putting the eight ball in the corner right pocket before turning to smile at him. "You owe me a beer."

"That I do, Blue Eyes. Rack 'em up and decide what we're playing for next."

Tall, dark and studly did as he was told, leaning over the pool table as he racked up the balls. Damn. That really was a fine ass, thigh muscles just strong as anything beneath it.

When Blue Eyes was done, Alex was given another once over. "I want a piece of that."

Oh, he did enjoy a man who knew what he wanted. His cock jerked, filling right up like it was trying to get the man's attention. "Works for me. I'll break, uh... You got a name?"

Oh, that grin widened, those blue eyes finding the bulge in his jeans fascinating. "They call me Rock. Short for the Rocketman"

"Oh, they do, do they?" He hooted, just loving it. "Well, I hope you've earned the name."

"You know it." Rock flexed and then chuckled and winked. "I'm a gunnery sergeant, but it's a multipurpose name, I assure you."

"I'm Alex. Alex Roberts." He let his look just linger on the man's chest, admiring. "Pleased."

Rock nodded. "You will be."

"Oh, strong and confident. I like that." He chuckled, turned and shot, sinking two. Not that he wiggled his ass in a victory dance, because that would just be wrong and possibly distracting to the marine. He thought he heard that purr again. He couldn't be sure now, but when he looked back, Rock was definitely focused on his ass.

"I'm stripes." He took two more shots before he gave it up, the last shot putting him damn near against that fine fucking body.

Heat and hardness pressed up against his ass as that big body leaned over him, big hands adjusting his slightly on the cue. "Try it again like that."

He arched, pushing back in a definite offer. "Like this?"

"Yeah, Alex. Just like that." That voice dragged over the back of his neck. "Just like that."

Rock backed off slowly.

Oh, fuck him raw. He took his shot, actually sinking the fucking ball. "You're good luck, Blue Eyes."

"You're pretty lucky yourself."

"You at Lackland or Fort Sam Houston?" He took his shot, stepping back as he went wide.

"Sam H. for special training. I'm stationed up in North Carolina." Rock took his shots, sinking several before missing. A Yankee by the sound of him, but with a body like that, Alex could forgive the man.

"Not going to get to play with us cowboys long, huh? It's a shame."

One hip leaned against the pool table, those blue eyes watching him. "I'm beginning to think it might be."

"Well, I'll just have to be right neighborly and make sure you remember it fondly."

Rock chuckled. "Sounds good to me, Alex."

"I have an apartment. Cold beer." Why waste time? He wanted himself a piece of that.

"Excellent. I've got over twelve hours before I have to report for duty." Rock straightened, and put his cue on the table. He was obviously done playing, too.

"I'm parked outside." Alex finished his beer, just fucking vibrating. Nothing like knowing you looked good, unless it was knowing somebody else thought you did, too.

Rock watched Alex while the man drove. The kid was a looker. Not too bad of a pool player either. Tight little ass. Rock smiled and adjusted himself, spreading his legs to accommodate his hard on. He'd enjoyed that tight ass snuggled up against him while they were playing pool, was looking forward to repeating the maneuver without the clothes or the other patrons.

All in all it was shaping up to be the best fucking Valentine's Day he'd had since high school.

If the kid sucked and fucked half as good as he played pool, it would be the best fucking Valentine's Day ever.

The country music was playing, not blaring, but Alex was humming along. Why the kid was in a joint like Sinatra's and not at some honky-tonk was beyond him. There was a stethoscope hanging from the rear-view mirror, along with an eagle feather and a crocheted Christmas tree. The whole cab smelled of Stetson cologne and antiseptic and something sweet and warm.

Alex looked over, grinned. "Sorry about the truck. She's a little ole thing and not used to hauling around big ole boys. We'll be at the apartment soon."

"Gets you from A to B, right?"

A long, thin hand patted the dashboard. "Solid little honey. Dropped a new transmission in her before I brought her down and her wiring's a little twitchy, but she's a good truck."

Nice hands, very tactile. This was gonna be fun. Alex didn't bounce, didn't chatter, just hummed along and drove, turning into a huge apartment complex and parking toward the back. "I'm on the third floor. 333 -- three blocks over from the beast." He got a wink and that long, tall drink of water hopped out of the truck. "There's beer in the fridge."

He chuckled and uncurled from the front seat, following that fine ass as Alex led the way.

"Beer sounds good." Alex sounded better, but Rock was a patient man and didn't have to be anywhere before fourteen-hundred hours tomorrow.

The tight little ass moved up those stairs, bobbing and swaying and fuck if the temptation wasn't to just reach out and squeeze. He was a big boy though, knew a man had to wait for a little privacy -- especially in a place like Texas. He started making plans though. They cleared the door and Alex wouldn't know what hit him.

"Lord have mercy, when my fucking lease is up I'm finding a house. With a yard and no goddamned stairs. God had meant us to climb stairs he wouldn't have invented elevators." The grumbling was light and easy, not even a hint of real upset or breathlessness in it.

Rock chuckled. "I don't think it was God that invented elevators."

The laugh he got in return was pure fucking sex, warm and wet and wicked. Fuck, if they didn't get in the kid's apartment soon he was going to throw caution to the winds and take Alex right up against the wall.

"Here we are. Apartment sweet apartment." The door swung open and Rock was let into a perfectly clean, straight, sterile little room.

"Nice." He closed the door and pulled Alex around by his arm, pushing him up against the door and pressing him in place with his own body. "Not as nice as you."

"You like what you see, Blue Eyes?" Thin hips rubbed against him, straightforward and hungry.

"Fuck, yes. Could barely keep my hands off that sweet ass all the way up those fucking stairs of yours."

"Okay, enough small talk. Want to kiss you." Alex's eyes were fucking grey -- really grey.

He rubbed his hips against Alex's, keeping his head back, lips just out of reach. "You do, do you?"

"Yep." Alex's eyes widened. "Oh, do you not kiss on the first date? 'Cause I can get that."

Rock chuckled. "I'll kiss you, Alex. Just wanted to

make sure you really wanted it."

Alex gave him another one of those chuckles, one he could feel in his balls. "Oh, kissing's one of those things that gets me off. Kissing, sucking, fucking -- I like to play, Rock."

"You sound like my kind of man, Alex." He pushed his hips again, rubbing his hard as nails prick along Alex's, growling slightly at the way their jeans got in the way.

"Mm... let's find out." Alex's hand cupped the back of his head and his mouth was taken in a slow, deep, bone-melting fucking kiss like nothing he'd ever felt.

He braced himself, hands against the wall, body against Alex's as his knees almost gave way under the force of that kiss. How could a kid like Alex kiss like this?

The fucking kiss went on and on, never fucking easing up, never letting go. Rock barely noticed the kid's hands working his belt buckle open and freeing his cock. He couldn't miss that warm hand with the clever fingers wrapping around his prick though. Pleasure shot through him, climbing up his spine and settling in the base of his skull. Between the kiss and those hands he was ready to go off like a Fourth of July rocket.

That tongue flicked and played, driving him higher and higher, then disappeared. "You want to come now or wait, Blue Eyes?"

The kid's eyes were flashing, voice hoarse and fucking *hungry*.

"Fuck 'or', kid -- I'll take both."

"Fucking A." Then those lips were sinking, even as the crinkle of a rubber sounded, latex surrounding his dick. Tight, incredible heat surrounded him as Alex took him down to the root in one, long swallow, the blond curls bobbing, skinny back tight against the wall.

Holy fucking Christ!

He started to fuck that sweet mouth, couldn't have stopped himself if he'd wanted to and he didn't fucking want to. Hands braced against the wall, he let the kid have him and damned if Alex didn't just take it all and ask for more.

Rock came with a shout. The fucking kid kept sucking, pulling slow and easy, moaning around his prick. He wasn't getting soft -- not with that sweet mouth working him like that. He let his hands drop to the kid's head, fingers moving through Alex's hair.

"Suck like a dream."

The happy sound vibrated through his cock, ending in his balls, kid's nose tickling in his pubes. Shit, he was going to come again and they'd barely cleared the door. Thing was, Alex's mouth wasn't fucking stopping, was just working and licking and sucking and playing his cock like there was nothing Alex'd rather do.

"Kid... you don't have to..." He'd been with a guy or two who were like that -- felt they had to suck you, had to make sure you got off before they'd even look to relieving themselves.

He hadn't pegged Alex as insecure like that, but you never knew.

Bright eyes, hot and fucking happy, shone up at him and Alex's hands cupped his balls. Then those lips slipped away. "You want me to stop?"

He shook his head, hand sliding over one of the smooth cheeks. Fuck, those eyes were grey, a man could get lost inside them. "I just don't want you to think you've got to is all."

"Told you -- like to suck. Your cock... shit, it's a piece of work."

He chuckled. "You like what you see, kid? Like the taste?"

"Hate fucking rubbers, don't tease." The kid rubbed

that long thin nose in his pubes, breathing deep. "Smell fucking fabulous and I'm not a kid, Blue Eyes. I reckon I'm older than I look."

He slid his hand along one of those pretty cheeks again. "Sorry, Alex, you're making me feel so good I forgot about the condom..."

Alex purred, humming into his crotch, lips moving open and hungry over his hips. "Fuck, Blue Eyes..." Heat flicked along his balls and then that mouth was sliding hot up his shaft. "I suck you off twice, you think you'll be able to get it up again?"

"Hell, yes, Alex. I'm a marine."

"I'll hold you to that." Cool hands ran up his stomach as that blond head went down and the world fucking stopped spinning.

Fucking shit.

He closed his eyes and dropped his head back, hips moving again. How had this kid, this sweet Texas boy, made him so fucking hard and needy again so quickly?

Alex took his cock, took him so deep that he fucking slid into that tight throat, *into* Alex. Fuck. Oh, Christ. Oh...

He came again, roaring with the strength of his orgasm.

He reached blindly for Alex's face, stroking through the blond curls and along the sucked in cheeks. Alex gentled his mouth, kept the heat and soft, sweet pressure on Rock's cock until the aftershocks faded, then slipped away.

"Fuck." He slid his hand beneath Alex's arms and tugged him up, bringing their mouths together. Kid tasted of the rubber mostly, but also something sweet and needy.

"Where's the bed?" he asked, hand sliding down over the close fitting jeans to cup Alex's hard prick through tight as hell denim.

"Down the hall. Want you." Hot and shuddering, Alex pushed into his hand, mouth nipping and sliding over his, grey eyes starving.

"You want this?" he asked, hand stroking hard. "Or you want me to fuck this sweet ass?" He slid his free hand around, cupping the tight butt, squeezing.

"Oh, fuck. Yes. Jesus. Bed, Rock. Please."

"You got it, Alex." He grabbed the kid's hand and dragged him down the hall. The first door was the toilet, the second yielded a bed.

Alex had his shirt off in a flash, mouth sliding over his shoulders. "Taste good. Fucking good."

"Yeah?" He returned the favor, pulling off Alex's shirt, sniffing the soft skin. "You smell good. I've been wanting more since the bar. I swear I could smell you underneath the smoke and the beer and the cologne."

Alex stretched, rubbing against him, popping open the painted-on jeans, mouth traveling over his neck. "Oh, man. You're making me hard enough to pound nails, Blue Eyes."

"Funny, I didn't see any construction going on."

There it was again, that 'oh, fuck me now' laugh, husky and happy and easy-going as hell. "I'm hoping there'll be some hammering going on soon."

"You got another condom and something slippery, cowboy?"

"Damned straight." Alex nodded toward the headboard on the bed. "Left hand drawer. Both in there."

"Straight?" Rock asked, raising an eyebrow. He gave the kid a grin and sauntered over to the drawer in question. He tossed the tube and several of the condoms onto the bed, stripping out of his jeans and skivvies and boots.

"Jesus, you're a good-looking man, Blue Eyes." Alex smiled and wriggled out of his jeans and boots, walking across the room to close the window, giving him a view of that sweet, high ass.

"That just might be the pot calling the kettle black, Alex."

He got a hold of the kid's arm and tugged him back to the bed, pushing him down and following. Long, skinny arms and legs wrapped around him, mouth immediately searching for him, eyes bright and laughing. Fuck, but Alex made him feel good, made him fucking feel amazing.

Alex's tongue pressed deep, eager cock painting his stomach with lines of pre-come, little sounds pressed deep in his mouth.

He found the lube with one hand and got some on his fingers to get Alex ready -- he wanted the kid to come on his cock. The kid was focused, needy, and fucking enjoying himself, throwing himself into the kisses and touches full-force. Rock couldn't remember the last time he'd been with anyone who enjoyed fucking this much. He pushed a finger against Alex, the kid's hole pulling him right in.

"Oh... Good..." His bottom lip was tested by careful teeth, the kid moving to ride his finger immediately.

"Fuck, yes." He groaned as that slick, grasping hole moved on his finger, cock throbbing.

Alex nodded, chuckling and murmuring with a happy sound. "Knew... knew you'd have great fucking hands when I saw them work the cue."

"Doesn't hurt that you're sex on a stick, Alex."

Rock pushed a second finger in with the first, Alex was tight, but hungry and his second finger was pulled in as eagerly as the first. The sounds got a little lower, Alex's feet falling to the bed, thighs parting for him. He fucked Alex with his fingers, mouth exploring along Alex's jaw and neck, tasting the fine skin.

His lips hit a spot on the kid's neck that made Alex jerk and cry out, the sound wild and desperate. "Oh, shit! Fuck!"

Latching his mouth around that spot, he pulled his fingers out of Alex's eager body and made quick work of the condom. He groaned around the skin in his mouth as his cock started to push into that tight as fuck heat. The hungry little hole pulled at him, thin hips moving in pulsating waves. There was a hand on his neck, another on his ass and encouragements moaned in a sweet as fuck southern drawl.

He pushed all the way in, moaning as his hips hit that fucking hot ass. He was a big guy, with a big, hard cock, so he waited to move, let Alex get used to his girth.

Hands tugged his head up, let him see those dancing eyes. "Oh, shit, you feel so fucking good, Blue Eyes. No more teasing. Want you to fuck me and make me come on that fabulous fucking cock." Then the kid leaned up and covered his mouth in a hard kiss.

Oh, fuck yeah.

He started out with long, slow thrusts. He could feel fucking everything.

The kid was doing anything but just sitting back and getting fucked. Rock's mouth was tasted, each thrust met, hands sliding over his shoulders and back. He shifted, bringing Alex's legs up over his arms and pushed in harder.

"Oh! Oh, fuck yes!" That thin body arched beneath him, ass grinding, riding his cock.

That's what he'd been waiting for and he started to pound in, hands wrapping around Alex's shoulders and letting the kid have everything he had. Alex took it all, took everything with a series of happy, soft cries. He thrust until he could feel his balls tighten and then he slipped a hand between them, wrapping it around Alex's cock. Alex shot at the first touch to his cock, jerking and shuddering, body clenching tight as he rode the orgasm. Those hot, silky muscles milked his cock, pulling his own climax from him and he shot into the condom.

They slumped onto the bed, Alex offering him a sloppy, sated kiss. "Good. Damn, Blue Eyes. You do a body good."

"Not so bad yourself, Alex Roberts." Rock settled next to the kid, not wanting to crush him. "You got a problem with me crashing here?"

Alex propped his head on his hand. "Well, that depends on two things. One, are you allergic to dogs and two, can we fuck again in the morning after breakfast?"

He frowned. "I didn't see a mutt. And you owe me a morning blow job, but I think fucking after breakfast would also be a go."

"He's crated on the balcony. He's a good puppy, but he likes to be outside come morning." Alex licked at the corner of his mouth. "What time do marines like their morning blow-jobs, Blue Eyes?"

"Mm..." He chased that tongue down, pulling it into his mouth to suck on. "Well I don't have to be back until fourteen hundred..."

"Mm... cool. I don't have to be at the hospital until three."

"Great. We can sleep in and then fuck the morning away."

Alex nodded. "Yeah. 'Night, Blue Eyes. Sweet dreams."

He chuckled and pulled Alex close, the kid's body warm against him. He thought maybe tonight they would be sweet.

By 8:30, Alex had taken Grimm for a walk, headed down to the pool to swim some laps, showered, sucked down a pot of coffee, read the paper, picked up the apartment, run a load of laundry down, and made cinnamon rolls.

He'd been quiet -- not hard. Christ, Bobby and Sissy both slept 'til noon and Momma wasn't exactly a morning person. He and Daddy'd crept around a sleeping...

Well, he doubted Daddy ever thought about creeping around something as fine as that marine on his bed.

Christ.

He'd actually been *sore* this morning. Stretched. Like he could still feel that cock inside him, fucking him.

Alex groaned, chuckling as he realized he was stroking his cock, humping his hand, slow and easy. Okay, 8:36 was close to eight forty-five which way damned near nine. Blowjob time. He shucked off his shorts, sliding under the sheets, mouth heading for those heavy balls. He licked and lapped Rock's nuts, fingers working the rubber open. His blue-eyed lover rumbled, legs shifting restlessly.

"Mmm..." He nuzzled, breathing deep on the rich male scent, rubbing his cheek against the soft inner thigh. Alex eased the condom down over Rock's morning wood, pumping slow and easy, to keep it full and ready for him.

God, he wanted a taste. The hospital lab could get results back in six days. Alex wondered if Rock would still be around, still be interested, next week.

"Fuck..." Rock's voice was sleepy. "Shit. Alex?"

"Yeah, Rock. Just your wake up call. Feeling good?"

"Fuck, yes. If all mornings started this way they'd have a hell of a lot more to recommend them." Rock groaned a little, hips pushing up into his hand.

Sean Michael

"No shit." He crawled up, sliding his lips over the thick, hot prick, pulling slow and easy. Learning where the little hot spots were, finding what made Rock shiver and shift in the sheets.

"Goddamned, your mouth is...fuck."

That made him hum, pull a bit harder. He loved giving head -- didn't know why, didn't care -- but he did. Loved the intimacy and the flavors and the feeling of having someone so close.

Rock's legs parted, opening to cradle him, and one of those big hands slid into his hair, stroking. He settled in, eyes closed, mouth working, hands stroking over fucking miles of muscles. A barely audible rumble vibrated Rock's belly. He chuckled, working that cock like the world's biggest Popsicle, searching for a louder sound.

"Oh, fuck, yeah." Rock's words were sort of moaned, the big guy's hips starting to push up whenever he pulled away.

Oh, yeah. That was so good. He cupped the heavy balls in his hands, rolling them gently. His tongue licked at the tip, pushing at the slit, instinctively looking for Rock's flavor.

"Fuck!" Rock jerked up, shoving deep.

He relaxed, letting Rock push deep, letting that hot, fucking cock in. Rock moaned, long and loud, both hands sliding over his head, holding him down. Alex hummed, sucking hard, head rubbing against those strong, warm hands. Oh, fuck. So goddamned good.

"Shit. Can't... shit." With that Rock started to push up, fucking his mouth.

He hummed louder, letting Rock know how good it was, how fucking hot, hands cupping Rock's hard ass. Rock made another noise, something like a roar or a loud purr and pushed up harder, jerking out of control and then shooting, filling the condom in long pulses.

21

Alex whimpered softly, wanting to taste so bad. He gentled his suction, bringing the marine down, cock rocking against the sheets. Those big hands slid through his hair and partway down his back, satisfied rumbles coming from the marine in his bed. He rubbed his cheek against Rock's hip, sucking slow and easy, in time with the touches to his hair.

"Shit, kid, you're going to keep me hard."

He chuckled, lifting his head to nuzzle Rock's belly, licking the salty skin as he disposed quickly of the condom. "You said fucking was on the plan. I figured I'd help out."

Rock rumbled. "You want a hand down there first?"

"Wouldn't say no at all, Blue Eyes." He started working his way up Rock's torso, moaning as his cock slid up that hard, hot leg.

One of Rock's big hands wrapped around his prick, pulling slowly. "That's a nice piece of meat you've got."

"Mm... gets me where I need to go." He grinned as Rock chuckled, nibbling along the strong shoulders, hips pushing into that hand.

"Oh, you're something all right." Rock squeezed around his cock, pumping harder.

"Oh, yeah. That's fucking sweet." He started licking the strong jaw, toes curling.

"You like it like that? You want it harder or softer or slower or faster, you just say so -- I can do this all day long if you want."

"Sounds perfect." Rock's palm grazed the head of his cock just so and he jerked, gasping against the column of skin. "Fuck!"

"Oh, you like *that*." Rock did it again, letting his palm slide more firmly along the top of Alex's cock.

"Oh, shit. Yeah. Yeah." He dipped his head, panting

against Rock's shoulder. "Again?"

Rock obliged and set up a new rhythm, pull and slide and push and pull and slide, over and over again, thumb grazing across his slit at random intervals. He was lost, humping against that hand, shudders rocking him hard and he was so fucking close. So...

"Close. Gonna. Oh, fuck..."

Rock's mouth covered his, tongue pushing in, taking the pleasure inside him right from the source. He came hard, crying out into Rock's lips, body shuddering. God, he loved sex. Just fucking loved it.

Rock kissed him long and hard and then pulled back. Rock offered a come-covered hand to him. "You gonna lick it off me?"

He groaned, nodding and grabbing the marine's thick as fuck wrist. Licking was his specialty. And if this didn't fill that fucking cock again? Nothing would. He started licking around the wrist, nipping at the nerves hidden there, jostling the veins just under the surface. Then the thumb, sucking it with a soft groan, before beginning to explore the wide, flat palm.

"Holy fucking shit." Rock's voice was almost a growl and without warning Rock rolled him to his back, Rock following him, pinning him beneath the marine's weight.

He arched into the sweet, fucking heat, sucking his spunk off Rock's thick, wide fingers. Rock shifted, humping against him slowly, blue eyes holding his as he sucked. Then a slick, wide finger nudged against his hole. He rode the sensations, humming around the fingers in his mouth, ass sliding on the finger penetrating it. Yeah. Fuck, yeah.

"You're a fucking jack-rabbit, kid. All long legs and fucking."

He chuckled, nipped the pad of Rock's index finger. "You gonna come hunt me, Blue Eyes?"

"Got my gun right here," Rock told him, thick cock nudging at his ass.

"Come get me then, I'm waitin'." He arched and rocked, looking for the burn of penetration, looking for that feeling again.

Rock took a moment to put on the condom and then pushed in, slow and easy.

"Oh, fuck, that's sweet." The burn wasn't as strong as last night, but deeper, an ache moving all the way through him.

"Uh-huh." Rock held his face in place and slowly brought their mouths together, tongue invading the same as that big, hard cock.

He relaxed, moaning softly as Rock filled him up. Those eyes were stunning -- so fucking blue and clear and bright. Not in a fucked up, eyes like jewels or ponds or any of that shit way, either. They were just fucking gorgeous and sexy and made him incredibly fucking hot.

"Fuck, you're tight and hot -- and that mouth. What a sexy motherfucker you are, Alex." With that Rock began to move, in and out in long, slow glides, slick flesh invading him over and over again.

Sweet Christ, that felt fucking amazing. Hot. Right. Sexy as anything. He rocked, moving right with it, feeling it. Needing it right *there*. Slow and steady and deep, Rock took him, pushing him closer and closer to the moon. They didn't talk, didn't scream or cry out or anything. Just fucked.

And fucked.

And fucked.

God in heaven, this man was amazing.

Those blue eyes watched him, those big hands held him, and that fat prick kept moving into him like Rock was never ever going to stop.

"Blue..." He arched and sobbed. "Good. So good."

"Yeah. Fucking out of this goddamned world."

Rock bit his bottom lip and then soothed it, sliding that hot, wet tongue over his skin. He nodded, leaning up and offering his mouth for another kiss. Rock took his mouth, fucked it like he owned it, hips moving faster, hips driving that thick cock deeper into him. He was whimpering, head spinning, jerking into each thrust, needing.

"Come for me, kid. I want to feel you coming on my cock."

"Not a kid." He grinned and then groaned as Rock pushed in deep and hard, sending him over the edge.

"Oh, yeah, fuck -- that's good, Alex. Good." Rock held still as his body convulsed and then the big guy was moving again, pounding into him for a few more minutes, pulling sweet shudders and aftershocks from him.

He held on with all he was, blinking and gasping and just... fuck, just holding on tight.

Finally Rock's face changed, the blue eyes going soft, unfocussed and Rock came with a quiet moan.

Alex groaned and licked the pleasure off those open lips, head fucking spinning. "Fuck. That was... fuck."

"Yeah."

Rock leaned down and kissed him, long and slow like there wasn't anything in the entire world to do but that. He could so handle that.

Pulling out, Rock slid over beside him, arms wrapping around him and pulling him along. The kiss just kept going on. Alex settled in, completely focused on exploring Rock's mouth. Rock's teeth were smooth, one just a little tilted in the bottom row. His bottom lip was full and the top was bristly and tickly. One of Rock's hands settled on his hip, heavy and hot.

He hoped Rock was comfortable, because he wasn't going anywhere, wasn't fucking moving until he was done with this fabulous fucking kiss. Rock's tongue explored his mouth, pushed and tasted, but didn't stop him from pushing and tasting back. His leg slid between Rock's, humming softly and sucking Rock's bottom lip.

Rock chuckled. "You're expecting a lot from me, Alex. Good thing I always deliver."

"Expecting?" He blinked up, frowning.

Rock squeezed his leg. "Don't worry, kid, I'm not as old as all that -- I'll get it back up again."

It took him a second and then he chuckled. "Oh, I'm not in a hurry. I was enjoying your mouth."

Rock gave him this smile, sorta surprised and incredulous and fucking pleased all at once. "Well then don't let me hold you back."

"That's what I was hoping to hear, Blue Eyes." He settled back, licking Rock's lips with a hum. Warm. Male. Not sweet, but good. Strong.

Rock let him take as long as he wanted, those blue eyes watching him, lips and tongue returning the favor, touching and sliding and exploring.

Eventually he got hard again, but it wasn't desperate and he was happy and relaxed. "Tell me, Marine, what're you doing in Texas?" He nipped that bottom lip again. "Besides fucking East Texas nurses, that is."

Rock chuckled, the sound deep and a little rough. "I told you -- guess I fucked it out of you." Rock looked pleased with himself. "Would you believe special maneuvers?"

He laughed, tickled all through. "You know? I think I can believe that, Blue. I do believe I can."

"Good." Rock's hands met in the small of his back, the big guy pulling him closer.

"Mm..." He wrapped his arms around that thick neck and drew that smiling face down for another kiss.

Rock gave it to him willingly, making it last, one big

hand still in the small of his back, the other holding onto his ass. He rocked slow and easy, humming into Rock's mouth, rubbing against the hot skin of Rock's belly. Against the strength of that hand. Rock rumbled, the sound starting in that sweet, ridged belly.

Oh... That felt good, made his motions a little more definite, a little more intense. Alex moaned -- Rock was like a playground, a sweet, hard, amazing fucking playground. More rumbles sounded, Rock's hands pulling him in now and one leg slid forward, heel wrapping behind his knees. He didn't know how long they shared the long, lazy touches, the kisses, the moans. He didn't fucking care.

Oh, he was *so* fucked.

Rock shifted him, moving him down a little, over a little, so that their cocks slid together.

He shivered, then chuckled at himself. When Rock arched an eyebrow, he grinned. "Feels fucking good. Warm."

"You one of those types that's cold all the time?"

"Not so long as it's seventy degrees." Alex grinned. "If God had intended cowboys to be cold, he wouldn't have put so many of us in the South."

Rock chuckled and pulled him closer, jostling their cocks and then rubbing them together.

"Mm..." He leaned in, licking at Rock's nipple, grinning as it peaked, their cocks sliding together, finding a rhythm.

"Fuck... your mouth."

"Yeah. Dying to taste your cock. Hate the latex." He fastened his lips around Rock's nipple, tugging.

Rock made a little noise, hand coming up from his back to hold his head in place. "Can't. You gotta play safe, kid."

"You don't have to tell me, Blue. I did my time in

the Infectious Diseases ward." He pulled harder, fingers finding the other nipple and teasing it to hardness.

Rock moaned for him, hand on his ass pulling him tighter into that hard body. His hips thrust harder, his free hand pushing between them to tease along their shafts.

"Oh yeah. Got good hands, too, kid."

Rock's prick was hot, thick, amazing. He rubbed along the ridge of the head, tickling the nerves, making that prick jump. Rock growled, the sound fucking hot. He let his thumb stroke the wet slit, teeth teasing a hard nipple, wanting that sound again.

Rock gave it to him, adding words this time. "You're not careful, you're going to make this old man shoot again, Alex."

"If I'm really careful, I'll blow your fucking mind, Blue." He tilted his head back, looking for a kiss.

Rock chuckled and murmured, "you can try," into his mouth.

He grinned, pushing into the kiss, tongue sliding into Rock's mouth. There was no trying about it, he was going to make this man fly. Without warning, Rock rolled him onto his back, that big, hard body following, pushing him into the mattress as Rock started to thrust against him. He cried out, kissing hard and deep, hand wrapping around Rock head, the other trapped against their cocks.

Rock was growling again, the sound hot and needy, wanting. Those hips drove their cocks together in a hard, fast rhythm. He drank every fucking sound down, wanting more of them. Fuck, this man was sex personified, strength and heat and hardness and those goddamned *eyes*.

Rock just kept moving against him, sliding their pricks together, sexy fucking growls and groans coming more and more frequently. He got his palm sliding over the head of Rock's cock, his own bumping the heel of his hand.

"Fuck!" Rock pulled out of the kiss, blue eyes gazing down at him, glazed over, but looking impressed at the same time.

"Yeah. What do you want, Blue?" He was still moving, rocking, gasping.

Rock nodded. "This is good. Fuck! Real good."

"Yes. Fuck, yes." He leaned up, licked the line of Rock's jaw. "Fucking amazing."

Rock nodded, tilting his head, giving him more skin to work on. He nibbled and licked on Rock's neck, sucking gently on pulse points and Adam's apple, careful not to leave a mark. He'd fucked military before -- marks above the collar were a definite no-no.

A shudder moved through the big body and Rock pressed harder against him, fucking flattening him against the mattress. He pushed back the best he could, thighs spread, hips jerking convulsively. Rock groaned, the sound vibrating in the man's throat against his lips. "Gonna come, kid."

"Yeah. Yeah. Gonna. Fuck!"

Their mouths came together hard, teeth clicking as heat and come and screams passed between them in close waves.

Rock rested their foreheads together, panting lightly, hips still jerking now and then, matching the shudders that rippled through that big body. "Good. Fucking good."

"Fuck, yeah."

Rock chuckled. "My CO's gonna wonder what I was up to, coming back off twenty-four hours exhausted."

Alex grinned. "Let's take a shower and I'll feed you. You're lucky, we can grab a quick nap before I take you wherever you need to go."

Rock grinned and gave him a wink. "No, if I'm lucky we won't be napping."

He laughed, warm and sated all through. "I do like how you think, Blue. Yes, sir, I do."

Rock nodded, voice just a little gruff. "You add coffee to the mix and this'll be a perfect morning."

"All I have to do is push the on button."

Rock laughed. "Oh, you've pushed it, Alex. You've pushed it hard."

"Good to hear it. You've done a fair amount of pushing yourself." He stole one more kiss and then got up. "Come on, you head for the shower, I'll start the coffee and join you."

"Sounds like a plan."

Rock got up, apparently unconcerned at wandering through his apartment naked. No wonder, the man was well built, not an ounce of fat anywhere, nothing but skin and muscles.

"Watch out for the hot water nozzle. I had to jerry rig it closed. Oh! And the toilet flushes with the chain on the side, not the handle. I had to rig that up too."

Rock chuckled. "You're quite the rigger, aren't you? Guess those hands are good at more than just making a man come."

"Hey, emergency triage's is my specialty. I just rig stuff up until the pros show." He grinned and watched that hard ass disappear into the bathroom. He sat for a second, thinking and blinking and shaking his head, before going to start the Mr. Coffee.

Yep. Utterly, completely, and unequivocally fucked.

No question about it.

"Get that sweet ass in here, Rigger, and show me how the fuck to turn the hot water on!" Rock's voice grumbled through the apartment and Alex grinned.

"Pushy, pushy, pushy." He grinned as Rock muttered something about being shown pushy if he had to take a cold shower.

Fucked. Happy, laughing, in-trouble, Momma-was-gonna-shit-a-brick fucked. He was one lucky son of a bitch. "Coming, Blue. Hold your horses!"

Pushy fucking marine. Alex hoped to hell Rock didn't have any plans for tomorrow.

CHAPTER TWO

Rock figured it was rude to just show up on a man's doorstep, but he'd put in his time, having a beer with the boys at some strip club and now it was time to feed his belly and his need. Besides, he didn't have Alex's number, just knew where the kid lived and he wasn't empty handed -- he had two boxes of pizza and a six-pack of the local brew.

He tossed some money at the taxi driver and headed on up the stairs, knocking on number three-thirty-three. He sure hoped he wasn't going to have to go home and take care of things by himself.

He'd had less than twenty-four hours with the kid and now, little more than twenty-four hours later and he was back for more. He couldn't remember the last time he'd enjoyed fucking this damned much. And he liked fucking. A lot.

The chaos that answered him had him bending over, laughing hard enough it hurt. The barking was first, then the door opened, Alex in nothing but soaking wet briefs, the puppy, huge fucking mutt of a puppy -- and the apartment -- sudsy as all fuck.

"Blue Eyes! Hey! Washing the dog."

He snorted and wiped his eyes with his free hand, the pizza and six pack somehow still in the other. "Oh, I think that dog is washing you."

The pup panted, looked totally fucking pleased with himself. Alex's grey eyes just rolled, grinned up at him. "Come on in. I'm near done."

"I don't know -- that beast looks like he's just seen a new victim to spray..." He winked and stepped in, finding a dry spot on the coffee table for the boxes of pizza and the beer. "Of course, you're only a tiny bit overdressed for what I have in mind, so I guess it evens out."

Alex chuckled, bending to drag the dog into the bathroom, showing him everything. Fuck, yeah. He started stripping. Pizza didn't taste bad cold and the beer could get put into the fridge sure enough.

The pup got rinsed and toweled off and plopped into the sunshine on the balcony to dry. "Let me get showered and I'll..."

Alex's words trailed off, eyes on his body. "Mmm... look at that."

"Yep, take a good long look and then come on over and get a good feel of it." And come to think of it, he could use a shower himself, he smelled of strip joint and straight boys.

Alex curled one finger in a come on gesture, temping him toward the bathroom. "Let's get slick."

"I do like the way you think, Alex. Like the way you suck even better." No reason to be shy about the way he enjoyed the kid's mouth.

That hot pink tongue slipped out, wet those parted lips. "Come and try again, then."

"I was hoping you'd offer." He followed Alex right into the bathroom, watching that sweet fucking ass as Alex bent to turn on the taps. Fuck. He groaned, stepping into the shower as soon as it was running. "Front and center, mister."

The briefs disappeared and then he had an armful of redneck, all slick and warm and grinning. He took that mouth he was already so fond of, kissing Alex hard, tongue just pushing in like he was going to push into that ass soon enough. Alex dove right in, meeting him headfirst, tongue fucking his lips.

Rock rubbed their bodies together, their cocks sliding, hot and silk and wet. Fuck. His hands slid down over Alex's back, reaching for that finer than fine ass. Oh, he did like how Alex said hello. That ass pushed back into his touch, wriggling, offering him all he wanted.

He pulled back, looking into those grey eyes. "Wanna fuck your mouth first, yeah?"

"Yeah." Alex reached up, snagged some condoms from the long narrow window above the shower. "Hell, yeah."

He loved how Alex was so well prepared, loved being able to just go without the fucking byplay of having to find the stuff they needed.

"Mmm..." Alex sank down, opening the condom and winking up. Then the kid did the trick with his tongue and his lips and slid the rubber right down, sucking right off. Look, ma. No hands.

Rock groaned, hands going into the curls plastered to Alex's head. Fuck. Sweet. Yeah, this was going to keep him fucking happy for the next two weeks. Hell, the memory of it was going to keep him happy for months to come.

That pretty mouth just drove him higher and higher, the suction making his eyes roll. Fuck, yes. He started to fuck, hips pushing his cock in deep over and over again and Alex not only took it, he encouraged it, helped, kept the suction good and hard. The look on Alex's face was something else -- pure fucking bliss. Then those hands slid up his thighs to roll his balls.

He roared, hands curling over Alex's shoulders as he pushed deep and came. Fuck. That was... the best fucking blowjob ever.

Alex just hummed, bringing him down before getting rid of the rubber.

He tugged on Alex, bringing the kid back up and taking that mouth again, ignoring the taste of the rubber. Anyone who sucked that that good deserved a good, hard reaming.

Luckily, he could more than oblige.

Alex opened right up, cock sliding, rocking against his belly, hotter than the muzzle of an M-13.

"Somebody's got a whole bunch of need. Good thing I've got just what you're wanting."

"Oh, hell yes. You're all about what I'm needing, Blue Eyes."

"You want it here in the shower or in your bed?" He could see benefits to either.

"Mmm... bed. Good and hard and deep, marine."

"Whatever you want, Alex. Whatever you want." He was already half hard again, those grey eyes full of want just turning him the hell on.

He got one of those full-on, sexy-as-fuck smiles. "You. C'mon. Bed. There's lube."

He turned off the taps and followed, grabbing a towel and drying off as he let his cock point the way -- straight at that sweet ass as Alex went down the hall ahead of him. The lean lines were easy on the eye, too. Long, thin spine, the barest dip and then that ass -- damn. He hurried the last few steps, rubbing up against Alex as they made it to the bed.

Those hands hit the bed, Alex bending, pushing that ass against his cock. He reached up for the lube, finding it on the little bedside table he'd left it on the day before, next to the condoms. He slicked his fingers up and pressed one against Alex's hole, sliding the tip in.

"Mmm... tease." The drawl was just full of want and laughter.

"I wouldn't want to go too fast," he drawled back. He slipped his finger out and pushed the tip of another one in. And then another. And then the first again.

Alex laughed, ass squeezing his finger. "Oh, I am going to have to beat you, marine."

He snorted. "I'd like to see you try."

And just for that he added his thumb to the mix, sending each finger only as far as the first knuckle before moving onto the next. That sweet little cowboy butt started riding his fingers, demanding a little more each time. It was fascinating and fucking sexy and he kept switching fingers, letting Alex do all the work until he just couldn't stand it anymore and he sank two right in deep.

"Fuck!" Alex's head came up, back just rippling. "Oh, shit. Do it again."

"Yeah. And again and again." And he did, pegging Alex's gland with each thrust of his fingers. Nothing got hidden, not a single response -- Alex just moved and groaned and took him and took him. Groaning, he let his fingers slide away and slid a rubber on. "Ready for me, Alex?"

"Fuck. Fuck, Blue Eyes. Ready? I need it. Now."

He chuckled, the sound fading away as he gloved up and pushed his cock into the best place it had ever been. Fuck. Alex was the most perfect fuck, mouth or ass, ever.

Alex started riding him, pushing and rocking, moving furiously. He wrapped his hands around Alex's hips, tugging him back harder, moving forward faster, and it was fucking awesome. The tight little hole worked his cock, the tight grip made sweeter by the low words, the heat of Alex's body.

He moved one hand around, finding Alex's cock and wrapping it in his fist, letting Alex's movements work it. Alex groaned, thrusts getting serious now, getting more definite. He bent over Alex's back, finding that spot that had made the kid wild yesterday, nibbling softly as he fucked hard.

Alex squeezed him like a fucking fist, just squeezed him tight as heat sprayed. He jerked a few more times, his own climax just... right there. With a groan, he came, filling up the condom as Alex's ass kept milking him.

They sort of panted together, easing down on the little bed. "Oh, Blue Eyes. That rocked."

He nodded, cock sliding out of sweet fucking heaven. "Yeah, it wasn't bad at all."

That lazy, sated chuckle was pure fucking sex. "I concur, marine."

"Excellent." He settled next to Alex, one hand finding the kid's hip, holding on possessively.

"Mmm..." That long lanky body cuddled right in, close as anything.

"Nap and then pizza and beer and then seeing what comes up?" It sure sounded like a plan to him. Maybe not in that order though, he imagined he could go for another suck before he ate.

"Works for me, Blue Eyes. You make some fine assed plans."

"Yep. Sometimes simple is best."

"You know it. Fucking. Sucking. Beer. Food. The periodic game on the tube."

"You know it." He tilted his head and took a kiss. "This mouth? Top of the fucking list."

Alex grinned, pushed right back into the kiss, reminding him exactly how good that mouth was.

He slid his hands down along Alex's back to that ass. Along with making good plans? He was flexible on changing them and right now? Another round of fucking before the nap was sounding really good.

Three nights of pizza was his limit and Alex grabbed his stew pot and started browning hamburger. He had the stuff for cornbread and... hrm.

No apples.

No cake-y stuff.

Ooh. Chocolate pie and someone else to eat it with.

Fucking A.

He turned up the radio, listening to the ball game, whistling and just having himself a ball. The knock he was waiting for came shortly after seven, Grimmy barking at the sound.

"It's unlocked, man." Man, time just flew on his day off.

The door opened a little. "It's unlocked, but is the beast gonna eat me?"

"Oh, sure the five month old puppy's going to eat the big marine."

"He's only five months? He's going to be a scary fucker when he's full grown."

"Yep. Gonna protect my ass from being burgled and eat his weight in kibble."

Rock laughed. "He is going to eat me then -- I'm here for that ass."

Alex laughed, wiped his hands off, heading into the front room. "Come and get it, Blue Eyes."

"Oh, that's what I like." Rock wasn't shy at all, just came right up to him and grabbed the goods, dropping a hard kiss on his mouth.

"Mmhmm." He laughed, diving right into the kiss, tongue pushing into Rock's lips. The kiss went on and on, and there was a nice, hot bulge in Rock's jeans pressing against him.

"Hungry marine." He rubbed against that heat, groaning. Shit this man rocked his world.

"Starving." He got a grin and then Rock sniffed. "Hey, something smells good."

"Chili, cornbread, pie." He grinned. "You *do* eat something besides pizza, right?"

"I'll eat anything you put in front of me." Oh, the look in those eyes was wicked.

"Ooooh..." He wiggled, pushed close. "Promises, promises."

"I believe I have delivered so far on any and all promises."

Alex looked up, smiling, nodding. "You have. Kiss me, marine. We're wasting daylight."

Rock laughed. "Alex. We don't need daylight to fuck."

He snorted. "Figure of speech, Yankee."

"Well if you mean hurry on up, you should just say so." Rock gave him a wink, squeezed his ass.

"Kiss me, Marine." Their laughter mingled, the kiss hot and sweet as fuck.

Rock picked him up by his ass, walked him over to the couch as they kissed. Good Lord and butter -- he did love him a strong man. Rock set him down on the couch, following him down, rubbing.

"Oh, fuck yes." He wrapped one leg around Rock's

ass, tugging them closer together.

"Fucking sexy, kid." Rock's fingers slid between them, working open their pants.

He nipped Rock's bottom lip. "Not a kid, marine."

Rock chuckled. "Gonna prove it to me, Rigger?"

Rigger? Jackass. "Could a kid suck you dry like I do?"

"I don't know... I can't quite remember how that went..."

"No? You sure... I'm pretty sure I demonstrated last night..."

"I have short term memory problems. I'll need another demonstration."

"Oh, I wonder if that's in my neuropsychology book..." He leaned back, working Rock's buckle open.

"Oh, that's a five dollar word -- I don't do those." Rock winked at him, shifted to his side, giving him more room to work.

"Grab the gloves, Blue Eyes." Alex got the jeans open, Rock's fat cock pushing free. "You want to fuck my mouth?"

"Oh. Fuck yes." No hesitation whatsoever.

He nodded, scooting down on the sofa. "Come on."

Rock stretched and grabbed a condom, pushing it down to him. He opened the package, worked it on with his fingers. "Man, I'd love to taste your cock."

"You know better than that, kid." One finger stroked his cheek.

"I didn't say I was going to do it, marine. Just that I want to." He nipped that finger.

"Tell me about it. That sweet fucking mouth without the glove? Damn."

He blushed, licked the tip of Rock's prick in thanks, then opened up. "Come take me."

"Yes, sir." Oh, those blue eyes shone down on him and that fat cock pushed into his lips. Fuck, yes. Fuck me, Marine. He moaned, just let Rock in and in. Rock shifted and pushed in all the way, movements slow and careful. He could see those blue eyes rolling in Rock's head. "Fuck. Just... fuck."

He hummed in agreement, hands sliding up to cup Rock's ass, squeeze and rub. Fuck was right. Fuck, yes.

Rock started fucking his mouth, that fat prick just pushing in over and over again, still careful, but not slow anymore. Alex moaned, just took it, jonesing on it. He fucking loved sucking. Loved it. Rock's hips pushed faster, harder, the care starting to slip, Rock's need taking over.

One finger slipped along Rock's crack, teasing the tiny hole. Rock's ass cheeks went tight, movements growing jerky. He could feel that fat cock throb, seem to get harder, knew it wouldn't be much longer. He buried his nose in the soft pubes, sucking hard, swallowing. Come on, come on, Blue Eyes.

Rock pushed in deep, cock throbbing as he roared. The muscles of Rock's ass tensed rhythmically beneath his hands. He whimpered, wanting to taste so fucking bad.

Rock shivered one more time and then pulled out, shifting to lie on his side on the couch. It wasn't strictly big enough for both of them, but Rock hauled him up and held him squished against the wide chest. It would do.

"It's all coming back to me," Rock told him with a wink.

"Yeah? Jogged your memory?"

"Yep. A kid couldn't suck like that." He got a wink, one big hand going down to grab his ass and tug him close, his prick sliding on that fabulous belly.

"Mmm..." Oh, yeah. That was nice. Just like that.

Rock's fingers slid into his crack, index finger finding his hole and teasing it as his body rocked and rolled against heat and muscles.

"Yeah. Oh, that's it." He just rode it, nice and easy. A little pre-supper screw.

Rock fucked him with that finger, mouth sliding against his, tongue hot and insistent between his lips. It didn't take him long, it all just felt too fucking good, too right. Rock purred, looking smug, looking like the fucking cock of the block.

Alex chuckled, grinned. "You ready for chili and cornbread?"

"Yeah, I could definitely eat. And I can't believe you cooked -- you didn't have to go to the trouble."

"Rock? I cook for *me*. A man cannot live on pizza alone. It's unnatural."

"No, a man needs a steak now and then in between." He was given a wink.

"Mmm. Steak. Pot roast. Fried chicken. Enchiladas. Chili. Come on. Let's eat."

"You can make all that?" Rock looked like he was almost drooling.

"Yep. Momma's fried chicken's better than mine, but she's got more practice."

"That settles it; I'm saving my money the rest of my visit here."

"For what, marine? Groceries?" The man needed someone to cook for him.

"Sure, I'll buy you groceries if you're making stuff like steak and fried chicken. Those beat pizza and burgers any day of the week." He was given a wink. "Man can't live on blow jobs alone."

Alex just cackled. "You buy the grub, I'll cook it up, Blue Eyes. I'm all about supporting the troops."

"Oh, now I'm not asking you to feed any troops, just one lone marine. I think I've got enough to keep you busy all on my ownsome."

"I think you do, Rocketman. I do. Come on and eat your chili. Otherwise that chocolate pie'll go to waste."

Rock stopped and stared at him. "Did you say chocolate *pie*?"

"Yeah..."

"I've never heard of a *pie* made out of chocolate, Alex." Oh, now, that marine? Was definitely drooling.

"You obviously were deprived as a boy, then." He led the way to the kitchen. Lord, lord.

"Yep. Deprived of a lot of things." He was given a wink and then Rock was moaning. "Oh, that all smells very good. Very."

Oh, lord. He was gonna have to call Momma.

All that time she was going on about the way to a man's heart and shit and they all laughed.

Looked like she was right.

Rock was in fucking heaven.

He'd been kissed breathless. Blown by the best fucking cocksucker he'd ever had. Eaten *homemade* cornbread and chili until he was gonna burst.

And now there was chocolate fucking pie.

Whoever invented this was a fucking genius.

He was on piece number two and Alex hadn't been stingy with the pieces either. He finished off the last bite and sat back with a heartfelt groan, opening his pants. He really was going to burst. "That was the best fucking thing I have ever eaten."

"You like, huh? My granny's recipe." Alex was stretched out, nibbling, looking relaxed as fuck.

"It must be a Southern thing -- I'd never heard of

it before." He was sure as hell going to put a bug in the COs ear though. See if it couldn't make its way onto the menu at the mess. No way it could match the pie he'd just had, but even half as good would be something.

"You just weren't raised right. Next thing you're going to tell me you never had blackberry cobbler."

"No, I don't do fruit."

"You're shitting me. No apple pie? Strawberry shortcake? Hell, grapes just for the hell of it?"

"Well I guess strawberry shortcake is okay. Why would I want grapes?" Rock was honestly confused.

"Cause they taste good?"

He made a face. "After I left home I didn't have to eat fruit or vegetables and I don't." Nasty things.

"Yeah? I like greens and stuff. Hell, I like food of all sorts, really. I'm easy." Alex settled on his back, stretching out. "I fucking love corn and green beans from the farm."

"Yeah, but you're a freak." He winked and patted his stomach. "That was fucking fine pie, Alex."

"Thank you, sir." The puppy bounced over, hopped right on Alex, tail wagging hard. Alex laughed, petting the big beast, spoiling it.

"That animal's gonna be even bigger when he's full grown and he'll keep expecting to climb into your lap."

"He'll learn. He's just a baby and he needs love." Grey eyes grinned over at him. "Gotta raise a happy pup, man."

"He's not gonna be much of a watchdog," Rock noted. Though big as that mutt was going to be, he was likely to scare folks off before they realized he was a big old softie.

"Long as he barks when someone comes knocking, that'll do. I found him, near to dead, in a box with a bunch of dead pups on the highway. Figure it was meant to be."

He chuckled. It said a lot about Alex, that he'd stop and look in the first place, that he'd bring the pup home in the second. "Stray pups and marines, eh?"

"You know it. Big ones."

Rock started laughing. He nodded and rubbed at his cock. "Very big."

"And very confident." Alex chuckled, licked his lips.

Such a pretty fucking mouth. Talented, too. "I've got nothing to be shy about."

"Nope. Man's as fine as you, he should know it."

"You said it." He nodded, enjoying the evening, belly full, body satisfied, even if his cock was taking an interest in that fine mouth and even finer ass. Finding someone you could just sit with and chew the fat, or not, was a rare thing.

"So tell me about North Carolina. You like it there?"

"Yeah, sure." He shrugged. It was a place to hang his hat. It was where he was stationed.

"Cool." Alex nodded, stretched a little.

"I guess you're one of those Texas is everything cowboy types." They had a few of those in his unit. He'd never been married to any one place himself.

"They train us to be that way in school." He got a grin, a wink.

He was glad for the wink or he wouldn't have been sure if Alex was serious or not. He chuckled, grinning back. "I have to admit I do enjoy me a nice friendly cowboy."

"I am, you know. *Very* friendly..." Oh, yeah. That grin was making promises.

"I've noticed. And I've enjoyed. *Very* much." His own smile accepted those promises, made a couple of his own. That ass? Sweetest fuck he'd had in forever.

Alex rolled up, crawled over between his legs. "Ditto, marine."

He purred, hand moving to slide through Alex's hair. "We do seem to be compatible." He winked, leaning down to kiss that hot mouth.

"Mmm... and you said you didn't use high-dollar words."

"Is that a high-dollar word? Let me try again." He tilted his head as if he were thinking. "We fuck good."

"Ugh. Marine make redneck come."

Rock laughed. "Yeah. Works pretty good the other way, too."

"No shit." Oh, there was something decent -- lap full of redneck.

He tilted Alex's head, took another kiss, fingers tugging that little grey t-shirt out of Alex's waistband. That tongue pushed right in, tasting him, blowing his mind all over again. He groaned, hands sliding down to cup that ass, tugging their bodies close together.

"Mmm... Blue Eyes." That kiss pushed into another, which pushed into another and another.

His hands squeezed and rubbed, rocked Alex against him. The need was building, slowly, but surely. They weren't in any hurry, and didn't that feel good, too, just moving slow and easy. He got Alex's t-shirt up, both of them loathe to break their kisses to get it right off, but in the end they did and he chuckled. "Fucking addictive, Rigger."

"Y'all and your nicknames." Alex licked his lips. "You got a real name?"

He snorted. "You've called me 'marine' as much as anything else. And yeah, I do. Sergeant James South at your service."

"Jim, huh?" Alex looked him over. "Rock suits you,

Blue Eyes."

He grinned and nodded. "As in rock hard and ready -- it sure does."

One hand cupped his cock, rubbing. "Hell, yes."

He purred. "Oh, you do know how to make a man feel good." He spread his legs, giving Alex better access.

"'s'why you keep coming back."

He nodded. "You got that right."

Alex winked, bent to kiss him again, tongue pressing deep. He was purring again, undulating against the man, hand landing on Alex's, keeping that rubbing going. It just fucking worked, the heat, the rubbing, the passion. Those eyes flared, thumb working the tip of his cock.

"I hear this is even better naked," he murmured. No way he was letting this kid make him shoot in his pants.

"Yeah? You think?" Alex didn't move though, just kept rubbing.

He nodded, groaning, hands finding Alex's ass and holding on. Fuck, yes.

He got another kiss, Alex just diving into him. It made him feel like the sexiest, hottest stud in town. Not that he wasn't, but this kid... man, he just cut straight to it. His cock was rubbed, stroked, Alex working him, dipping into his jeans.

"Oh, thank fuck." He grinned, pushing up into Alex's hands.

"Mmm..." His cock was squeezed, Alex's thumb working the tip.

He found Alex's zipper, tugging it down. He wasn't a greedy lover.

"Mmm." The sound pushed into his lips, tongue sliding against his.

His hand wrapped around Alex's cock, holding that heat in his hand. Oh, yeah, he loved fucking. They just rocked together, pushing and moaning. Alex shifted a little, got their cocks together, got their fingers working together.

"Yeah, just like that."

He grinned, one hand still on Alex's ass, the other finding the back of his head, tilting it so he could take a good, deep kiss. Alex just opened up, tongue sliding against his, fingers getting tighter. He moved their hands faster, hips starting to push, the heat growing between them.

Alex started sucking his tongue, pulling in time with their hips. His eyes rolled in his head. Fuck. That mouth. His hips started jerking, hands tightening. Alex grunted, thighs going tight against him, kiss never even slowing.

His orgasm just slid over him, like a wave, spunk shooting over their hands. It didn't take long before heat added to his, Alex jerking, grunting soft and low.

"Nice..." He grinned, took another long kiss.

"Mmhmm." Alex settled against him, relaxed and lazy.

"Yep." He nodded, hands sliding on Alex 's back. Nice, smooth skin. He purred.

Alex kissed his jaw. "Can you spend the night?"

"I can. Got an early wake up though." Was nowhere else he wanted to spend his night. Just as soon as he'd napped, he'd offer to nail Alex to his mattress again.

"I got an alarm clock and a shift at seven, so I'm up at five."

Rock groaned, but he nodded, too. "Roll call's at six tomorrow. One too many assholes out partying all night every night and not showing up with their A game." And he was going to have a few choice words to say to them, too.

"Blah." Alex settled in, eyes closing. "Good thing we're young and full of energy."

Rock held on, his own eyes closing. "Yeah, well I

think the booze had something to do with their condition. They've got to learn that fucking gives you energy, booze just leaves you with a hangover."

"Mmhmm..." Alex nodded, sort of.

He chuckled. Nothing like a good meal and coming a time or two to make a man sleepy. "Your ass is mine when we move to the bed," he murmured, one hand sliding down to squeeze the ass in question.

"Good deal." Soft snores filled the air, Alex snuggling in.

Yeah. He was certainly getting a very good deal.

He was still grinning as he started snoring himself.

Alex headed up the stairs to the apartment, the wind killer cold and wet. Damn, it sucked that this was the last bit of weather Rock was getting to see in Texas. Not as bad as it sucked that the marine was leaving, but still high on the scale.

Still, it was probably a good thing. He had midterms coming up, then his last bit of practicals and finals and he didn't want to fuck up now.

Well, okay.

He just wanted to *fuck* now.

And wasn't there someone up there looking out for redneck cowboys who weren't exactly straight and narrow because there was his marine, coming up the stairs behind him.

"Hey, marine. How's it hanging?"

"Oh, pretty good, I'd say." Those blue-blue eyes were smiling up at him from two stairs down.

He grinned down, nodded. "Good to hear. Very good to hear."

Rock held up his hands, a bag in each. "Fried chicken," he said, lifting his right hand. "Cake." Rock lifted the other. "I didn't think food would be on your mind, it being your last chance to take a ride on the Rocketman and all."

"Nope. I can eat anytime." He opened the door, grabbed Grim to let him out on the balcony.

Rock was right on his ass, pressing him up against the balcony door when he came back in. Their mouths met, Rock's tongue just invading. He groaned, pushing up against Rock, rubbing good and hard, cock just aching for it. One of those big hands landed on his ass, the other slid into his hair, tilting his head just so, kiss going deeper.

His eyes rolled, his hands landing on Rock's shoulders and holding on. Fuck. Fuck, more. Rock's body slammed against his, pushing him hard against the balcony door. Fuck, yes. He bucked, rubbing furiously. Need. Fuck.

The hand at his ass slid around, tearing at the button on his jeans as a low growl filled his mouth. He shook, gasping, hips pumping up into Rock's touch.

"Fucking need you," muttered Rock, getting his jeans open, zipper down. That big hand wrapped right around his cock and started tugging.

"Yeah. Yeah. Fuck." He arched, pushing up and up, just shaking with it.

"Condom?" Rock's blue eyes looked into him.

"In my pocket. Come on."

Rock fished it out and handed it over. "Open it up and put it on, Alex. Gonna give you a memory to live on."

Alex nodded, biting his bottom lip, fingers sliding the rubber down over that fat fucking prick.

Rock laughed. "Alex. Put it on *your* cock."

"Oh. Oops. I was sorta focused..." His cheeks flamed, but he was laughing as he gloved himself up.

"You can do me after." Rock winked at him and then slowly went to his knees.

Oh. Oh, sweet fuck. His hands ghosted over Rock's high and tight, the dark hair tickling his palm. His cock bobbed, begging for it, for the touch of that mouth. Rock made this little purring noise and gave him a last look before those blue eyes focused on his prick. Rock licked at the tip and then took it into his mouth, sucking on the head.

"Oh..." He stretched, every fucking muscle he had going tight with wanting it.

Rock hummed around his flesh, and went slowly, so slowly down on him. He leaned back, watching, just stunned. The heat and pressure was going to drive him fucking mad. Rock went all the way down and swallowed and then slowly backed off again.

"Sweet fuck, that's hot, Blue Eyes. Damn." He started rocking, nice and slow, pushing into Rock's mouth.

Rock increased the suction for him, but let him fuck that mouth. Blue eyes turned up to him, looking straight up into his.

Oh. Fuck. Oh. So fucking blue. "Beautiful motherfucking man."

That purr around his cock was something else and Rock's hands wrapped around his ass, encouraging his movements. His moan was all about wanting and needing and damn if he didn't just start moving, start fucking those hot lips. Rock's hands slid into his jeans, one finger teasing his hole.

"Oh, yeah. Yeah." He nodded. That's it. That's just enough to... Yeah.

Rock pulled harder and pushed that finger all the way in. He could see it in Rock's eyes, the 'come for me.' He did too, spunk just pouring from him, filling the rubber, everything fucking shorting out.

Rock pulled off slowly, smug, cocky smile on his face. "Oh yeah. You liked that."

"Uh-huh. Damn. Just. Damn." Like wasn't near strong enough a word.

Rock chuckled and kissed his hip before standing again. "Come on, Cowboy. Take me to bed and put that same look in my eyes."

"Uh-huh. Bed." He nodded, tugging Rock up, still swaying a little.

Laughing, Rock put one shoulder in his belly and picked him up, hauling him down the hall.

He laughed, squeezing Rock's ass. "Neanderthal!"

"That's short for All American Class A Stud, isn't it?"

His laughter echoed down the hall. "How did you guess?"

"I'm smart as well as studly." Rock tossed him onto the bed, just grinning down at him.

He grinned back up. "You know it. Smartest marine I've ever fucked."

"Best fucking marine you've ever fucked, too." Rock stripped the rest of his clothes off. "Get naked, Rigger."

Alex snorted, mock-saluting before getting naked.

Then Rock was on the bed with him, eyes on his, that fat cock hard, red, leaking.

"How do you want it?" What do you want to fucking remember, marine?

"Your ass, tight and hot. And then your mouth. Never had anything like your mouth, Alex."

"Sounds fucking perfect." He reached up, pulled Rock down. "Let's get started."

"You got it, Rabbit." Rock's mouth came down on his, the hard body pressing him into the bed.

He'd have chuckled at the nickname, but his mouth was busy. Fuck, his whole body was busy. Rock's hands slid on him, fingers finding his nipples and pinching, tugging.

"Fuck!" He loved that, made him absolutely mad for more.

Purring, Rock pinched again before his fingers moved over to the other side.

"Evil tease." He bit his lip, bucked.

Rock slid that fat, hard prick along his cock. "Does this feel like teasing?"

"Mmm... no fucking way. That feels like heaven."

"I thought so." Rock's hips kept working, kept stroking against his. Then Rock bent his head and wrapped hot lips around his right nipple.

Alex's hand slipped around Rock's head, holding that mouth right fucking there. Shit, yes. Rock hummed and purred, tongue working his nipple like a pro, one hot hand sliding down between his legs. His breath was just huffing out of him, fuck it felt good. He spread, thighs just giving it right up. Rock's finger teased at his opening, stroking his skin, pushing in.

"Fuck, yes." He bore down, rocking, riding the touch.

Rock purred, the sound vibrating around his nipple. "Fucking tight, Alex."

His body jerked, taking more in, eyes just rolling. "Fuck. More."

Rock sat back and that finger disappeared as he reached over for the lube. It wasn't long though before Rock was leaning in over him again, two slick fingers pushing right in. He braced himself on Rock's shoulders, rocking good and hard, fucking himself. Oh, yeah. That's what he needed.

"Sexy fucker," Rock murmured, eyes on his ass, watching as another finger pushed in.

"Oh..." His motions slowed, entire body into it, riding hard, grinding.

"Save some for me. I want you coming on my cock."

Even as he said the words, Rock's fingers curled and pushed deep, finding his gland.

"There! Oh, fuck. Again." His shoulders left the bed, belly going tight as a drum.

"Right here?" Rock asked, grinning down at him, nailing that spot again.

"Uh...uh-huh. There." Oh, shit. Yes.

"Good."

Rock kept pegging his gland, bending to lick at his nipple again, then the sweet spot on his neck and then his mouth. He reached down, squeezed the base of his cock, just trying to hold on. Rock groaned against his lips and then those thick fingers disappeared, the condom wrapper made a crinkling noise and blunt heat pushed into him.

He nodded furiously. Oh. Yes. Fuck. Need. Rock didn't tease, didn't make him beg, just pushed that fat cock into him, filling him up. They groaned together, the sound proving how good it was. Those blue, blue eyes looked into his own, filling up his sight as Rock set a nice, easy rhythm. He just rode it, that fat cock sinking in and in and in, filling him. Taking him. Rock's breath brushed his face, colored by groans and moans and the occasional grunt. The thick cock spread him, stretched him, made him feel so good.

He leaned up, took Rock's mouth, kissing the man hard. Rock moved faster in response, pushing into him with hard, solid thrusts that he could feel all the way to his toes, to the top of his head. Oh, he was going to be fucking ruined for anybody else after this.

It didn't seem Rock was ever going to stop, he just slowly sped up again and again, moving harder and faster and just sending him high. His eyes rolled, heart pounding, balls tight as shit, aching. One of Rock's hands slid around his prick, started to pull in time with those thrusts. It was hot and all he could see was blue.

He came with a low cry, entire body shaking.

Rock just purred. "Love that smell." Rock kept moving, a little faster, a little harder, jerking into him now.

"Mmm..." He spread, let Rock in deep, let Rock fill him.

"So fucking good," Rock told him, humping hard for a moment longer. Then Rock roared, thick cock throbbing inside him.

Oh, so fucking hot. So fine. Damn. Damn.

Rock collapsed onto him, one arm braced by his shoulder, keeping Rock's full weight from him.

He groaned, eyes just rolling. "Damn."

Rock nodded and gave him a hard kiss. "You said it."

"Uh-huh." Alex swallowed, moaning low.

"Best fuck ever, Alex. That's what you are."

"It's been a fucking amazing two weeks, Jim." He didn't know how else to say it. How to say it was gonna suck to lose this.

Rock nodded, fingers wandering over his belly. "I've got a whole new appreciation for special training."

"Can you stay the night, man?"

Rock nodded. "My bag's already on the bus home. Put clean skivvies on before coming out." He was given a grin. "Didn't think I'd be wearing 'em long enough to need a new pair in the morning."

"You thought right." He leaned up, kissed Rock's jaw. "C'mere, marine. I'm not giving you back quite yet."

Rock rolled back on top of him. "I just may make the MPs come drag me away."

"That sounds fair to me." He took a hard, deep kiss. He could so handle that.

Seriously.

***

Rock glanced at the clock, groaning.

Too fucking early.

And he had to be up and gone in just over an hour.

Gone away from San Antonio and Alex, and that was a crying fucking shame. Kid was a hot fuck, sucked like a dream and could cook to boot. Wasn't half bad to be around, either. Knew his way around a football game.

Well there was time enough for one last suck, another fuck. He reached over for Alex. Alex turned toward him, just wrapped around him and started rubbing.

Oh yeah, he was going to miss this.

One of his hands landed on Alex's ass, the other found one of those sensitive little titties and started tugging. Alex pushed low, deep cries into his mouth, just giving it all up. Fuck, he'd never known anyone who loved it this much. Fucking addictive, that need.

It was easy to reach for a rubber, slide it on his cock. The kid made it easy. He took one more hot kiss from Alex, and then let that mouth go, let it make the trip on down to his cock. Alex sucked him down like the kid was starving and desperate to make sure he didn't forget his stay in Texas.

Like he was going to forget that mouth.

Groaning, he slid his hands in Alex's hair, hips starting to shift just a little. Alex nodded, deep-throating him, nose in his pubes. He made a noise, something between a moan and a shout. "Oh fuck, don't stop."

He got a soft, deep moan, Alex not stopping at all. He watched as his cock disappeared between Alex's lips, sliding deep over and over again. Fuck, it made his balls ache with need. Those grey eyes just watched him, the look happy and horny, fucking hot.

"You're something else," Rock murmured, hips

starting to snap.

Long hands landed on his ass, encouraging his motions.

"Fuck, yes!" With that he just let go, fucking Alex 's mouth like it was the last time.

The kid just took and took and took, accepting every fucking thing he gave. With an honest to god roar, he came, filling the condom. The kid whimpered, mouth working him, drawing out each little aftershock.

He purred, just pleased as fuck. "You keep that up, I'll stay hard for you. Fuck you through the mattress before I go."

Alex nodded, sucking good and hard, head bobbing slow.

"Yeah, that's it... just like that." He wondered if he could sneak the kid on the bus.

Oh, fuck, those hums sent shocks straight to his balls. Alex had him whimpering -- *him*.

His balls were rolled, weighed, Alex's hands warm as fuck. There was a part of him that would have been happy just letting Alex suck him off again, but he wasn't a selfish man and he slid his hand over Alex's cheek. "Come on up here and ride me."

"Oh, hell yes." He got a huge grin, Alex scooting up.

He popped off the condom as their mouths met, tossing it as they kissed. Alex was like that energizer bunny and Rock appreciated a man who loved fucking. The kid's hot cock rubbed along his thigh, wet-tipped and needy, hips just rocking. He reached over for the lube, getting his fingers nice and slick before finding Alex's hole with them, pushing in nice and easy.

"Oh, fuck yes. More." The words were low and soft, whispered against his lips.

Purring, Rock pushed a third finger in alongside the

first two. Alex was all hot silk inside. Fuck, it was a good place to sink into. Alex groaned, thighs parted, just riding him, rocking up onto his fingers. He got another condom onto his cock with his free hand, eyes on Alex's, watching the pleasure chase across the kid's face.

"Don't stop. Gotta make this last."

"I'll make it good, Rigger." He let his fingers slide free and pushed his cock up in their place, letting Alex's own motions tug him in. Alex pulled him in deep, that tight ass squeezing and holding him. Groaning, he wrapped his hands around Alex's hips, fingers digging into the warm skin.

"Yeah. Fuck, yes." Those grey eyes were wide open, watching him.

"You know it." He pulled Alex down to meet his thrust, groaning at the way Alex's tight heat felt around him.

The long body arched, bucking and riding, belly going tight. So fucking pretty. So fucking hot. And, for another hour, all his. He pushed up harder, faster, prick dragging against silky flesh.

"Shit. 's so fucking good. So hot." Alex's drawl was all about sex and wanting.

He just nodded, growled and wrapped one hand around Alex's cock, stroking nice and slow. The low groan was just right, deep and raw. He watched and fucked and jacked, just sinking into it, into Alex.

"Close. Close. Fuck. Want to last..." Those long hands grabbed the headboard behind him, entire body moving faster.

He slowed his thrusts, slowed the pull of his hand. "You know any football stats?" he teased.

Alex laughed, head tossing. "I thought it was supposed to be baseball..."

Fuck, that sound was sweet, so was the husky tone in

Alex's voice. "Well I did bring my bat..." he winked.

"Bastard." He got another laugh, low and husky. He just chuckled. "You got the greatest laugh, Blue Eyes."

"And you're not hurting my ego one little bit."

"Mmm... gotta love a man with a big... ego."

He snorted and laughed some more and that was just enough to take the edge off, give them a chance to spend more time fucking before they came.

Shit, it was something else, watching how Alex rode him, enjoyed him. He could have done this all day. He wished he did have all day. One more day of fucking this fine cowboy.

They shared a slow, deep kiss, Alex shivering and squeezing his cock. He purred and took another kiss, moving smooth and slow, just right. Just fucking right. Alex's body clenched around him in time with the kiss, with the push of that hot tongue. So fucking good.

He moved a little faster, pushing in a little deeper, humming deep in his chest. They weren't going to be able to stop this time, bodies slamming together, skin slapping.

"Show me. Show me how good it is."

Alex whimpered, jerked, heat spraying out over his hand, his belly. He grunted, the heat around his prick fucking unbelievable and tight, just milking him. He jerked a few more times and then roared, filling the condom.

That long, fine cowboy leaned down, rested against him. "Damn."

"Uh-huh. You said it, Alex." His fingers stroked over Alex's skinny back, fingertips counting vertebrae.

"Yeah." Alex held him for a few minutes, then sighed. "You want a quick shower, marine? Coffee's programmed to start."

"You got a hankering to get wet together one more

time?" He could handle that.

"I most sincerely do, Blue Eyes."

"Excellent." He grinned and kissed Alex's nose. "Come on, Rigger. Time's a wasting."

"Yep. Up and at 'em, marine."

"Oh, I've already been up and at 'em. But I imagine I can give you one last minute of joy to remember me by."

Alex nodded, swatted his ass. "Somehow? I don't see forgetting you, Rock."

"No, I imagine I'm pretty unforgettable." Rock grinned and led the way to the shower, knowing Alex's eyes were on his ass.

"No shit. No shit at all."

He got the shower going, nice and hot just the way Alex liked it.

"Come on, Cowboy. Saddle up."

CHAPTER THREE

He spent a long time looking at the empty spot on the bed.

Just looking at the spot that had held somebody last night.

And the night before.

And the night before that.

And the twelve nights before that.

Fuck, Alex missed him already.

Momma'd warned him that God had a sense of humor, that if you gave Him half a chance, He'd prove it to you. One thing Alex knew beyond a shadow of a doubt was that Momma was always right about this sort of thing.

He wondered what Momma was gonna say about the mess he was in now.

Damned near graduated, damned near licensed, finally well and truly over George – lousy, son of a bitch bastard, may he have boils on his nuts and rot in hell – and on with the business of living. Then what does he go and do?

Fall for a gruff fucking marine with the bluest goddamned eyes he'd ever seen. A marine for chrissake. A marine with a sweet, fat cock and a terrible sense of humor that played a fairly good game of pool, didn't dance and fucked like a dream.

Shit.

Alex chuckled and shook his head. North Carolina – it wasn't Texas, but it wasn't Yankee country either.

Ten weeks 'til graduation was plenty of time to get packed up and start applying for work and preparing his speech for the first time he could call the big man local.

Momma would understand.

He prayed Rock would.

Rock settled on the old green couch and put his feet up on the coffee table.

Ah, home sweet home.

Not that the trip to San Antonio had been bad. Just the opposite, in fact. He couldn't remember a time he'd enjoyed training as much.

Of course, it wasn't the training he'd enjoyed.

Wasn't the training that was making his prick hard, either.

He undid his BDUs and wrapped a hand around himself, closing his eyes as he remembered a certain lanky cowboy with the sweetest ass he'd had in a long, long time. Maybe ever. Fucking tight and hot and it just milked him dry every single fucking time.

And the kid could suck. Fuck, that had been sweet.

Hot and sexy and making him blow faster than he'd blown in a long time. Shit, just the memory of it had him humping up into his hand, body all tight and eager and rushing to the finish.

Grey fucking eyes and hair so blond it was almost goddamned white. Shit, but Alex was sex on a stick -- the whole fucking package.

Rock reached down with his free hand and fondled his balls, slid one finger back further, teasing himself for a moment as he remembered that agile tongue poking at his slit.

Oh, yeah. Sucking and fucking and just begging for it every second. Alex was grade A American Slut. Fucking perfect.

He came, spunk splashing over his hand.

Fucking perfect.

Except for one thing.

The cowboy lived in fucking San Antonio.

Momma and Daddy sat, listened, nodded. Finally, when he'd said his piece, Daddy nodded again and stood. "Sounds like you thought it out, Son. Sure wish it wasn't so far. Kinda hoping you'd come home to stay."

Then Daddy went for a walk, leaving him with Momma and her teary eyes and bright red shirt just sitting at the dining table, fiddling with the lace edge of Granny's tablecloth.

"So, Baby, you got the job?"

"Yes, ma'am."

"And they're gonna teach you to work outta them helicopters?"

He nodded. "Yes, ma'am."

"And the money's good?"

"Yes, ma'am."

"You got a place to live?" She sniffled again, wiped her eyes.

"No, ma'am, but my credit's good and the market is, too. Thinking 'bout buying something in a few months."

Her eyebrows raised. "You thinkin' of stayin'?"

He nodded. "Yes, ma'am." That all depended on the situation when he got there. That all depended on Rock.

"What's his name?"

"Ma'am?"

"Don't you 'ma'am' me, Jeremy Alexander Roberts!" Momma's hand slammed down on the table, rattling the salt and peppers. "Who's so special you're leaving Texas?"

He looked down, hearing 'leaving me' clear as day in his head. "His name's Jim. Jim South. He's a marine." Oh, God. Momma knew. It must be real.

"And why haven't I met him?"

"He... uh... he doesn't exactly know I'm coming, Momma."

Momma's eyes did this wide-narrow-wide thing and then she sighed like the weight of the world was on her shoulders. "It's like that, is it?"

"Yes, ma'am."

She stood, the chair legs squeaking loud against the floor. "I expect you to bring him home for Christmas. Now, go help your daddy in the shed. I've got biscuits to put on."

"Yes, ma'am."

He stood and was headed for the door when he heard her voice, just a little teary. "Everything'll be fine, baby boy. I have faith. Love you."

"Yes, Momma. I love you, too."

It shouldn't have made him feel better, but it did.

CHAPTER FOUR

Two fucking months of 24/7 training, two fucking weeks of OJT, and he'd finally gotten three days off in a row. Three days.

Three days to go find Rock and convince the big lug he wasn't a stalker.

Really.

Honestly.

Sergeant Jim South lived in a little apartment complex outside of post. Three-forty-two. Alex had been sitting and watching the door for a little less than an hour, trying to figure out what to say.

"Hi, Rock. Wanna fuck?"

"Hey, Rocketman. I'm here."

"Hello, Blue. I missed you."

Fuck... this was harder than he'd thought.

His salvation came in the form of a Dominos

deliveryman heading for Rock's door. Alex shot out of his new Jeep and waved the kid down. "Hey! You delivering to three-forty-two?"

The teenager backed up a step and nodded.

"Cool. Tell me how much I owe you and I'll take it in. I'm fucking glad I caught you." He turned on his Sunday-best smile, gave the kid a healthy tip and before he could talk himself out of it, was knocking on Rock's door, double pepperoni burning his hand.

The door opened and there Rock was, wearing only a pair of shorts, going for his wallet. "Eleven-seventy, right?"

"I'd settle for a couple of pieces and a beer, Blue Eyes." Please, God, don't let him be pissed off. Please.

Rock blinked. "Alex?"

"Yeah." He didn't babble, just looked in those eyes. "Can I come in?"

Rock looked confused, but took a step back and held the door wide. "You quit your day job?"

He brought in the pizza. "I graduated in May and got an offer on Bragg working as a flight medic. Finally finished my training and thought I'd look up an old friend."

His entire fucking body was tight, fucking freaked out. What the *fuck* was he going to do if Rock threw him out or worse, laughed in his face and then threw him out?

Well, besides going back to his apartment and getting shitfaced, anyway.

"You didn't have to pay for the pizza," Rock told him, taking the box from him. The marine nodded at the couch as he dumped the box on the seen better days coffee table.

Rock opened it up and grabbed a slice, wolfing half of it down in a couple of bites. "Help yourself. I'll get us a couple cold ones."

"Thanks." God, he was as nervous as a long-tailed cat in a room full of rocking chairs. Maybe he should have just called. Or sent a note. Or just waited 'til they ran into each other. Maybe he should just go.

Then Rock came strolling back in, pizza gone, a beer in either hand, and it was too late to go gracefully. "So you like working for Uncle Sam?"

"It's not bad. Interesting people. I like the work." He accepted the beer and took a long, slow swig. Oh, yeah, that hit the spot.

"Have some of the pizza -- you need some meat on your bones." Rock helped himself to another slice.

"Had a busy few months is all. Too much work, not enough play." He took another sip of the beer, looking over at Rock. "You're looking good."

Rock puffed up a little for him. "I keep in shape."

Alex nodded, biting his bottom lip hard. "Fuck, yeah." He finished the beer, gathering up his courage. "You gonna throw a shit-fit if I kiss you hello?"

"Hell no, isn't that what you're here for?" Those blue eyes were twinkling at him.

"One of the things, yeah." He put the beer bottle down and scooted closer to Rock, brushing his lips against Rock's. Oh, yeah. Yeah. That was it. "Just one."

One of Rock's eyebrows rose, but so did one of those big hands, settling at the back of his neck and holding him close as Rock's tongue pushed into his mouth, plundering. He pushed right back, hands cupping Rock's cheeks as he fell into the kiss, moaning long and low. Sweet Jesus! He'd needed for fucking months. Months.

Rock's free hand slid down over his back, only stopping when it reached his ass. He was pressed closer to that hard body, kiss never breaking. Alex moved to straddle Rock's hips, spread open and pressed close, rubbing against that sweet, hard stomach. He was going to fucking kiss this man until they both goddamned died.

Or Rock agreed to fuck him regularly, whichever came first.

The big hands held him, warm and solid and right there. Rock's mouth was hot and wet and tasted like pizza and a hint of mint toothpaste and something indefinable that was *Rock* that he hadn't tasted since February.

He whimpered, so hard he hurt, balls sore and heavy in his jeans. "Blue. God."

Rock chuckled. "Not quite, but flattery will get you laid."

He laughed, grinning against Rock's lips. "Kisses like those will get your cock sucked until your fucking brains melt, marine."

"Well then shut up and let me give you another one." Rock's mouth covered his again, hard and eager and thorough.

He just melted, moving until their groins pressed together and pushing hard, steady, picking up Rock's rhythm from their kiss. Rock's hand on his ass encouraged his movements. He reached down, popping Rock's fly open, then his own, wanting skin on skin.

Rock made a rumbling sound that he hadn't heard or felt since February and the tongue fucking his mouth moved faster, pressed deeper. He shuddered, rocking harder, faster. He was going to fucking come all over Rock's cock and then he was going to find a motherfucking bed and fuck that sweet body until Sunday, God willing.

The big hands on his ass tightened, Rock pulling him closer against that hard body. Alex groaned, pushing hard as he shot his load, tongue sliding deep into Rock's mouth. That rumble was back, Rock's hands gentling on his ass, the big guy still rocking him softly against hard belly, hard cock, hard man.

"Feels so fucking good." He nibbled Rock's bottom lip. "Good to see you, Blue Eyes."

Rock chuckled and captured his mouth again. "Good to see you, too, Alex." Rock rubbed them together again. "You gonna let me fuck you into my mattress now?"

"I think I am. Yes." He nodded, licking the corner of Rock's mouth.

"Good."

The muscles beneath his thighs bunched and then Rock was standing, hands on his ass holding him in place as the big guy headed down the short hall. He wrapped his arms around Rock's neck, licking and nipping at the strong jaw as they moved, filling himself with Rock's flavor.

"You'd best be careful or I'm likely to drop you," growled Rock.

"You won't drop me." He moved on to the thick column of throat, licking away the salt.

"Sure of that, are you?"

"Yep." God, this man smelled fucking good. He scraped his teeth along one collarbone.

That sent a shudder through Rock and he *was* dropped, right onto the bed, Rock following him down.

He groaned as Rock's weight landed on him, overwhelming his senses. "Blue... Fuck."

"That's the idea, Alex."

Rock's weight lifted off him, the big guy stripping in front of him, not putting on a show or going quick, just taking off his clothes like he had all fucking day. Alex tugged off his shirt and wiggled out of the rest of his clothes, eyes never leaving Rock.

Rock grinned at him, blue eyes shining. "You been working out, Alex?"

"Been working hard. Trying to keep up with the guys

I'm supposed to help."

"Shows. You're looking good."

Then Rock was on him again, weight pressing him into the bed, all that hard, smooth skin hot against his own. He didn't wait, just wrapped himself around Rock, arms and legs, rubbing their bodies together in long, undulating waves.

"Want to fuck you," Rock murmured, stretching past him to reach for something on the dresser.

"Good, then we're on the same page. I'm not in the mood for knitting doilies." He arched into Rock's body, groaning at the feel of that amazing fucking cock.

Rock chuckled, sliding against him. Then a thick finger was teasing at his hole, slick and cool with lube. "I don't even know what a doily is, Alex."

"Well, then, good thing we're fucking instead." He pressed down toward that finger, hungry again, wanting.

"Fuck, you're something else," said Rock, finger pushing in deep.

He groaned, gripping Rock's shoulders with his hands as his started riding that thick finger. "Oh, yeah. I've been wanting..."

"Yeah? Everyone else leave you wanting in comparison after having the Rocketman?" Rock's finger fucked him deep and hard.

"No one else had a fucking shot." He fastened his stupid, traitorous mouth over Rock's skin, licking and sucking and shutting himself the fuck up.

Rock just chuckled, sounding pleased. There was the sound of the condom package opening and then that wide finger slipped out of his body to be replaced by that thick cock. "No more waiting." Without teasing, Rock started to push slowly in.

Alex rubbed his cheek against Rock's, his knees coming up and back to give the big man room. "Yes. Oh, fuck, yes." He'd waited for months to be filled like this, fucked like this and fuck, it was as good as he remembered, better, because now he knew what Blue's sheets fucking felt like under his bare back.

Rock didn't say anything, just sort of nodded and rumbled, those blue eyes gazing down at him as Rock started to fuck him. Long, slow strokes going in, coming back out and in again. Rock set a hard, solid rhythm. Alex just relaxed into it, body meeting each thrust, rolling and dancing against those hard as fuck muscles, squeezing and milking that thick cock. God, he loved fucking this man.

"Fucking good." Rock groaned, movements speeding. One big hand slid between them, fingers wrapping around his prick and pulling in time with each thrust.

"Yeah. Good." Alex shuddered, balls tightening, toes curling. "Good."

That thick cock kept pounding into him, Rock moving like he wasn't ever going to stop, was just going to pound him into oblivion.

He moaned and shifted, the slide of that cock over his prostate making him cry out. "Oh, shit! There! Again!"

"Right there?" Rock pushed in again, nodding as his whole body arched up into the thrust.

"Yes! Fuck! Please!" He was going to shoot, fuck yeah. Yeah.

Rock moved faster, harder, pushing against his gland every single time. He just gave it up, moaning low and blowing his load, entire body jerking and tightening on Rock's cock, flying. Moaning, Rock kept plowing into him, strong thrusts losing their rhythm and becoming jerky. The big guy moaned again and came.

He licked Rock's shoulder, arms wrapping around the big man's waist as Rock settled. Rock slid out of him and got rid of the condom, one hand sliding over his hip, holding him close. Alex sighed happily and pressed close without a word. If Rock wanted him to leave, Rock could tell him to. He was where he wanted to be.

Rock woke up slowly, the early evening sun shining in. Evening? The octopus clutching him shifted. Right. Post sex nap. With Alex, the kid from San Antone. Posted here, what were the odds? Not that he was complaining, he hadn't had a decent blowjob since coming back to Bragg.

The kid slowly untangled, going from sound asleep to wide-awake in a matter of heartbeats. "Hey, Rock. Guess I conked out on you. Sorry."

He grinned. "Going to sleep after sex is a time-honored tradition, kid. As is waking up to more sex. I seem to remember that mouth of yours being a piece of heaven..."

Alex grinned back, grey eyes shining. "Handy, since I have very found memories of sucking your cock."

He reached up and grabbed another condom off his dresser, handing it to Alex. "Perfect."

"No. Perfect would be bareback, but I'll take damned close, thanks."

He touched one of the high cheeks with his fingers. The kid was going to be in town for a while; there was no reason they couldn't get some tests done...

Alex scooted down his belly, nuzzling and licking, long fingers stroking his cock to fullness and then smoothing the condom over it. Groaning, Rock shifted, getting more comfortable. His hands stayed with Alex, touching the kid's face, his hair, the curve of an ear.

Alex's mouth dropped over the head of his cock, tongue pushing hard, suction sweet and steady. Oh, fuck, yes. He arched up into that hot mouth and then settled,

Sean Michael

forcing himself to stay still and enjoy the blowjob the way Alex wanted to give it to him. The kid sure could suck.

He managed another ten or twelve deep breaths before Alex got serious -- head bobbing in slow motion, drawing the pleasure up through every fucking part of his body.

"Shit, Alex..." He slid his hands through the kid's hair, trying hard not to hold him down and just fuck his mouth. Any fucking second though...

That got him a low hum that vibrated from the tip of his cock all the way down to his balls. He roared, hands tightening on the kid's head, hips pushing his prick up into Alex's mouth. The kid didn't even flinch, just took him in deep, pulling hard like Alex wanted it as bad as he did.

Fuck, it was good.

He started to hump up hard, the tip of his prick slamming into the back of Alex's throat, the kid just kept taking it, sucking harder the harder he thrust. Alex's hands slid under his ass, pulling him deeper, pulling him *in*. Well shit. He just kept thrusting as hard as he could, body starting to shake. Oh, fuck he was going to come.

With a roar, he did, calling out the kid's name.

The suction eased, but didn't cease, Alex finding a comfortable spot and just working the aftershocks, making him shiver. He dragged his hand along Alex's head, petting as he murmured his appreciation. A smooth cheek rubbed against his belly, grey eyes closed.

"Fucking awesome, kid."

"Yeah. Feels good." The hot tongue swiped over the tip, hunting a taste. "Want to taste you one day."

"I've got my yearly physical in a few weeks. Should have the results back soon after that."

He was presuming, could be the kid wouldn't want to hang around an older guy like him on a regular basis.

Still, it had been Alex who'd looked *him* up.

"Cool. Mine was two days ago." His belly was given another kiss and a lick. "Should know in a week."

Rock nodded. "A month or so then. What're we going to do to fill the time?"

"Buy a case of rubbers and fuck madly in anticipation." Those grey eyes were laughing.

He chuckled. "Sounds like a plan, kid. Sounds like a plan." He was still stroking the soft hair, cut a lot shorter than he remembered. Alex got rid of the condom, cleaned him up, then started licking the way up his belly. "Fucking sex on a stick, Alex."

"I just know what I like." That long, thin nose nuzzled his nipple, then those lips teased it to hardness.

He moaned, shifting as his cock twitched. "Like I said -- sex on a stick."

"Mm..." Teeth grazed over his nipple and then Alex moved on, heading across his chest.

He slid his hand down Alex's back, following the long curve of spine. A soft hum floated over his chest, Alex's cock hard against his hip, rubbing slow and easy. He matched the noise with a rumble, hand sliding to cup one perfect ass cheek, pulling Alex a little tighter against him.

"Oh. Good." His other nipple was nibbled and teased, Rock licking the nub.

"Yeah, real good." He pulled Alex over into the cradle of his thighs, sighing as their cocks slid together. Yeah, that was it.

He put one hand at the back of Alex' neck, the other on the kid's ass and just gave himself up to that sweet mouth and hard, hot cock sliding alongside his own. Purring moans tickled his nipple, Alex's hands sliding over his skin, massaging and rubbing. Fuck, it felt good.

He couldn't remember the last time he'd been ready

to go again so quickly. Except maybe the end of February on the last day he'd spent in San Antone. The kid could suck and fuck like nobody's business, Alex felt good around him, simple as that.

The kid traveled up his shoulder, nuzzling his pits briefly with a shudder and then moving on to his neck. "Fuck, Blue. So sweet."

"You like what you taste, kid?"

"Yeah." Alex moved up further, licking at his jaw. "Yeah, Rock."

He nodded. Fuck the kid made him feel like a god.

Grey eyes twinkled into his, sexy as fuck. Then those lips covered his, taking his mouth in a slow, bone-melting kiss that made him fucking ache. He rumbled, sliding their hips together. Shit, a man could get used to this.

Soft whimpers poured into his mouth, Alex moving faster, shivering. He brought his knees up, holding Alex close, feeling the slide of those skinny hips between his thighs.

"Oh, fuck. Blue Eyes." Alex's hips started jerking, their kisses growing sloppy and hungry.

"That's the idea, kid." He bit at Alex's lips, nibbling and tasting and licking.

"Blue..." A long, sweet moan brushed over his lips and the kid pressed hard, coming hot over his skin.

The smell pushed up between their bodies, making him gasp, his cock twitching hard.

"Oh, shit. Shit, yeah." Alex reached down, wrapped a hand around his come-slick cock. "You want this?"

"Fuck yeah." He pushed up, cock sliding through Alex's hand.

"Mmm... hot. Fucking hot." That hand started moving on him, gripping firm, thumb working the tip.

He groaned and moved with the rhythm Alex was setting, the sensations sweet and hot and fucking good.

"Yeah. Fucking sexy, Blue Eyes."

Shit, that sweet as fuck, wanton as shit voice was going send him right over. He moaned, body bucking up hard as he came. Alex purred over his jaw, lips sliding and fingers tugging and just pulling out one aftershock after another. He shuddered and shivered and held Alex tight.

Alex settled beside him, warm and loose, lips brushing his jaw. "Wow."

"Yeah, fucking wow."

He yanked at the blankets and pulled them up, covering them both. Hunger was probably going to drive him out of bed sooner or later, but he was thinking aside from that, he was going to keep the kid right here until duty called. And from the way the kid was snuggled right up, cheek resting on his shoulder like it belonged there, the kid wasn't going to have the slightest fucking problem with that.

Alex woke up early-early, like three a.m. early, the mixture of strange bed and hot body and early night fucking with his clock.

He found the bathroom, then the kitchen. Then the coffeepot.

Okay. That worked. Now. Coffee.

Where the fuck would the man keep his coffee?

It wasn't like there were a whole lot of places to keep it. Short on counter and cupboard space, the room was fairly small. There was a tiny window over the sink, too, only four cabinets up top, two on either side of the window, and four larger ones below. They were painted blue, which matched the little gauze curtain thing on the window. He made the mistake of looking too closely and found it full of dust that had likely not been disturbed in several years. He supposed it depended on how long

Rock had been living there.

There was small stove with a microwave on a shelf above it and a good-sized fridge that proved to be mostly empty aside from beer and a few take out containers. The coffee turned out to be in a big can on the top shelf of the fridge.

Cool.

He fixed a pot -- scrubbing the thing beforehand because, damn. Then Alex sat at the little Formica table, waiting for the shit to perk.

Drip.

Whatever.

Fuck, he couldn't believe he'd fucking done this.

The coffee smelled almost ready when Rock came stumbling into the kitchen, butt naked, Glock in one hand. The glare and tension eased when Rock saw it was him. "Fuck -- what time is it?"

"Early." He arched an eyebrow. "If you're gonna shoot me, do it before I get my first cup. I'd hate to be awake for it."

Rock blinked down at his weapon and flipped on the safety before putting it on top of the fridge. "Fuck, no -- I thought I had a burglar."

"Nah. I just was hunting for the Folgers."

Rock leaned against the counter, just sort of staring at him out of sleepy eyes. "You got somewhere you need to be?"

"Uh-uh. Well, at some point I gotta feed Grimmy, but I left him a lot." He let his eyes drag over Rock's body, admiring.

Rock's prick took notice of his look, perking right on up and Rock gave him slow grin. "Well, I can think of one good reason to be up then, but you'd have better luck with it back in bed."

"The coffee'll keep." He stood, his own cock taking

an interest.

"'Til there's daylight anyway." Rock's grin grew and one big hand reached out for him and tugged him up against all those muscles.

"Mmm..." Oh, yeah. That wasn't bad at all. "Bed, marine. Your body's making all sorts of promises."

"You know I'm good for it." Rock's arm went around his waist and he was half dragged down the little hall and back into Rock's bedroom.

"Hell, yes." He got himself a handful of rock-hard marine ass, squeezed it.

Rock gave him a little rumble and pushed him down onto the bed. "How do you want it, Alex?"

"That depends on you, Blue Eyes. You want a nice easy fuck and then an early breakfast or a hard, hot fuck that puts me back to sleep until after daylight?"

"Oh, I'm all for sleeping in, Rigger. Let's go with the hard fuck and the sleeping until daylight and then I'll take you out to IHOP."

"Gotta love a good plan." He grinned, hand wrapping around Rock's cock and stroking. "Fucking *and* waffles."

Rock just laughed, blue eyes dancing down at him. "Oh, I do appreciate a man who loves cock and knows how to fill his stomach."

"Knowing what you want is the secret to happiness."

"Well I guess that's why I'm happy. I pretty much know what I want and I'm not shy about asking for it. Now get over here and let me at your ass."

"Bossy fucking marine." He crowed, launched himself at Rock.

Rock laughed, arms grabbing him, holding him tight. "You love it."

"Who? Me?" He pressed closer, kissing that smile

good and hard.

Rock purred. "Yeah, you, Rigger." Those big hands landed on his ass and squeezed.

Alex groaned, tongue pushing in, fucking those lips in short, sharp stabs. Rock's mouth opened to let him in, fingers teasing his ass. He got his leg around Rock's, spreading some, holding on. One finger pushed into him and then pulled out. In and out, over and over again and it took a minute for him to realize Rock was moving in rhythm with his tongue. He groaned low, rocking with it, heart just pounding, toes curled. Damn.

"Fucking tight, Alex. You were the sweetest fuck I ever had. Still are." Those blue eyes were so warm.

Oh. Oh, thank God. "Then you don't mind that I'm more local now?"

"Mind? Why the fuck would I mind a chance at that mouth and this ass on a regular basis?"

"Just checking." He dove back into the kiss, just going with it.

Rock's chuckles filled his mouth, that finger inside him becoming two -- hot and thick, just right. He groaned, riding good and slow, just feeling it all through. Rock's prick was huge and hot against his belly, promising him another hell of a ride. He reached out, fingers stroking and sliding, jacking Rock off.

That prompted a third finger being pushed into him. "You about ready for a piece of me?"

"Fuck yes. Hard and deep." Alex nodded, heart just pounding.

Rock's fingers slid away and they rolled, Rock putting him on the bottom, back against the sheets, Rock's eyes boring down into his as the condom was put on. Things went from playful to intense, just like that and Alex? Man, he just went with it, pushing up into those amazing fucking muscles and making offers. Rock's cock pushed into him, fat and hot, filling him like nothing else ever.

"Oh..." He arched, still stretched from earlier, the burn fucking sweet.

Rock slid all the way in, only stopping when he was deep. "You good, Alex?"

"Good? Good's nowhere near as fine as this is."

Rock chuckled and started to move, nice and slow and deep to start.

"Oh, fuck yes." He reached up, hands on Rock's shoulders and fucking held on.

That cock just pounded into him, good solid thrusts that he'd be feeling for days. He groaned, legs wrapped around Rock's waist, pulling Rock in closer. One of Rock's hands went behind him, cupping one ass cheek and tugging him into each thrust. Rock's lips met his, just sort of dancing against his own.

He was going to fucking burn alive.

Alex squeezed, holding that blue-blue gaze, fucking flying. Groaning, Rock moved harder, tongue pushing in between his lips. The rhythm sped up, Rock's skin slapping against his ass. Then that big hand wrapped around his cock, holding him tight and hot.

He groaned, eyes rolling, hips just bucking. "Fuck, yes."

"Got it in one," growled Rock, body shining with sweat.

"Come on, more. Gotta..." His eyes rolled, hips snapping. "Gotta tire me out."

"I can go all night long, Rigger. All fucking night long."

"I know." It was why he left Texas.

Rock grinned ferociously and kept thrusting, pushing deep.

"Fuck." His eyes rolled, toes curling. He felt it everywhere, just burning.

"You're something else, Rabbit," murmured Rock, those eyes drilling him as surely as that cock.

"Don't stop, Blue Eyes. I need."

"You feel me stopping?" Rock bent and kissed him. "Not stopping."

"Good. Damn." The fucking room was spinning.

That rumble came from Rock again, the big man in him and around him, all his senses just filled with Blue and the heavy scent of sex, need.

His whole body went tight, balls drawing up. "Soon. Soon."

"Any time you want. I'm right behind you." That growl just slid right down his spine.

He shot hard enough his eyes rolled. Rock's roar chased the pleasure in his balls, the big guy jerking into him a couple more times and then collapsing down onto him, all hot and hard and sweaty. He hummed, eyes closing, relaxing into the mattress.

Rock pulled out slowly and collapsed next to him. "Fuck, that was something."

"No shit, Blue Eyes." He cuddled, stretched. "Sleep?"

"That was the plan." One big hand landed on his hip, held him against Rock's body.

"Mmhmm." Oh, hell yeah. That was it.

"And just think, pancakes and doing it all over again when we wake up."

"You know it, Blue Eyes." He stretched and snuggled in. Yeah. Nap. Food. Fucking.

Sheer goddamned perfection.

It had been a hell of a weekend.

And Alex cooking him Sunday dinner was the capper.

A fucking roast, potatoes, salad -- which he'd pointedly ignored -- and chocolate pie for dessert and the promise of more fucking before the day was done. Not to mention the possibility of repeating the last two days next weekend.

There was no bad here.

"You're one hell of a cook, Alex." He patted his belly. "One hell of a cook."

"Have to feed myself somehow, man."

He laughed and shook his head. "That's what take-out's for, Rigger."

"Man does not live on pizza alone, Blue Eyes." Alex stretched out, looking relaxed and happy and fine.

"Nope. There's also sex." He winked and reached over, patting Alex's thigh.

"Is that a high calorie meal?" Alex spread for him, easy as, well, pie.

"Can be. We both come out clean and you can eat all you can handle." Fuck, that would be something, that mouth with no rubber interfering.

"Mmm... promises, promises." Alex scooted closer, licking his lips.

"That mouth makes a man want to make promises." All sorts of promises.

"No shit?" Any closer and he would have a cowboy on his lap. He couldn't see any bad there, either.

"No shit, Alex." He let his hand drift up, fingertips teasing Alex's balls through his jeans.

"Mmm... Gonna make you chocolate pie more often..."

"You can make me chocolate pie every night if you want. I promise not to get tired of it." He winked, fingers pushing a little harder.

"You would. Chocolate pie has to be cut with brownies and the periodic cobbler."

He tilted his head, honestly considering that. "I don't know.... I tell you what I'll never get tired of though and that's a good blowjob. You don't need to cut that with anything."

Alex's laugh was pure fucking sex, the finest thing he'd ever heard. With a bit of a growl, he moved his fingers on up, curled them around that hot bulge in Alex's jeans.

"Mmm... oh, that feels fine." Long fingers landed on his shoulders, sliding toward his neck.

"You feel pretty good yourself, Rigger." He grinned at the look Alex gave him at the nickname. Kid was just going to have to get used to it.

"Rigger." Alex chuckled, taking one kiss after another.

He grinned and put his free hand behind Alex's head, tilting it and turning the next kiss into something long and deep. Alex opened right up, sucking on his tongue, hands holding his head. He purred, hand moving on Alex's cock, stroking right through his jeans. Kid had a mouth on him. Pure fucking heaven.

The kiss went on and on, stealing his breath, his fucking good sense. He squeezed that hard prick, thumb sliding up to pop open the top button of those sinfully tight jeans. Alex sucked in for him, the breath rocking them together. Fuck, but everything about the kid made him hard as fuck.

Groaning, he started in on the zipper, inching it down over Alex's cock. That hard cock just jumped out to meet his touch, hot and wet-tipped.

"Fuck, that's sweet." He wrapped his hand around it, thumb sliding across the liquid heat at the tip.

"Oh. Oh, fuck. 's good." Rigger's eyes rolled. Well, wasn't Alex just a sensual fucker. A grade A prime slut.

Chuckling, Rock slowed his hand a little, let his

thumbnail drag over that little slit. A full body shudder rocked Rigger, a dull flush coming up. It made him purr, fuck but he liked getting a reaction from the man he was fucking.

"Damn, you make me feel like I'm fixin' to catch fire."

"That's the idea." He leaned in to lick at Alex's neck. There was a spot. Oh, right fucking there.

"Rock. Rock, oh. Oh, hell yes." That? Was a damned sweet spot. He let his tongue play it while his hand continued to work that long cock. Taking his time. Alex moved slowly, steadily, deep moans filling the air.

He pushed Alex's t-shirt up with his free hand and left that sweet spot on Alex's neck, going for the sensitive little nipples instead. Those little bits of flesh were hard, trying to get his attention. He purred around one, teasing the tip with his tongue before wrapping his lips around it and sucking, looking to drive Alex wild.

"Blue. Sweet fuck." Those fingers tightened, Alex bucking, eyes rolling.

"Yeah, that's the idea." Uh-huh. A long, slow, sweet fuck.

He got a nod, a soft gasp. "Yeah. Yeah, good idea."

He bit down on Alex's nipple, shaking his head a bit, letting the motions pull on the little bit of hard flesh. His hand tightened around Alex's prick, sliding over the silky heat. He got a cry for that, that long body going stiff and still.

Come on, Rabbit, give it up for me. He worried that little bit of flesh, tongue flicking across the very tip as he let his thumb flick across the slit in Alex's prick again.

Alex jerked, heat pouring over his fingers, scent of spunk sharp in the room. He growled in triumph, hand still moving, pulling every sensation he could out of the long body. Deep, rough little sounds filled the air, Alex melting, moaning.

"You staying the night?" he asked. No use getting something started that they couldn't finish. "I have to be up at oh- five hundred."

"I got tomorrow off, but I'll make coffee."

"You don't need to get up -- long as you lock the door when you go."

If the man was staying though, they could keep on taking their time. He pushed Alex's t-shirt up and off. Oh, those little nipples were pink and hard. Fucking fine. He flicked a finger across one, rumbling softly as it went tighter. That responsiveness was fucking sexy.

"Mmm..." That fat cock just jerked, the tip wet.

He chuckled. "You didn't even go soft, Rigger. You looking forward to getting fucked again?"

"Me? Would I do that?"

His chuckles turned to purrs and he went for one of those hard little nipples, murmuring against it. "That's why you're here, isn't it? For a piece of the Rocketman. A nice, large piece."

"You know it. Need it." Oh, that was sweet.

"I've got what you need right here," he growled, latching onto Alex's nipple, sucking.

"Blue!" That cry just echoed, rang through the apartment.

A man could get used to a sound like that. He started tugging off Alex's jeans, lips sealed tight around that little bit of hard flesh the whole time. Alex was shaking, eyes wide and watching him, so close.

He met those grey eyes and slowly let Alex's nipple go. "You wait for me this time, Rabbit. I aim to be inside you when you blow this time."

He got a low groan, a nod. "Yeah. Yeah, okay. Damn, that. Damn."

"You're swelling my head, kid." He winked and

pulled back long enough to strip, pulling off his wifebeater and yanking open his jeans.

"That shouldn't be all I'm swelling..."

"Come and see for yourself," he said, slowly pumping his freed cock.

Those eyes were hot and burning on him, just focused and needy and wanting. Damn.

"Get the condom, Alex. You're going to ride me all night long."

"Uh-huh." Mmm... Had to love that need.

He sat down against the back of the couch, slouching just a little, legs spread, his cock pointing straight up. Then he grabbed hold of Alex and tugged him over.

"I'm gonna open that sweet ass of yours. Get it all ready for this."

Alex groaned, hands reaching for his prick, hands hot, sure. "P...promises, promises."

"More than a promise, Alex." He found the lube pushed down into the cushions and slicked up two fingers, sliding them along Alex's crack.

Those lean thighs spread wide. "Hell, yes."

He purred, letting his fingers slide right in. Alex was still a little loose from earlier -- they'd been doing a lot of fucking this weekend, the kid was going to be sore, but he was willing to lay odds it would be a good sore and Alex would be back next weekend for more of the same. And hot inside. Fuck. His cock throbbed in anticipation.

"Mmm... 's good." Alex leaned in, nuzzling into his throat.

He let his head drop back, rumbling softly as his fingers worked that sweet ass. The kid was careful, never marking or sucking, just tasting, letting that tongue drag.

"Shit, that mouth is worth your weight in gold." He pushed a third finger in, stretching them all wide inside

Alex.

"Oh..." Alex shuddered, starting to move slow and careful.

"You like that, Rigger? What about this?" He found that little gland and pegged it hard.

"Fuck!" Alex bucked, body going tight-tight.

"Yep, you know what we're doing all right." He grinned and winked and kept pressing his fingers against that little spot. Alex just panted, eyes closed, just riding it. "Yeah, that's it. I know you love it."

"Uh-huh..." That lean body rocked, moving for him.

He kept his fingers stretching and pressing, watching Alex move until he couldn't stand it anymore and then he let his fingers slide on out.

"Want you, Rigger. Now."

"Yeah. Yeah, fuck me. Please." Rig spread, shifting, begging for his prick.

He got the rubber on -- fuck he was looking forward to doing this skin on skin -- and rubbed the top of his prick against that sweet, hot ass. Alex bore down, head falling back, a sweet groan just pouring out as he pushed in. His hands went to Alex's waist, holding on, a low groan of his own sounding. "Ride me, cowboy," he whispered.

"Fuck, yes." Those long hands landed on his shoulders, Alex moving, rocking, just riding him nice and easy. It felt so fucking good, Alex's body sliding on his cock, squeezing and releasing him.

"Mmm..." Alex's mouth slid over his shoulder, his throat, his jaw.

He tightened his hands, bringing Alex down a little harder, a little faster, speeding them just a little.

"So fucking hot. Makes leaving Texas less awful."

He just purred, pleased as punch. He knew the kid loved Texas something fierce, had seen that when he'd been down there. He turned Alex's face up, taking that mouth with his own. Fuck, those kisses were...

Shit.

He stopped thinking, just felt. His eyes were caught by grey, his whole body focused on the heat and glide of his cock inside Alex.

"Blue..." Teeth tested his bottom lip.

"Right here. Right fucking here." He planted his feet and started thrusting up, hips pushing his cock in deeper.

"Yeah. Yeah. Right... right there."

"Uh-huh." Yeah, he saw the way those grey eyes lit up every time he pushed in.

Alex leaned back, cock rubbing his belly, leaving wet kisses. He could get used to this being a real Sunday night regular thing. The thought made him thrust up harder, faster and he wrapped one hand around Alex's prick.

He got a cry, ass tightening, milking him.

"Oh yeah, just like that." He thrust harder, hand squeezing tight as Alex's cock pushed through it.

Alex just nodded, moving faster, bouncing on his cock.

"Soon, kid, soon." He growled a little, hips working hard, pushing up.

"Uh-huh. Like now..." Alex went tight, shaking as he came.

He just roared, Alex's body pulling the spunk right out of his prick, making him shake it was so fucking strong, so fucking good.

"So fine." Alex slumped into him. "Damn."

"You're not so bad yourself, Rigger. Not so bad at all." He chuckled, fingers lazy on Alex's back. "Pretty fucking good, in fact."

"Mmm... Fucking. Good."

"You got that right." Fucking very good. "'m glad you decided to give leaving Texas a try."

"Yeah. Yeah, me too, Blue Eyes."

He purred, hands sliding on Alex's warm skin. "Come to bed. You can give me a wake-up call in the morning."

"Mmm... I get the feeling you're not talking about coffee..."

"That's because you're a smart man, Rigger. A very smart man." He gave Alex a wink and flexed, his cock throbbing inside Alex's body.

"Mmhmm... Smart and lucky and well-fucked."

"You got that right." Rock grinned and took another kiss.

Oh, yeah. He was pretty fucking pleased this cowboy had left Texas.

CHAPTER FIVE

Oh, man. He was loving the sunshine. Alex was stretched out on his balcony in nothing but tiny tiny cutoffs, sweat and a smile. Grimmy was snoring beside him, the smell of cocoa butter filled the air and his beer was fucking cold.

Hallelujah.

He reached out with his toes, turned George Strait up *just* a little bit. Damn, if he closed his eyes it could almost be Texas.

A loud knock sounded. Oh, that had to be his marine. He'd casually invited Rock to come to his place this weekend and Rock had said he'd likely show up after his football game at the base.

"'s open!" He really hoped it wasn't an axe-murderer. He didn't want to move.

Door opened and closed. "Alex? I brought pizza."

Good lord and butter, did the man live on the stuff?

He grinned. "Yeah? You can stay. There's beer in the fridge. And a chocolate pie and possibly a couple steaks."

"Well fuck me blind and call me happy. I love pizza for breakfast." Rock appeared at the door to the balcony, giving him a grin. "Aren't you a sight for sore eyes. I can't remember a week ever being so fucking long." Rock's eyes met his and then wandered, settling just south of his belly button.

Oh, now, weren't those eyes just the finest thing? "You been busy, Blue Eyes?"

"Same old, same old." Rock shrugged, leaning against the door. "Seems the weekends have more going for them."

His cock started to fill, balls drawing up a little. "Yeah?"

Rock grinned. "Oh yeah." Another sweep of those blue eyes and Rock turned and headed back in.

He rolled up, swigging the last of his beer as he headed in. "I should probably dunk my head in the shower."

"What a coincidence..."

"Hmm?" He lifted his face for a quick kiss, knowing he was slick and probably smelled sweaty.

Rock just purred, the kiss a lot more than quick. Those big hands slid around him, cupping his ass.

"Gonna get you... uh... Oh, fuck, you feel good... All sweaty."

"I happen to like sweaty. All fucking male. It's hot."

"Perv." Alex just moaned, pressing closer, cock good and hard now.

"You think that makes me a perv? Just wait 'til you see what I have in mind for your ass."

Rock's mouth closed over his again, the kiss deep, hard. Sweet fuck, yes. He arched into it, hips rolling and to hell with Rock's clothes. Rock's hands squeezed his ass, fingers pressing the seam into his crack. A low rumble vibrated from Rock's chest, going right through him. He wrapped one leg around Rock's hip, rubbing them together, squeezing them together. Oh, yeah. Just. Like. That.

"Sweet as fuck," growled Rock, one hand sliding along his leg.

"More." He climbed right up that fine fucking body.

Rock supported him, hands on his ass, legs spreading slightly to take his weight. Solid as his namesake, Rock kept kissing him, and never once did Alex feel like he was going to fall or be let go. Oh, fucking yes. Alex dove into the kiss, hotter now than he was outside, cock like a spike.

One of Rock's hands moved around to work on opening his cut-offs. There was another growl as the button proved stubborn.

"Hold me." He didn't wait to see if Rock listened, just reached down, opened both their jeans, slid two zippers down. "There. There."

Rock chuckled. "You've done this before."

"Never promised to be a virgin, you beautiful fucking man. Just searching for a perfect cock." Found it too, hadn't he?

Rock's chuckles turned into laughter. "I'd say your search is over right here, Rigger."

That fat, fine prick pushed against his own, Rock sliding them together.

"Mmm... vain motherfucker." He arched and rode it, humming low.

Rock didn't back down one bit. "I can back it up."

"You can. Hell, I'm all for backing it up."

Rock chuckled and actually backed up a few steps,

just grinning at him. A moment later their mouths were together again, the kiss hard and deep, tongues twisting, echoing the thrusting movements of their hips that slid their pricks together.

Mmm... Happy fucking day. Hops and heat and marine -- fuck, yes, Alex was thinking he might just stay right there for a minute.

"You smell fucking good," muttered Rock. "Gonna smell even better soon."

"Uh-huh. More. Gonna smell like us." Shut *up*, Alex. Just fuck the pretty marine.

Rock grunted and backed up a couple more steps, leaning against the wall. Then one big hand wrapped around their cocks, tugging firmly.

"Fuck yes." He bent his head down, hips jerking, fucking that palm, just like that.

"Come on, Rig. Give it up to me." Rock's thumb slid across the head of his prick.

He grunted, bit out his 'yes' and shot, entire body into it. Rock moaned, hand continuing to move hard and fast and then more heat splashed between them and yeah, that smelled like sex. Him and Rock sex.

Fucking wonderful sex. "Mmm..."

Rock gave him a long, lazy kiss. "You still wanting that shower, Rigger?"

"Mmhmm. Shower. Wet and slick and soapy, what's not to like?"

"My thoughts exactly." Rock didn't put him down, just readjusted the hold on his ass and walked down the hall with him.

"You are a strong man, Blue Eyes." He rested his chin on Rock's shoulder, fingers exploring.

Rock nodded. "I'm a marine."

"I noticed that." Alex chuckled, grinned against Rock's throat. "Possibly it was the haircut that gave you away."

Rock laughed. "You think?"

He was set down, Rock grinning at him, beautiful cock hanging out of his open jeans. "Those shorts you're wearing are likely illegal."

"These? No... They're just redneck Speedo." Alex winked, shimmied a little. "Pocket for my pocketknife and smokes."

Rock laughed again, smile looking just grand on that face, those blue eyes dancing. "There's no question I can see what you're packing in those and I don't see any pocketknives or smokes. However, I do like what I see. I like it a lot."

Mmm... Nothing like a man who knew how to appreciate what he had to offer. "You sure you don't see any weapons in here?" He bent over, spread a little as he turned the water on.

Rock made a rumbling purr of a sound and before he could stand, Rock was there, rubbing up against his ass. "No weapons. Just the finest ass this side of the equator."

He rubbed right back, humming, offering a little ride 'em cowboy action. Rock's hands slid around to grab onto his hips, the rubbing getting a little more vigorous. While they were at it, Rock grabbed his cutoffs and tugged them on down his legs. Rock's cock was that much hotter without the denim in between.

"Mmm... Someone's needing again." Had to love a short recovery period.

"Yeah, you're fucking inspiring." Rock pushed off his own jeans and toed off his boots and then rubbed against him again, cock just sliding along his ass. "You do have condoms in here, right?"

"Medicine cabinet, where they belong."

"Were they the first thing you unpacked?" Rock

asked, hand staying on his ass as the medicine cabinet door was opened, the condoms found.

"No. My lube was. I don't need rubbers to jack off." And really, it was the coffee maker and the phone. Momma was too fucking wigged about him being out here.

Rock chuckled, but the sound was distracted and a moment later one of Rock's thick fingers pushed into him.

He grunted, got a better stance on the tile floor. "You want to do this in the shower?"

"Oh yeah, good plan. Hot water. Let me just get you all slicked up and ready for the Rocketman first." One finger was suddenly two, Rock spreading him, searching for his gland.

Rig arched, helping out, riding that touch until... "Oh. Fuck! Right there."

Rock rumbled happily, working that spot, just nailing his gland. Oh. Okay. Fuck yes. Good marine. Very, very good. His hips rolled, ass pushing back against Rock's thick fingers. Rock's cock slid along the back of his thigh, leaking, like a hot, hard reminder that it was still there, still wanting.

"Sexy fucking slut," muttered Rock.

"That... that a problem, marine?" He fucking loved this, loved the stretch of those fingers.

"Not from where I'm standing."

A third finger pushed in, the stretch increasing, but Rock was a generous man and kept the focus on his gland. Moaning had graduated to panting, little cries pushing from him, just like that, desperate and harsh.

Rock kept it up a little longer before those fingers slowed. "You about ready for the real thing?"

He nodded, back arching like a bitch in heat, burning top to bottom. "Now, Blue Eyes. Fuck me."

"Thought you wanted it in the shower?" Those fingers disappeared though, big hands grabbing his hips and rocking him back onto that thick cock.

"Fuck the shower." He spread wider, eyes rolling up. Yes. Yes, right there.

"No, Alex. I think I'll stick with fucking you."

And fuck him Rock did, pulling him right back all the way onto that cock, the heat so deep inside him. Oh, yeah. Good fucking plan. He got one leg propped up on the tub, letting Rock in deeper and deeper. Rock groaned, hands tightening on his hips, pulling him into driving thrusts. He just went with it, just rode it with deep, low cries. Yeah. Come on. Blue.

Rock kept thrusting and he just knew Rock would do it all fucking day if that's what he wanted. "Fucking good, Rig."

"Yes. Fucking perfect." He arched, hand working his own cock in time.

"Perfect fucking," said Rock, changing the angle and finding his gland again.

"There!" His hand scrabbled on the tile, eyes rolling.

"Oh yeah. Yeah." Rock kept pegging his gland, kept working it, working him, just pounding him.

His orgasm barreled down on him like a freight train, entire body tensing and shaking as he shot.

"Oh, fuck!" Rock jerked into him, cock throbbing as he filled the condom.

He slumped against the tile, panting, gasping. Damn.

Rock kept hold of his hip with one hand, the other petting his back, sliding along his spine. "Fucking good, Alex."

"You know it, marine. Worth chocolate pie and steak."

"Oh, good sex *and* chocolate pie and steak? I'm one happy fucking man."

"Hell, there's even beer." They moved into the shower, the spray still mostly warm.

Rock chuckled. "Cool. Sure beats drinking it alone at home."

"Well, you know, if there's a weekend, you're welcome to my beer."

"That goes both ways, too. Wouldn't want the stuff in my fridge to go off." Rock grabbed the soap and started running those big hands over him.

"Sounds fair." Hell, he could leave the big man leftovers, save the pizza budget.

"I bet there's even beer at a pool hall or two that's needing drinking."

"You think? They have beer at those out here?"

Rock popped him in the ass. "They do. I'll prove it to you next Friday."

"Sounds fair. You buy the beer, I'll kick your butt at pool." He rubbed against Rock, sudsing them both up.

Rock chuckled, the sound nice and husky. "You mean you'll try."

"Trying's for wimps. I will." He kissed that smile, winking. "And make you like it."

"Oh-ho! You think so, do you?" Rock growled a little and crowded him against the tile. "You think you can make me like getting my butt kicked at pool?"

"Absolutely. Me? Bent over the pool table, legs spread? What's not to like?"

"Oh, someone's gonna be cheating, I see."

"Cheating? Me? Never!" He pushed up against all those muscles. Fuck, he liked this game.

Rock pushed back, rubbing against him. "That ass is definitely a cheating tool."

"This cowboy thing?" He wiggled the ass in

question.

"That's the one." Rock reached around him, grabbed him, squeezed.

"Mmm... Your hands feel pretty nice on that."

"Yeah? Maybe I'll do some cheating of my own." Rock leaned in, kissing him nice and easy.

He hummed into the kiss, those pretty blue eyes just happy as hell.

Rock suddenly jerked and jumped. "Fuck! That's cold."

He scrambled for the faucet, laughing and trying to avoid the spray. "Out. Outoutoutout."

Rock puffed up, blocking him from the spray. "I've got you covered -- Run!"

Oh, that man? Just a keeper. He grabbed a towel, wrapping it around Rock as soon as the water was off.

Laughing, Rock pressed close. "You gonna warm me all up now?"

He snuggled in, rubbing all those muscles down. "You know it, Blue Eyes."

"You got great hands. They're almost as good as that mouth."

"Just almost." He could spend, oh... ten or twelve years working those muscles. Maybe thirteen.

"I'm not sure there's anything as good as that mouth, Alex."

He used it, lips trailing over those fine fucking muscles. "You taste good. Your test in soon?"

"It sure as fuck had better be."

Rock cupped his cheek, slid his thumb between Rig's lips. "I want to feel this full on, sucking my brains out."

He moaned, lips wrapped around that thick thumb, sucking hard, head just bobbing. Wanted to taste Rock, drink that beautiful son of a bitch down.

"Soon, Rabbit. Fucking soon." Those blue eyes just

stared right into him.

It was a whimper that left him, the sound almost embarrassing with its need. Rock's thumb popped out of his mouth and he was given a hard kiss. Oh, yeah. Soon. Soon, but until then? Until then, this would so do.

Rock grabbed a piece of pizza and sat back, opening his mail.

Bill, bill, fucking advertisements, envelope from the lab. Oh. Fucking A.

He opened it, knowing it would clear him. Hell, he was dialing the phone before he had the paper out of the envelope. "Come on, Rigger, pick up so I can give you the good news."

"'lo? God *damn* it, Grimmy! Hold still! You're still soapy!" He heard the phone clatter onto the floor. "Motherfucker! Oh, you big bastard. That best not be Momma on the phone or I'm shaving your stinky ass!"

Rock just laughed, his humor only increasing when a glance at the lab results proved him right on the clean results.

"Hey. Sorry. Bath time. Hello."

"You want to shave that ass, I'll hold the beast down for you, Rigger."

"Rocketman? Hey. How's it hanging, man? Happy Friday. We still meeting for pool?"

"We could. Or you could come over here and get a proper taste of the Rocketman."

"Hmm? Grimmy, get *down*. Christ on a crutch. What do you mea..." He heard a splash. "We got results for you, man?"

"Yep. Cleaner than any whistle and harder'n nails right now, Rig. I'd hate to have to give my hand a work out..."

"Don't you fucking dare. I'll be over in a half hour."

"If you let the mutt drip dry I bet you could make it in fifteen."

He hung up the phone, chuckling, going back to his pizza.

It wasn't fifteen, but it was closer to twenty than thirty when a freshly showered cowboy knocked on his door, looking good in old jeans and a tight t-shirt. He pulled Alex in without even a hello, mouth closing over the one that he was counting on sending him right to fucking heaven.

Alex dove into the kiss, just meeting him head-on, fucking stealing his breath. He closed the door with one hand, the other finding Alex's ass and tugging him close. Those long fingers were already between them, working his jeans open, fishing for his cock. Oh yeah, he wasn't interested in pussyfooting around with this either. He let the kiss end and put his hands on Alex's shoulders, helping him find his knees.

"Fuck, yes. This all for me?" Alex didn't fuck around, just swallowed his cock down with a happy sound.

Jesus fucking Christ. "Every fucking inch."

Oh, as fucking great as that mouth was before, this was... Fuck. Fuck, yes.

He widened his stance, eyes rolling in his skull. He was going to fucking die and be fucking happy about it. Alex took him in deep, took him all the way down, nose buried in his pubes before pulling back. He watched, the sight awesome, the way it felt something fucking else.

Those grey eyes stared up at him, hotter than hell. "Come on, Blue Eyes. Fuck my mouth."

"Oh, you're a fucking wet dream." Growling, he wrapped his hands around Rig's head and started to move, taking what he needed, giving Rig what he wanted.

Sweet fuck. The whole world shorted out, nothing but Alex and that mouth, that tongue. He wanted it to last for fucking ever, but it was too damned good and in too too short a time he was shouting, coming hard. Rigger drank him down, and he could fucking feel it. Feel each swallow.

He moaned, fingers sliding over Rig's hollowed cheeks. "Fanfuckingtastic, Alex."

That mouth cleaned him off, eyes closing.

"That? Was worth the fucking wait." He kept patting Rigger, fingers sliding through the short curls.

Rigger sucked the tip of his prick, tongue fucking the slit, so gentle, so careful.

"Fuck." He groaned, a shudder going through him. He'd known it was going to be good without the rubbers -- Alex was a big enough cockhound he *knew* that. But he hadn't known just how fucking good.

"Mmmhmmmm..." Alex nodded, eyes lit up. Those fingers were on his balls, stroking, pulling.

"Keeping me hard, good man. Gonna take that sweet fucking ass without anything between me and it." He felt Alex's groan all the way along his cock. Oh, somebody wanted that. Yeah, he wanted it, too. It didn't look like either of them were in a hurry to move on though, not with that hot, wet mouth making fucking magic on his cock. He'd let Rigger take all the sweet fucking time he wanted.

The sweet suction never stopped, just continued, driving him crazy. He never even started going soft, his cock hard as diamonds inside what he was thinking was heaven. Christ, how did anyone ever even begin to think with that mouth available?

Eyes closing, he groaned, fingers sliding along Alex's stretched lips. Alex nibbled at his fingertips, teeth teasing.

He chuckled. "Sexy motherfucker." Sexy enough he was surprised he was still standing. "Bed."

Alex looked up, blinking, nodding. "Bed."

"Yeah. The flat soft thing." He tugged at Alex. Come on. It was time to get horizontal.

Alex stood, jeans rasping Rock's sensitive cock. "Yeah. Yeah, Blue Eyes."

He put a hand on the back of Alex's neck, kissing the swollen lips. Fuck, he could taste himself there. Alex opened, pressing into him, rubbing, so hard. He stepped out of his jeans and started walking back toward his bedroom, all without breaking the kiss, his tongue fucking Rigger's mouth. Deep, rough sounds pushed into his lips, Rig hard as hell.

As soon as he got them into the bedroom he attacked Rig's clothes, getting his hands on Rig's skin.

"Yeah. Yeah, fuck yes." Alex helped, tugging and shimmying out of his clothes.

He reached for Alex's nipples as soon as they came into view. Oh, yeah. Those eyes went wide, Rig pushing close and almost fucking his belly. He dove back into Rig's mouth, playing the little titties, rubbing their bodies together. Rig's cock left wet kisses all along his belly, Rig's fingers digging into his shoulders. Groaning, he pulled Rig down onto the bed, rolling them so he was on top, hips driving his cock along Alex's skin.

"Fuck me. Come on. Let me feel your cock." Rig's fingers dug into his ass, demanding.

"Slut," he muttered, reaching over for the lube.

"Yes. I never have. Never been bareback. Want to know."

"Me neither, Rabbit. Never cared to break that rule." Alex was different though, something worth changing his ways for.

Alex drew him down, the kiss deep and something

special, something hotter than hell. He could fucking lose himself in this mouth, in this man. He slicked up his fingers, sliding two in, finesse just blown away by sheer fucking need. Alex squeezed him, ass milking him.

Oh, sweet fuck, it was going to be a hell of a ride.

He pushed in another finger, getting Alex stretched out quickly.

"Come on. Don't play. I need it. Need you."

He growled and pushed Rigger's legs up over his shoulders, lining up and pushing right into that fucking beautiful heat.

"Oh..." Alex purred as his eyes rolled right up into his head. Fuck yes. It was hot and tight and about enough to blow his head right off.

"That's. Damn, Jim. Damn."

He nodded, bending to bring their mouths together, the kiss slow and deep.

Then he started to move.

Oh, fuck, it was hot and he could just bury himself inside Alex for fucking ever. He moved slowly, feeling it all, the pleasure intense, deep. Alex rode him, moving on his cock. He just stared into Alex's grey eyes, fucking caught in the pleasure, in the heat.

"Fuck, Rocketman. This is... " Alex smiled suddenly, face lit up. "When we're done can we do it again?"

"Fuck yes." He thrust. "And again." He thrust again. "And again."

"Oh, good. Good plan. I love this plan."

"Yeah, I'm kind of fond of it myself." Rock grinned, groaned as he thrust again, Rig's body squeezing his cock hard. "Very fond."

"Mmm... All the... all the positions. All the fucking fun."

"Fuck, yeah." He purred, thrust harder.

Rigger jerked, coming with a surprised cry. "Blue!"

"Fuck!" His hips snapped, the pleasure just flowing from him. "Fuck, yeah."

He groaned, Alex still riding him nice and easy, eyes closed.

Oh yeah, he could do this awhile. A nice long while.

"Eight ball in the corner pocket." Alex made his shot, just winning the game, grinning up at Chon. "Your turn to buy the round."

He was waiting on Rock, it was Friday night and they'd been meeting here pretty regular. A couple of games of pool, a few beers, then they'd head to a soft bed for some hard fucking.

Alex had won three games out of five and was feeling pretty good -- six beers good -- but he'd be feeling better if that marine would show. He could use a bit of food, really.

He was just starting on beer number seven when Rock walked in the door, looking mighty, mighty fine. He covered his moan behind a cough. Oh, yeah. Food. Less beer. More food. Fuck, that man was hot. Rock nodded at him, gave him a grin and headed for the bar, sitting at a stool and talking to the bartender.

He turned back to the pool table, managing a decent break and sinking a couple. "You're stripes."

The game went fairly easy, Chon as tipsy as he was.

Rock wandered over with his second beer in hand.

"Howdy, marine." He nodded, swaying just a touch. "How goes it?"

"'m hungry. You?"

"Yeah. Been experiencing a liquid diet this evening and it's catching me."

Rock chuckled. "You 'bout ready to go then? Catch a meal?"

"Yeah. You driving?" He made his last shot, scratching on the eight. "Damnit. It's yours, Chon. I'm done."

"I'll just take your money for the next round then and see you next week," Chon answered with a grin.

He handed over a ten-spot and chuckled. "Pricey date, asshole, considering you never put out. You ready, marine?"

"Born ready." Rock finished his beer and put it on an empty table, walking out ahead of him, giving him a real nice view of that fine ass.

He weaved through the tables, following easily. They hit the door and the wind whapped him hard, making him shiver. "Damn! It got chilly. Happy weekend, Blue."

Rock gave him a grin. "I'm sure it will be. Parsons dropped me off, gimme your keys."

"Pushy bastard." He grinned and handed them over with a grin. "What're you hungry for?"

"Oh, I think you know what I'm hungry for." Rock gave him another grin. "Let's get some take out on the way back to my place though -- you need something non-liquid in your diet."

"Yeah. Y'all are running late tonight. Somebody got their panties in a wad on base?" He slid into the passenger side, automatically reaching to click the radio to something they could both handle -- classic rock. Wooboy.

"Something like that." Rock got the jeep started and pulled into the road. "What, aside from me, do you want to eat?"

"Let's swing by Dairy Dart for burgers and milkshakes. That's quick and cheap and gets us closer to a place where I can suck that sweet cock." Nice thing about Rock, he didn't need any romancing.

"If you weren't in such dire need of actual food,

you'd be sucking it now." Rock gave him a wink.

Alex snorted. "And you'd be raiding my fridge between thrusts if we didn't feed you, so don't go there."

Rock chuckled and pulled into the drive-through, ordering for them both. He leaned his head back, just listening to that low voice, letting it pour over him.

The food was put in his lap. "Give me a burger -- might as well eat while we're driving."

"Huh? Sure. Sorry, got to listening to you talk and floated some. How much do I owe you?" He found Rock's burger -- no veggies, extra meat, extra cheese, ketchup, and unwrapped it.

"You give me a blow job when we get home and we'll call it even," Rock told him around a mouthful of meat.

"Sounds like a fair deal." Alex grabbed his burger and ate slow enough not to make himself sick.

By the time they hit Rock's place, the burgers were gone and the milkshakes were nearly finished, Rock still munching on a few fries. "You gonna make it up the stairs, cowboy?"

"I reckon I'll manage just fine." He grinned, a hell of a lot steadier with food in his belly and a marine close at hand.

They headed up, Rock close enough to his ass he could *feel* that heat. "I can smell you under all that beer and smoke," murmured Rock.

His steps stuttered, balls tightening in a heartbeat. "Oh."

One big hand ghosted across his ass and then Rock was ahead of him, getting the door unlocked. That man was going to fucking *kill* him one day.

Damn, he was lucky.

Alex followed Rock in, grinning at Grim's happy bark. The pup loved Rock beyond good sense, drove the marine batshit. Amused the fuck out of him, though.

Rock's hand got a hold of his collar and dragged him in. "What's got you grinning?"

"You, Blue Eyes. You're happy-making." Alex leaned in for a kiss, tongue sliding over warm, still-salty lips.

Rock gave a little growl, mouth opening wide, tongue sliding into his mouth. Humming, he pushed close, hips moving to a slow waltz purring through his head. Delicious. There wasn't anything about the flavors of his man he didn't like. Big hands slid around to his ass, sliding with his movements. Oh, yeah. Sweet. Fucking *perfect*. He wrapped his arms around Rock's neck, fingers working on the tight muscles.

Rock brought him in a little closer, letting him feel that hot package up close and personal. Alex fed Rock a little moan, hips rocking forward and rubbing. Fuck, but he was wanting. Rock rumbled and the hands on his ass squeezed.

"Somebody," Rock said, stopping to give him a kiss before going on. "Promised me a blow job."

"Is that so?" He grinned, licking Rock's lips. "Well, now. I wouldn't be one to back down on a promise, Blue Eyes. You want to head toward my bed?"

"I hear that's where you do your best work."

One eyebrow lifted slowly, his fingers sliding over Rock's prick. "Talk to yourself often, old man?"

Rock chuckled, hips pushing into his touch. He started walking them backwards, playfully leading Rock by the prick, teasing shamelessly. Rock chuckled again, the sound more husky, sexier. And that smile, oh, that one was his.

"Slut."

"Yours." He met those blue eyes without an ounce of worry, fingers sliding open Rock's fly.

Rock nodded. "I guess you are at that."

He nodded and let it go, easing down to his knees before that beautiful body. They both knew what was what.

Rock groaned, hands sliding into his hair. "Oh yeah."

He fished that heavy, hard cock out, lips wrapping around the head to kiss.

This groan was louder. "Fuck, yeah."

He spent his own sweet time licking and exploring, using tongue and lips to give Rock as much as the marine could bear. Rock finally growled, hands tightening on his head, holding him still as those hips went to work, pushing the huge prick in and out of his mouth. Moaning, he relaxed, letting Rock take what was needed, letting Rock give what was needed. Rock fucked his mouth hard, groans growing louder, hands tightening on his head.

"Rig! Fuck!" Blue shot down his throat.

He swallowed hard, throat working around that sweet cock, body throbbing. Rock was purring for him, hands sliding through his hair, along his cheeks and neck. He relaxed, moaning and licking, purring. Loving on Blue's cock.

"Oh, Fuck, Rigger. We shoulda made it to the bed."

"Mmm... we'll make it, Blue Eyes."

"You keep licking that like it's a never-ending popsicle and I'm not."

"You're not?" He chuckled and kissed Rock's belly. "You're still damned stunning."

"And you've got the best mouth ever." Rock grabbed him under his arms and hauled him up, bringing their mouths together. He wrapped himself around Rock with a soft cry, hips rubbing against hot muscles just a little frantically. Hands dropping to his ass, Rock pulled him in tighter and shuffled them toward the bed.

"Blue... Fucking good." His whispers slid into hungry

lips, his fingers massaging Rock's scalp.

Rock pushed him down onto the bed, following him down, pressing him into the mattress. "Fucking... good."

"Yeah. Hot. Rock. Shit." He arched, moaning as the friction tightened his balls.

Rock's fingers tugged at his shirt, pulling it off and then going for his jeans, working them down until they hit the tops of his cowboy boots. He toed off his boots, managing to do it without losing the mood or racking Rock -- both of which were an accomplishment. Rock took care of the jeans and then worked quickly on his own duds, leaving them both naked and pressed together.

"Fuck, you're nice and warm, Blue." He pushed closer, one leg wrapping around Rock's fine-as-fuck ass.

Rock chuckled. "And you're always cold, cowboy."

Rock's hot lips pressed against his, tongue splitting them apart and pushing in. Alex fastened his lips around Rock's tongue and started sucking, moaning as their hips picked up the rhythm. Fuck. Oh, fuck yes. Rock's hands slid over him, fingertips finding his nipples and scraping across them. That made him whimper, drew a full-body shudder from him. Christ, he was sensitive there.

Rock fed a noise into his mouth and his fingers lingered, sliding around his nipples and tugging and flicking. He knew he was making desperate, needy sounds, knew his body was pushing up into Rock and demanding more, but he couldn't stop, not even if he wanted to.

Rock kissed back from his mouth to his ear and rumbled softly. "Like that, don't you, Rabbit?"

"Oh, fuck. Blue. Yes. Fuck, yes." His toes curled as Rock's voice slid right the *fuck* down his spine.

Rock licked at the skin behind his ear, breath hot against him as those fucking fingers kept pulling and tugging and sending him into fucking orbit.

Oh, God. He was going to come -- just like this, just with those fingers on his... "Blue!"

Rock growled, hips pushing hard against him, nails just barely scratching across his nipples. He shot hard enough that he saw stars, entire body shaking with the aftermath.

"Sweet," murmured Rock, weight sliding to the side, one arm and leg staying on him, holding him close.

Alex made some noise that was supposed to be a 'yes' and didn't quite manage it, snuggling close. Rock's chuckle sounded sleepy. It was a good thing they'd already eaten.

He dropped a soft kiss on Rock's throat, eyes falling closed. Yeah. Damned fine.

It was shaping up to be an A-1 weekend.

Rock couldn't find his favorite pair of jeans. He'd checked the chair in his bedroom, the floor, under the bed, he went out and checked the front room and kitchen, the bathroom.

Growling, he went back to the kitchen where he'd last seen Alex. He stopped for a moment, enjoying the cowboy in his kitchen. He was getting used to Rigger being around.

"Hey. I can't find my fucking jeans. The ones with the little hole in the thigh." His favorite, most comfortable jeans and Rigger had better not have thrown them out. He wasn't *that* used to the man being around.

"I washed 'em. I got something all over mine yesterday. They're in your bottom drawer with the others."

"Oh." He offered Rigger a sheepish smile. "Sorry, I'd left 'em on the floor last time I took 'em off."

Rigger chuckled, grinned and wandered over, hands landing on his stomach. "I needed some jeans to fill the load up."

He grinned, flexing the muscles in his stomach for Rigger. "I'm more used to doing them when they step up and remind me. I might like this way better."

"You think?" Rigger wasn't really paying attention, eyes on his abs, pink tongue wetting those talented lips.

"Oh, I don't think, Rigger. It's against policy." He winked, his own eyes on that mouth.

Alex chuckled, leaned in to lick the hollow of his throat, hands moving down. He just purred and let his head drop back, letting Rigger lick and touch any damn part of him Rig wanted. This beat having someone wash his fucking jeans any day of the week.

"Mmm... taste good, Blue Eyes."

"Eat as much as you want..." he offered. Grinning, he slid his hands over Rigger, searching for the bottom of his t-shirt. He got a chuckle, a sharp nip then that mouth was moving again, searching out his nipples. He tugged off Rigger's t-shirt and let his hands wander over that smooth skin, encouraging Rigger to keep going.

Rigger hummed, licking and loving on him, moaning low.

"Fucking amazing mouth, Rigger. Never had its equal. Never." It was fucking magic.

"Flattery will get you sucked off, Blue Eyes."

His cock throbbed and he grinned. "Then I'll have to keep flattering."

"You know it." Rigger cupped his cock, thumbs sliding along the shaft.

He groaned and brought their mouths together, kissing Rigger hard, his hands cupping Rigger's head, tilting it so his tongue could press deep. Oh. Oh, he fucking loved that, the way Rigger gave it up.

He rumbled happily, the sound coming from somewhere deep inside him, hands finding Rigger's ass and squeezing. Rigger pushed back into his hands, rocking a little, rubbing.

"Someone's wearing too many clothes," he noted, fingers working Rigger's jeans.

"Yeah? Damn that clean laundry." Alex chuckled, licking at his lips, moaning low. Those eyes just looked at him like he was a fucking god.

He just put his head back and laughed, not even thinking on how happy it made him having Rigger in his arms. He took Rigger's mouth, hands working those sinfully tight jeans off and suddenly no one was overdressed and they were skin on fucking skin.

Rigger climbed him like he was a fucking mountain, legs sliding around his waist. He grabbed hold of that ass as their cocks slid together, spreading his own legs a bit so he didn't overbalance. No way was he fucking dropping this load.

"Oh. Blue. Yeah." Rigger nodded, moaned.

He started moving them, pushing their cocks together over and over as their mouths met, tongues tangling. Rigger was right there, hand reaching down to work their pricks. Growling, he took a step backward and leaned against the wall, working his hips harder.

"Oh. Oh, fuck yes." Rigger grinned, the look a little wild.

He laughed and dove in for another kiss, taking Rigger's mouth hard. Rigger's hand clenched, squeezing good and hard.

"That's it, just like that." He purred and pushed into Rigger's hand, feeling fucking awesome.

"Uh-huh. Fuck." Rigger pushed, hips rocking, grinding against him.

"Nah, this is just rubbing off," he muttered. "Fucking comes after."

"Mmm... Excellent plan, Blue Eyes. Fucking...

mmm... yeah. There."

"Uh-huh." He grunted and rocked harder, hands tight on Rigger's sweet ass, tugging him in close again and again.

Rigger took another kiss, sucking his tongue, desperate little sounds filling his mouth. He squeezed Rigger's ass as his balls tightened up, the pleasure shooting through him and out his cock.

Rigger groaned, hand moving faster now that it was slick, dragging over their pricks. "Fucking hot."

"Show me how hot, Rigger. Fucking come for me." He let one finger tease its way into Rigger's ass.

"Oh. Oh, hell yes." Rigger's body clenched, heat spraying everywhere.

He purred at the smell of them together: strong, hot and pure male. Relaxing back against the wall, he brought their lips back together. Rigger hummed, those eyes just dancing for him.

As their mouths pulled apart, Rock straightened and headed for the bedroom, arms still full of hot man. "You ready for round two, Rigger?"

"I'm all about multiple rounds, Blue Eyes."

He nodded. "That's one of the things I liked about you from the start."

"And I thought it was all about my mouth." Rigger winked, snuggled in.

He just laughed. "Well I'll tell you that that was a big part of it. But man cannot live on blowjobs alone. Can't say I'd mind trying, though." Fuck, Rigger's laugh was just pure sex.

He put Rig down on his bed, purring at the lean length of the man. And he'd be fucked if just the sight of Rigger didn't make his prick work its way back to life, just like that.

"Gotta love a man with a short recovery period."

Rigger chuckled, stretching out for him.

"You're an inspiration." He gave Rigger a wink and climbed up onto the bed. "Not that I would complain if you wanted to do some sucking, make sure I'm really ready for the next round."

"Well, bring it on, marine." Rigger scooted down, lips parted and wet and looking so fucking good.

He climbed up at Rigger slid down, straddling the man's shoulders, cock sliding against those magic lips.

"Mmm..." Rigger's hands slid around his hips, fingers on his ass.

"Oh yeah. You do love your work, don't you?" And so did he. Fuck, that mouth was making him all but drool.

"Not work, Blue. All fucking pleasure."

He just purred at that. A fucking god, that was what Rigger made him feel like. Then that mouth dropped over him, Rigger's hands finding the small of his back, rubbing in lazy circles. "Fuck!" Oh yes.

Moaning he leaned forward to grab onto the headboard, eyes on where his cock disappeared into Rigger's mouth. Oh, sweet fuck -- wet and red, those lips were stretched around him, eager and hungry, begging for him.

He started to move -- it would have taken a better man than him to hold still -- watching and feeling it as Rigger just took him in and in and held him close, lips dragging reluctantly as he pulled out again. The look on Rigger's face was... it made a man fucking feel ten feel tall and invincible. And that look, that feeling, they were almost as good as the sex.

Rigger did something with his tongue and Rock's eyes rolled back in his head, the pleasure shooting up his spine. Almost. Rigger focused on the tip of his cock, lightning just rocking him.

"Shit, Rigger, you'll make me come."

Rigger let him go. "Mmm. You promised to fuck me."

"I did." And that ass was fucking sweet. And his. Oh yeah, right now it had his fucking name on it.

"Come on then. In me. Deep and hard."

"You know it." He reached over for the lube, getting his fingers nice and slick before rubbing them along Rigger's crease.

That hot little hole twitched, begging for him and he let one finger slide in to the hilt. Rigger's whole body jerked, rippled, arched for him.

"So fucking sexy, Rigger. Gonna make you feel fucking amazing."

"Oh, hell yes. So fucking hot for you." All stretched out and wanting, blond curls crowning that full cock.

"I know." Like a fucking furnace around his fingers. Rock pulled them away, settling in place between Rigger's legs. He hauled Rigger's legs up over his arms, spreading Rigger wide and lining up with that stretched little hole.

"Deep and hard, Blue Eyes. Remind me there's good outside of Texas."

"I've got your good outside of Texas right here, Rabbit." He growled a little, pushing in nice and slow, not stopping until his hips were pressed up tight against Rigger's ass. "Fucking sweet."

Rigger's lips were parted, eyes wide and happy and sexy as fuck. Groaning, Rock started to move, putting his whole body into each slow thrust.

"Oh. Oh, fuck yes." Rigger moaned, body clinging to him.

"You said it." He grinned wildly and kept on moving, pushing into Rigger again and again.

Rigger reached up, hands wrapping around the headboard.

"Oh, fuck, you're something." He leaned in to take one of those little nipples into his mouth, teeth threatening before he set up some suction.

"Rock! Oh. Oh, fuck. Please. Yes."

He worked the one tiny tit and then moved on over to the other one, sucking in time with his thrusts. Rigger bucked, driving himself down on Rock's prick, flushing dark. Rock roared a little, moved harder, working with Rigger.

"There. Right. Fucking. There." Rigger went fist-tight.

"Here, Rigger?" He asked, nailing that same spot over again. Rigger didn't answer, just wailed, ass squeezing him tight. "Oh yeah, right here." Harder, faster, he kept moving, driving Rigger hard.

"Blue. Blue. Need. Fuck. Fuck, please!"

"I've got what you need." He wrapped one hand around Rigger's hard as nails prick and started tugging in time with his thrusts.

"Yeah. Yeah. Need you. Oh, fuck." Rigger let go of the headboard and curled up, grabbing his shoulders.

"Show me. Fucking show me." Their mouths crashed together, his hips going a mile a minute.

Heat sprayed between them, Rigger milking his cock, jerking on his prick. Roaring, he slammed into Rigger, coming hard.

Rigger licked his lips then slumped down on the bed, panting. "Goddamn."

He collapsed, letting Rigger take most of his weight. "You said it." He was panting, trying to find his breath. Feeling fucking fine.

"Uh-huh." Rigger octopussed right around him, cuddling in.

"Comfortable?"

"Mmhmm." Rigger nodded, sort of licking at his

skin, sort of dozing.

He chuckled and settled half on Rigger, half off. He could nap awhile. Rigger hummed, relaxing, fingers slowly petting his belly.

Oh yeah. He could nap here awhile. Maybe even longer.

There was nothing like a rough and tumble game of football at the park on a hot day to make a man full on horny.

It was hot enough they'd been playing skins versus skins, not even bothering with shirts, everyone half naked, gleaming with sweat. Hot, male skin that was slick under your hand, the pure musk of sweat heavy in the air. It was a fucking sweet way to spend the afternoon. He'd been half hard all game and had bowed out of the post-game chicanery at the bar, opting instead to take his need down to Alex's apartment.

Rock sure as fuck hoped the man was home.

He lucked out, too. He could see that tanned body in the grass, teaching that big-assed creature Rigger called a dog to catch a Frisbee. Sweaty and shining, wearing nothing but a pair of cut-offs that were tiny enough that Rock *knew* Alex wasn't wearing any skivvies, the good old boy looked *fine*.

He adjusted himself and grabbed the bag of take-out he'd picked up, more glad now for the cover it would provide until they got in.

He called out as he headed toward Rigger. "Hey, cowboy. How's it hanging?"

That got him a wide grin and a nod as Grim barreled across the grass toward him. "Not half-bad, Rocketman. What you up to? Grimmy, you jump up on him and I'll whup you!"

Grim stopped short and gave him a happy bark, tail wagging hard.

He chuckled and gave the dog a quick pet. "I brought food. Let's go in and eat."

"Cool. Thanks." Rigger stretched under the sun, giving him a peek of white-blond curls before he was presented with a view of a tight cowboy butt and sweaty inner thighs as keys and Frisbee were grabbed. "Fuck, it's a pretty day out here. Love this weather."

He groaned, cock fucking throbbing. "Get the fuck inside, Rigger. Now."

"Low blood sugar makes you growly, marine." Rigger snapped a leash on Grim's collar and they headed in to the cool, dark, too-fucking-neat for real people apartment. "You want a beer?"

"No, I don't want a fucking beer."

He managed to wait until Rigger had the door closed. The bag of take-out didn't make it to the floor before he had Rigger slammed up against the wall, taking a good, hard kiss. Rigger gave a gasp, lips parting before that good old boy just melted, giving it up without a bit of worry, fingers slip-sliding over his shoulders.

Fuck, but the man smelled good: raw and real and fucking awesome. He could feel that hard, hot cock rubbing against his hip, held tight in that old denim. That was better than awesome, as was the mouth that was working its magic against his own. Fuck, but Rig was a sweet lay.

Rock could feel those lean muscles rippling, smell the mixture of salt and sunshine and sheer fucking hunger floating up beneath them. And those eyes. Fuck. You never had any doubt about that boy paying attention.

He got a hand between them and undid the top button of the had to be illegal in fifty states cut-offs.

"Fuck, yes." Alex's hands held his head, tilting him

for another kiss, tongue thrusting deep.

He groaned into the kiss, getting Rigger's zipper down and then that sweet fucking cock was in his hand, hot and damp. That got him a sharp nip to his bottom lip, Rigger humping his palm nice and steady. He stopped long enough to get his own shorts down and then it was cock on cock, both in his hand. So fucking hot.

"Fuck! Blue!" Rigger's hand joined his, palm working the heads, making his fucking knees weak.

He slid his free hand around Rigger, pushing into the back of those itty-bitty shorts and stroking his fingers along Rigger's crease. Rigger pushed back, offering. He was too wired to wait, so he just slid one finger inside his Rabbit and kept tugging on their cocks.

"Shit! Blue! Fucking hungry!" Rock didn't know which one of them Alex was talking about, didn't really figure it mattered.

He nodded, finger pushing in as deep as he could like this. "I'll do you right once we've got the edge off," he growled.

Rigger jerked against him, grey eyes going wide as spunk sprayed, hole clenching around him. The smell was what did it, that strong musk just making him roar and shoot his own load over their fingers.

He was leaning hard against Rigger when that slut drew their hands up, licking them clean. He groaned, prick twitching hard. "You are one sexy fucker."

Oh shit, that chuckle was distilled sex. "I got inspiration."

He preened a little and then gave Rigger a hard kiss. Oh yeah, his cock was more than a little interested in round two. "What do you say we get horizontal and see if I can't inspire you some more?"

"You want a shower first? I'm definitely not smelling like roses."

"You can have a shower after, I want your skin like it is." If he wanted fucking roses, he'd date some chick with a large perfume bottle.

Rigger took a long, hard kiss. "Such a romantic. Come fuck my ass until I fly, Blue Eyes."

"You don't have to ask me twice."

He followed Alex down to the bedroom, cock filling just right at the sight. Hell, you didn't have to ask him at all.

CHAPTER SIX

Rock let himself into his apartment and tossed his gear in the bedroom. He emptied his pockets, fishing out the key he'd had made and tossing it onto the coffee table in the living room. A quick shower later and he was in the kitchen in a clean t-shirt and sweats, looking for a beer.

There was a knock on the door, so he grabbed two and went to let Rig in.

"Hey Blue Eyes. How's it hanging?" The long body lounged against the doorframe, a bag of burgers in his hands. "Hungry?"

"Hey, Rigger, come on in. And I'm always hungry." He held out the extra beer. "Thirsty?"

"I could use a swig, yeah." Rigger grinned, eyes dancing as he pushed his way in. "You're looking good."

He nodded. He was. Still it was nice of Rigger to notice. "Thanks."

He pointed Rigger into the living room with his beer. "You need ketchup or anything like that?" It was fast food -- they didn't need plates.

"Nope. Got what I need." One decent thing about Rigger, the man was self-sufficient.

"Cool." He sat down in his old armchair and helped himself to a burger; loaded up, just the way he liked them. "Thanks," he said around a mouthful.

"Hmm-mmm. 's good. Fries?" Alex pushed over a bag with two containers of fries and a second burger.

He nodded and snagged a container of fries, making a face when they weren't salted enough. He wasn't the kind of guy that poured ketchup on his fries, but he liked them hot and he liked them salty.

Grunting, he got up, nodding in the general direction of the key. "Getting salt and another couple of brews. That's for you."

"Yeah?" Rig's voice was pleased and, by the time he got back from the kitchen, the key was gone. "Thanks, Rocketman."

He made a noise, plunked the two new beers on the table between them and salted his fries.

"That extra burger for me?" he asked as he finished off the last mouthful of his first.

"Yep. Double meat, double cheese, no pickles."

"Cool. Thanks."

He made short work of the rest of his fries and his second burger and then sat back with his beer, just relaxing and watching as Rigger slowly made his way through some fries.

"I've got a three-day," Rock noted casually.

"Yeah? Me, too." Rigger guzzled some beer and toed off his shoes, lounging on the sofa. Man looked good, too, lean and relaxed, tan and loose-limbed. "You got plans?"

He chuckled. "Well, I was hoping to get laid."

"Only once? Blue, you're not shooting high enough." Alex winked, thighs parting. "I was hoping for seventy-two hours of sex and beer and food, cut with a nice crash 'em up flick or two."

He grinned. "It sounds like you put a good thought into that. Tell you what, add in a couple of hours for watching the game and you've got a deal."

"Works for me. Hell, I'll even blow you during half-time." Rigger finished his beer, grinning from ear to ear.

Laughing, he put down his own bottle and petted his thigh. "Well come on then, time's a wastin'."

Never one to hesitate when fucking was offered, Rigger walked over and straddled his lap, arms wrapping around his neck. He slid his hands around Rigger's waist, pulling the tight fitting t-shirt out of Rigger's jeans so he could touch skin. Rigger's talented as fuck mouth closed over his.

Yeah, this was a good start to a three-day.

Rigger tasted salty and hot, hands like fire on his skin. A hard prick rubbed against his belly, Alex ready and wanting. He popped the button of Rigger's jeans, carefully working the zipper past the hard cock and then tugging it out. It didn't take a moment to pull his own prick out of his sweats and once he had them both in his hand he started stroking.

"Fuck yeah. Sexy motherfucker." Rigger was humming, sucking on his bottom lip, eyes lit up and hot.

He growled in the back of his throat, his free hand sliding between Rigger and Rigger's jeans, cupping that sexy little cowboy butt. His t-shirt was tugged up and off, Rigger feeding him a soft sound as those hands slid over his skin. Squeezing their pricks tighter together, he stroked faster, feeling the touches settling in his balls.

"Oh, fuck. Fuck. Want you." Alex rocked harder, fingers sliding over his nipples, nails just scratching.

"Right here, Rigger." He growled, getting close as their bodies moved together.

Rigger pushed their lips together again, kissing hard, long, jerking against him. He swiped his thumb over the heads of their cocks, moaning as he shot.

"Oh, shit. Fucking *hot*." Rigger reached down and brushed against him, eyes blazing as long fingers, wet with his spunk, were sucked into that amazing goddamned mouth.

He growled, cock twitching and staying hard. Another touch, another taste and Rigger was coming, heat spurting over his hand, splashing against his belly. He grabbed the back of Rigger's head, tilting that head and taking a long, hard kiss.

Alex melted against him, lips open and just flavored with his come.

The next seventy-two hours promised to be a hell of a good ride.

Rock wasn't much for mornings. Oh, he got up when he needed to and did his PT and showed up at work awake and able to do his job. But that didn't mean he liked it. And that didn't mean that all but the greenest baby green knew better than to come and bug him before noon if they could help it.

Alex on the other hand was a morning person as far as Rock could tell, but the man had quickly learned to go do his awake thing where it didn't disturb Rock. Which was good, because what Rock couldn't abide was folks who were in your face with how chipper and awake they were in the morning.

Still, there was something nice about smelling breakfast already cooked when you woke up on a Saturday. Knowing the coffee would be fresh and things sort of put to rights. Hell, half the time Rigger had fucking grocery shopping done and was just coming in from his run with that dog.

Oh, yeah. That was always a fine sight, the gleaming, golden body dressed in nothing but running shorts, all sun-warmed and relaxed and hungry for him. Some things made mornings more tolerable and that was one that was better than all the coffee in the world.

He cracked open an eye, wondering what time it was and where Rigger was at.

The clock said eleven-thirty -- Christ, Rigger might have fucking redecorated, changed the oil and cleaned the carburetors in both trucks and... wait just a fucking minute. Rigger was still curled up against him, doing that fucked-up octopus impression.

He grumbled. Something was fucking wrong.

"Rigger? You sick?"

Those grey eyes opened slowly, almost reluctantly. Hell, Rock hadn't realized how tense Rigger had been until his Rabbit relaxed, melting into him. "No. Had an evil friggin' migraine when I woke up at four; took some meds and came back to bed. Feeling fine now, thank the Lord for small favors." He got a bright, warm smile and a soft kiss. "Morning, Blue Eyes. How's it hanging?"

"High and hard, Rigger." He nudged Alex with his morning wood. "Glad you're okay -- I don't do sick well."

Rigger's hand wrapped around his prick, rubbing slow and easy. "Mm... I'm fine. Didn't get dick accomplished this morning, though."

"So you do it later." He pushed into Rigger's hand, not trying to speed the pace, just deepening the strokes.

"Yeah. Make you come out with me..." Rigger's voice was distracted, lips sliding toward his cock.

Oh, he wasn't sure about that -- his days off were days off, not days to go running around the place. But he knew better than to argue with the man about to take your prick into his mouth so he just growled, encouraging Rigger to suck him. Besides, he played his cards right, he could just keep his own personal slut in bed until Monday.

Rigger's tongue slid over the tip first, cheek resting on his belly, eyelashes tickling his skin. Then those sweet lips just covered the head, tugging lazily, tongue working the slit. His body jerked, stomach muscles jumping against Rigger's cheek.

Rigger sucked him with a lazy focus, keeping him hot and wanting, but not pushing him over to hot need, not teasing. They could do this all fucking day as far as he was concerned. He rumbled, letting Rigger know how good it was and his hands drifted down, sliding over Rigger's hair and face. The soft humming vibrated his cock, Rigger nestling into the touches. Rigger's cock slid against his leg, one warm hand was rolling his balls, just tugging on the sac. He moved his leg, rubbing against Rigger's prick.

Slowly, so slowly he barely noticed, Rigger started taking all of him down, holding the head of his cock in that long fucking throat, lips pulling at the very base of his prick. He growled, hips starting to thrust as he was pushed from hot and unrushed to hungry and wanting. Fuck, but Rigger just took whatever he gave -- took it deeper, harder, faster and then fucking begged for more. He'd never known anyone who loved sucking as much as Rigger did. He moved his leg with each push into Rigger's mouth, giving back as much sensation as he could.

He growled and rumbled -- it wouldn't be long now.

Rigger's nose buried itself in his pubes, the humming and tight suction combining to something huge. He roared as the pleasure built in his balls and the base of his spine, shooting out hard from his cock. Rigger swallowed hard, pulling each pulse out of him, milking his cock for all it was worth.

He growled, petting the blond hair. "'s good, Rig."

"Mm... yeah." That cheek settled against his belly again, eyes closing. "Happy weekend, Blue Eyes."

Yeah. It was.

He stroked Rigger's head. "Good morning to you, too."

Rock scowled at the vegetables and kept pushing the cart past them. He could see the meat at the other end of the aisle and that's where he was headed.

Rigger had been appalled by the state of his fridge and insisted they come and shop so Alex could make him a real meal.

Rock thought that pizza and burgers and fried chicken *were* real meals, but Rigger seemed pretty convinced that his cupboard was bare and frankly, he enjoyed the way that ass looked in his kitchen, so he figured it was worth having to come to the grocery and shop next to Suzie homemaker and her brood. And this way he could make sure Rigger didn't bring in a bunch of vegetables.

Oh, chips. He veered off into the chip aisle. "Maybe this wasn't such a bad idea after all," he teased. "I am out of nacho chips and Cheetos."

"Ass. Grab some popcorn, too." Grey eyes grinned over at him, dancing a little.

He grinned right back. "You're not going to toss in a bunch of salad and carrots and shit while my back's turned, are you?" Okay, so maybe this grocery-shopping thing wasn't quite the hell he was expecting.

"Probably. Okra too. I'm wily that way."

"I don't even *know* what okra is and already I hate it. Sounds like something that's like number three or four on America's Most Wanted list. You know -- on the list so you know the name sounds familiar, but far enough down you don't actually recognize it." He didn't know why anyone would want to ruin a good meal by throwing vegetables on the plate. Lots of people did though, so he could forgive it in Rigger.

"Okra's fried, Rock. You can eat it without turning in your he-man macho card."

"You sure? 'cause I just picked up a life-time membership and I'd hate to have to do the work toward that all over again." He gave Rigger a wink and filled the cart with chips and popcorn and Cheetos and a couple jars of salsa, another of some cheese dip.

"That queso is nasty." Alex's nose wrinkled. "And yeah, you can't have chicken fry without okra."

"I'm not driving to Texas to buy you queso, Rigger." He shook his head and grinned. "You don't need okra for steak."

He turned the cart back toward the meat aisle. He was planning on buying a bunch of steak and some of those pre-made hamburger dealies. He knew Rigger didn't think he could cook, but he had more than a passing hand at grilling.

"Mmm. Steak. Grab a packet of stew meat and some hamburger meat. I want spaghetti and meatballs."

He could do that. He remembered the meals Rigger had cooked back in San Antonio. He could definitely do that. "Extra hamburger meat if we're having chili, right?"

"Yeah. They don't make chili meat here. Bizarre fucking state."

"There's special meat in chili? Wow they're right -- you do learn something new every day." He gave Rigger a wink. "So if you're making chili then you need stuff to make cornbread, right?"

He was never going to eat at the mess again if Rig indulged him.

"I can make cornbread. I have a craving for blueberry muffins. I'll get a mix. Me and Grim can't eat a whole dozen." Rigger winked, grinned. Brat.

Of course Rock could be a brat, too. "If you're going to be baking it would be a crime not to have something chocolate."

"Chocolate? You like chocolate? I heard it's good for you." Random odds and ends got dumped into the basket. Weird shit like flour and cinnamon and garlic powder.

He swatted Alex's ass. "It's never done me any harm." He flexed for a moment, showing off his muscles for Rigger.

Those eyes ran over his body, just appreciating the hell out of him. "You got that right, Blue."

He purred. Okay, so there was a definite drawback to this shopping for groceries thing. He couldn't lay Rigger down over the cart and fuck him blind.

"Come on," he growled. "We're done here, right?"

"Need, uh... Something?"

"What?" he demanded, wanting nothing more than to be back at his apartment so he could do something about that 'fuck me now' look Rigger was sporting. "What the fuck do you need? Let's get it already."

"A six pack and a carton of Marlboros. I'll get the rest later."

"A couple of six packs and we can skip the fucking Marlboros." He'd never liked the smell.

"I've smoked too damn long to stop now, man." They headed to the beer aisle.

"You taste too good to turn your mouth into an ashtray, Rigger."

He got a look, a raised eyebrow. "It's not like I'm a chain smoker, man. I just need one every now and again."

Rock shrugged. He wasn't the man's momma, but he didn't want those things stinking up his house. Or his man. "I just don't see the point in wasting your money when you're not going to be smoking them this weekend."

"I'm not? You got other plans for my mouth?"

He gave Rigger a look, his prick going full on hard at just the thought. "You know it."

Rigger grabbed a case of Bud. "I guess we're ready, then."

He grunted and nodded, pleased that Rigger hadn't made a big deal of it. "I guess we are at that."

He trailed Alex as the man headed toward the checkout, watching that sweet ass ahead of him. Oh yeah, he was more than ready.

CHAPTER SEVEN

lex pulled into Rock's driveway, grabbing the pizza box off the front seat. Rock's old truck sat in its spot and he'd never been so glad to see that Chevy.

The fight two weeks ago hadn't lasted any time. He'd bitched about something, Rock snapped at him. He snarled back and Rock told him to back the fuck off, nobody'd made him come east to begin with. Right. Rock was right. Nobody'd made him. Hell, nobody'd even asked.

So he'd backed the fuck off. Hell, he'd backed all the way to the fucking Florida Keys for two weeks helping to train Royal Air Force medics in some nasty assed swamps.

He'd flown in bright and early, fetched Grimmy from the kennel, bathed and napped before grabbing a case of beer and a pepperoni and green pepper from the pizza joint. Surely two weeks was long enough.

Alex walked up to the door, hand poised to knock when he heard Rock's low moan. He grinned, prick paying attention. He could *see* it, see Rock leaning back on that old couch, cock in hand, stroking off. Fucking hot.

He juggled the beer, digging in his pocket for the keys, wriggling a little now from lack of room. He'd fished them out, was searching for the blue one when he heard another moan and a "Yes, Sarge. Fuck. Again." Rock's response was muffled, horny, encouraging.

Oh.

Oh, shit.

Right.

He moved back, careful not to drop or fall or get found out. Right. Okay. Time to go, then. Shit.

Alex put the beer in the Jeep and trashed the pizza in the big-assed container outside Rock's place. He let the Jeep slide back onto the street before he started it, digging his cigarettes out of the glove compartment and pushing in the lighter.

Okay, then -- home. Get Grimmy and some cash and head out to the beach for a few days. Then back to work. Get shit done. Maybe look into some extra training that would get him out of North Carolina for awhile.

After all, nobody'd made him come east to begin with. Nobody. Hell, nobody'd even asked.

Rock ordered another beer, leaning back against the bar to watch the pool games going on. Luke had told him about a place closer to the main drag where the rest of the cherries hung, but he wasn't really interested in picking anyone up tonight. He just wanted a beer, maybe a few games of pool and to go home for a nice long fuck with the promise of getting woken up with a blowjob.

Unfortunately Rigger had gone AWOL about three weeks earlier, walked out over some stupid shit or the other. He'd expected Rigger would come back after he cooled down but the man never had. It was a fucking shame, the man sucked like a dream, the barebacking was fucking hot, and he'd gotten fucking used to having Rigger around.

Those were the breaks.

The door opened and, speak of the devil, in walked Lucifer himself, skinny ass dressed in jeans and a black t-shirt, cigarette held tight in his teeth. Rigger didn't avoid him, didn't do much more than greet a few regulars and then sidle up to the bar and order a beer. "Hey there, Rock. How goes?"

He raised an eyebrow and shrugged. "It goes. You?"

"Been busy as fuck, but I reckon I'll make it." Rigger paid for the beer, downed about half of it.

"Yeah? You busy tonight?" he asked casually.

Rigger shook his head. "No, thank God for small favors. What're you up to this evening?"

"Thought maybe a beer or two, some bar munchies, maybe a game of pool. Find someone for some weekend fun." He looked over into Rigger's eyes. Rigger could be that someone; hell, Rigger had been that someone before the cowboy took off just as suddenly as he'd come in the first place.

Those grey eyes were still, quiet like the sky before a storm hit. "Sounds like a hell of a plan. I reckoned on having a few myself. Seems like I haven't been in here for a month of Sundays."

"Three weeks," he pointed out. Not that he'd meant to, but now that he had it kind of hung between them, almost like a challenge.

"Yeah." Rigger nodded. "I got called out to Florida at o-dark thirty that Saturday morning. Didn't get in 'til last Friday night."

Well that explained a thing or two. He nodded and had some more of his beer. "And here I was thinking you were a man who held a grudge."

"Not really my style." Rigger finished his beer and ordered another. "Life's too short and all that."

"Well all right then, why don't we pool our resources? We're guaranteed a good weekend that way."

He got another long look and then nodded. "Sure. Sounds like it'll work. Want to shoot some pool?"

"Sure. Or we could skip the pool and just head back to my place." It had been long enough since he'd had his pipes cleaned. Cherries could be fun, but they knew next to shit about blowjobs.

"Let me finish my beer and I'll follow you out."

"Sure." He had a few mouthfuls left on his own and he wasn't in any real hurry.

Rigger chatted idly to the bartender, to a couple of wing nuts who walked over. Lazy, easy, Rigger just sort of fit. He watched, munching on some beer nuts as he waited.

Finally that beer was drained and Rig stood, leaving a tip on the bar. "You ready to go?"

"Yep." He nodded at the bartender and headed out.

The burnt orange jeep was parked a few spots over and he got a nice look at that cowboy butt as Rig climbed in. "See you in a few, Rocketman."

He nodded, took his last look at Rig and got into his own truck. The trip home was uneventful, Rigger pulling in a couple moments after him and following him upstairs.

The door shut behind Rigger with a click. "You want

to start at the sofa?"

"You pacing yourself?" he asked with a grin.

"Just finding out which way the wind is blowing, Rock." He got a quick grin. "And seeing whether to park my ass out here or just dispense with the pleasantries."

"You're the one who left mad and took three weeks to come back, Rigger." He wasn't sure exactly what it was Rigger was wanting. He couldn't even remember what the argument was fucking about, he sure as shit wasn't apologizing for it.

Rigger blinked, one eyebrow arching. "You wanted me to back off. I backed off. I'm just trying to figure out if we're going to sit and neck or get right to the fucking. It's not like you asked me here to talk."

"Cool. I can do fucking a whole lot better'n talking." He pulled Rigger to him and closed their mouths together.

Rigger tasted like cigarettes and beer and a hint of whiskey, but that tongue was familiar, quick and hungry, pushing into his lips. He groaned, hands reaching back for that ass, pulling Rigger in tight against him. That lean cowboy body pushed right up close, rocking and moving against him, making him fucking ache.

Fuck, he'd missed this more than he'd thought. He put his hands on Rigger's shoulders, not pushing hard, just making his wants known. A soft noise pushed into his mouth and Rigger went to those bony knees, unfastening his jeans and pushing them down around his hips, tongue sliding over the line of his pubes.

He moaned, hands sliding idly over the blond almost-curls, letting Rigger take his time, work his magic. The kisses and caresses and strokes were fucking hot, almost as hot as that mouth dropping over his cock, lips rolling a rubber on just like a pro.

"What the fuck?"

Rigger gave him a quick, odd look, then lifted his head. "You want me to stop?"

"Shit no -- you can lose the fucking rubber though."

"I don't think so. I told you, I don't bareback with someone who's playing the field."

"Who's playing the fucking field?" Jesus fucking Christ he was losing the mood.

"Look, don't bullshit me, okay? I stopped by last Friday after I got in, you were busy. Cool, barring the fact that you ought to look into weatherproofing your door, the moans come right through." Rigger shook his head. "Nobody made any commitments and that's fine. I'm a great fuckbuddy, but I play safe."

"Well fuck, Rigger -- you should have come in -- you've got a goddamned key, don't you?" He shook his head. "You could have helped with the cherry, taught him a thing or two. Yeah, cherry, pure as the driven fucking snow -- and I used fucking condoms."

"I never suggested you didn't, asshole." Rigger sighed, rubbed the back of his neck. "I'm not sure how it is I'm not being reasonable, Rock. Last time I checked, it was rude to walk in when your... when someone's having sex. Do you want to play or not?"

"Yeah, I want to play, dickwad." He glared and then guided his prick back to Rigger's mouth. He wasn't even sure what the fuck Rigger's problem was, but fucking was always better than arguing about shit.

Ducking his head, Rigger went back to work. That hot mouth worked his cock, tongue knowing just where he liked it, just where to tease. Just how to make him ache. He closed his eyes and let that talented as fuck mouth send him soaring. It didn't take long before he was buried in Rigger's throat, that blond head bobbing strong and steady, taking him all the way.

He roared, coming hard. Rigger sucked and licked

until every fucking aftershock was over, mouth gentle now, soft against him. He rumbled, the sound turning into a half-growl as he pulled out and had to deal with the condom. Rigger slowly got to his feet, lips swollen, red.

Rock reached out, tracing the soft mouth. "What the fuck is going on, Rigger?"

Rigger kissed his fingers, eyes dull, unhappy. "Nothing, Rock. I think getting testing and riding bare meant something to me it didn't to you. That's cool. No stress from this old boy, but if you... if we're going to fuck other guys, we'd best be safe."

"And I told you, I was safe -- I don't ride bare with anyone else." He growled, he still didn't get what Rigger was so sore about, it wasn't like he wanted the cherries to stick around or nothing. "I'm just helping some cherry boys find their way, Rigger."

"And if I go up to Raleigh, find me a few hard bodies to play with when you're off in the field? You comfortable with that, so long as I cover my cock?"

He grunted. "Long as they're cherry, fine."

Rigger arched an eyebrow, gave him a look.

"What? I'm only doing cherries. Performing a public service, I might add. And it's not like I knew you were on duty -- all I fucking knew was you were pissed off and left and didn't come back for three fucking weeks." He glared at Rigger. How dare that cowboy give him a *look*. "Not a single fucking phone call -- don't be talking to me about how getting tested and riding bare fucking meant something to you."

"I came over as soon as I got back into town. You didn't seem like you wanted to be disturbed. Damnit, Rock, you wanted me to back off and I got called out. My fucking answering machine said where I was, or didn't you bother to call?" Rigger lifted his chin, eyes flashing.

He glared back. "You were the one who was pissed off."

"I wasn't the only one."

"Fine, it was all my goddamned fault." He turned on his heel and headed for the kitchen. "I need a fucking beer."

"Look, I didn't come to fight." Rigger's voice was quiet, low. "I was missing your company. I'll get on home. Try again another day."

"I'm not interested in fighting either, Rigger. I'm all about the fucking, you know that."

"Yeah, I know." Rigger nodded. "I won't ask for anything else from you, Jim."

"I don't know what else you want from me, Alex."

"Why is it I'm always talking in circles with you?" Rigger sighed. "Look -- I'm not comfortable going bareback if we're going to fuck other people on the side. Simple as that. No bullshit."

"I'm not going out looking to fuck other people, Rigger. Look, when I was a baby green, there was a Sarge took care of me, showed me the ropes. Now I pass the tradition on, that's the way it works."

"Okay, fine. I'm not asking you to stop. I just... Hell, Rock, it's a risk -- you want to take a risk? Then we either take it together where I get to be involved or I don't want to take it at all."

"I've got no problem with that. Long as next time you head off on a tour you let me know where you're at." No problem at all -- hadn't he just been thinking Rigger could teach the cherries a thing or three?

Rigger nodded. "That's more than fair."

"So we're good?"

Those grey eyes met his, warm and sure. "Yeah, I reckon we're good."

"'bout fucking time." He went back up to Rigger

and shoved him up against the wall, taking his mouth so the talking could fucking stop and the fucking could fucking start.

That lanky slut of a cowboy wrapped around him, kissing hard, tongue fucking his mouth hard and sure. He grabbed Rigger's butt and shifted, hauling both their asses toward the bedroom. He was suddenly in the mood to pound Rigger through the fucking mattress.

Rigger chuckled, lips trailing along his jaw. "No long chats on the sofa, Blue Eyes?" That hot fucking tongue licked at his ear.

"You want some fucking foreplay?" He dropped Rigger back onto the floor in the doorway to the bedroom and stripped off his own clothes, turning to shake his ass. "There. Now let's get on with the good stuff."

"Man, the romance is *thick* tonight." Rigger popped him hard on the ass, laughing.

"Romance is for the weak, Rigger." He grabbed his Jackrabbit and took another kiss, pushing Rigger down onto the bed as it went on and on.

"Don't fucking need romance, Rocketman." Rigger rubbed up against him, fucking hard and hot. Fucking *sweet*.

"That's my Jackrabbit." He reached under the pillows for the lube, slicking up his fingers and sliding two into Rigger.

"Oh, fuck... Yeah, Blue. Yeah." Rigger danced on his fucking fingers, rocking hard, taking him deep.

Oh yeah. No cherry could fucking do this. He didn't spend a whole lot of time finger fucking Rigger. They both knew what they wanted, why they were here.

"Hard and fast, Blue Eyes. I want to feel you in my fucking skull." The words were harsh, hungry. Fucking slut.

He wasn't going to leave his Rabbit wanting. He

pushed in, slow and deep, holding there for a moment, eyes on Rigger's, letting their limbs settle and then he started fucking. Hard and fast, just like Rigger wanted.

"Yes. Christ, I want you." The words were gasped and then Rigger took his mouth, tongue and eyes speaking clear enough for fucking anybody.

He made his own reply with his cock, working Rigger's gland as hard as he could. Rigger jerked, entire body flushing. Harsh, hungry gasps filled his mouth as Rigger rode hard, fucking slamming their bodies together. He just kept his focus on those grey eyes and fucked with everything he had. Yeah. This was the good stuff.

Rock could see when Rigger got close, those too-fucking-pretty grey eyes growing dark and wide, fastened onto him like he was a fucking god come to save needy rednecks. He grabbed Rigger's prick in his hand, tugging hard as he nailed that sweet gland one more time.

There -- Rigger convulsed, spunk spraying between them, that tight fucking ass milking him. He let it go, let Rigger's ass have his load. The kisses lasted until after the last aftershocks, deep and slow.

He let himself down slowly, staying buried deep, letting Rigger have his weight for awhile. A low hum sounded, Rigger holding on tight, hands sliding over his head, his neck. He stayed as he was, grunting to let Rigger know it was good. Fucking good.

Rigger's lips brushed against his throat and it didn't take long before that cowboy was snuggled in, holding on and sound asleep in his arms.

It was shaping up to be a pretty fucking glorious weekend.

Alex woke up before dawn, headed right for the kitchen, hunting for coffee.

Jesus fuck. Fuck. What the fuck was wrong with him?

It was bad enough that he went looking for Rock like a lovelorn idiot. Bad enough that he'd ended up on his knees within four minutes of walking in the door. Now he was fucking agreeing to have threesomes? Screwing without fucking protection?

His momma'd kick his ass.

He started the coffee after cleaning the machine and the pot. Then he went out to the front porch to sit and smoke and think and smoke and think.

Fuck.

The sun had been up a couple of hours and he was through most of a pack when he heard Rock stirring.

Wasn't long after that the marine was out on the porch with him in a pair of PT shorts and little else, cup of coffee in his hand. "Morning," Rock grunted.

"Morning." He was queasy as all fuck, trembling a little from the caffeine and nicotine.

Rock sat and blinked a little, groaning once he got the coffee cup up to his mouth. After a few sips Rock put down the cup. "Got to admit, I was expecting a blow as my wake up call instead of a cup of coffee."

"Been up a long time. Couldn't sleep." He wasn't going to apologize. Damn it.

"Something wrong with my bed?"

"No. I just kept thinking." Kept kicking myself in the ass. Kept trying to figure out what the fuck I'm doing.

"Oh, now that there's dangerous. Thinking I mean." Rock gave him a wink and a grin. One hand reached out and squeezed his thigh. "Less thinking, more fucking. That's my motto."

He closed his eyes, nodded. "That's a great goddamned motto."

Rock stood and stretched then reached out a hand to

him. "Come on, Rigger. That's enough thinking for one morning."

His hand fit right into Rock's and he stood up, hushing Momma's voice in his head. "We'll have to talk about last night, but not now."

Rock gave him a look, but just led him in and down the hall. "Mornings are definitely not for talking, Alex."

"No shit. Is it morning still?"

Rock snorted. "Fuck yes. It's nowhere near noon. Which on a Saturday morning means why the fuck are we out of bed?"

Rock corrected that matter, pulling him down onto the mattress, mouth covering his in a hard kiss. He moaned, the kiss making his head spin, making his heart pound. Rock rolled him on the bed, hands tugging off his t-shirt and cut-offs, roaming over his skin.

Oh. Oh, fuck yes. That was what he'd been thinking. Just that.

One hand found his nipples, tugging gently on one, pinching the other. Rock's PT shorts were rough against his skin as Rock rubbed them together. He shoved Rock's shorts down, trying to get to that fat fucking cock.

Rock helped. "This what you're after, Rigger?" That fucking fine prick leapt out at him, hot and solid.

"You know it. Fuck. Need."

"Yeah, I know it. Fucking hard for you, Rigger. For that amazing fucking mouth and that sweet as fuck ass."

Fuck, that felt good. So good to hear. Rock's hand fisted his cock and then slid down to tug at his balls. He made a deep sound, the noise rolling out of him.

"How do you want it, Rigger? Mouth or ass?" Rock grinned and thrust against his thigh. "Both?"

"In for a penny, in for a pound, marine." He arched up, pushing right back.

"I've got lots of pounds," growled Rock, mouth

closing over his again, a hard rhythm starting as Rock slid against him again and again, their cocks rubbing, bumping.

"Fuck. Yes. Need." He leaned in, bit down on that shoulder.

Rock growled and pushed harder against him before rolling onto his back. "Suck me, Rigger. Want that fanfuckingtastic mouth around my cock."

"The cherry didn't learn how to do it right?" He winked, slid down to kiss the tip.

"Fuck no. Shit, Rigger after you there isn't anyone who knows how to do it right."

He groaned, sucked the head of that fine prick right down.

"Oh, yeah." Rock moaned, the sound low and desperate, needy.

His own cock jerked, opening to take more in. Rock's thick fingers slid through his hair, groans steadily filling the air. Alex tugged Rock closer, in deeper. Need.

"Fuck." Rock's hips started rocking, pushing the hot flesh deep.

He nodded. Yeah. Fuck. He didn't want to think anymore. Harder and faster, Rock took what he needed, gave Alex exactly what *he* needed, fucking his mouth. He groaned, soaring, flying with it, nipples hard, cock throbbing.

"Yeah. Yeah, Rig!" Rock shouted, hips snapping as he came. Heat and salt poured down Alex's throat.

Swallowing and tugging, he drew out each aftershock, each pulse of pleasure.

Rock shuddered, hands stroking over his head. "Fucking good."

He nodded, humming low,· hips just rocking and fucking the air.

"Keep me up, Rigger and I'll fuck you nice and

hard."

He nodded, groaned, tongue flicking Rock's slit, pushing in.

"Oh yeah. Fuck." Rock groaned, fingers stroking over his cheeks, his ears, down along his neck.

The prick in his mouth never even started to go soft. His eyes closed, a deep moan pushing right out of him. Those fine fucking hands...

Rock let him suck and play for awhile and then those hands slid beneath his arms. "Come on now, Rigger. That ass is mine."

"All fucking yours, Rocketman. I'm needing." Fucking followed it from Texas.

"I've got what you need, right here."

Rock reached up and snagged the tube of lube, slicking up a couple of fingers and pushing them right into him. Those blue eyes held his as he was stretched. He squeezed, moaning as he felt the touch deep inside.

"So fucking tight." Rock pushed a third finger in, curling and finding his gland.

"Blue!" His knees bent, cradling Rock between his legs.

A low groan was his answer, Rock's head bending, warm lips surrounding one of his nipples, hot tongue flicking across the tip.

"Oh. Oh, sweet fuck. Rock. Damn." Lightning shot through him, hot and bright and sweet as fuck.

"Oh, right there." Rock nudged his gland again, fingers stretching and playing and making him crazed.

All he could do was nod, whimpering, hips rocking and riding Rock's touch. Rock's mouth moved over to his other nipple, sucking on it. He fucking flew, the burn and stretch perfect. Rock's fingers played him for awhile and then they disappeared, that fat cock pushing right into him.

"Oh, hell yes. More." He was more than willing to be demanding.

Grunting, Rock gave him what he wanted, pushing in harder, really letting him have it. It was a bit of a challenge, but he managed to get his hands up, fingers wrapped around the headboard. Oh, yeah. That so helped.

"Oh, fuck, yes." Rock nodded and thrust even harder.

"Yeah. Rock. Oh, fuck that's sweet. Deep. Damn."

Rock nodded, bending to lick at his collarbone, to nip at his nipple. His grunt would have been embarrassing, had a lesser man been fucking him.

"Oh yeah." Rock nodded, moved harder still. One big hand wrapped around his cock, tugging. Oh, okay. Fuck yeah. Just. Like. Fucking. That. Rock only grunted, hand and cock coordinated.

"Yes. Yes, fuck. Rock. Gonna." His toes curled, legs drawing up and back.

"Yeah, Rigger. Give it to me."

Heat sprayed over his belly, ass squeezing, milking Rock's prick. Rock roared, hips jerking, heat filling him.

Yeah. Damn. That was. Oh, hell yes.

Groaning, Rock collapsed, cock slipping free.

"Morning."

Rock made a rumbling noise, the sound vibrating in the muscled chest. "And a fine morning it is, too. Best in *weeks*."

He nodded, cheek rubbing on Rock's chest. Fuck, yes.

Rock shifted to lie on his back and tugged him right up against the warm body, hand sliding on his arm.

"Mmm... You smell fucking good," he said

"You don't smell so bad yourself, Rigger. Man and sex. The fucking perfect combination."

He grinned, cheeks heating. Okay, for a growly marine? Rock could give a compliment.

Rock chuckled and tilted his head, took a good, hard kiss. "I like you in my bed, Rigger."

"Yeah? I like being here." He focused on those lips. "You... the whole threesome thing. How does it work? I mean, you don't worry they're trying to screw you over?"

"You mean me and the cherry marines?"

"No. I mean us and the cherry marines." They were going to get that shit straight, right away.

"Right. Well I -- we -- don't play with anyone who hasn't gone through basic. I'm not stupid, Alex and I'm not looking to be outed." Rock shrugged. "I have a... what do they call it? Gaydar? I can tell the ones who are prime cherry meat. The ones who are going to need a bit of a helping hand."

He nodded. "You seemed to know about me right off."

"Oh, you didn't need any kind of helping hand." Rock chuckled and squeezed his hip. "But yeah, I knew. Hell with the way you were packing those jeans I'd have been crushed if I was wrong."

"Flattery will get you sucked blind, marine." Alex grinned, legs twining with Rock's. Fuck that man was hot.

"Then you'd best prepare for it being laid on nice and thick, because that mouth? Sheer fucking heaven." Rock took another kiss, this one slow and deep, as one leg wrapped behind his and tugged him in closer. He let himself just ease right down, let himself trust that strength. Each kiss flowed into another, Rock taking his time, one hand sliding along Rig's skin as they kissed.

Oh, man. He was so deeply fucked.

Alex moaned, lips parting, tongue sliding against

Rock's. Of course, that deeply fucked part might have been apparent when he crossed the Louisiana state line.

CHAPTER EIGHT

It was pitch black and he was fucking filthy and tired and needing a little -- fuck that, a lot of Rock -- so Alex stumbled over and used his key for the first time, praying like hell that Rock didn't shoot him.

The damned thing stuck, but he jiggled it, cussing up a storm as it started pouring. "Come on you bitch! Open!"

The door was suddenly flung open, and he was grabbed, a thick arm coming around his neck, putting him in a choke hold. Rock's growl was fierce.

"Rock, it you're going to kill me, do it quick. I've had a long fucking day."

"Fucking Christ, Rigger, what are you doing skulking about?" Rock growled, hold loosening as the door was closed.

"Tired. Needed." He pushed up and took a quick

kiss. "Your place is closer."

"Well why didn't you say so?" Rock's hands settled beneath his ass and he was lifted against the hard body and carried off to Rock's bedroom.

Oh, thank God. He wrapped his arms around Rock's neck, holding on, lips sliding over Rock's jaw. Rock put him in the big bed and started stripping him with that focus his Blue had.

"Oh... Fuck, yes. Need you." He shivered, reaching up, brushing Rock's lips, jaw.

Rock pushed off his jeans and then that hard body was pressing him down into the mattress.

Moaning, he wrapped around those hot muscles, pressing close. "Blue..."

Rock rumbled for him, prick like a brand along his skin. Two fingers went into him, slick and thick, stretching him, finding his gland and pegging it hard.

"Oh... Oh, fuck. Yes. Blue." His shoulders raised up off the mattress as he pushed down, hips jerking. "Again. Please."

Rock obliged him, over and over, stroking those big fingers inside him. Panting, eyes rolling, Alex just went with it, holding onto Rock's shoulders as he flew, higher and higher.

Rock's fingers disappeared, leaving him empty, still needing, still caught high. He whimpered, reaching for Rock with a long, low cry, needing so fucking bad he hurt. Then there was Rock's prick, pushing at his hole, wanting in.

Yes. Fuck, yes. He pushed down hard, shuddering at the burn and stretch and sweet fucking pleasure. Just there. God. Just right fucking there. Rock's growl was low, fierce, a warning and then he was being nailed to the mattress, Rock thrusting hard and fast.

"Yes! Blue!" He shook and came hard, room spinning

as they slammed together, cock not even fading as Rock kept fucking him, pushing him hard.

"So fucking tight," muttered Rock, not even slowing down.

"Made for this." He could touch now, hands and lips trailing, the need manageable, rich, right.

"Fucking perfect." His Blue's face was strong, full of pleasure.

"Yes. Oh..." He brought their lips together, body one long line of wanting.

Rock's tongue slid into his mouth, hot and wet and good. He sort of melted, his belly going raw with heat and the pleasure filling him, top to bottom. Except for his prick. That was harder than diamonds and Rock wrapped one big hand around it, tugging.

When he shot again, all he knew was that fat, sweet cock that his body bore down on, those blue-blue eyes. Heat filled him, Rock's eyes never leaving his even as his Blue came.

He relaxed, just sinking into the soft mattress, fucked completely boneless. Rock rested half against him, half on him, nuzzling into his neck, licking the sweat from his skin.

"Mmm... needed you." He moaned and snuggled, already three-quarters asleep.

"Got me," growled Rock, arm solid across him, hand on his hip.

He nodded, petting and humming, already dreaming of taking a long bath, floating, swimming. "Count on it."

Rock pulled up in his truck, grunting happily as he saw Rigger's jeep in the visitor's parking. He'd called the man that afternoon, told Rigger he had a three-day and he was bringing home a cherry baby green marine.

He gave Sammy a smile and nodded at the bucket of chicken, the bag of biscuits and fries and gravy. He'd hump their gear in. "Come on, there's someone I want you to meet."

Startled green eyes met his. "Oh. I thought we were..." The kid blushed up fucking red and Rock chuckled.

"We are, kid. Rigger's gonna join us is all. Trust me -- we won't lead you wrong."

"'kay, Sarge."

Rock nodded and led the way in, dumping their gear just inside the door. He wanted a blowjob in the worst way, but he'd settle for a kiss from that talented as fuck mouth before they showed Sammy the ropes.

"Rigger?"

"Yeah, Rocketman. In the kitchen." The smell of chocolate filled the air. Oh. Brownies. Damn, that cowboy was good to him.

"Come on, Sammy, bring supper." He grinned and put a hand on the back of the kid's neck, guiding him into the kitchen.

"Hey, Rigger. Brought you home dinner and entertainment for the evening."

"Hey." Alex gave the cherry a nod, a smile. "Chicken and biscuits?"

Sammy handed over the bag and bucket. "Yes, sir."

Rock snorted. "He's no sir, this is Rigger Roberts. Rig, this is Sam Bonnely."

"Pleased, Sam. You want a beer?" Rigger gave the kid a tentative smile, the natural charm peeking through the nerves.

"Yes, please!"

"Me, too. Is that brownies I smell, Rigger?" Rock pulled dishes out of the cupboard, handing them over to the kid who caught on quickly and set the table.

"Yep. With pecans and without. Taking half to the base on Monday." Three longnecks were pulled out, offered around.

"Thanks." Rock took a nice long drink. This was different from how it usually went: eating in front of the television, fucking. Maybe some life lessons when everyone'd come a few times. "We should eat."

"Cool." Rig sat down, opening up containers and grabbing a drumstick. "Where you from, Sam?"

"Hawaii, sir, I mean Rigger."

Rock grabbed a couple of thighs and helped himself to some biscuits and gravy.

"No shit? For real?" Rigger turned on the full-on, gee-you're-interesting-talk-to-me-I'm-southern thing.

"Yeah. You ever been?"

Rock just ate, more'n happy to have Rigger keep the conversation going while he filled his belly.

"Oh, Lord no. Want to though. I fucking *love* the ocean. One happy benefit of heading out here."

"It's really beautiful and laid back, you know? Man, basic was a *shock*."

Rock chuckled. He'd bet. "You out back home?"

Sam shrugged. "Kinda a little. My folks know, my best friend."

Rock grunted. "It's different here, yeah? The only people who know are gonna be people who bark up the same tree you do. That's just the way it works."

Sam nodded, pouring gravy on his biscuits. "I didn't even think there were gay marines."

Rigger chuckled. "There are gay marines?"

Rock shook his head. "Nope, I don't believe there are."

Sam grinned. "I get it." He nodded. "I do."

"Cool. So, tell me about Hawaii." Rigger leaned back, one bare foot sliding up Rock's leg, those grey eyes twinkling.

Rock smiled and spread his legs, giving Rigger room to work as the kid nattered on about Hawaii, looking more animated than he'd seen Sam in the two weeks the baby greens had been with his unit. Rigger grinned, managed to look interested while that foot moved higher and higher. Rock knew he wasn't managing to look interested in much but Rigger's smile and his foot and frankly, he didn't care.

He groaned and Sam looked over at him, stopping mid-sentence. "Sorry, kid. You about done with your dinner?"

"The Sarge isn't a conversationalist, dude. He's a man of action."

Rock nodded. "Less talking, more fucking -- that's my motto."

Sam grinned. "I like the sound of that."

Rock grunted. "Good. Then let's go find the couch. Kitchen tables don't make the best spot for fucking."

"Is that one of the gems of wisdom I should make sure I remember, Sarge?"

Rock laughed and swatted the kid. This one wasn't going to need more than a night to get him happily on his way.

Rig's fingers slid over the kitchen table, stroking the wood. "Poor table. I almost feel sorry for it."

"Come on, Rig. You don't want splinters in your ass." He winked at Rigger and stood. They had a cherry to pop.

Rigger nodded, winked back. Those thin hips bumped his. "Splinters? Ow."

Chuckling, he put one arm around Rigger and the other around Sammy and headed them down to the couch. He rarely brought the baby greens into bed. This night was for fucking, not sleeping.

He got the kid between him and Rigger on the couch and then leaned in for his kiss. It had been too long since he'd last tasted Rig and tonight was the first night they hadn't fallen on each other the minute he'd coming in the door. Rigger searched his eyes a second, then moved in for it, kind of feeling him out, seeing how far they would go.

He pushed his tongue into Rigger's mouth, just taking it. Let the kid see real passion, see how the pros did it. It took a minute, then Rigger melted, pushed into the kiss with a happy little moan, tongue sliding against his.

He purred himself and grinned into the kiss when Sam's moan joined theirs. He looked over at the kid as their lips parted. "You want a taste, kid?"

"I didn't think most guys kissed," Sam said quietly. "They never do in the pornos."

Rock snorted.

"Porn is joyless." Rigger winked. "Kissing is God's gift to people."

Rock nodded. "Kissing is good, kid. You've got to enjoy it all, yeah? Fucking is a full body experience."

"Balls to bones." Rig leaned over, lips just brushing the kid's, making them wet. "Balls to fucking bones."

Sam whimpered, lips parting and sort of following Rigger's. It was sweet and wanton, needy.

He leaned in himself, licking Rigger's lips first and then Sammy's, pushing his tongue right into the kid's sweet mouth. They started kissing, one long lazy taste after another. Rigger tasted familiar, hot, pure sex. The kid was eager and sweet.

He wanted more though, wanted that hot sexy mouth on his cock. He pulled out of the kissing and leaned back on the couch. "I need, Rig."

Those eyes dragged down his body, Alex licking his lips, admiring all the way. "Mmm... I reckon I got some of what you're needing, Rocketman."

"I'm counting on it." He popped the buttons on his BDUs, his cock pushing hard to get out. "Watch and learn," he told Sammy.

Rigger slid over, settled against him for a second, lips on his ear. "Never done this with somebody watching."

"You don't have to if you don't want to," he murmured, eyes on Rig's grey ones. If Rigger just wanted to watch him do the kid, he didn't have a problem with that.

"Like there's ever been a time I didn't want to."

He chuckled. Yeah, that was his slut. He purred a little, hands sliding into Rigger's hair as he took another nice, long kiss. Then he pushed up with his hips, wanting.

Rigger smiled against his lips. "Horndog." Then that lean body was between his legs, spreading them wide, lips hot on his balls.

"I won't deny that accusation," he muttered, voice a low growl.

Rigger's hands slid up his legs, petting and stroking him while that fine fucking mouth slid down and down and down. He let the growl come right out, fingers pushing through Rigger's hair. "Yeah, yeah, like that."

He felt the low hum, the sweet, deep vibrations surrounding his cock.

The kid made a soft sound next to him and he grinned over. "You paying attention?" he asked, voice husky. "Because this is the best mouth in fucking forever." Rigger pulled on him harder, tongue sliding around and licking, driving him fucking crazy. He didn't know if Sam answered, or even if the kid was paying attention, as all of his attention was on that mouth and his cock. He groaned, hips starting to move.

"Can I... can I touch him?" Sam leaned close, eyes on Rigger's bobbing head.

"You've got good instincts, kid. Never do anything someone doesn't want. Rig? Sam wants to know if he can touch you."

Those lips left his cock, Rigger smiling over at the kid. "Sure, a kind touch can't hurt."

"Just don't distract him too much." Rock winked over at Sam.

The kid laughed. "He didn't look like much was going to distract him."

"Cherry, this?" Rigger licked, all the way up his cock, tongue fucking the slit twice. "Is the finest cock on Earth. No distracting."

He growled and nodded. "No distracting."

"I got it."

"Good." He grunted and tugged Rigger's head a little to encourage him to get back to it.

Rigger smiled, then that son of a bitch deep throated him, had his hips bucking off the couch. He roared, shudders moving through him as his hips started fucking Rigger's mouth.

"Oh, wow," murmured Sammy. "Oh, fuck."

Oh, sweet fuck. No one did that like Rigger. Not fucking anyone. He thrust up a few more times, whole body shaking as his balls emptied, pouring his pleasure down Rigger's throat. Rigger took him in deep, drank him down, didn't lose a single fucking drop.

He just purred, relaxing back against the couch. "Fuck, that was a good one." Like they all weren't.

His balls were nuzzled, licked, loved on.

Sam reached over and touched his cock, Rigger's lips. "Wow. It is real."

He nodded. "Yeah, kid. As real as it gets."

Rigger licked the kid's fingertips, nodding. "It is. And fuck it's good."

Sammy moaned softly and swallowed. "You say that

like you're the one who got the blow job."

"Hey, giving is as good as getting, you know?" Alex licked the tip of his cock, crawled back up into his lap. Rock groaned and took a long kiss, tasting himself in Rigger's mouth.

"So... can I try?" Sam asked.

"Try what, kid?" Rigger was hard, rubbing idly against his belly.

"S...sucking you?" Sam suddenly looked less sure of himself, shy.

Rock chuckled and gave the kid a grin. "Not too many guys are going to say no to that."

"Rubbers are in the drawer in the end table." Rigger turned, draped himself over Rock's legs, ass to cock, thighs spread. "This okay?"

"It's just perfect," muttered Rock, rubbing a little.

Sam nodded, looking at Rigger like he was a buffet before tripping over his feet on the way to get the condoms.

"You guys don't use these?" Sam asked, coming back with the rubbers.

"We did. Then we got tested. Agreed to go bareback with each other only." Rock's voice rumbled against his back.

Rigger nodded, leaned his head back for a kiss. "Yep. Gotta be safe." Rock licked at his lips and then pushed that hot tongue into his mouth, kissing him nice and hard.

"I've been practicing on myself," Sam admitted. "But it seems different putting it on another guy."

It couldn't have been helping that the kid looked about as turned on as he possibly could be: cheeks flushed, eyes a little wild, lips red from licking.

"Well, I swear I won't be nasty about it. You just take your time, I'll be hard while you try."

Sam got on his knees between Rigger's legs, giving him a tremulous smile before focusing on getting Rig's cock out of his pants.

Rigger hummed, stroking the kid's short hair. "No stress, now. We're having fun."

Yeah, he knew Rigger would do it right, knew the man couldn't resist a cherry. He helped the kid undo Rigger's jeans, and slid his fingers up under Rigger's t-shirt. Rigger arched, cock pushing out, ass pressing back against him.

He groaned, wanting in Rigger's ass. And Sam wanted Rigger's cock, the kid eagerly working on the condom.

"Mmm. That's right. You got nice hands, Sam."

"Yeah?" Sam beamed up at Rigger and Rock chuckled silently. This was going so much fucking better with Rigger. Man knew how to put the cherries at ease.

Rigger's finger traced the kid's face. "Yeah. Nice and strong. Warm. Touch me some more."

"I can do that." The kid just beamed up at Rigger, hands sliding on his cock, feeling Rigger up. "So hot."

"Oh, hell yeah. Fucking hot." Rigger just pushed up, letting the kid touch, letting the kid know it was good.

Sammy bent and licked at the tip of Rigger's cock, made a bit of a face and then wrapped his lips around the tip of Rigger's prick. Rock purred. Not bad for a beginner. It didn't hurt that Rigger liked that, liked to have the tip worked, good and hard, almost enough to burn. Then Sam proved he'd been paying attention, head bobbing on Rigger's cock. Not taking Rigger all the way in, but moving with enthusiasm.

"Oh, hell yes. Yeah, kid. Just like that."

Rock reached out and added his strokes over Sam's head to Rigger's. "You're doing great, kid."

Sam just kept bobbing, kept moving on Rigger's prick.

"Mmm..." Rigger grunted, a dull flush crawling up

the flat belly.

Rock slid his hands up along that belly, pulling the t-shirt higher so he could play with Rigger's nipples. "He's close kid."

Sam moved faster.

"Oh, fuck." Rigger's nipples went tight and hard, just begging for him to touch and tug and pull. He obliged, loving how sensitive Rigger was there, how he could make his cowboy squirm. Rigger started moving, hips rocking so careful, trying not to push the kid.

The kid pulled off with a bit of a gasp, lips swollen and red. "Am I doing it okay?"

"Oh fuck. Yes. Don't stop. Rock. I need it."

"You're doing great, kid. Finish him off." He put his hand on Sam's head, pushing him back to Rigger's prick.

Rigger nodded, moaning low, the sound needy. "Yeah, fucking close now. Need it good and hard."

Rock grabbed hold of Rigger's balls, cupping and tugging them, his other hand teasing one of those pretty little nipples. "Come on, kid. Bring him home."

Sam nodded and took Rigger's cock back in that pretty mouth, head bobbing nice and quick. Rigger's ass rubbed back against Rock, demanding, rocking. Those long thighs squeezed against him, Alex crying out, jerking.

He purred. "Gonna fuck the kid and then this ass is mine, Rig. All fucking mine."

"Fuck yes. Fucking yours." Rigger's eyes were wide, focused on him, showing him everything as Rigger came. He took Rigger's mouth, kissing hard as he patted Sam on the head. Good boy.

Alex slumped back against him. "Damn. Damn kid. That was fine."

Sam beamed, cheeks flushed. "Thanks, I... I kind of... came."

Rock chuckled. "Good for you, kid."

Rigger's head bobbed a little. "You gotta like what you're doing, yeah?"

"I liked it. I liked it a lot."

Rock grunted. "Good. That's the whole deal, Sammy."

"Mmhmm. Brownies or more fucking?"

"Oh, brownies. Always fuel both fires, kid. Especially if chocolate dessert is involved." Rock grinned, feeling lazy and happy.

Bringing Rigger in on this looking out for the new gay boys thing? Was a great idea.

Alex woke at six, blinking at the clock before settling back down. Fuck that, they'd been up late playing with Sammy. He was going back to sleep. He cuddled right in, legs twining with Rock's, cheek on Rock's shoulder. Oh, hell yeah. That was nice.

Rock grunted, arm circling him, tugging him closer.

"Mmm..." He dozed off, dreaming of flying, of fucking. Rock's cock was what woke him again, poking insistently at his hip. He reached down, stroked it, still sort of floating.

Rock rumbled and dropped a kiss on his head. "Gonna give me a wake-up call, Rigger?"

"Mmm... you wake up horny, Blue Eyes." He moaned, lips parting.

"I do when I wake up with you all over me," murmured Rock, tilting his chin up for a kiss.

"Mmm... morning." He settled on top, hands stroking over Rock's muscles. Oh, yeah. That felt good.

Rock rumbled. "Yeah. Fuck, that feels good."

He grinned, nodded, mouth open as he slid down Rock's belly. Rock's rumbling got louder, making the muscles under his mouth vibrate. That fat cock was waiting for him, tip glistening. He opened his mouth, tongue lapping at the tip, moaning low at the salt there, the heat. Rock growled, legs spreading wide to cradle his body. His fingers rolled Rock's balls, stroked the sac, the dark curls wiry and slick against his fingers.

Rock's hands found his hair, sliding through it and cupping his head. Rock didn't try to guide him, the touches were just soft, there. For him. Oh, yeah. He was liking this, touches and purrs, moans and growls. It had been fun playing with the kid, but this? This was what he wanted. He focused on the tip, licking the ridge, the slit. That had Rock's fingers curling in his hair, the moan soft and low, fucking needy.

Alex hummed, taking more in, head just starting to bob. He could feel the tension in Rock's thighs, could feel his marine trying not to push up into his mouth. He slid one hand under Rock's ass, pulled up. Come on, Blue Eyes. Fuck me. His permission was obviously all Rock was waiting for. There was a grunt, a bit of a growl and Rock's hands cupped his head, holding him in place as those hips started to work, pushing that fucking fat prick into his mouth. He opened wide, groaning, swallowing around Rock's prick.

Oh, sweet fuck. Yes.

Rock's moans were low and needy, those hips pushing harder, deeper. He relaxed his throat, nose buried in Rock's pubes. Yes.

Rock just roared, coming down his throat. Swallowing, pulling, Alex took every drop in, every fucking drop.

Rock finally collapsed back against the bed, hands patting. "Good fucking morning."

Fuck yes. He nodded, hips fucking the sheets. Rock tugged on him, encouraging him to slide up the hard body.

One hand wrapped around his prick, stroking easily.

"Oh. Oh, fuck. Yes." He arched, offering Rock his lips.

Rock took them, tongue fucking his mouth, one hand on his ass, the other working his cock just right. He didn't take long at all, come just pouring out of him, moan torn from him.

"Oh yeah, Rig. Fucking love that smell."

"Uh-huh." Alex just sort of melted, humming low.

Rock rumbled, hand stroking along his back. "Nice."

"Mmm... Feels fucking great, Blue Eyes."

"Yep, not bad for an old-timer." Rock puffed up a bit, muscles flexing, moving, showing off for him.

Alex snorted, fingers tracing each muscle, each inch of skin. Rock made them jump and move for him, putting on a show.

"Oooo... look at that stud!"

He got a smack on the ass. "I am."

"You are." He nodded. "Worth leaving Texas for."

Oh fuck.

Fuck.

Shut *up*, Jeremy Alexander Roberts!

"You know it."

"Yeah." He leaned down, took a slow, deep kiss.

Rock opened for him, letting him in, hand going behind his head to keep him right there in the kiss. He fucked Rock's lips, moaning low, diving into the kiss. Those strong arms wrapped around him, holding him close as a moan filled his mouth. Oh, yeah. He pushed it harder, kissing Rock with all he had. He could feel Rock's prick go hard again between them, one of Rock's fingers teasing his crack. Somebody was going to get to ride that fat prick this morning and it looked like the lucky cowboy was him. That thick finger found his hole and pushed against it, pushed in.

He moaned, thighs spreading, letting Rock in.

"Oh yeah. Fuck, you're hot. Tight."

There was only one more thing to say to that. "More."

Rock chuckled, looked happy. "Slut."

"Yeah, but I'm your slut."

Rock chuckled. "Through and through." A second finger pushed into him.

He nodded, bearing down, needing it. "Balls to bones. Fuck, you have fine hands."

"All the better to fuck you with." Oh, those blue eyes just shone at him.

"Oh, yeah? I'm a big fan of that idea, marine."

Rock growled. "Me, too. You ready for your ride?"

"You know it." He moved to straddle that fat, fine prick.

Rock's hands slid onto his hips, guiding him, those eyes watching him, full of heat.

He stretched, reaching for the lube, slicking one hand and stroking Rock's prick.

Groaning, Rock pushed up into his hand. "Those hands aren't so bad, either."

"Yeah? Not my mouth, but not half bad." He worked the tip, thumb rubbing.

Rock chuckled, groaned some more, hips pushing up again. "Not half fucking bad at all."

Rigger just hummed, licked his lips, watching. "Fucking *fine*."

"You know it." That chest just puffed right up for him, that whole body fucking fine.

"Mmhmm..." He leaned down, kept touching while he sucked one nipple.

Rock's hands went tight on his hips. "Fuck."

He nodded. Yes. Fuck. Rock's hands moved his hips,

trying to get him lined up with that hard prick. He moved easy, wanting it, wanting to feel Rock in deep. Rock pulled him down onto that fat cock, hips pushing up to go deep.

"Oh." His head rolled, eyes wide as they focused on the ceiling. "Damn. Blue. More."

"Yeah. Fuck more." Rock grunted and started moving, hips pushing up into him, hands pulling him down.

He was still stretched from last night, Rock slamming into him, pounding him through the mattress.

"So fucking hot." Rock pushed up again, cock sliding across his gland just like that.

His eyes went wide, hips rocking furiously for a second. Oh, shit yeah. Just like that. "More."

"Fuck, yeah." Rock nodded and pulled him down harder, giving him more.

How exactly did he manage mornings before this kind of sex? Rock just kept pushing into him, cock sliding right past his gland every time.

"Fuck. Gonna. Christ. Rock." He moved a little faster, just slamming himself down.

"Yeah, that's the idea, Rabbit." The words were growled, Rock's body meeting his hard.

"Uh-huh." He jerked, coming so hard it hurt, ached deep in his balls.

Rock's roar preceded the heat that filled him, those blue eyes holding his.

Oh. Damn. Wow.

Just wow.

Rock pulled him down onto that great big chest, hands sliding on his back. "Remind me again why we ever get out of bed?"

"Paychecks and food."

Rock grunted. "Good point."

"I have them once in a blue moon."

That earned him a chuckle, Rock's touches lazy and slow.

"Mmm... we ought to get up. I'm thinking pancakes and good coffee at the IHOP." He was starving.

"Another good idea. That moon must be really blue."

He bit at one nipple. "Watch out, marine. I'll start having them more often."

Rock jerked at the bite and smacked his ass. "Can't have that."

"God, no. Ideas lead to thinking and that's nasty shit."

"Yep. No thinking."

He nodded, grinning ear-to-ear. Fucking was way better than thinking.

Any goddamn day.

CHAPTER NINE

Rock pulled up at Rig's apartment building and slammed the door of his truck behind him. He took the stairs two at a time, grumbling as he went.

Fucking stubborn cowboy.

They'd argued over the weekend, Rigger cleaning his little apartment like the fucking president was coming to visit or something and he'd had enough and growled and Rigger had growled back. One thing led to another and before he knew it he was reminding Rigger that he'd never asked the cowboy to follow him out here and well, that had put an end to the argument, hadn't it?

Alex had just turned and left, just like that.

Considering the last time they'd argued it had been three fucking weeks before he saw Rigger again, Rock figured he was going to have to take matters into his own hands this time.

He rapped on Rigger's door, that damned mutt starting to bark. He growled back. Come on, he was missing the fucking Thanksgiving parade. He knocked again, louder this time.

"It's motherfucking Thanksgiving. I'm not buying whatever the fuck you're selling." Oh, someone was snarling.

The door flew open, Rigger wearing nothing but a sweater and a pair of briefs.

"Interesting outfit." He leaned against the doorjamb, crossing his arms. He felt better, knowing he wasn't the only one out of sorts from fighting. Hell, he was here because it would be a crime to waste that mouth and ass when there was a four day holiday happening.

"Fuck off." Rigger turned and went into the apartment, grabbing the mutt's collar.

He walked in, letting the door close behind him. "I'd rather just fuck."

The place smelled like turkey and apples and coffee and bread and shit. The sofa bed was pulled out, blankets pushed into a nest.

Rigger grabbed some empty bottles, trashed them. "Let me get some pants on."

"You don't have to on my account." He watched Rigger move around and realized he was hungry, not for food, not for some random encounter, but for Rigger. "But you're obviously still pissed off at me."

"No." He got a look, a shrug. "I'm not pissed at you. Want some coffee?"

"No." He went over to Rigger and took ahold of his face, tilting it up and taking a kiss. "I want you."

Rigger looked into his eyes, searching them for a second and then he had an armful of cowboy, the kiss sharp and burning. He grunted. Yeah, that's what he wanted. What he fucking needed. Fucking perfect mouth. His tongue slid with Rigger's, his arms circling Rigger, hands finding that ass. Those long arms wrapped around his neck, holding on tight, tugging them close together.

He deepened the kiss, just devouring Rigger's mouth, hands sliding into the tighty whities to squeeze Rigger's ass skin on skin. Rigger pressed closer, whimpering, rocking them together, that hard prick insistent on his hip. His own cock was pushing against his zipper, just fucking aching. He dragged them over to the sofa bed, hands pushing Rigger's underwear down past his hips and then sweeping up and pulling the sweater off.

He wanted skin; he wanted to fuck Rigger's ass until they were both screaming from it.

"You too. Skin. Fuck, Rock. I want."

"Uh-huh." He grunted his response, and worked off his t-shirt and then his jeans, nearly ripping off a layer of skin tugging down his zipper. There were disadvantages to going commando. But when his cock pushed out and slid along Rigger's skin, he remembered the fucking advantages and they were tumbling to the bed, rubbing hard.

Rigger arched, lips wrapped around his tongue, sucking hard enough to make his head spin. He had no fucking clue where the lube was with the sofa bed pulled out, so he forced a finger between their lips, pushing it into Rigger's mouth. Rigger sucked hard, fellating his finger, eyes hot and burning for it. His prick jerked. Fuck, he needed it bad.

Pulling his finger away, he reached around Rigger, working the tip into that hot body.

"Yes." Rigger was hotter than hell, tight and perfect against his finger.

He offered Rigger two fingers from his other hand, eyes watching the grey of Rigger's. Those lips opened, wrapped around his fingers and pulled, sucking hard. He groaned, hips pumping, rubbing his cock against Rigger's skin. Fuck, that mouth...

He pulled his fingers out with a pop, the need like a fucking freight train, rushing and unstoppable. They went into Rigger, nice and easy, stretching Rig out for his cock.

Rigger undulated under him, spread and panting. "Fuck me. That's so fucking good."

"I'm gonna fuck you, Rig. Gonna fuck you hard and deep." He growled, fingers pushing, searching.

Rigger's head lifted when he found it, eyes fucking huge and burning. "Yes!"

"Right there, huh?" Rock pegged it a couple of times and then pulled his fingers out. He shifted, bringing his cock up to Rigger's mouth. "Slick me up, Rig."

That mouth dropped over him hard, the suction and hunger enough to make him roar, make his head slam back.

"Fuck! Enough." He was going to come like a ton of bricks down Rigger's throat any second now.

Rigger leaned back, panting, watching him with wet, swollen lips. "What?"

"That mouth is too fucking good and I want that ass." He shifted back down, pushing Rigger's legs up over his shoulders.

Rigger bent, spread so pretty. "All yours. Deep and hard, Blue Eyes."

"You know it." He nodded and pushed right in. He knew what he needed, knew what Rig needed.

They groaned together, the sound raw and right -- the first right thing he'd heard in a few days. He bent Rigger double and kissed him and then he started to move, deep and hard. Rigger took him in, eyes burning, staring up at him as they moved and slammed together. It all went into each thrust, the frustration and anger, three days pent up need. He growled, moving harder, faster.

"Blue Eyes. Please. Fuck." Rigger reached down, pumping his own prick, driving them higher and higher.

He nodded. "I'm fucking."

Harder and harder he pushed, just letting Rig have it all, those grey eyes wide with pleasure.

"Gonna." Rigger squeezed him tight-tight, ass clenched around him.

"Fuck!" He roared, hips snapping, jerking into Rigger a few more times before he came hard.

"Yes. Fuck, yes." Rigger panted, rocking against him, lips on his shoulder.

He shifted, letting Rigger's legs down off his shoulders without slipping out of that hot, clutching body.

"Fucking good, Rig."

"Happy fucking Thanksgiving, Blue Eyes."

Rock chuckled, his cock moving inside Rig, making him moan. "Yeah. Happy fucking... Thanksgiving."

Rigger squeezed him, nodded. "Glad to see you. Cooked food, just in case."

He shuddered, cock throbbing. "Thought I smelled turkey."

The squeezes came again and again, rhythmic and good. "Rolls and sweet potatoes. Dressing. Pecan pie."

He groaned, half for that ass squeezing his cock, half for that menu. "Can't remember the last time Thanksgiving included real food," he admitted.

"I never had one where I wasn't at home."

"Well this year you're having it with me." He grunted, thrust once for emphasis.

"Yeah." He got a smile, one that made it worth driving over, without a question.

He thrust again, just because he could, and then again because it felt so fucking good.

"Mmm... that's good. Good. Damn." Rig rolled them, landed on top of him, riding nice and easy.

Groaning, he rolled his hips, working with Rigger's movements.

"So fucking hot." Rigger moaned, leaned down, licked at his lips.

"Fuck, yes." He opened his mouth and sucked on Rigger's tongue.

Rigger tasted like him and coffee and donuts. Mmm... somebody had donuts in the kitchen. He pushed up hard on the next thrust. "Taste good," he told Rig.

"Feels fucking amazing. Don't stop."

"You see me trying to stop?"

"Nope." Rigger laughed, leaned up, riding him hard.

He met each drop of Rigger's body, pushing up into that heat over and over. Fuck, Rig was hot and tight.

Rig's fingers found his nipples, twisting and tugging, pulling.

He arched, cock going deep. "Fuck yes."

"Beautiful fucking man. Right there."

"Right there?" he asked, thrusting in again.

"Uh-huh. Uh-huh." Rigger rocked, biting down on his own lip as they moved together.

He slid his hand around Rigger, letting Rigger's own rocking slide that prick along his palm.

"Sweet fuck, yes. Getting close, Blue Eyes." Yeah, he could feel it.

"Give it up, Rig. You know you want to."

Rig nodded, eyes rolling, breath huffing from him. It took two more pushes before heat splashed over his hand.

The smell of Rig along with that ass squeezing his cock so fucking hard sent him over and he moaned, hips bucking, pushing himself deeper as he came again.

Rig slumped down against him with a plop and a hum. "Hey."

"Hey." He nibbled at Rig's lips. "I didn't have breakfast," he noted.

"No? There's cinnamon rolls and donuts in the kitchen. Good coffee."

"Yeah? Sounds good." Almost as good as lying beneath his own private redneck slut.

"Yeah. Sounds better than ever."

Four days of fucking and eating turkey dinner and a ton of leftovers. It didn't get much better than this. Of course Sunday afternoon meant it was almost time to start getting back to the reality of his own apartment and having to get up early tomorrow for PT and getting on base by o eight hundred.

But not quite yet.

He and Rig were currently sitting on the couch, watching stuff blow up on the TV. Not bad in and of itself. Add that warm, sexy body plastered to his, a beer in one hand and a plate of brownies on the coffee table and he was one happy marine.

Rig was dozing in and out, all cuddly and lazy, the pup pushing at his hands every now and again to get some love. Rock had to chuckle, wondering if that automatic response that had Rig petting the beast would work with other stuff as well.

He let his hand drift over to stroke one of Rig's nipples through his t-shirt. Well, he'd be damned. That little nub went rock-hard, Rig's cheek just nuzzling him. That kind of response was golden. He stroked his thumb across the hard little bit of flesh again, his cock perking up. That got him a moan, another nuzzle, a little shift. He rumbled happily, sliding his other hand over to Rig's hip.

"Mmm." God, the man was a slut, pushing closer, rubbing and sliding them together.

Chuckling, he tugged on Rigger's hip, turning the man to lie on him front to front. Oh yeah, that was nice. A couple too many pairs of jeans, but it was a start.

"Blue Eyes. Smell good..." That soft tongue trailed along his throat.

He chuckled, hand sliding along Rig's back. "Yeah? You do, too. *We* do." They did. Smelled fucking fantastic, like really good sex.

"Mmhmm." Lazy, cuddly, octopus Rig.

He tilted Rig's head, brought their mouths together for a nice, lazy kiss. Rig was as lethal like this as in full-out slut-mode. Maybe even more lethal. He wasn't even trying, hell he wasn't even all awake and yet he was all sex. Rock growled softly, hands working their way beneath Rig's t-shirt. That got him a soft little moan, Rig pressing closer.

He rolled them, putting Rig under him, growling a little. He took the kiss up a notch, tongue pushing into Rig's mouth. Rig pushed up, lips wrapping around his tongue as Rig sucked. He worked that t-shirt up, fingers searching for those pretty little nipples. He found them and it was electric, Rig groaning, bucking up under him. He kept sliding across them, tugging and pulling, loving the way Rig moved beneath him.

"Blue Eyes. Damn. Fuck. Please, I want..." Rig whimpered, rolling that hard cock against him.

"Oh, you want something?" He chuckled, pushed his hips down hard.

"Yeah..." Rig's eyes rolled. "Do it again."

"Anything you want, Rig." He pushed again, pinched Rig's nipples at the same time.

"Oh." Rig groaned. "Fuck. Fuck."

"Pushy, pushy," he murmured, just grinning.

"Uh-huh. Your point?"

He laughed and rubbed them together, grinding Rig into the couch. "There's my point."

"Mmm... good point. Damn." Rig's shoulders left the couch, lips parted, hungry for him.

He met that kiss head on, tongue just invading as his hips kept pushing, humping against Rig. Fuck, things went from lazy to wild in no time, that lean body fucking twisting and turning beneath him. He tore off his own clothes and then pushed Rig's t-shirt right off, managing to only break the kiss for a second. The damned jeans were next, too fucking tight for easy disposal and he growled into the kiss, fingers threatening the seams.

Rig groaned, half-helping, half-complicating things. "Fuck. More. Damn, don't stop now."

"You're saying yes, but your jeans are saying no." He winked down and yanked, not caring if he ripped anything.

Rig leaned up and bit his lip, wriggling until one long leg came free. "Yours now."

He growled happily, hand sliding beneath Rig's ass, thumb finding Rig's hot, long crease. He pushed against the wrinkled flesh of Rig's hole. That deep groan felt damned good, Rig's motions beneath him growing more and more desperate. He let his thumb push in, groaning as Rig's body pulled it right in, eager and needy.

"Blue Eyes..." Rig rippled, eyes wide, fastened on him.

"You want me, Rig? Want a piece of the Rocketman?" He slid his thumb away, pushed two fingers in.

"No. Want all you got. Every fucking inch."

He moaned. Hell, yeah. "That's what you're going to get." He nodded and pushed another finger in, stretching Rig fast and easy.

Fucking slut just took him in and begged for more, riding him, riding his fingers. He tongue fucked Rig's mouth, fingers pushing quickly. He couldn't wait long, he wanted this sweet fucking ass in the worst way.

"Come on. Come on, now. Show me why I left Texas, Jim."

"You know it." He let his fingers pull away, let his cock replace them. Rig's body just swallowed him right up, making him groan. "Oh, fuck, yes."

"Yeah..." Rig arched, hips rocking, riding him nice and steady.

He nodded, bending to nip at Rig's nipples, teeth just grazing the hard little nub. He felt that, deep inside Rig, the lean body jerking and squeezing tight. He did it again, loving that sensitivity, that immediate response. His hands wrapped around Rig's hips and he fucked harder, driving himself deep.

"Oh, hell. Yeah. There. Right like fucking that, man." Rig's head came up off the sofa.

He moved his head over to work Rig's other nipple, but his aim with his cock stayed right where it was, making Rigger writhe and moan.

"Fuck. Fuck." Those knees were spread wide, Rig holding them, spreading himself open. Sexiest fucking thing he'd ever seen and he'd seen a lot.

Growling, he pushed harder, just giving it all to Rig. Rig gasped, toes-curling, entire body clenching as the man shot without a touch to his cock.

"Oh, fuck. Rig." He nodded, thrust, roaring out his own pleasure as Rig's body milked the spunk right out of him.

"I. Oh. Fuck." Rig's eyes just rolled.

He grunted and nodded. "Yeah. Fuck."

Letting himself down carefully, he let Rig take his weight, purring at the heat of all that skin.

"Mmm...hell of a way to spend a holiday, man."

"I can't think of a better way."

"You sticking around for Christmas?"

"Well they're going to come arrest me if I don't get up and go in tomorrow." He winked.

"Yeah, yeah, yeah. You know what I mean. You going to see your folks?"

Rock snorted. Yeah, right. Not in this lifetime, not in the next. "No."

"Momma wants me to come home, but I was thinking on staying here. Saving my pennies some."

"Yeah? I usually grab dinner at the base and they show that Scrooge movie in the mess." He wouldn't say no to a decent meal like the one they'd had for Thanksgiving.

"I get two weeks leave. I could do you better than that."

"Yeah, I imagine you could at that." He gave Rig a grin. "Definitely sounds better than what they serve at the base."

"Mmhmm. Ham and cookies and whatever movies we want." Rig grinned back. "Way better than Scrooge."

"Hell yes. Sounds like a plan." He gave Rig a hard kiss. Sounded like a damned good plan.

In fact, add in some lube and a couple of showers with his favorite redneck? It might even sound like a wet dream.

CHAPTER TEN

Rock was playing pool with Wilson, watching the kid's ass every time he bent over the table to take his shot. Pretty fucking sweet, but then the cherries always were.

He had a beer in one hand, his pool cue in the other and fresh meat in front of him. If Rigger would come on and show up, it would be a perfect Friday night.

Wilson was a cocky little thing around the pool table and Rock figured it was going to work out perfectly. He'd not mentioned anything more than pool to the kid, he figured once Rig got here and they'd played a couple, they could start playing for sexual favors and let nature take its course. With Rig nature always coursed toward pure fucking pleasure.

Wilson scratched his next ball and Rock drank down the rest of his beer, the dark malt taste heavy in his mouth, lingering. He glanced at the clock. Eight ten. Rig was late. Shaking his head, Rock bent over the table more than he really needed to for his shot, but it was good to give Wilson a taste, let the cherry start wanting before he knew he could have.

He heard the guys hoot and holler, everybody knew Rig. Everybody liked the man. It wasn't long at all before Rig wandered over, beer in hand. "How's it hanging, man?"

"High and hard," he replied, giving Rig a grin and a lazy once over. "You?"

"Not bad. Been a long day." He got a smile, the cherry got a nod. "Hey there."

"Yeah, I was thinking you were a little on the late side." He nodded at Wilson. "That's the kid I was telling you about earlier this week, the baby green. Name's Wilson. Hey W, this is Rigger."

Rigger smiled over. "Pleased to meet you. Who's winning? Y'all eaten?"

"Nah, we've been waiting on you and the kid's winning. He's an aggressive player."

Wilson smiled, sank two more balls and then came over to shake Rig's hand. "You play?"

"Every now and again, yeah." Rig nodded, settled down into a chair with his beer. "Thank God it's Friday."

"I'll play you for eats," Wilson suggested.

Rock laughed. "That's okay, kid. My treat."

"Yeah? I want a hamburger and fries. I missed lunch." Rig swigged his beer, settled. "I'll pay you back tomorrow, Rocketman."

"I said it was my treat." He handed the kid two twenties and sat across from Rig. "I'll have a burger and fries, too, get what you want and beers all around."

After the kid walked off, Rig gave him a smile. "Good

to see you, Blue Eyes."

"Yeah, you're a sight for sore eyes." He looked Rig up and down and rumbled a little.

"We were up in the bird three times today. Two training accidents and a wreck. Glad I'm off for a couple."

"Sounds rough. We've been training baby greens all week, no deaths, but there were a couple of times it came close." He craned his neck and watched Wilson hand over his money, fingers tapping on the bar. "Of course baby greens mean cherries..."

"Yeah? You pick that one?"

"Yep. A Sarge special." He winked at Rig.

Rig chuckled. "Let's see how he does, then."

"Just don't bet your paycheck at pool, he's a shark."

He got a grin, grey eyes twinkling. "Better than you?"

"Only if he gets really, really lucky. You think he's going to get lucky tonight?"

"It's a possibility, if he's a good marine."

Rock chuckled and grinned. "You mean like me?"

"No, with you? It's a guarantee. He's still on probation."

"Probation?" He raised an eyebrow. "You're putting my cherries on probation now?"

He got an eyebrow raised right back. "I'm just saying that if I'm not feeling it, I'm not fucking it."

He supposed that was fair. "As long as you're feeling me, Rig."

The smile warmed right up, made his cock jerk. "Balls to bones, Rock."

It was a good thing the kid showed back up with the beer right then because he was heading into forgetting where the fuck they were.

"You order us eats, Wilson?"

"Yes, sir."

He cuffed the kid upside the head.

"He's not a 'sir', he works for a living." Rig grinned, grabbed a pool cue. "Who's playing me?"

"Go on, kid, I've got a beer to finish." Rock shifted his chair so he could watch that ass in motion. He knew Rig would put on a show for him.

Rig racked up, the long legs and tight ass fine in the thin, thin scrubs. Rock spread his own legs as his cock filled his BDUs. Damn, Rig was something else. The kid on the other hand was all bounce and bluster. A fucking puppy.

The game went fairly quick, Wilson slapping Rig on the back hard enough to make the man wince. "Kicked your ass, man! Kicked your fucking ass!"

Rock shook his head. He wasn't exactly the king of finesse himself, but Wilson was going to make him look like a master.

"Good game, man." Rig wandered over to him, admiring him. "Food here yet?"

The waiter was coming with it, so he nodded, grinned. "Come on, kid, pull up a chair. It's chow time."

Wilson sat, rubbing his hands. "Do I get to whip your ass next, Sarge?"

"Fuck off, kid."

Rig settled, stealing his lettuce and tomato as he took it off. "Where are you from, Wilson?"

"New York City, man. Best city in the world."

Rock chuckled. Now that was not the way to win the boy from Texas over.

"It's sure big, I'll give you that."

Rock chuckled, eating happily. "I bet that's all he'll give you though."

"You ever been to New York, Rigger?" Wilson

asked.

"No, sir. Never had the slightest desire to, really. Houston was big enough for me."

"Oh, you gotta see New York. It's the center of the universe." The kid was grinning, and he winked.

"You obviously haven't ever been to Texas." Rig chuckled, eating slowly, leg just touching his.

"Nope. Don't really plan to either." Oh, this poor cherry needed pointers in more than just sex and the single gay marine area. Rock just shook his head and stole fries off Rig's plate.

Rig stole his pickles in return. "Texas is a beautiful place, man. Everything a man could need. Well, mostly."

"So why'd you leave, man?"

"Oh, I had a good reason." Rigger smiled, drank deep from that beer. It was enough to make a marine want to drag a certain nurse home and fuck him blind.

He growled a little. "Well I'm done, let's get this game going, kid."

He gave Rig a look. "I'll be ready to go once I've showed the kid how to play."

"Cool." Rig's eyes were burning, wanting him, making promises. "Kick ass, marine."

"I will." He winked at the kid, but gave Rig a head on look. Oh, yeah, that ass was his. ASAP.

This game was faster than all the others; he sank ball after ball, focused on nothing but winning.

The kid was pouting by the time he was done. "Man, you were holding back earlier!"

"Nah, Wilson. I just needed some food." He turned to Rig. "You see that? That's how a marine does it, Rig."

"I saw, Rocketman. You done?"

"I am. We playing?"

"We are." Rig stood, threw a bill on the table for a tip. "See you around, Yankee."

Rock chuckled. And that was where Wilson had gone wrong. You didn't have to be from Texas for Rig to like you, but if you flaunted it, you were in trouble.

"See you Monday, Wilson."

"You guys going already?"

"We are indeed."

"All right, see you Monday, Sarge. Good to meet you, Texas."

The kid got a smile, a nod, and then Rig was off. Focused fucking redneck. Of course he was following that ass pretty closely, now wasn't he?

He shook his head as he went. It was the first time he'd picked a cherry to initiate and not followed through. Somehow he couldn't work up any upset about it.

They headed toward his place. He needed to let Grimmy out and his food was better, no question. Alex hoped Rock wasn't pissed about the whole turning down the cherry thing, but he was tired and so not in the mood for games. He pulled into a space, grabbing his bag while he waited for Rock's truck to stop.

Rock pulled into an empty spot a couple over and got out, grabbing his pack. "You still got that pair of jeans you were washing a couple weeks ago? This all needs a wash."

"Yeah. You got some sweats and t-shirts too. You're set." He'd do laundry tomorrow. "Come on up."

"Yeah, won't need underwear." Rock gave him a wink and came along with him. "It just gets in the way."

"You know it. Morning wake up calls require access."

"Fuck, yes." Rock gave him a grin, leaning against the wall as he worked his key into the lock.

He grinned right back, popping the lock. "Come in,

I'm going to walk my beast. You grab a beer."

"Walk your beast?" Rock grinned and grabbed his crotch. "I've got your beast right here and it's not a walk it needs."

Oh, that made him laugh, loud and long, happy in a way he hadn't been all fucking day. "Man, I needed me a dose of that."

"What you need is a good hard fuck. Make that walk a quick one." Rock stopped him before he could go out, kissing him nice and deep, making Grimmy bark. "You know what's waiting for you when you get back."

"I do." Thank God for favors large and small.

He got Grimmy out, the pup desperate to do his business. "Such a good boy. Good pup. What a good Grimmy."

Grimmy barked up happily at him.

One of his downstairs neighbors walked by with her little poodle, her long blond hair up in a pony tail. She gave him a big smile. "Hi there, Alex."

"Hey Jenny. How's Miss Ursula doing?" The poodle was a sweetie, if a little high-strung.

"Really good. That shedding problem stopped as soon as I got rid of that big noisy fan. My poor baby didn't like the noise, did you sweetums? Your boy is looking as drooly as ever." She flirted madly with him, blue eyes just gazing up at him like he'd hung the moon or something. She'd done a lot of hinting, but never asked him outright for his number or a date.

"He's a goober. I have to run, a friend's upstairs waiting on me. Come by some time, we'll take the pups to the dog park." Sweet girl. Way high-strung, though.

"Oh, okay. It was nice talking to you, Alex." She gave him a smile and headed toward the dog park.

He clicked to Grim, headed back into the apartment. Toward Rock.

Rock was on the couch, a beer in one hand, the TV remote in the other, looking right at home. He got a grin as he came in.

"Look who's lounging on my couch."

"Look who's not over here sucking my cock."

He hooted. "Ah, romance, thy name is Rocketman."

"Hey, you want romance, go back to the bar. You want me, I'm right here." Those blue eyes were looking right into him.

"I know what I want, Blue Eyes." He made his way across the floor, cock throbbing in his jeans.

"Yeah, I figured you did." Rock spread his legs, beer carefully put on the little table beside him.

"You going to show me what you got?" Not that he wasn't drooling for it.

Rock chuckled and opened his BDUs, one button at a time, his fat cock all but leaping out. "There you go. All yours."

"Mmm... All mine." He licked his lips, settled between Rock's legs. "So fucking fine, Rock."

One of Rock's hands slid into his hair. "A mouth like yours deserves a cock like mine."

"You know it. Excellent fit." He moaned as his lips circled the tip of that heavy prick, tongue lapping at the head.

Rock groaned. "Fuck, yeah."

He nodded, head bobbing a little, just taking it slow and easy. Some dudes had meditation, some had weightlifting. He sucked cock. Rock's legs spread wider, hips pushing that fat prick into his mouth.

"Mmm..." He opened wider, took more and more in, groaning low as Rock filled him up.

Rock's purrs and moans filled the air, the heat in his mouth incredible. He ran his hands up along Rock's legs, fingers just brushing the heavy balls.

"Oh yeah. So fucking good." Rock's fingers slid along his stretched lips. "Fucking good."

He nibbled the tips of Rock's fingers, then started bobbing hi head. Hell, yes.

Groaning, Rock started to move with him, thighs clenching, hips pushing Rock's cock deep. He slid his hands under Rock's ass, encouraging the man to move, to fuck his lips. Rock cried out, hips moving freely now, pushing into his mouth over and over.

Oh, fuck yes. Rigger relaxed, taking more and more into his throat. Rock pushed and pushed, fucking his mouth, just giving it to him. Finally his nose was buried in Rock's pubes, cock buried in his throat.

Rock's roar was sweet, those thick fingers curling around his head as hot spunk spilled down his throat. He damn near creamed his jeans, hand dropping down to rub frantically at his cock.

"Yeah, Rig. Fucking come for me."

He dropped his head on Rock's belly, grunting hard, just losing it.

Rock's belly vibrated with a low rumble. "Nice one."

He just nodded, panting. "You up for a nice two?"

Rock laughed, rubbed that fine cock against his neck. "Fuck, yes."

"Excellent." He kissed the top ridge of dark curls.

Rock's hand slid through his hair, fingers eventually finding his mouth again. "Poor cherry really missed out."

"Someone'll help him. I wasn't in the space to entertain."

"As long as you're in the mood to entertain me."

"Always." He kissed the tip of Rock's prick.

Rock's cock jerked for him and one hand went under

his arm, hauling him up. Rock's lips found his, tongue pushing right on in. He moaned, opening up, thighs parting and straddling Rock. Rock's fingers landed on his ass, so hot through the thin material of his scrubs. He was rocked forward, their pricks sliding together. He moaned, cock filling again, belly rippling and tight.

"Too many clothes, Rabbit." Rock's fingers slid beneath his scrub top, tugging it off, fingertips hot as they dragged up along his torso.

He nodded, pulling Rock's t-shirt off. "I'm a big fucking fan of naked."

Rock grinned. "How about a big fan of fucking naked?" He got a wink before Rock grabbed either side of his scrub pants and tore them apart.

"Bastard!" He pushed in, tweaked one of Rock's nipples good and hard. Fuck, the man was *strong*.

Rock grunted, pushing up into his touch. "What? I couldn't get them off with your legs all spread out like that."

"Sure. Neanderthal."

Rock just chuckled. "Oh, you gonna start sweetalking me now?"

That got him chuckling, fingers sliding over Rock's ribs, searching for ticklish spots.

"Oh ho!" Rock's fingers retaliated, making him squirm, their bodies rubbing together.

Rigger started laughing, arching away from Rock's hands as he tried to keep hold with his own. Rock's chuckles were low, deep, one hand landing on his ass and making sure he didn't arch right off. Oh, that hand was fine. Strong. Hot. Damn.

"Come on, Rig. Get my jeans off so we can get this party started properly."

"Oh, hell yeah." He reached down, pushing and shoving at the material, freeing those muscles for him.

Rock wriggled and helped as much as he could with two hands wrapped around Rig's body, and then they were both naked, bodies rubbing. Rock's cock was fully hard again, sliding against his own. His head fell back, a low groan sounding, heat flaring in the pit of his belly.

"Gonna fuck you, Rig. Take that sweet ass all the way to fucking heaven."

"Promise?" He stretched up, cock sliding all the way.

"Fuck, yes." Rock's hand slid under the couch cushions, pulling out the lube. "Gonna watch you slick yourself up, Rig."

His cheeks flushed, but he nodded, holding his fingers out. That made him feel exposed and hot and sexy all at once. The look in those blue eyes was so hot, threatening to burn him up. Rock squeezed the tube, getting the slick all over his fingers. He braced himself on Rock's shoulder, reaching back, fingers pressing deep.

"Fuck. Would you look at that." And Rock was looking, eyes riveted.

Oh, man. That made him just burn for it. He started riding his fingers, giving Rock a show. Rock's hips were moving in rhythm with his own, a low rumble coming from the muscled chest. He could feel each growl, each purr, each motion of air against his skin, his nipples going hard as stones.

Rock just kept moving with him, kept making low noises of pleasure. "Don't be too long, Rig. I want in."

"Fuck me. Now." He could be a touch demanding. Sometimes.

Rock nodded. "Yes." Rock's hand grabbed his wrist, pulled out his fingers. Then that fat prick lined right up at his hole, started pushing in. He cried out, bore down and took Rock in to the root.

"Fuck!" Rock's whole body bucked, those big hands

landing on his hips, holding on.

They found their rhythm -- good, hard, steady, deep. Like good music, good beer. Rock leaned up and tongued his nipples, breath hot on his skin.

"Fuck. Hot. Hot, Blue Eyes."

"You know it." Rock growled, nibbling on his flesh, taking a nipple between his teeth and tugging.

Heat flooded him and he moved faster, harder, cock like a stone.

"So fucking good," muttered Rock, hips just pumping.

"Uh-huh. More. Fuck."

"All you fucking want, Rig." Rock's hands held him hard, hips snapping up to fill him deep. He reached down, stroking his cock, pulling hard. "Yeah, that's it, Rabbit. Give it to me. Show me how good it is."

"So good. Sweet fuck, Blue. It's fucking amazing."

He jerked, coming with a low cry. Rock's hands went tight on his hips, fat prick fucking and fucking, pushing into him as Rock found his release with a roar. He leaned in, panting hard, just blinking. Damn.

Rock rumbled, hands warm on his back, sliding idly. "Fucking good, Rig."

"Uh-huh." He just nodded, cuddled.

Rock grunted and shifted a little, settling more firmly on the couch.

"Mmm... you comfortable?"

"I'll do."

"You did."

Rock chuckled, moving against him. A moment later the blanket he kept at the end of the couch landed over him.

"Mmm... Feels good, Rocketman. Great way to start the weekend."

"Fuck, yeah. Nothing that starts with fucking is

gonna be a bad thing."

"You got that right."

"I know it." Rock petted his back, a low rumble vibrating all those lovely muscles beneath him.

Rigger closed his eyes, sighed. Man, this was the life. Just like this.

CHAPTER ELEVEN

Rock parked his car in front of Rig's apartment, locked his door and went back to the truck bed. If he shouldered his pack first and hoisted the tree over his other shoulder, he could probably handle the case of beer with one hand. He could make it as far as Rig's place as long as he didn't meet anyone in the stairwell.

Grunting, wishing he'd worn his gloves, he loaded up and headed in. Luck was with him and he didn't run into anyone. He kicked at Rig's door. "Come on, Rigger, open up."

"Coming. Coming!" The door opened, the smell of chocolate, sugar and cinnamon rushing out at him.

Oh, now that smell was worth fighting Christmas shoppers to buy Rig's big stupid mutt a big old bone, not to mention the look the blue haired wrapping ladies had given him.

"Ho, ho ho." He grinned, pretending the tree wasn't trying to fucking chew through his jacket.

"Oh, wow. Wow. Come in. Come in. Oh, too fucking *cool*, marine!" Rigger was *bouncing*, grey eyes dancing madly.

He grinned. Oh yeah, so fucking worth it. "Yeah? All I got was tinsel to decorate it."

"My folks sent a huge ass care package."

He was drawn into the apartment, the damned dog decorated with a bow. He laughed, Grimmy barking at him.

"You got decorations in the huge ass care package?" He really hadn't wanted to mess with all the froufrou crap the store'd had.

"Yep. A star, some balls, some garland. All sorts of shit."

"Cool." He tossed the case on the couch, his pack on the floor. "Where do you want the tree?"

"Uh. Set it by the balcony right now, 'kay? Did it come with a stand?"

"A what?" He set the tree down, grunting and straightening it as it tried to fall over.

"One of those stand doolies? You know, to hold it up?" Rig got down on hands and knees, right in front of him.

"Mmm... looking good, Rig." Stand doolie? Did he look like Susie homemaker?

"Hold it still; I'll jerry-rig something." It took a few minutes, some ass wriggling, an old metal bowl and an electric drill, but sure as shit, Rigger did something down there to make the tree stand up.

He chuckled, sliding his hand over Rig's ass as Rig stood. "Is there anything you can't jerry-rig together?"

"Nope. It's a gift."

"Speaking of gifts." He turned Rig's face up to his,

mouth landing hard, tongue pushing deep.

Oh, now. That was just fine, Rig slamming up against him, hips to shoulders. His hands landed on that sweet ass, holding on tight, squeezing as his tongue fucked Rig's mouth. Fuck, a whole ten-days of this might just make his cock fall off. Rig leaned in, rubbing, stroking against him. Or maybe not.

"Gonna unwrap you now," he growled, fingers grabbing the bottom of Rig's sweater.

"Mmm... Ho ho ho." Rig lifted his arms, helping out.

He laughed, getting the sweater and then the shirt off Rig. That gave him access to those sweet little titties that he knew would bud right up under his touch.

Rig shivered, stepped closer. "Man, the air's got a bite."

"Air's not the only thing with bite," he noted, fingers reaching out, pinching.

"No?" Rig's lips parted, entire body going stiff with a harsh moan. "Fuck."

"Yeah, it's coming, Rigger. It's coming."

"Good. I'll keep you in Christmas cookies, you keep me warm like that."

"Oh, you've got a deal." He grabbed ahold of Rig's other nipple and gave it the same treatment before pulling him in and devouring his mouth again. Rig tasted fucking sweet, all sugar and cinnamon and coffee. Oh, man. Just like Christmas.

He slid his hands along the lean body, fingers returning again and again to those sensitive little nipples. Rig's hands were just as busy, working his belt open, tugging his jacket off. Oh yeah, losing the pants would work. He popped open Rig's top button, feeling that prick trying to push the zipper right open.

Rig moaned, tongue pushing into his lips, fucking

them slow and steady. There was nothing fucking like it and he stumbled back toward the couch, helping Rig's cock escape his jeans.

"Wasn't even fucking horny 'til you came."

"Yeah, well that's what happens when you open the door to a class A stud." He winked, one hand circling Rig's cock, the other tugging Rig's jeans down.

"Mmhmm." Rig arched up into his touch, sexy little smile on those swollen lips. "Merry Christmas to me."

He chuckled and nodded, puffing up some. Rig did make him feel all stud, there was no doubt about that.

"I know what I'm wanting." He traced Rig's lips. Finest mouth in the US, he had no doubt about that either.

"Mmm..." Rig's lips wrapped around his fingers, sucking and nipping. "Yeah. Yeah, want it."

Fuck, the noises that Rig pulled out of him with that mouth. Fucking purrs and groans just from the way Rig was working his fucking fingers. Rock's hips bucked and pulled Rig back onto the couch before his knees could threaten to buckle.

"Gonna fuck my mouth, Rock?" Fuck, look at those eyes shine.

"You know it." Rock circled Rig's mouth with his fingers again, just rumbling happily. Shit, this was shaping up to be the most amazing holiday ever. Rig just nodded, lips open, tongue flicking at his fingers.

A shudder went through him, his prick so fucking hard it hurt. "Rig..."

"Yeah, Blue Eyes. Take what you need."

He nodded and pushed on Rig's shoulders, moving Rig down between his legs. He opened up his pants, shoved them off his ass so Rig could get to his balls as well as his cock -- he knew what he wanted and that was the full Rigger treatment.

Those fucking grey eyes just gleamed at him, Rig's tongue slipping out to lick and slide over his sac as his pants were eased the rest of the way off. Groaning, he slid his hands through Rig's hair, the curls longer now, fully formed. Rig was in need of a good cut, but damn those curls were soft as they slid through his fingers, grasping at him as if asking for him to tighten his hold and have at Rig's mouth.

Rig spread him a little, tongue slipping behind his balls, hands tugging at his hips. He spread his legs wider and shifted down, giving himself over to Rig, to that talented mouth and amazing tongue. "Fuck. 's good."

"Mmhmm." Rig's tongue slid across his hole, so hot, so wet.

He gasped, legs spreading wider on their own, ass sliding to offer himself to Rig. Damn..

"Oh, yeah. Blue." Those thumbs spread him wider, tongue moving, pressing right against him.

"Fuck. Rig. Fuck." His fingers twisted in those curls, hips bucking a little as Rig's tongue sent electricity right through him. Oh, yeah. Rig was fucking him, that tongue hot and sure, driving him out of his fucking mind. "Rabbit... shit." He whimpered, hips finding Rig's rhythm, his eyes just rolling.

Rig pushed up, mouth dropped over his cock, fingers pushing deep and pegging his gland, just like that. With a roar he tightened his fingers around Rig's head and he rocked between those fingers and that mouth, just fucking flying. Rig didn't pull back, didn't let up, sucked him down all the way.

He just moved between fingers and mouth, riding it until he roared again, come pulsing from his cock. Rig drank him down, fingers stroking deep inside him. He shuddered through his orgasm, groaning and jerking.

Rig settled against his belly, finger sliding free. "So

fine."

He just kind of growled, out of words, out of thoughts, just fucking feeling. As Rig closed his eyes, the brush of the long eyelashes tickled. He chuckled and petted Rig's face. "Damn. If I don't survive this holiday, at least I'll have gone happy."

He got a hum, Rig pushing closer. "I'm a fan of happy, marine."

He nodded and tugged on Rig, encouraging him up. "Speaking of happy..."

He wrapped a hand around Rig's prick. "Someone's still needing."

"Uh-uh." Rig nodded, whimpering softly, pushing right into his touch.

He let his thumb play across the tip, pushed it against the leaking slit. Rig moaned, lips parting, tongue flicking out.

"Sexy fucker," Rock told him, working Rig's prick hard, free hand sliding down Rig's back, cupping his ass.

"You have. You have a point?"

"I had one. You took very good care of it." He winked, teased a finger along Rig's crease.

"I did. Tasted fucking good to me."

Oh, that made him purr, made him feel every inch the stud he was. His cock jerked, started filling again. Rig made sure to let him know it was noticed, too, rubbing and scooting closer. He pushed his finger against Rig's hole, letting Rig know the interest was returned a hundred percent.

"Mmm... yeah." Rig pressed back against his touch, moaned low.

He pushed his finger in, groaning at the tight heat. Fucking perfect. His cock grew harder. Rig was moaning for him, moving slow and steady, riding his touch. That hot, tight, silky skin spasmed around his fingers, slid along his flesh. He groaned and took Rig's mouth again, the kiss hard. Rig squeezed him, eyes wide and watching as the kiss went deeper.

It was so fucking sexy the way Rig just plain fucking enjoyed sex. All of it. He pushed his tongue deep into Rigger's mouth, finger pushing deep as well, hitting Rig's gland. Rig was wild beneath him, rocking and groaning, heart just pounding. He pushed in another finger, thinking Rig was the only guy he knew who loved this as much as the fucking, the preparation, the stretching, the little grunts and groans and kisses shared between them. Rig made everything fucking sexy.

"Just gonna ride you to town, marine. Lord, that's right."

"Merry fucking Christmas to me." Another finger and he spread Rig wide. "So fucking hot and tight."

"Take every single inch of you."

"You ready for it? Ready for every fucking inch?" Rock pulled out his fingers, spread Rig's legs further apart.

"Uh-huh. Every one. Don't tease."

"No plans for teasing, Rigger. I just want to fuck you." He pressed in, all the way in, just sinking into pure pleasure.

"Oh, good. Damn. Blue Eyes." Rig's eyes rolled, lips parted, swollen, hungry.

"You know it. You fucking know it." He started to move, watching Rig's face as he thrust.

Rig looked like he was over the fucking moon, heart pounding, lips open. Rock wrapped his hand around Rig's prick, squeezing the burning hot flesh as he fucked.

"Yeah. Yeah." He got a whimper, Rig bucking into the touch. "Merry fucking Christmas to me."

"That's right. Merry fucking Christmas."

He moved harder, faster, just giving it to Rig, fucking

and stroking and sending them both flying. Heat sprayed over his fingers, the scent hitting him straight on. Fuck, yes! Roaring, he jerked into Rig's body, filling Rig with his spunk.

Rig moaned, slumping. "Good."

"Uh-huh." He pulled out and settled back on the couch, tugging Rig around until he had his very own octopus. "Already beats last year's Christmas."

"And we haven't gotten to presents or cookies yet."

"There's cookies? Hot damn. I am one lucky fucking marine."

"And whatever's in the care package."

He grinned. It was cute that Rig's parents still sent him a care package. His own gift was in his bag. It was even wrapped, thanks to the little blue haired ladies at the mall.

Rig chuckled, snuggling. "There might even be fudge."

"Fudge? I didn't even realize I'd been such a good marine this year." He gave Rig a wink, patted the sweet ass.

"Mmm... you've been a very good marine."

"You haven't been bad yourself, Alex. That mouth alone should get you on Santa's nice list."

"You going to help me decorate the tree?"

He grunted. "Yeah, sure." After all, it *was* Christmas.

They got in well before midnight. The pool hall had been swamped and they'd neither one been able to have more than one or two since they took their own vehicles. Rig wasn't complain-ing. He'd had a dance or four, played some pool, but it was time to take it home for some more direct partying. That spread out on his sofa kind.

He threw it into park and headed up, only about three steps behind Rock. Tight jeans and a simple navy t-shirt. Fuck, but Rock looked fine. "You sure you don't want to be out somewhere at midnight?"

"Yep." Knowing what he wanted had never been one of his hang-ups.

Rock only grunted in reply, but it was a happy sounding grunt and he took the last stairs a little quicker. They'd learned some shit about each other in the last few days. Like how Rock loved the food he made in Momma's honor, and how he could get a little testy if teased about missing poker night at Christmas Eve at home. Of course Rock had managed to distract him right out of being testy, those thick fingers knew just how to make him forget about anything else.

Rock rolled his eyes as they got to his apartment and Grimmy started barking. "Didn't he go out just before we left?"

"Yep." He grinned, grabbed the leash and prepared to get puppy-tackled. "Didn't you have a dog when you were a little boy, man?"

"Nope. My mother said they were too messy. She liked the place clean." Rock chuckled as Grimmy bounded out the door as soon as it was opened. "You want company while he pees?"

"Surely do." They headed back down, laughing as Grimmy bounced in the cold air. "My mom cleans a lot, but when you have boys and horses and Julies and cattle and dogs and and and..." Hell, Daddy's woodshop alone was damn scary, dirt-wise.

Rock shrugged. "It was good training for the marines. I knew how to keep my bunk clean and avoided the fucking toothbrush scrubbing as much as possible." Rock didn't talk much about his family.

Rig chuckled. "We had to make the bed in the

morning and then we each got a list of chores. I did the yard and the dishes and washed the cars. Then I fed the chickens and got eggs and took care of my horse."

"Lots of animals," Rock noted. "It was just me and my sister and boys didn't do dishes. That was girl's work."

"Oh, lord." Rig laughed out loud, tickled. "Man, I can just *see* someone saying that to Momma. She'd have his balls hung out on the clothesline."

Rock's hand went down to his crotch and he winced, then winked. "Thanks for the warning."

"Anytime, Blue. I got plans for those that don't involve clothespins."

Rock snorted. "I would sure as hell hope not."

Rock glanced at his watch. "Are we supposed to have bubbly stuff or something tonight?"

"It's in the fridge. Just a half bottle." Rock had mentioned about forty times he didn't like it. Never let it be said Rig couldn't take a hint.

Rock nodded. "So we'll toast the New Year. I'm not singing that stupid song though."

"Okay." He could handle that. He didn't think it was really English anyway. "How do you feel about midnight kissing?"

"Oh, now you know how I feel about kissing. The time doesn't matter." Rock's eyes just shone at him.

He shivered and it wasn't all about the cold in the air. "He's done his business, marine. Upstairs."

"Hallefuckinglujah." Rock didn't need to be told twice, turning an abrupt about face and heading for the apartment building. It was dark and quiet and Rig dared a quick feel of that ass before running Grimmy up the stairs.

"Oh-ho, someone's feeling his oats." Rock was right behind him though, now wasn't he, crowding him as he opened the door.

"Didn't feel like oats to me..." They stumbled in, Grimmy just letting him pull the leash out before going to get a drink and a bone.

"I hope not. Of course you should probably double check."

Oh ho! Ladies and gentlemen, we have ourselves a randy marine. He stepped close, hands sliding around to get himself a double handful of heaven.

"Well?" asked Rock, hands imitating his, finding his ass and squeezing.

"Fucking *fine*, Blue Eyes." He smiled up, starting to warm up.

"You know it," murmured Rock, mouth coming down over his, the kiss hot and hard, Rock's tongue pushing between his lips.

He couldn't have helped the little cry if he'd wanted to, and he didn't, diving right in and giving it up. Rock's chest rumbled with a pleased sound, just vibrating against him as the kiss got deeper, Rock taking everything he gave.

"We'll... we'll miss midnight." He bucked and rubbed their cocks together, eyes rolling a little.

Rock snorted. "We can stop if that's what you want."

"Stop?" Oh, Rock was fucking kidding.

The corner of Rock's lips twitched. "I wouldn't want to stand in the way of another important redneck tradition..."

"Oh... You bastard. For that? No black-eyed peas for you..." He tackled Rock, managing to bring them both down to the floor with a thud.

Rock's breath whooshed from him and he gave a coughing laugh. "I'm not sure that doesn't make me lucky."

Rig took advantage of the situation, fingers digging in, finding Rock's ticklish spots.

Rock bucked and wriggled beneath him. "Bitch!"

"Not even a little." He tickled hard, just cackling.

"Well thank fuck for that." Rock rolled them suddenly, pinning him beneath the large body. His breath huffed out of him, body arching instinctively.

"Slut," Rock accused, though his eyes were shining again, body pushing him back down into the floor.

"Yeah. Yeah, yours."

Rock growled and brought their mouths together, fingers sliding along his ribs, but the tickling never materialized, instead those fingers stroked, touched. Oh. Oh, hell yes. Yes. He hummed, just melting, balls to bones.

Rock's tongue invaded, fingers pulling apart the buttons on his shirt, fingers hot against his skin. He sucked, moaning low, stretching out beneath Rock, just feeling it. Rock groaned low, hand tugging at his belt-buckle, undoing it, working on the button, his zipper. He sucked his belly in, helping out those thick fingers.

"Yeah, just like that." Rock tugged his jeans down, the back of one hand sliding along his cock.

The touch rocked through him, made his stomach tight. "Mmm... Blue."

"Right fucking here," murmured Rock, mouth sliding over his jaw and down his neck, finding that spot that made him just wild. His eyes flashed open, balls drawing tight as stones. The sucking and licking continued, Rock's fingers finding his nipple and flicking across it.

"Fuck. Oh. Do it again." He wasn't about to beg, but ask nicely? That he could do. Practically purring, Rock did, fingers playing over his nipple, tongue sliding on his skin. His toes curled, breath gasping from him. "Yeah..."

Rock did it again, then those thick fingers slid down over his belly, headed toward his cock. His hips rolled, pushed up toward the touch. Yeah. Yeah, just like that. Rock's fingers wrapped around his prick, fingers sliding across the tip, spreading the liquid dripping slowly from him. Rock's teeth dragged along his neck.

"Oh, sweet fuck. Fuck. Blue. Yes. Sweet fuck, yes."

"Just like that?" Rock asked, squeezing his cock. Those teeth kept sliding along his skin.

"Just like that. More. Just like that."

"It's gonna mark you," Rock warned, fingers tightening again.

"Got more than a week before I go back." He twisted, chin lifting, balls drawing tight.

A low purr was his answer, Rock's teeth hard on his neck, lips wrapping around his skin, sucking. The sound he made was part whimper, part moan, hips pushing up, cock fucking Rock's hand.

"Want you," growled Rock, the words vibrating over his skin.

"Yours. Yours. Now. Fuck." He nodded, toes curling. "Now."

Rock's hand left his, his Blue's jeans coming off like that. "Lube?" One thick finger slid along his crease.

"In the coffee table..." He spread farther, pushing toward the touch.

Rock grunted, finger and heat disappearing as he went for the tube in the coffee table. That finger returned as Rock kissed him, pushing into him, opening him up. He grabbed his knees and spread, riding and grunting, taking all Rock gave.

"Fucking sexy," muttered Rock, pushing another finger into him. "Love the way you just take it. Want it."

"Made for this. Made to fuck."

"Yeah. Yeah, you fucking are." Rock nodded, pushing yet another finger into him, finger-fucking him hard.

"Oh. Oh, fuck. Yes." He bucked, driving himself deeper.

The sucking kiss on his neck faded, Rock watching his body move, eyes like a brand on his skin, so fucking hot. His cock was dripping, entire focus on his body, his ass.

Growling, Rock pulled his fingers away, settling between his legs. "Fucking want you."

He just nodded, panting. Yes. Fuck, yes. Rock pushed two thumbs into him for a moment and then they were gone too and it was that thick cock, hot and hard and spreading him open.

He damn near screamed, need pouring through him in a huge wave. He reached down, grabbed the base of his cock and squeezed. "Fuck!"

"Yep. A nice long, hard one." True to his word, Rock started to move, thrusting with brute fucking force.

Oh, hell. Yes. Everything spun, his heart pounded. His balls just ached. One of Rock's hands was by his head, thumb stroking his neck now and then. The other was near his waist, arm like a band of heat along his skin. Those eyes. Fuck, those blue eyes just bore into his own, Rock right *there* with him.

"Close. Oh, shit, Blue. So fucking close."

Rock grinned down at him. "The longer you last, the better it gets."

He nodded, panting, holding onto his cock with a death grip. "Okay. Okay. Hold on."

"You hold on, I'm busy." Rock gave him a wink and shifted, hitting his gland.

"Oh!" His eyes rolled, head slamming against the floor. "Fuck."

"Fuck yeah, right there." Rock bent to kiss him, pounding the spot over and over again.

He started coming and coming and just didn't fucking stop. Rock didn't stop either, just kept plunging into him, and then his mouth was filled with a roar, Rock's spunk hot as it shot into him. Rig panted, blinking up at Rock, dazed all through. Rock finally stilled, lying against him, most of that weight on Rock's arms. "Will that ring in the new year right for you, Rigger?"

"Uh-huh."

Rock grunted. "Good."

Then Rock rolled, sliding out and landing next to him. One strong arm curled around him, pulling him over against Rock's hard body. He just snuggled in, couldn't do anything else. Rock's fingers slid on his skin, warm and sure, like the man himself. "This was a good holiday."

"It was." Rig grinned, moaned just a little. "Next year, we'll have to go see the farm."

"If it's that or go back to the mess at the base, you've got a deal."

"Cool. You'd like Daddy. He's a big believer in beer and football and fudge."

"Sounds like a good man who knows what's important in life." Rock gave him a smile, sitting up with a grunt. "Speaking of which, I know there's a cold beer in the fridge. And I can hear that fudge calling my name."

He nodded and stayed right where he was, comfortable enough for the moment. Happy New Year to him.

CHAPTER TWELVE

Snow. Rig stood at the window and blinked. There was white shit falling from the fucking sky. Fucking unreal. Grimmy was curled up in the middle of the bed, snoring to beat the band and Rig nodded. Yep. Good plan. He was not going out today. Not going to buy donuts at noon and wake up the bear in that cave. Nope.

Staying home.

In bed.

Under the covers.

Until this shit stopped.

He pulled on a pair of sweatpants and curled around Grimmy, falling back to sleep in no time.

It was banging that woke him. Took him a moment to realize it was someone at the door.

"Coming." Rig cleared his throat as Grimmy bounded off the bed, barking his damned fool head off.

"Coming!"

He opened the door, only half-dressed, hand rubbing the back of his neck.

Rock pushed in past him, closing the door, a large frown creasing Rock's forehead. "What's wrong?"

"Wrong? 'sides the fact that it's fucking *cold* out there and *snowing*? Nothing." He pushed Rock's jacket off, muttering about the cold and the weather and the grey and the goddamned audacity of *winter*.

Rock blinked. "You didn't come over, didn't answer your phone and took five fucking minutes to get your door because of a little snow? It's not even sticking on the ground, Rigger."

"I didn't leave the house because of the snow, Yankee. I didn't hear the fucking phone because Grimmy snores like a damned freight train and it took me a bit to answer the door 'cause I was sleeping, which is the only thing to do in this frigging weather." He shivered and went to grab a sweater or two, turning the heat up as he passed by. "You want some coffee, Rock?"

Rock followed him, laughing. "You know, cowboy, you seem to have missed the best thing to do in this weather."

"Hmm? What's that, Blue Eyes? Fly down to Mexico?" He bent down, digging through his dresser for something warm.

Rock's hand slid between his legs, grabbing him through his sweats. "Not quite."

"Oh." Rig blinked and grinned wide as he stood. Oh, yeah. He could handle a bit of skin-on-skin. "Bet the sheets are still warm."

"Yeah? Bet we could warm 'em up if they aren't."

"You think?" Rig pushed into Rock's arms, taking the long, slow, hey-Blue-happy-weekend-how's-it-going-stud-I've-missed-you kiss that he needed. Rock's answer was just as non-verbal, kiss getting deeper, hands moving over him, solid and warm. Rig just hummed into the kisses, leading Rock to the bed, slow and sure. He unbuttoned Rock's flannel shirt as they moved, fingers searching out skin. Rock gave him one of those rumbling noises and slid those big hands into his sweatpants to cup his ass.

Oh, yeah. That felt fucking sweet. He pushed back into the touch, hips rocking and eager.

"Always so fucking willing," murmured Rock. "I do like that in a man."

"Just know who I need." He pushed Rock's shirt off and went to work on the jeans, needing to bare that fat cock to his touch, his lips.

"Oh yeah." Rock's hands tightened and his lips were taken again, the kiss deep and hard and *Rock*.

By the time they were naked, his head was swimming and Rock was growling steadily into his lips. They settled into the sheets, Rig teasing one tiny nipple, hand rolling Rock's nuts. Rock pulled off his t-shirt and helped him get his sweatpants off and then he was pressed against acres of warm skin, hard muscles.

"So fucking good, Blue Eyes." He arched into the heat, tilting his head to get another kiss, one hand wrapped around Rock's hip, sliding their cocks together.

"Really fucking good" Rock agreed. Rock turned them, pushed him down into the mattress, moving against him. He groaned, hands sliding over Rock's spine, finding the little sweet spots, making the growls darker, louder.

"Want you," growled Rock, pushing against him harder.

"You got me, Blue." He raised his knees, offering.

"Good." Rock leaned up and found the tube that was kept under the pillows, making a show of popping it open and slicking up those fingers. Rig grinned and started nuzzling and licking at Rock's ears, Rock's jaw, kissing and tasting and encouraging his Blue with all he was.

"Slut," murmured Rock, voice just as fond as could be, and one finger slid into him, just like that.

"Yours." Rig moaned and started riding, body clenching around that one finger. "More, Blue. Need you."

Rock just gazed down at him, blue eyes hotter than July, warming him straight through as a second finger pushed in with the first.

"Yes..." That sent a nice long ripple soaring up through him, body shivering and lips parting as he wanted.

"Fucking hot, Rig." Another finger slid into him, Rock stretching him wide.

"Oh. Oh fuck, yeah. Blue..." His motions slowed, eyes closed as he rode those thick fingers, moans pushed right out of him.

Rock's mouth covered his, tongue pushing deep, just like those fingers. He fucking dissolved -- hot and horny and happy and oh, yeah. Life was fucking *sweet*. Rig fastened his lips around Rock's tongue, sucking slow and steady. Rock growled and those thick fingers slid away, only to be replaced by the solid heat of Rock's prick. Rock didn't tease or play or make him wait, just pushed right on in, spreading him wide.

He took everything Rock offered, whispering his need into those hot lips, letting his Blue know how good it all felt. Rock took him with long, slow strokes, mouth hard on his, eyes just blazing at him. He traced the corner of those eyes, lost in them, fucking perfect. Rock's movements got harder, faster, one hand moving between them to grab his cock. Rig nodded, shoulders rolling up as he met each thrust, slamming between hand and cock. Rock just kept moving, sending him flying higher and higher, wrapping them together in sweet fucking pleasure.

When he came, Rig cried out, heat flooding from the top of his head, shooting from his cock. Rock made a soft noise, licking at his lips for a moment, letting him shudder through his orgasm before thrusting again. It wasn't long before those thrusts became jerks, Rock roaring as he came.

"Mmm... so fucking good." Rig held on, licking the salt from Rock's shoulders and throat. "So warm."

Rock chuckled, the sound husky, sated. "So you're not still cold?"

"Nope. 'm good. You're gonna have to stay, though. Just in case it gets worse." He took another kiss. "I'll make chili and cornbread."

"That sounds like a fair deal."

Rock groaned as he pulled out. "I could use a nap anyway." There was a hopeful glint in those blue eyes.

Rig chuckled. The man loved his morning blowjobs, even when they came during the afternoon naps. "Mmm... naps are good."

Then he leaned over and licked Rock's lips. "Waking up from naps is even better." Rock's grin was answer enough.

His Blue settled and one arm went around him, pulling him up against the hard body. Rigger snuggled in, pulling the blankets up around them, head settling on Rock's shoulder. When Rock fell asleep he'd get up and start puttering. He looked out the window, at the frost on the glass, the snow blowing.

Better yet, maybe he'd just snuggle a little longer.

Rock juggled the deli take out bag, making sure he didn't end up wearing the soup, the new comforter from JC Penney and the bag from Rite-Aid full of over the counter cold remedies and banged on the door to Rig's apartment.

"It's only a cold," Rig had told him. That had been two days ago and he hadn't seen or heard from Rig and damn it he was worried. He banged the door again. Harder. He'd break it down if he had to.

He heard a harsh cough and a croaked, "Comin', damnit. Hold up!" Then the door opened up, Rig blinked over at him. "Rock? Hey."

He grunted. "You look like shit."

"Thank you?" Rig chuckled, the sound ending in a cough. "Come on in. You want some coffee?"

"No. I'll get myself a beer in a minute. Go sit." He dumped the bags on the coffee table. "I brought crap. To make you feel better."

"Oh." Rig sat, sorting through the stuff, sniffling. "Wow. You did good, Rock. Thank you." Rig pulled the comforter out and wrapped up in it... "Oh... Soft."

Rock puffed up. "Chicken soup. From that place over on Ratcliffe. Supposedly homemade."

"Oh, you're fucking good to me." Those grey eyes fastened onto him, just shining. "Thank you. Come sit for a spell?"

"Let me get my beer." He did, bringing one out for Rig, too. Just in case. Besides, he could always have it if Rig didn't want it. He sat next to Rig. "You going to be okay?"

"Oh, I reckon. Just wore out." Rig took a couple of pills and leaned against his side, handing him the remote.

He grunted and put his arm around Rig, idly flipping the channels. That was all the invitation Rigger needed, snuggling right into him with a soft sigh, hand stroking against his belly. He spread his legs, hips sliding slightly, pushing up toward Rig's hand.

"Mmm..." Rig hummed, hand sliding down farther. "So hot."

"You're sick..." he murmured, pushing into Rig's hand.

"Uh-huh. Hate being stuffy -- no blow jobs." Rig nuzzled. "Fucking need your cock."

"Yeah. Need your mouth. Soon enough, yeah?" He petted Rig's head.

"Yeah." Rig's hand wrapped around his cock, stroking slow and steady. He groaned. He probably shouldn't let Rig do this. The man needed his sleep. Still, he just went with it, wishing like hell it was Rig's mouth. He missed that fine mouth. Rig leaned, pushing his sweats down and freeing his cock. "Just a lick."

He groaned. "You're sick..." But fuck, he wasn't going to say no.

"You'll make me feel better..." Rig's tongue dragged over the tip of his cock.

He wasn't going to argue that. Instead, he just spread his legs wider and slid his hand through Rig's curls. Man needed a haircut in the worst way. Rig didn't suck him, but instead licked him, root to tip, over and over, hands working his shaft.

Oh, Rig was going to fucking kill him dead. Yeah. What a way to go. Rig's cheek was hot against his belly, but the soft sounds were happy, peaceful, pure sex. One hand in Rig's hair, the other on his redneck's back, just touching, keeping them together. Then he slid a hand down to cup Rig's balls, rolling them, squeezing just enough to make him arch and moan.

"Fuck, Rig..." There was nothing like that mouth, those hands. Fuck it was good.

A low hum answered him, Rig's tongue slowly fucking the slit of his prick.

"Jesus fuck, Rig!" Hands clenching, Rock came

hard. Rig took it, moaning around his cock like he was the one giving Rig the blowjob. Fucking slut. He petted Rig's head. "Fucking awesome, Rabbit."

"Mmm..." Rig settled, curling up against him with a happy sigh. "Needed that."

He purred. "Yeah. Me, too."

He put his arm around Rig, tugging his Rabbit in close again. Rig relaxed against him and closed those grey eyes, snuggling and cuddling and asleep almost immediately, wrapped in the comforter.

He flipped channels until he found football and then settled. All almost right with the world.

CHAPTER THIRTEEN

Rock shook his head and handed Williams two twenties. Poor bastard hadn't brought enough to buy his wife roses. Fucking florists jacked the prices up every Valentine's Day, like clockwork. Made him fucking glad he wasn't involved with women. Men didn't expect roses or fucking chocolates just because someone had declared the day romance day.

Snorting, Rock climbed into his truck, waved to Williams and the boys and headed off to Rig's place. He knew exactly what Rig was expecting and he had that bad boy as standard equipment, right in his lap. The thought made him chuckle and he was whistling as he pulled into a parking spot in front of Rig's apartment building.

He threw his bag over his shoulder and headed up, rapping on the door in short order.

"Come on in. I'm up to my elbows in gun oil." Oh

yeah, that was his Rig. No flowers, no candy, just fucking gun oil.

Chuckling, Rock let himself in, giving Grimmy a pat on the head before pushing him off. "Hey, Rig, how's it hanging?"

"Can't complain, Blue Eyes. Can't complain one bit." He got a grin, Rig cleaning and oiling a pistol. The man knew how to take care of a weapon. It was enough to make a marine proud.

"Nice piece. You keeping up with target practice?" He put his bag by the door and hung up his jacket, toed off his boots.

"Had to qualify today on the range. There's some rumbling about my teams taking some day trips into unfriendly areas."

Rock frowned, the thought of Rig being out there unsettling. He shook it off. "Well if you can shoot the way you can take care of your weapon I imagine you qualified with flying colors."

"Sharpshooter. I'm point man for our team until Rodriquez gets back."

Rock grunted. "You be careful out there."

"Always." Rig got everything cleaned up and packed away, unfolding up from the ground. "Turn the hot water on for me, marine."

"Now how did you know I was hoping to start the evening getting naked with you?" Grinning, he headed for the bathroom, leaning over the tub to get the shower started. He knew fucking well Rig had meant the sink tap so he could clean up, but Rock wasn't a marine for nothing and he knew how to seize an opportunity.

Still, his own personal redneck was right there, pressed snug against him as he bent over. "So fucking fine, Blue."

He pushed his ass back against Rig. "You know it."

Shower on, he straightened and turned, hands moving to cup Rig's ass and tug him in snug again.

"Mmm... hey." Rig gave him a grin, leaned in to trace his lips with that hot little tongue. He chased it down with his own, and then captured it with his lips, sucking. Fucking hot.

Rig kept those oily hands held away, which gave him perfect opportunity to touch and feel. He pushed Rig's t-shirt up, hands sliding on the hot skin, fingers searching out the places that made Rig's breath catch and that cock jerk inside those fucking tight jeans Rig wore.

"Oh. Oh, damn. Let me... I need to wash my... Oh..."

"That's right, we're supposed to be getting naked." He pulled the t-shirt right off and then started in on the jeans, watching as Rig's prick leapt out eagerly. Rig smelled good, rich and male and right. The hint of gun oil just made the man that much sexier. He pushed Rig's jeans down past the knee, trusting Rig would get them the rest of the way off as he let his hands wander. He stroked Rig's belly, fingers of one hand stroking up toward the nipples, the other moving down to the long cock.

"Fuck, your hands are something." Rig's head fell back, entire body undulating.

"They work." He winked and leaned in, lips sliding along Rig's neck, stopping to suck on Rig's Adam's apple.

"Sweet fuck, yes. They work." The words vibrated against his lips and Rock groaned, pinching one of Rig's nipples.

"Rock!" Rig jerked, "No fair. I can't touch you."

"No? A little gun oil never hurt a marine, Rigger."

"Oh, fucking A." Rig's hands slid over his arms, just a little slick.

Purring, he tugged his own t-shirt off and undid his

BDUs, pushing them down off his ass. "Yeah, fucking A."

"Oh... miles and miles of skin and it's all for me..." Rig stepped back toward the shower.

He kicked his pants the rest of the way off and pulled off his socks and then followed, purring again as the water started to splash over Rig's skin. Rig stretched, moving under the water, giving him an unconscious show. His cock was standing at full attention, saluting the sight in front of him.

He followed Rig right into the water, taking Rig's mouth. Rig pushed into the kiss, rubbing against him. He reached for Rig's ass, pulling Rig even closer, their cocks slipping and sliding together.

"Mmm." Slippery, horny redneck. Just what a man needed.

He knew this was all the candy and flowers Rig needed. Just show up ready to fuck, ready to spend the night fucking pounding into Rig's sweet ass or letting Rig suck him off and they were good to go.

He groaned, fucking Rig's mouth with his tongue. Rig grabbed the soap, started sudsing him up, making him twist and beg for it.

"Tease," he accused, pushing his cock along Rig's slick belly.

"Nope. I put out." Rig's hands wrapped around his prick, stroking.

He groaned, head dropping back as he pushed into Rig's touches. "You do. And how."

"Over and over and over. Beautiful motherfucker."

He flexed, the action automatic, letting Rig see him. Rig made him feel every inch the stud he was. Rig's moan felt good too, balls to bones. He ran his hands over Rig's lean body, thumbs finding those sweet little titties, playing them lazily.

"You called me a tease." Rig arched a little.

"Hey, I put out, too." He pinched harder.

"Oh, fuck yes. You put out like none other, Blue Eyes."

"You know it." He growled a little, pushing Rig up against the tiles and taking that fucking sweet mouth.

Rig gave him a cry, fingers pulling him closer. He ground against Rig, pushing Rig hard against the tiles. He could do closer; one leg propped up against the side of the tub, thighs spreading. Such a fucking sexy slut. Rock shifted, rubbing his cock along Rig's balls and behind them, the heat there incredible. Rig arched, belly rubbing against his, cock hard and hot, throbbing. He loved the way Rig wanted him, just giving it all up. His hands held Rig's hips and he slid one down to Rig's ass.

"Oh, hell yes. Yeah, Blue." Those lean hips started rocking, pushing against him.

"You want it? Want a piece of the Rocketman?" It wasn't even a question.

"No." Those eyes were shining. "All. I need it all."

He growled, pushing Rig hard against the tile. "You've got it." He slid his finger into Rig's ass. He just slipped right into that heat, Rig's muscles rippling around him. Rig was as tight today as he'd been a year ago. Just as eager, too and Rock pushed a second finger in, stretching that fine, fine ass.

"Yeah. Yeah. Just like that. Fucking fine, Blue Eyes."

"No, Rigger, just like *this*." He curled his fingers, pegging Rig's gland.

"Rock!" Oh, hell yes. Look at that. Flushed cheeks, tight muscles, cries just echoing. Grinning fiercely, he hit that spot again, nailing it over and over. Rig twisted, cock throbbing between them.

"Yeah, that's what I'm talking about." He grunted

and pegged it harder.

Shudders rocked Rigger, forehead falling against his shoulder. "Oh..."

So fucking sexy. "Now, Rig. Time for the real thing."

"Fuck yes. Please." Teeth scraped his shoulder. "Please."

He growled, pulled out his fingers and turned Rig around to face the tile. Best fucking ass ever, staring him right in the face. Rig spread wide, offered it up. Right there, no question, no hesitation. He took one ass cheek in each hand and exposed that little hole he'd been stretching. With a groan, he pushed into the best heat ever. Rig's cry echoed, hands sliding up along the tile.

"Uh-huh." Head on Rig's shoulder, he pushed until he was all the way in. All the fucking way.

They moved together, sliding and shifting, moans bouncing off the tile. Rig's heat was fucking perfection. He slid one hand around, grabbing hold of Rig's prick, sliding and tugging.

"Oh, yeah. Fuck, you're..." Rig chuckled, squeezed. Yeah. Yeah, he was.

He groaned at the squeeze and moved harder, faster, getting them where they needed to go and loving every fucking second of the journey. Rig was right there with him, all the way. He leaned in, nuzzling against Rig's neck, breathing in the wet, male smell. "Fucking close."

"Yeah. Yeah. Fill me up."

"You first," he growled, squeezing Rig's prick, pushing in hard. Rig jerked, sobbing low, cock throbbing in his hand, ass just milking him.

"Yes." He roared, letting all the pleasure out as he filled Rig deep.

They ended together, slumped against the tile, panting. He licked the water off Rig's shoulder and neck, groaning. It felt good, resting against Rig's heat, the water pounding down on his back.

"Mmm... Yeah. Happy anniversary to you, too, Blue Eyes. Damn."

He chuckled. "I knew you didn't want fucking roses."

"Shit no. I wanted fucking."

"That's my Rabbit." He squeezed Rig and then straightened, turned off the water.

"You off all weekend, Blue?" Warm, sure hands stripped the water off him.

"I sure am. All yours."

"Mmm... perfect."

He puffed up. "You know it." Grinning, he tugged Rig in, bringing their mouths close. "You're not so bad yourself."

"You know it, marine."

"I do." He squeezed Rig's ass in his hands. His stomach growled and he chuckled. "Am I ordering pizza?"

"Mmhmm. Got a brisket for tomorrow."

"Oh yeah? Chocolate pie for dessert?"

"Only if there are pancakes on Sunday."

He chuckled. There wasn't much that he cooked, but he made a mean pancake. "You got it."

Rig grinned, nodded. "I want green peppers and pepperoni on mine."

"I'm getting the big meat one." He gave Rig a wink.

Rigger's laugh just rang out. "Oh, you are the big meat one. Funny man."

He chuckled and grinned and gave Rig another long kiss. Damn, the man made him feel good. Had right from the very start. He grunted. "There's something in my bag for you. Saw it and figured your wall could use some decorating."

It wasn't a big deal.

Not at all.

"Yeah? You got something on the kitchen table." Rig grinned, leaned in and took another of those kisses. "Not a bad first year, Blue Eyes. Not bad at all."

He nodded. Nope, as years went, it had been a pretty fucking good one. "It's not a Valentine's gift or anything," he clarified. "It just happens I saw it the other night and had the cash on me for it."

"Cool. Yours is just something I found at the Wal-Mart."

Rock went to his pack and pulled out the painting he'd found. Velvet dogs playing pool. It wasn't wrapped, but it was still in the plastic bag so good enough.

Rig laughed hard, eyes just dancing. "Oh. Oh, fuck! That's fucking *perfect*!"

A Wal-Mart sack was handed over to him as Rig went to hang the painting up. Oh. Rambo on tape.

"Cool, now we have something to do in between fucking and blowing." He wrapped an arm around Rig and tugged him in for another kiss.

"Yep. We're set for bear."

"You want bear?" He growled, mouth open, showing his teeth, and then winked.

Rigger just laughed. "Blue. Bear. Marine. You. Call for pizza."

He nodded and grunted. "Yes. Me Rock. Me call for pizza." Chuckling, he headed for the phone, eyes watching Rigger.

"Good marine. Beer?"

He grunted again. "Me want beer."

Rock ordered the pizzas and found his jeans, took out the wallet and put both near the door for easy access. Then he went into the kitchen, hunting that ass. He found it too, upended by the fridge, digging for something. Oh, wasn't he just the luckiest marine going? He went right up to Rig and rubbed his growing cock against that hot, sweet flesh.

Rig jumped a little, wiggled. "I was looking to see if there was any cheesecake left."

"Oh, I'd say there was plenty of cheesecake here." He grinned, squeezed Rig's hips, tugging him back.

Rig stood up, beer in hand. "That's *beefcake*, now."

"I'm glad you know it when you see it." He grabbed hold of the beer, and slid it along Rig's belly.

"Ooo!" Rig went tight, muscles rippling and sexy as fuck.

He moaned, backing Rig up and closing the fridge door. "You're something else," he murmured, sliding the beer over Rig's belly again, just to feel Rig move. Oh, those little nipples drew up, tight as pebbles, Rig shuddering and shivering. "You like that?" He moved the cold to those little nipples.

"Cold! Cold. Fuck." Rig gasped, eyes closing a little.

"Yeah, look at your cock rise up for it though." He chuckled and put the beer on the counter, sliding his cold hand around that pretty cock. That earned him a sharp cry, Rig just bucking.

"Fucking sex on a stick, Rigger." He bit at Rig's earlobe and found one of those tight little nipples with his free hand, tugging and squeezing it.

"I. Damn. Damn, Jim..." Oh, somebody was right there, loving it. Needing it.

It made him rumble with pleasure, hand squeezing and tugging the long prick, fingers playing one nipple and then the other as he nibbled that sweet spot on Rig's neck.

"Nobody gets to me like you do... Fuck..." Rig's hands were on his shoulders, holding on.

"That's because there isn't anyone like me." He slid his mouth up along Rig's neck, over the solid jaw, heading right for that mouth.

"Not a fucking soul."

"You got that right." He pushed his tongue into Rig's mouth, kissing him hard. There was nothing, nothing like that mouth, giving it up. He growled, pushing Rig up against the counter. Rig arched, hips rocking, rubbing against him, cock hard and dripping for him again. Such a huge fucking slut.

And all his.

He deepened the kiss, hands grabbing that ass now and grinding them together. Rig cried out, tongue fucking his lips. His own prick was hard, fucking needy again. He was always fucking hard for Rig.

Rig shifted until their cocks were side-by-side, in his hand. "Yes."

He growled the word back. "Yes."

Hand wrapping around both pricks, he started moving it, looking into those grey eyes. He felt like a god, caught in that look, in the center of that focus. As the pleasure built, starting in his balls and crawling up his back, he fucking knew he was a god -- Rig and pleasure making that real.

"Yeah. Yeah. Rock. Blue Eyes..."

"Right here. Right fucking here."

"Uh-huh..." Heat sprayed over his fingers, the scent of sex and Rig strong.

Groaning, he bucked, that smell sending him over, his come joining Rig's on their bellies.

"Wow." Rig panted, eyes rolling.

"Yeah. Happy fucking wow." He grinned, took a long slow kiss and then grabbed his beer and sauntered back out to the front room.

CHAPTER FOURTEEN

He found a house.

It wasn't big – twelve hundred seventy two square feet. Three bedrooms. One bath. Nice backyard. Garage. Off-white trim and grey brick exterior. It was on a corner lot, about twenty minutes from base. The fence was in good shape, the plumbing, too. His lease was up next month and Rock's was up the month after.

He had a nice kitchen table and a comfortable easy chair and a hell of a stereo. Rock had a sofa and a big bed and a good-sized TV. His futon could go in the spare room; Rock's gear could be stowed in the garage.

They'd save a fortune on rent and gas. Daddy said he'd spring for a good used washer and dryer for a housewarming gift.

Rig nodded, picked up his list of pros and cons, looking at it, going over it again.

He found a house.

Now he'd just have to catch him a roommate.

Rig had looked at ten dozen and thirty two houses, had talked to mortgage lenders, had gotten loan approval on the little 3-1-1 with a fenced back yard for Grimmy and a nice big tree in the front yard he'd found. The plumbing was pretty good, and the central heat and air was new and there was a shed in the back yard. It wasn't perfect, but it was his, or would be in short order.

First things first, though, now that he had all those ducks in a row. He needed to find a certain marine who just got home from maneuvers and see what he thought about being roommates and helping make a house payment.

Rig smoothed his palms on his jeans and knocked, almost shaking from nerves. He'd never asked anyone to move in with him before.

The door opened, Rock standing there wearing nothing more than a pair of shorts. "Well aren't you a sight for sore eyes?"

Rock moved back, giving him room to come in.

"Hey there, marine." Rig scooted in, eyes fastened on that beautiful body, those amazing fucking eyes. "How's it hanging?"

"Fucking needy." Rock closed the door firmly and gathered him in for a long, hard kiss. Rig stretched out along that hard heat, lips opening eagerly. Fuck, yeah. Hi, Blue Eyes. Good to see you. Looking fine. Smell fucking hot. So fucking fine.

Rock's hands closed over his ass, pulling him up against that fucking fat prick, hot even through shorts and denim. Rig whimpered, one leg lifting to wrap around Rock's waist, rubbing their groins together. Rock grunted and pushed him up against the wall, humping hard against him. He wrapped his arms around Rock's neck, crying out as his other leg lifted, ass settling in Rock's hands.

Rock just went to town, humping, moving against him with intent, not seeming to care they weren't naked. Old Blue Eyes was going to make him cream his jeans at this rate. Fucking hungry marine. Rig dove into the kiss, crying out with pure hunger and happiness, flying on the want and the need.

Rock's lips wrapped around his tongue, sucking as Rock's fingers spread on his ass. Oh, sweet! He gave a sharp cry, hips bucking as he came hard enough to make his balls hurt. Rock growled and thrust against him a couple more times before going stiff.

"Mmm... missed you, too." Rig grinned, took another kiss. "Let's say hi again."

"I don't recall either of us actually saying hi in the first place." Rock gave him a wink and let him down, leading the way into the apartment. "You want a beer?"

"I'm cool." He grinned and stripped off his t-shirt, sweat making them both shine. "Sticky, but cool."

Rock tossed him a box of tissues and headed to the kitchen. Rig rolled his eyes and went to the bathroom and wiped up... off... whatever... before heading back to the front room. By then Rock was out from the kitchen with his beer, wearing nothing but his boxers and a grin.

"Looking damned fine, Blue Eyes." He stretched out, eyes trailing over that tanned skin.

"Nothing like maneuvers and c-rations to put a man in top shape." Rock sat down in his chair, grinning at him.

He grinned back. "I've been busting my hump this week, too." Not subtle, but hell, this was Rock.

"I'd like to bust it for you." Rock gave him a wink and took a swig. "What's up?"

"I've been looking at houses and I think I've found

one." He met Rock's eyes. "Thought maybe I could get you to come take a look, see what you think, see if you like it."

"I could have a look, make sure you aren't getting ripped off."

"I..." He swallowed. "I was hoping you could have a look and see if you might be interested in moving in, in splitting bills."

One of Rock's eyebrows went up, but he didn't say no outright or laugh. "Been awhile since I've had a roomie. I suppose if I moved in with anyone it would be you."

Rig nodded. "There're three bedrooms, a good sized bathroom. Yard for the dog. Big-assed garage and the mortgage is less than either of us are paying right now." His belly was twitching.

"Sounds like a good deal if the place is right." Rock reached out with a foot and nudged him. "Mr. Responsible."

"That's right. Well... that and if Grimmy gets any bigger? He's going to eat a hole into apartment two-twenty-four."

Rock chuckled. "Can't have that."

"That's what I reckoned." Rig tilted his head. "There's something to be said for regular morning blowjobs."

Rock chuckled, hand sliding down into his shorts, adjusting that fine prick that had perked at the mention of blowjobs. "You stacking the deck?"

"Yep." He nodded, licking his lips. "I reckon only a fool doesn't play to win."

Rock laughed. "You drive a hard bargain. I'll take a look at this house of yours, Rig."

"Yeah? Cool." He wasn't beaming. He *wasn't*! He was just... really, really happy.

Rock laughed again and winked, stroking his cock. "How cool?"

He leaned forward, ending on his knees with his cheek nuzzling that prick. "Pretty fucking cool."

Rock rumbled, hand sliding through his hair.

"Smell good." He nuzzled, breathing against those heavy balls.

Rock pushed down his shorts and rubbed that sweet prick over Rig's face. Rig lips parted, tongue licking the hint of come off the hot flesh. Rock's legs spread wider. Rig slid his hands under Rock's ass, thumb rubbing the soft inner thighs.

"Fucking sexy cowboy."

"Sexy fucking marine." Rock chuckled, stroking his face. Rig closed his eyes, focusing on that hot, stiff prick, nuzzling and licking, taking the flavor in.

"This gonna be my wake up call every morning, Rig?"

"Every fucking morning you're hard and wanting it, Blue Eyes."

"I could live with that."

"Yeah? Good." He took the head in his mouth, sucking strong and steady.

Rock groaned. "Fuck, for that mouth, Rig, I'll pay the fucking mortgage myself."

He chuckled, tongue fucking the slit, the knot in his belly gone.

"Oh fuck, yes." Rock's hands were moving over his head, hips beginning to move just a little.

Oh, yeah. He hunched over, taking more in, humming as that cock slid over his tongue. Rock purred and rumbled for him, fingers not quite holding him in place yet, more just encouraging his movements. Rig just lost himself in the tastes and texture. He knew Rock's prick intimately -- knew where to lick, where to tease, where to settle to make the big guy crazy with wanting. Rock groaned and moaned, hips starting to move rhythmically.

227

Hot sexy bastard. Rig started deep-throating, just relaxed and took that fat cock in and in.

"Fucking shit, you're something else."

He hummed. He was fucking happy, was what he was. Rock moaned again, hands starting to hold his head now, that fat prick pushing in and out. He let one of his hands slide over, teasing Rock's hole, circling it. Rock growled, hips moving faster, hands getting harder in his hair. He let his finger slide into his mouth on the next downward stroke, then went back to that tight little hole, pushing in.

"Fuck!" Rock squeezed his finger tight, spunk shooting deep into his mouth. Swallowing hard, Rig took it all, then slowly brought Rock down, fingers moving to slide over and stroke those strong thighs. Rock petted his head, rumbling from deep in his belly. His cheek came to rest on Rock's thigh, lips brushing that skin.

"So you want me to move in," said Rock, fingers still moving over his head, his face.

"I do." He nodded. More than just about anything.

"You know I'm a lousy roommate. I hog the bed. My brand of cooking involves the phone and the doorbell. I fucking hate vacuuming."

He nodded again. "I don't sleep in, spoil my dog and tend to sing when I'm working in the garage."

"Long as you know what you're getting into."

Rig lifted his head, met Rock's eyes. "I wouldn't have asked if I wasn't sure."

"Well all right then. I can buy that stereo system I want with the money I save on rent."

Oh. Oh fuck, yes. He crawled up along Rock's body. "Reckon your bed will go in the master. We'll put my little one in one of the extra bedrooms."

"I'll leave the interior decorating to you," Rock told him with a grin and a nod toward the plain walls around them.

"Good plan. I'll leave the ordering the cable to you." Rig took a long, hot kiss.

"You're paying half, right? I'm getting the sports network." Rock gave him a grin and another kiss. "'Course I might be too busy to be doing much watching."

"I'm thinking I could occupy you a bit, here and there." He reached down and cupped those heavy balls.

"I'll bet you could." Rock's hands slid down and cupped his ass. "In fact I'm counting on it."

"Oh, good." Rig brought their lips together again, rocking into those strong hands, moaning just a touch.

Rock growled and slid those hands into the back of his jeans, cupping his bare ass and squeezing.

"Mmm... feels good." His toes curled, cock throbbing in his jeans.

"Yeah? I can make it feel even better." Rock's hands slid out of his jeans and around to open them.

He leaned down, licking at Rock's neck, moaning soft and steady. Rock got his jeans opened and pushed off, thick fingers starting to tease at his hole.

"You've got the hottest fucking hands, Blue Eyes." He got himself settled, straddling Rock's lap.

"You're biased," Rock answered with a grin, one of those hands reaching down into the magazine holder and coming up with some lube.

"Mmm... not a bit. Keep touching, though, so I can make real fucking sure."

"Wasn't planning on stopping anytime soon."

Without ceremony, Rock slid one finger into him. He groaned, rocked back against the pressure, hips riding it.

"Slut," growled Rock, eyes warm.

"Yeah." He nodded, licking Rock's lips. "For you."

Rock just growled again and added another finger, free hand on his hip, guiding his movements. He rested his forehead on Rock's, eyelids drooping, body dancing on those thick fingers.

"Fucking sexy, Rig." Rock's fingers kept working him, finding his gland and playing it.

He fucking whimpered, belly clenching. "Oh, shit. Rock... So fucking hot."

"You ready for a piece of this?" Rock asked, hand circling his own cock and pumping. "Ready to ride?"

"You're a fucking machine. Always so fucking hard." Rig's smile was wild, horny and hungry. "Fuck, yes, I'm ready."

"I'm just the fucking best," Rock told him.

The fingers inside him disappeared, Rock tugging him forward, pressing that fat prick against him. "Ride."

He leaned back, stretching out as he sank down, entire body bowing with the pleasure.

"Shit, that's good." Rock's hands at his waist encouraged him down all the way.

His balls snuggled against Rock's pubes, his hole stretched and tight, entire body thrumming. Fucking perfect. Rock was making those deep rumbly noises that meant he was fucking happy, feeling fucking fine. His hands found purchase on the arms of the recliner, stabilizing himself as he began to move, fucking himself on that fat cock. Rock's hands on his hips helped, bringing him down with more and more force.

He let his eyes close, focusing on nothing but the way their bodies slammed together, fierce and hard and fucking hot. Rock's hands grew tighter, the strong hips pushing up into him now, too.

"Fuck, yes. Oh, shit. Good." They shifted and slid until... "Fuck! Rock!"

"Right fucking there," muttered Rock, pulling him down even harder now, nailing him every time.

"Shit! Please!" He grabbed his cock, started pulling,

bringing himself off.

"That's it -- come on my cock."

Rig threw his head back and shot hard, toes curling, balls fucking hurting as they emptied. Rock roared, cock throbbing as it filled him with spunk. He collapsed on Rock's chest, breathing hard, wore plumb out. Rock's arms slid around him, holding him against the warm, hard body.

He brushed a lazy kiss against the hollow of Rock's throat, humming softly as he floated on the edges of sleep. He got a bit of a rumble in reply, Rock settling in the chair and shifting him to lie just right against the wide chest.

The last thought he had before he fell asleep was that he needed to call the realtor, needed to get the keys to show his Blue their new house.

CHAPTER FIFTEEN

Rig pulled up to Rock's apartment, the back end of his little truck filled with broken down boxes and tape and old newspaper.

Moving.

Into the house.

Next fucking Friday.

Too cool!

His apartment was finished, all the shit he'd unpacked, repacked, Momma and Daddy hauling the rest of his stuff up in a few weeks. He found a parking space as close to Rock's door as he could and grabbed a load of cardboard, nudging the door with his elbow. "Open up, Rocketman. My hands are full."

The door opened, Rock giving him a grin. "You in there somewhere with all those boxes?"

He chuckled. "Theoretically, yeah. Lemme in. I

wasn't sure how many you'd need."

"I don't have that much stuff, Rig," Rock told him, chuckling.

"Christ, Blue Eyes, you got your whole kitchen and your weapons and your magazines will fill twelve of these." He dumped his load and headed out for another. "What're we ordering for supper?"

"The usual. It's on its way." Rock followed him out.

"Cool." He handed Rock the lion's share of the boxes and grabbed the tape and newspaper and the case of beer. "There's a cheesecake in the cab. Can you grab it?"

"Cheesecake? Hell yes, I can grab it."

"Yeah, it's chocolate. Looked good." Like he didn't know what would make the packing easier.

"Chocolate. Awesome."

He could feel Rock's eyes on his ass as they headed back to the apartment. He gave it his best sway as he walked. These were his tightest, thinnest jeans, just about see-through in spots. Rock was practically purring by the time they got in.

The cake was dumped on the coffee table, the boxes next to them and then he had a mouthful of Rock. He pushed close, rubbing against the acres and acres of beautiful fucking muscles. Rock's hands slid down his back and grabbed his ass.

He pushed back into Rock's touch, moaning. "Oh, fuck. Your hands are hot, Blue. Fucking sweet."

"All the better to hold you with."

"Ooo... gonna show me your big teeth and your big cock, Gramma?" Oh, fuck. He loved when Rock was playing. Fucking loved it.

"You brought the treats, it would only be fair."

Rig moaned, cupping Rock's prick and rubbing. "Mmm... what a big cock you have..."

"All the better to fuck you with."

"Oh, yeah. Screw Gramma. I want to play with the Big, Bad Rock."

"I don't want to screw Gramma, I want to screw you."

"I'm all yours." He pushed up into another kiss, hands tugging at Rock's shirt.

"I know it." Rock raised his arms, letting Rig pull off the shirt before grabbing his ass again.

Rigger let his hands explore those amazing muscles, fingers tweaking those tight little nipples as he passed by. Rock groaned and took his mouth again, kissing hard. He wrapped one leg around Rock's hip, hands sliding to hold onto those strong shoulders. Rock pulled him in tight, their chests rubbing together, skin on skin, cocks finding each other even through their jeans.

"'s so fucking good." His words were gasped into Rock's lips as they humped and rocked together.

Rock growled an agreement, hands hard and hot on his ass. Rig arched, groaning. Oh, shit. He was going to shoot and didn't have a change of clothes in the truck and he hated wearing soggy jeans and Rock's shorts would just fall off his ass and... Oh...

Rock wasn't stopping, just jerking against him, one hand letting go long enough to flick fingers across his nipples.

"Fuck! Rock!" He jerked as he came, hips pushing hard, mouth open on a cry.

"Yeah, you're fucking Rock." His Blue chuckled, the sound husky and ending on a moan. Even through Rock's jeans he could smell the heavy musk of Rock's spunk.

"Oh, fuck yes." He grinned, nipped at Rock's bottom lip. Sexy motherfucker.

"You need to get yourself a new pair of jeans, Rig -- if you're expecting me to ever get anything done with you around."

"Hmm? These are my hanging around the house jeans, Blue Eyes." He took another quick kiss. "Guess I could cut them down into shorts, though..."

Rock laughed. "Oh yeah, that's going to make you less fuckable."

He grinned. "Rock... Blue... I am *so* not going for less fuckable."

"As long as we're on the same page." Rock gave him a wink. "You want a beer? Pizza'll be here any minute. I'm going to go change."

"Yeah. You got a pair of sweats I can borrow?" He gave Rock a wink and started shimmying out of his soggy jeans. "Like from when you were a ninety-pound teenager?"

"I was never a ninety-pound teenager," Rock told him, eyes on his body.

"Never?" He managed to get his boots off, then the jeans and socks, standing proud and naked for his lover. "How about ninety-five-pounds?"

"Maybe when I was a pre-teen." Rock flexed for him.

He groaned, took a step forward, fingers trailing up that fine fucking six-pack. "Mmm... I'm a lucky redneck."

"You know it."

Those big hands cupped his ass again. He snuggled back into the touch, hips rocking and rubbing.

"Pizza's coming any minute," Rock murmured, mouth on his neck.

"Yeah? Maybe they'll get lost..." He lifted his chin, moaning.

Rock laughed. "We can hope."

"Mmhmm... I'm thinking we deserve an orgasm for every other box we pack. Sound like a plan?"

He was warm and liquid, happy and right the fuck where he wanted to be.

"Sounds like a plan, Cowboy."

Rock lifted him by the ass and walked him back to the bed. "I packed a couple of boxes before you showed up -- time to collect on the first orgasm."

He wrapped his arms around Rock's neck, chuckling. "Oh, most definitely. You deserve one just for sheer fucking initiative."

"Yep, my thoughts exactly." Rock pulled off his jeans, using his undies to wipe himself off.

"So, Blue Eyes, how do you want orgasm number one or is that two? Suck? Fuck? Hand job?" His eyes trailed over Rock's skin, his hands exploring like they both hadn't just come.

"Yes." Rock's cock was already hard, like they both hadn't just come.

"Mmm..." He leaned and licked the tip of that sweet as fuck prick. "Taste good."

Rock groaned for him, legs spreading a little. Rig leaned in, licking again, then wrapping his lips around the head and tugging gently. Rock's thick fingers slid through his hair, rubbing his scalp as a low groan sounded. He kept his touch light, focusing on the tip, sucking and sliding, carefully fucking the slit with his tongue.

"Fucking awesome." He could feel Rock's thighs go hard, his Blue fighting not to thrust.

He hummed, tugging a little harder, fingers cupping Rock's balls. The doorbell rang, making Rock groan.

"Oh, fuck." He wrinkled his nose. "They didn't get lost."

Growling, Rock grabbed a pair of BDUs from the floor, carefully tucking his prick away. "Don't go anywhere."

"Not a chance, Blue Eyes." He settled on the bed,

stretching out tall. "Not a fucking chance."

Rock gave him one last head to toe look, eyes hot, before heading off to answer the door. He turned so he could watch Rock move, pay for the pizza, growling low at the pretty little thing delivering. The pizza landed on the coffee table, Rock taking no time in coming back to him.

"Mmm... here kitty, kitty, kitty." He stretched again, arching and popping his back.

Rock chuckled, opening his pants and letting that fat prick free. "No pussies here, Rig."

He grinned, reaching for his lover. "Nope. Come here, Blue Eyes. Fuck my mouth."

"My pleasure." Rock gave him a wink as he climbed up onto the bed and straddled his face. "Yours, too."

"Fuck, yes." He wrapped his fingers around Rock's hips, lips already open and waiting. Rock fed that magnificent cock into his mouth, his Blue leaning forward to grab hold of the headboard. Oh. Oh, fuck. Yes. He moaned, tongue sliding all the way down the shaft, passion making him ache. Rock moaned and started moving, slowly fucking his mouth, almost gentle. Rig took advantage of the motions, tongue and lips doing their best to drive Rock out of his fucking mind. By the sound of the moans and groans it was working.

He just sank into it, focusing on nothing more than that sweet prick, the slide on his tongue, their scents filling the room. Faster and faster Rock moved, moans and grunts filling the air, words interspersed with the sounds telling him how fucking good it was. Rig took him deep, nose burying in those warm curls.

"Oh fuck, yes." Rock spilled into his mouth, spunk pouring down his throat as that fat prick throbbed.

He swallowed his lover down, just fucking purring around Rock's flesh, tongue sliding over the tip, searching for after-shocks. Rock jerked and shuddered for him, all but fucking purring. He looked up, grinning into those blue-blue eyes, lips tugging on the tip of Rock's cock again, sending sensation through those fired-up nerves.

"Fucking shit, Rig." Oh, someone liked that. Rig did it again. Rock's reply was a moan this time, hips rolling that prick in his mouth. He slid his fingers along Rock's crease, teasing that little hole as he sucked. Fucking sweet.

"Rig..." his name was purred, Rock starting to move again, pushing into his mouth and then back against his fingers. He slid his finger into his mouth, slicking it, then reached back to Rock's hole, pushing in deep with one smooth stroke.

"Fuck, Rig!" Rock moved faster, fucking his mouth hard. His Blue's cries were back, more desperate now, needy.

He found the smooth gland deep inside and started working it, pushing hard, fingers stroking again and again. He could see the muscles in Rock's arms and stomach working hard, could feel the thick thighs trembling with effort. Then Rock was roaring, coming again. Fucking A. He swallowed and pulled, taking every fucking drop before letting Rock slide free.

Rock dropped down next to him with a groan. "Fuck. That was awesome."

"Mmm... yeah." He nuzzled one hard little nipple with his nose, grinning wide. "You owe me two packed boxes."

"Put it on my tab."

Rig started chuckling, nipping that sweet bit of flesh before settling close. "Asshole."

"Yep." Rock's arm went around him. "Naptime. Then supper. Then you'll get your boxes."

"Mmm... Good plan." He stretched, cock snug

against Rock's hip, cheek on that strong shoulder.

Rock's hand slid idly up and down along his back, slowing as Rock fell asleep. He drifted, slowly cataloging all the crap Rock had strewn about. Pretty soon they'd be napping in their house.

Their bed.

Pretty fucking cool.

He yawned, tugging the covers over them. Oh, yeah. Really fucking cool.

CHAPTER SIXTEEN

Rock grabbed a beer and wandered into the front room. He hadn't been unhappy at his old apartment -- it had everything he needed and moving was a fucking pain in the ass. He caught sight of Rig's ass encased in tight, thin jeans as the man bent to grab books out of a box, filling up the shelves. Of course he hadn't been married to the old place either and the perks at this one were fucking sweet.

"Hey, Rabbit -- you planning on taking a break today?"

Rig turned, gave him a long, slow grin that was pure fucking sex. "That depends, I reckon, on what plans you might have for this old boy."

"Location might be different, but the plans are the same. Fuck you through the floor."

"You always have the best plans." Rig pulled off his

shirt, draped it over a box. "Don't think we've fucked in here yet."

"Nope. We've hit the bedrooms and the bathroom, but here and the kitchen are left." He waggled his eyebrows. "Until now."

"Gotta love a man with a goal." Rig walked around the boxes, that tight little ass swaying as he moved, closing the space between them.

He set his beer down on one of the shelves and took off his t-shirt -- no reason for them not to start out naked. Rig unbuckled the painted on jeans, filling cock pushing out the thin material. He growled and grabbed Rig around the waist, pulling him in close as their mouths came together. Screw it -- they could get naked as they went.

A low cry pushed into his mouth, Rig's arms wrapping around his neck as their bellies rubbed together. He sucked on Rig's tongue, hands pushing down into the open jeans to grab that sweet ass and squeeze. Those talented as fuck hands rubbed at his neck and shoulders, hips rolling and jerking under his touch. Grey eyes watched him, happy and horny. He was feeling pretty fucking happy and horny himself.

He pushed Rig's jeans down, one hand coming around to grab Rig's hard, hot prick.

"Mmm... feels fucking good." Rig reached down and started tugging his jeans open.

Rock couldn't argue with that.

He groaned as his hard prick suddenly had room, air like a fucking kiss. Then he and Rig were pressed together, heat on heat and it was fucking perfect. Rig's cock slid along his own, hot and smooth. The touch of the soft curls was cooler, almost tickling, silk on his skin. He kicked off his jeans and leaned back against the wall, legs slightly spread. Rig fit just perfectly, hot and tight and right against him.

They slid and rocked together, growls and moans covering the slide of skin on skin. His hands stayed on Rig's ass, guiding Rig's movements. Rig's hands moved constantly, pinching and stroking and playing with him, making him crazy. He was torn between rubbing off until they both came or pushing Rig up against the wall and fucking his ass. Rig tweaked his nipple, teeth nipping his bottom lip, teasing bastard.

That made his decision for him and he flipped them, coming off the wall and putting Rig there, face first. "Spread 'em, cowboy."

"Ooooh! You going to search me, Blue?" Rig spread, ass wriggling, sexy as fuck chuckle sounding.

He snorted. "Yeah, I think you're hiding contraband."

He pushed at Rig's hole with one finger.

"Mm... not yet, but I'm hoping." Rig pushed back, fucking hungry little hole taking him in.

He groaned, working Rig with his finger, loving the way his cowboy's body just swallowed him up. Rig stretched along the wall, body clenching around him, so fucking hot and tight, muscles rippling. He pushed in two more fingers, fucking Rig with three now, moaning at the heat, the tightness.

"Oh... Oh, fuck. Yeah. Good." Rig's head fell back; he was panting hard, hips snapping.

"Wait for me," Rock warned, pulling his fingers out and pushing in with his prick. Nice and easy, just like that.

Rig groaned, hand dropping to squeeze the base of that prick. "Oh, Blue... Sweet fucking cock feels so goddamned good."

"Just like your fucking ass. So fucking good." He groaned and starting fucking his Rabbit.

Rig cried out, arms stretched up against the wall, entire fucking body into it. Riding him. Fucking him. Fucking perfect. He reached around, grabbing hold of Rig's cock, working both ass and prick as hard as he could.

It didn't take long before Rig was bucking, ass squeezing around him, dark flush crawling up Rig's spine. "Blue..."

"Yeah, that's it, Rig. Right there -- fucking come on my cock."

"Right there... Oh..." Rig's voice faded into a sweet moan as he shot, the scent of spunk rich and male and fucking right.

He groaned at the scent, at the way Rig's ass squeezed his prick so fucking hard. Another groan and he was coming, filling Rig's ass up. They rested together, breathing slowing down, the back of Rig's neck salty and hot to his tongue. He stroked his hands along Rig's sides, enjoying the hot and sweat feeling of Rig's skin.

"Mmm... 'm liking this room-by-room fucking thing." Rig hummed, stretching tall. "Maybe after we'll have to go wall by wall."

He nodded. "Piece of furniture by piece of furniture, too."

"Oh, hell yes. Over the table, the sofa, bent over the sink..."

"You know it. Then we'll start on tattooing your ass with carpet patterns."

Rig's chuckling made that sweet ass squeeze his prick. "By then we'll have finished unpacking."

"Only if I lose my powers of persuasion."

Rig tilted back, twisting to take a long kiss. "Somehow I don't see that happening."

"Neither do I," he murmured, pushing in deep again, making Rig groan.

Oh yeah, this place had a whole lot more going for it than his old apartment.

CHAPTER SEVENTEEN

There was a Clint Eastwood movie on the TV, just audible over the electric screwdriver. He'd built a nice wall unit of shelves for their movies and cassettes and CDs and shit. He'd done them just like Daddy'd shown him, stained them a dark brown. They were looking fine and would stop that whole piling shit on the floor thing that drove him crazy.

Rig grinned. Man, wasn't he all grown up? Making fucking furniture for his own fucking house. He stripped off his shirt and grabbed a chair, perching precariously to bolt the top edges in.

"Are you looking to commit suicide, or just break a few bones?" growled Rock from behind him.

"Hmm?" He turned his head, tilting, almost losing his balance.

Rock shook his head and moved forward, big hand

steadying his legs. "You're going to take a fucking header, Rig."

"Oh, I'm okay." Still, didn't that feel good, that big, hot hand on his thigh. "You like the shelves?"

"I don't know as I was too busy noticing you about to break your neck." Rock's hands squeezed. "I'll get a proper look once you're down."

"Mmm..." He grinned, set in the last two screws, leaning toward Rock's touch.

Rock shook his head and chuckled. "Slut."

"Yep. Yours." He wriggled, just a little. "You can't blame me."

"Blame would imply I thought it was a bad thing." Rock smacked his ass. "And no wriggling until you're down."

"Who was wriggling?" He set the screwdriver down on a shelf and turned, letting himself slide along Rock.

Rock purred, arms wrapping around him, mouth sliding over his. Oh. Kisses. He pushed right into Rock's heat, lips open, tongue flicking out for a taste. Rock's tongue slid on his, hands moving over him. His hands wrapped around Rock's head, holding them close together. He poured himself -- his pleasure, his heat, his happiness with the world at large -- into the kiss, losing himself in it.

Rock rumbled happily, slowly moving them back to the couch. Rig moaned, following easily, body in synch with his Blue. Rock's hands pulled off his clothes, fingers warm on his skin. Not one to hesitate when it came to the naked, his Rock. He chuckled into the kiss, vibrating and wanting. Rock's own clothes went next and then he was pulled against all those hard, hot muscles.

"Oh..." He rubbed, he couldn't help it. He needed.

"Gonna let me fuck that sweet ass?"

"As often as you want, Blue Eyes." And then maybe

more.

Rock chuckled, tugging him down onto the couch. They landed together, belly-to-belly, both moaning at the sensation. Rock's fingers slid down to his ass, teasing along his crease. He spread, hips rocking back, making it clear what he wanted, what he needed. Rock's fingers slid one by one past his hole, each dipping in for a moment before disappearing again.

The touches left his skin tingling, his cock throbbing against Rock's belly. "Tease."

Rock chuckled. "You love it."

"Who? Me?" He brought their lips together, catching their laughter.

One of those teasing fingers slid right into him, started fucking him soft and slow.

"Oh..." He arched, undulating nice and easy, eyes dropping closed. Sweet fuck, Blue was good at that, knew just how to make him fly. One finger became two and Rock found his gland, pegging it. Rig jerked, eyes flying open, lips parting. "Blue! There!"

"Right here?" Rock asked, voice low and growly as those fingers slid deep again.

"Oh. Oh, yeah. Fuck. Blue..." He humped against that strong belly, going from wanting to needing just like that.

Rock's cock was hard, hot as it slid along his balls, those fingers moving hard and fast inside him.

"More. Fuck. Please. Blue." He was babbling, eyes rolling, but he didn't care, didn't care about anything but more, please.

Rock kept pegging his gland, moving faster and faster. He arched, heels digging into the sofa, crying out as his balls tightened.

"Wait for me, Rabbit." Rock's fingers disappeared and he was shifted to straddle Rock's waist, that fat prick nudging at his hole.

He threw his head back, panting, a low, animalistic sound escaping him as he took Rock in deep. Rock growled, hips shoving that fat prick even deeper.

"Hold up. Fuck, gonna make me come, Blue. Let me..." He reached down, squeezed his cock hard, breath coming in shallow gasps.

"So come -- you'll get it up again." The grip turned to a few quick, hard strokes, his body needing now, ass squeezing Rock tight. Rock's hands slid along his thighs to brush his balls, hips pushing that fat prick deep again.

"Oh. Oh, fuck, that's sweet. Fucking made for this, Blue Eyes."

"Fuck yeah." Rock kept moving, thrusting up into him, fat prick head sliding past his gland over and over.

He closed his eyes, riding, bouncing up and down on the thick shaft, fucking flying. One of Rock's hands slid up over his belly to his chest, tweaking first one nipple and then the other. He bucked, eyes rolling, sparks shooting down his belly. Rock was moaning, bucking, fucking him hard.

He leaned down, took a long, hard kiss, eyes fastened onto Rock's, sinking. Rock's tongue pushed into the kiss, fucking his mouth like that hard cock was fucking his ass. He wrapped his lips around Rock's tongue, sucking hard, moaning low. Mouth and ass and tits and cock were all connected, shooting fire straight to his balls.

He came hard, toes curling, body jerking hard. Rock roared, pushing hard into him several more times before filing him with heat.

Rig moaned, leaning in, relaxing against his Blue, cuddling. "Good."

Rock chuckled and hugged him. "Always is."

"Uh-huh." He kissed Rock's shoulder.

Rock waved toward the entertainment unit. "So is

this your way of saying I'm messy?"

"Nope. This is my way of saying we have a shit-load of shoot-'em up movies and the harder for Grimmy to gnaw on, the better."

His momma didn't raise no fools.

Well... there was Bobby, but he was a throwback.

Rock chuckled. "Right."

He grinned. "It's a good-looking set of shelves."

"I've always liked your shelves." Rock grabbed his ass, squeezed.

He wiggled, squeezed Rock's prick, still buried inside him. "They're a good fit."

Rock groaned, eyes rolling slightly. "A fucking A fit."

"Yeah. Just... Just right."

Rock purred, hands sliding up his back. His lips found Rock's throat, leaving teasing little kisses. "Feels fucking good, Rabbit."

He nodded, offering little licks, little nips. "Always."

"You wanting to go again?"

"Again? You're ambitious."

"You're the one milking my cock like you're wanting another go round." Rock grinned up at him, eyes hot.

"I can't help it, feels so fucking fine." He met Rock's eyes. "You fill me up."

Rock purred for him again. "I guess I do at that."

He squeezed again. "Beautiful bastard."

"Takes one to know one." Rock winked at him, one hand working between them, tweaking a nipple.

He peeped, toes curling, eyes wide. "Shit!"

Chuckling, Rock plucked his nipple again.

"Blue..." Rig's spine arched, eyes closing, lips parting.

"You like that, Rabbit?" Rock did it again, knowing

fucking well that he did.

He nodded, clenching around Rock's prick, trying to make Rock as crazy as he felt. Rock's moans told him he was doing a pretty good job, as did the way that cock started to buck up into him. Yeah. Fuck. Sweet. He closed his eyes, belly rippling, nipple going tight. Rock kept tugging on the tiny bit of flesh, kept pushing up past his gland, like the man hadn't just worked him hard moments ago.

"Oh..." His toes curled. "Gonna. Blue. Fuck."

"Yes. Do it, Rabbit. Come on my cock."

He whimpered, head thrown back, eyes rolling furiously. His balls drew up tight, cock throbbing at Blue's words.

"Fucking amazing, Rabbit." Rock's words were groans.

"Yeah. Fuck, Blue." Seed sprayed against Rock's belly.

Rock roared, filling him with heat even as he came. He slumped, panting, eyes rolling. Rock gathered him close, arms holding him tight. Rig hummed and cuddled, snuggling in for the duration. Rock purred, the sound happy, easy. He let his eyes close. He'd worry about filling the shelves and being a grownup house-type owner later.

After he was finished with his post-well-fucked nap.

Rock was watching television.

It didn't really matter what was on, he was just enjoying the twenty-nine inch picture, stereo sound. The remote had fifty million buttons and would supposedly work from the back bedroom. Pretty fucking cool.

Nothing like watching football on a big screen. He'd bought it just today, along with a new VCR because Rig's was making the tapes stick. He'd even managed to set everything just the way they wanted it without a hitch. Not bad at all for a Saturday evening.

Still, there was something missing. Something fucking crucial to a fucking good time.

Rig came wandering in, bowl of steaming popcorn in his hands, two beers in those long fingers. "You pick out a movie, yet?"

"That new Arnie flick is playing on HBO. Starts in about twenty." He grabbed one of the bottles, grinning at Rig.

"Too cool." Rig settled in next to him, putting the popcorn on his lap.

He put his arm around Rig's shoulders, taking a big handful of popcorn and munching away. He nodded to the remote. "You should give it a try -- I'm surprised they don't expect you to have a license to drive it."

Rig looked over the remote, blinking. "Christ, I've seen choppers with less buttons..."

He grinned. "Yep."

He watched Rig flip channels for a minute and then nudged the thin ribs. "We've got twenty minutes before the movie starts."

"We do." Those grey eyes were twinkling, focused on the TV. "Whatever will we do to pass the time?"

"I've got an idea or two." He put the popcorn down on the coffee table, grinning over at Rig as he took another long drink.

Rig leaned over, put the remote down, then turned to slide one hand up his thigh. "An idea or two? Really?"

"Yep." Rock put his beer down on the coffee table, too, hauling Rig in for a kiss.

He wasn't the coy type.

Fortunately, his own personal slut was never slow on the draw, fingers moving to cup his cock and balls while those sweet lips opened right up. He stroked his hands over Rig's shoulders, fingers tickling the skin of Rig's neck as his tongue pushed in deep. A low moan slid into his mouth, almost a purr. Rig's eyes were bright, warm, full of wanting.

Oh yeah, he recognized that look. Counted on it.

His hands moved to pull Rig's t-shirt off, lips clinging before parting long enough to get it over Rig's head. Then his hands were on Rig's jeans, playing with the waistband, with the button.

"Mmm..." His Rabbit moved closer, straddling his thigh and starting to rock. "Good..."

"Better without the pesky jeans," he noted, pulling the top button open and teasing the zipper down. He slid one hand down the back of Rig's jeans to grab that sweet ass.

"Oh, yeah." Rig nodded, ass rocking into his touch. "Yours too. Want that fat cock."

"You want it, you got it."

He got his own jeans open, arched up and tugged hard, pulling them off his ass to the tops of his thighs.

"Mmm..." Rig fucking licked those parted lips, hands wrapping around his cock and stroking.

"Slut."

"Yep. Yours."

"Yes." He pushed Rig off his leg, pulling the tight jeans off. "Want you."

Rig nodded, scrabbling around for the lube and slicking up two long fingers before reaching back to slide them deep in that sweet, tight, little hole.

Oh fuck.

That was a beautiful thing.

Shoving his own jeans right off, Rock moaned, licked his lips. So fucking hot. Rig ducked his head, panting as he rode his own fingers, the scent of need and sweat and want heavy in the air.

"Enough," he growled. "Need you."

"Yeah. Now. How?"

He patted his own thighs. "Come ride me."

"Fuck, yes." Rig shuddered as those fingers slid free, then settled atop his thighs, straddling. "Fuck me."

"Hell, yes."

Grinning, he guided his prick to Rig's hole and brought his Rabbit down onto him. It pulled a groan out of him, the way that Rig's body just swallowed him up. Tight and burning hot, Rig's muscles rippled around him, squeezing and keeping him held deep. He ran his hands along Rig's thighs, the tension and need building between them until he couldn't go another second without moving. Hands grabbing Rig's hips again, he started to thrust.

Rig leaned in, brought their lips together, sharing breath as they fucked, little grunts and moans filling the air. He growled and groaned, hands tight on Rig's skin, digging in as he pulled Rig down onto him. Rig rode him hard, stiff prick rubbing liquid heat all over his belly, head thrown back in pleasure.

"Sexy fucker," he muttered, drawing his fingers across the tip of Rig's cock.

"Mmm... make me need, Blue." Rig jerked, body clenching around his prick.

He nodded. He knew all about that, about the feeling in his balls that begged him to fuck harder, faster. He just kept fucking, one hand wrapping around Rig's prick. The soft keening that filled the air made him ache, Rig's spine bowing, orgasm starting deep within him. Rig's ass rippled around his prick, drawing his own climax from him, making him roar as he shot.

His Rabbit settled against his chest, breath coming quick and light against his throat. "Good."

"Yep, you can't mess with perfection."

A soft chuckle tickled his jaw as Rig nodded. "You

got that shit right, Blue Eyes."

He nodded; he knew.

He tilted Rig's head just a bit and took a kiss, long and deep.

All in all, pretty fucking good for a Saturday evening.

There was nothing fucking worse than being stuck on hold with the fucking cable company. Rock had been watching the game and then the television had gone snowy and that had been that.

Fifteen minutes later and he still hadn't talked to a human being and he was about ready to tear whoever did finally come onto the line a new one. The fucking telephone was going to grow into his ear.

Rig wandered in from the backyard, eyebrow arched. "What's up, Rocketman? Ordering pizza?"

"No. Fucking cable's out. I'm waiting for a goddamned operator."

"Blah. Want me to go see if Grimmy chewed through the cable?" Rig wrinkled his nose and poured two glasses of Coke, handing him one.

He growled. "If that mutt's responsible, he's sleeping outside for a week."

"If Grimmy did it, I'll fix it." Rig gave him a look. "If you'd quit throwing his bones away, he wouldn't chew on the cables, you know."

"He leaves those smelly drooly things everywhere." Rock shook his head. How long were they going to keep him on fucking hold?

"He's a good pup. Dogs are drooly, nature of the beast and all." Rig shook his head, giving that mutt a grin as it heard its name and blundered in. "Aren't you good, baby?" He rolled his eyes, groaning as the recording came on again to thank him for staying on the line and maintaining his call priority. Rig gave the dog a good scratching, then scooted over to him, hands trailing over his belly. "What about you, Rocketman? Are you good?"

He growled lightly, shifted to spread his legs. "I'm stuck on fucking hold, what do you think?"

"I think you're sexy when you're rumbly." Those grey eyes danced at him, one hand sliding over his cock.

He growled again, this time from pleasure, hips pushing up to keep his prick in contact with Rig's hand. Rig kept the pressure steady, gentle and good, fingertips dancing over his nuts. He undid the button of his jeans and pulled the zipper down one-handed, grinning a little now.

"Watch it, Blue Eyes, you almost look happy." Rigger gave him a smile and leaned up to taste his mouth, hand sliding in his jeans.

He groaned into Rig's mouth, almost dropping the phone.

"Sexy bastard. Make me want you." Rig's free hand settled at his nape, rubbing.

He purred. "You want me? Good."

"Always." He got another kiss, this one slow and deep.

"Well I'm not going anywhere," he told Rig, waggling his eyebrows.

"You're a spoiled marine, fishing for blowjobs while you're on the phone." Rig chuckled at him, thumb sliding over the tip of his cock.

He moaned, voice going husky, rough. "I've been on hold for almost a half a fucking hour -- I think I deserve a fucking blow job."

"Yeah? You're a patient man, Blue Eyes." Rig sank down on those bony knees, whispering against his prick,

"Too bad I'm not."

Then he was sucked in deep.

He called out, free hand wrapping in Rig's hair. "Fucking good, Rig."

Rig hummed, tongue sliding around his cock, taking him in deep. He purred, just rumbled. Fuck, that was sweet. He watched Rig work, eyes closed, cheeks flushed, the look on his Rabbit's face pure fucking happy.

He let the phone drop and pushed his other hand through that blond hair as well. Some things were better'n cable.

Rig's hands slid up along his thighs, stroking and petting. He growled, hips starting to hump up into that perfect fucking mouth. Rig took everything, everything he had to give, moaning low and sweet around his cock. Those grey eyes flashing up at him was all he needed and with a shout he came hard down Rig's throat.

Rig swallowed around his cock, drinking him down, eyes fastened on his face. He purred, fingers stroking Rig's face. Rig hummed, nuzzling into his hand.

The phone made a noise and he leaned over, picked it up off the floor.

"-name is Tanya, how may I help you today."

Grinning, he hit the off button.

The cable could fucking wait.

Popcorn.

Check.

Good movies with explosions and cars and guns.

Check.

Beer.

Check.

Rig went and put on a pair of sweats and a t-shirt and grabbed a comforter.

"Come on, Blue Eyes. It's time for the movies."

Rock did two more sit ups and grunted. "You want me to take a shower first?"

"No, you're fine. I'll just wipe you down." He leaned down and licked Rock's shoulder. "Either that or rub you with the popcorn."

Rock chuckled. "Kinky as being rubbed with popcorn sounds, I'd rather you use that awesome mouth of yours."

He grinned, taking another long, lazy lick, the blanket falling from his hands. Rock's fingers slid through his hair, big hand moving to wrap around his head.

"Mmm..." He let himself settle on his knees, mouth trailing over that hot, damp skin, licking and lapping, teeth testing the hard little nipples.

He got a sweet grunt for his efforts and Rock's other hand slid along his back, fingers pushing underneath his sweater to stroke the skin of his back. Each ripple of that hard belly was next, Rig licking and lapping, tongue sliding and teasing along the elastic waistband of Rock's PT shorts.

Rock slowly lay back down, belly muscles rippling under his tongue. That fat prick was straining at Rock's shorts, trying to work free. He let his tongue slide beneath the waistband, licking and teasing, just brushing the tip of that cock. Rock groaned, hands squeezing and then opening again, stroking, petting, only pushing his head down a little bit.

Rig chuckled and licked again, flicking that slick slit, taunting.

"Oh fuck, Rig. You're going to kill me."

"Hmm... no, Blue Eyes. Going to suck you until you don't want me anymore." He slid the waistband of Rock's shorts down a little, lips circling the sweet cock.

Rock snorted, the sound turning into a moan. "Never

gonna happen."

He grinned, lips sinking down a little farther, hands pushing Rock's shorts lower. Damned right. Rock was his. He was given another groan, Rock's hips and legs shifting restlessly. Oh, he loved that -- the need, the scent, the fucking feeling of that hard cock on his tongue.

Rock's hips pushed up harder, sending more of the hot prick into his mouth. He relaxed, moaned, took it all in. Fuck. Yes. Please.

"Fuck, yes. Please." Rock's words echoed his thoughts, his Blue humping up into his mouth.

Rig whimpered, pulling hard, his own cock swollen and throbbing in his sweatpants. With a growl, Rock's hands wrapped around his head, held him in place as Rock fucked his face. Beautiful, hard, sexy fucker. Rigger swallowed and hummed, taking Rock down to the root.

"Oh, fuck!" Rock's prick jerked hard on his tongue, come splashing down his throat.

He drank Rock down, head bobbing, rubbing against those huge hands. His Blue purred, stroking his head, hips settling. He lowered himself, mouth easing, cleaning that fat prick off, finding each soft little shiver of aftershock.

"Fucking amazing," murmured Rock.

Oh. He purred, nuzzling that sweet belly.

Rock's hands slid over his shoulders and down, hooking under his arms and tugging, not forcing him up, but strongly suggesting it. He slid up Rock's body, moving until he could give Rock a kiss. Oh, yeah. Good.

Rock's hand was behind his head again, tilting him so Rock could plunder his mouth, tongue fucking owning him. Rig melted, sinking into Rock with a low cry, toes curling, cock hard in his sweats. Rock's other hand slid into the back of his sweats, grabbing his ass and pressing him against the hard body.

"Mmm... yes." He started rubbing, moaning as his

hips rocked, his dick sliding against the soft sweats. "So good."

"Yep. Almost perfect."

"Almost?" He sucked at Rock's bottom lip, purring low.

Rock winked. "Yep. Almost."

He pushed the sweats away from his prick, whimpering at the touch of Rock's skin.

There was that sexy growl. "There you go. Fucking perfect."

"Blue..." He shivered, pushing harder, eyes closing as he rubbed himself off.

"Right here, Rabbit," Rock murmured, licking at his lips, hands helping him move.

"Oh... So fucking hot. Made for this." His lips parted, he was gasping and panting, needing so bad.

Rock growled, the sound vibrating along his skin. His toes curled, cock jerking as he shot, shivering against Rock.

Rock's hands slid over his skin. "Nice."

Rig snuggled, breathing hard. "Uh-huh. Damn. Melted me."

"As usual." Rock sounded smug, happy and sated. Just about the perfect combination in his Blue.

"Mmhmm. Wanna snuggle and eat popcorn and watch shit explode?" He petted Rock's belly, humming softly.

"Fuck yes. Especially if there's more coming on tap."

"You can count on it. We got all night." He kissed Rock's shoulder.

"Popcorn, shit exploding, cocks exploding. Who could ask for anything more?" Rock gave him a wink and a grin and hauled them both up off the ground. "I'll even let you bring the blanket."

"You're so good to me, Blue Eyes." He grabbed the blanket and the last thing on his list.

Rock.

Check.

CHAPTER EIGHTEEN

Rig left Grimmy overnight at the vets, making himself ignore those sad little whimpers. The little shit had broken through the gate to the kitchen and dumped over the trash, grabbing a bunch of chicken wrapped in foil and eating it. Rig hadn't even cleaned the mess, just took one look at Grimmy heaving up blood, picked up his baby and ran like hell.

Doc Rogers said everything would be fine, that Grimmy would need a couple of days of observation, just to make sure.

Still.

Damn, he hated leaving those sad eyes.

Rig stopped and picked up some supper and headed home to clean the floor up, fix that fucking door gate, and fret over his pup.

Rock grunted as he came in. "Mutt all right?"

"Gonna be, yeah." He put supper on the coffee table and headed toward the kitchen. "He's unhappy, but the vet says he can come home in a few days."

Rock gave a grunt that might have been "good".

He got to the kitchen to find there was nothing for him to do. The garbage was cleaned up, so was the bloody puke. Hell, even the recycling was gone, out in the garage he presumed.

Rig closed his eyes and said a little prayer of thanks for a certain, blue-eyed marine. "You want a Coke, Blue, or a beer?"

"Whatever you're having'll do."

He grabbed two cokes from the fridge and headed back in, sitting down close enough to feel Rock's warmth. "Thank you."

Rock gave him another grunt -- marine speak for "you're welcome". A warm, solid arm came around his shoulders after Rock opened his coke. "You good?"

"Yeah. Little shit scared the life out of me, but I'm good." He leaned into Rock, toeing off his shoes, resting.

His shoulder was massaged, Rock drinking some Coke.

Rig let his eyes close, let himself relax. Let himself just feel those hands, listen to that sound of Rock's heart. Rock seemed content to just sit with him, to let him soak up comfort.

He must have fallen asleep, because he woke up with his head in Rock's lap, cheek resting against that sweet cock. "Mmm... smell good."

Rock chuckled. "That's because I showered while you were out."

Rig shook his head, rubbing that sweet prick. No. That smell was *Rock*. Rock's fingers slid through his hair, encouraged him to press his mouth against the bulge.

"Mmm..." He opened his mouth, licking and breathing hot air over that sweet prick before turning his head to breathe against the heavy nuts.

"Fucking sweet," murmured Rock, hands petting, sliding down to rub at his shoulders.

Yeah. Yeah, it was. Just about the closest thing to just right he knew. Rig kept blowing, kept rubbing, keeping the rhythm slow. Rock didn't try to hurry him, just kept touching him back.

Eventually just touching through the cloth wasn't enough, wasn't near enough, and he loosened the waistband of Rock's sweats, hunting for skin. That fat prick popped out eagerly, Rock's low moan sounding as it was freed. His own moan answered Rock, tongue sliding along the shaft. It jerked beneath his tongue and Rock's hips pushed up.

He took his own sweet time, licking and nuzzling and humming over that fat prick.

"Oh, Fuck, Rig." The hands in his hair tightened, and Rock's hips moved with little motions.

"Mmm... yeah." His mouth was open, the flavors of Rock filling it.

Rock's hand helped now, bringing his mouth down further. His head bobbed and he moaned, lips fastening around that cock and pulling, sucking.

"That's it. Oh fuck." Rock's hands held his head, his Blue's hips moving, pushing that fat prick in and out of his mouth.

He relaxed, opened up to it, took Rock deeper and deeper. Fucking flying. So fucking good. Rock roared suddenly and spunk shot down his throat. He swallowed Blue down, licking and lapping at that sweet cock, drawing out each tremor, each bit of sensation. Rock was practically purring for him.

Then one of his lover's hands slid beneath his arm

and tugged him up. "Come here, cowboy, let me have a taste."

He went easy, melting against Rock's strength, lips open for Rock's kiss. Fuck, yeah. One of Rock's hands slid into the back of his jeans, grabbing his ass, the other popped open his button and slid down his zipper, wrapping around his prick and tugging as Rock's tongue invaded his mouth.

Rig moaned, hips rocking sure and steady, thrusting up into Rock's touch. He fastened around Rock's tongue, pulling, sucking, fucking needing his man. Rock knew what he liked, knew how to work the tip of his cock and the back of the head with one thick thumb. He fastened onto those blue-blue eyes, gasping. Fuck. Fuck, yes.

The hand down his backside slid along his crease, the hand on his cock tightening, tugging harder. His orgasm hit him hard, sliding up his spine and slamming him in the back of the head as he shot.

Rock purred. "Sweet."

"Mmm... yeah. Is." He leaned in for a second, recovering. "Got amazing fucking hands, Blue Eyes."

"Not nearly as good as your mouth, but they'll do." Rock gave him a grin and a hug.

"They'll more than do." He kissed Rock's jaw.

"Good." Rock gave him another kiss. "You about ready to head to bed, see what else our hands and mouths can get up to?"

"Fuck, yes. You're the best thing that's happened to my ass all day." He grinned and took a kiss. Hell, Blue was the best thing that happened to his ass. Period.

"Well then you're in luck because I have plans for that ass."

"Fucking A." He stood and helped Rock to his feet. "Come on down the hall and tell me all about your plans. Keep me busy."

"Oh, I'll keep you busy all right. Keep you busy as long as you need."

Rock herded him toward the bedroom.

He followed, nodding. Two days. At least two days.

Then they could switch to celebrating Grimmy's homecoming.

Rig was a pretty upbeat guy, pretty even and Rock appreciated the lack of drama. Some days though, the man would come in like the world was on his shoulders. Rock would wait, see if there would be fucking or if Rig would disappear into his workshop and do shit with tools. Some days Rock took it out of Rig's hands.

This was one of those days.

He started growling the minute Rig came in, that haunted look in those grey eyes. He took Rig's arm and pulled his cowboy along the hall and into the bedroom, without a single word. Rig stumbled along behind, not fighting -- not following, but not fighting.

"Nothing fucking matters here but this," he muttered as they got to the bed and he grabbed Rig's crotch. He didn't let Rig answer, taking that sweet fucking mouth. Rig was stiff and still for a heartbeat, maybe two, and then a soft cry sounded, Rig melting in his arms. That long body wrapped around him, arms and legs holding him tight.

He growled. Yeah, that was it, just let it all go. He grabbed himself a double handful of ass and just kissed Rig hard. Rig opened to him, the stunned, haunted look fading into heat, want. Little sounds started -- the softest purrs and hums that were the start of what he was looking for. He growled some more and put Rig on the bed, following that sweet body down and starting in on the clothes.

"Oh, shit. Blue. I..." Rig tugged at his t-shirt, moaning low. "Been a bad day."

He growled, nuzzling Rig's neck as he got the scrub shirt off. "No talking. Just let me..."

"Mmm... 'kay." Rig stretched and rubbed, hands holding his head. He knew Rig wanted this, wanted the escape and heat as much as Rock needed to give it.

He worked Rig's pants off as he slowly made his way down to those sensitive as fuck titties, taking his sweet time, licking and sucking too softly to leave marks on his way down. Rig arched, hands fastening onto the headboard, nipples hardening into little stones under his tongue. Yeah. Fuck yeah. He pushed Rig's scrub bottoms off, wrapping his fingers around that sweet fucking prick.

"Blue! Hot! Fuck!" Rig's thighs parted, hips pushing that hard prick into his hand.

"Yeah, Rabbit, I got you now." He sucked hard on one of those little stone titties and tugged that sweet prick.

"Yes. Oh, Blue. Don't stop. Need it. Need you. Don't stop..." Desperate and needy, Rig rocked beneath him, hot and sweet and hungry.

"Not going to stop." He licked his way down to Rig's prick, lapping at the tip and then taking it in, letting his fingers play Rig's nipples.

"Fuck!" Rig went still, cock throbbing on his tongue, spunk spraying for him, his Rabbit wanting, eager.

He sucked it all down, took Rig's heat into him and lapped that prick clean and then worked his way down to lick at Rig's ball sac. Rig moaned, legs sliding on the sheets, slow and lazy, like he was swimming.

"So good. Blue."

"I know," he murmured, nosing Rig's balls out of the way, licking the skin behind them.

"Oh... Oh, fuck... Melt my fucking mind." Those long thighs parted for him, a sweet whimper sounding.

He just growled softly, hands pushing Rig's ass open, tongue finding that hot hole and pushing in, wanting that pure Rig taste. Rig's knee drew up, parting for him, offering him that tight little hole, not holding anything back. He plunged his tongue in, rumbling. Oh yeah, just take a taste, get Rig slick and then he was gonna slide his prick home.

Rig was babbling -- soft, nonsensical, drawled bullshit that meant nothing more than Rock had his Rabbit's full attention, that that quick fucking mind didn't care about a goddamned thing but getting fucked and feeling good. He fucked Rig with his tongue until that sweet little hole was quivering and wet.

There was lube under the pillow and Rock had himself slicked up as quick as anything and just like that he surged up, sliding home.

"Oh..." Rig's eyes went wide, lips parted and wet as that fucking tight body took him in, held him fucking close.

He purred, bending to take another kiss and then he started to thrust. Each motion was met with a low cry, a squeeze, a ripple of Rig's body, those long-fingered hands sliding over his body, stroking him, touching. He wrapped his hand around Rig's prick, holding himself up with the other, intent on sending his cowboy to the fucking moon.

"I... Oh...Oh, fuck. Blue. Yes. Good." Rig's body flushed, a low keening filled the air.

He nodded, grunted, filling Rig over and over again with hard surges into the tight body. Rig's eyes went wide, harsh, needy cries pushed right into the air, burning cock pushed right into his hand.

"That's it, Rabbit, come on my cock."

"Blue. Oh, Blue." Rig arched, throat working as his fingers were sprayed, that sweet cock jerking in his hand.

He roared, Rig's body squeezing him tight, pulling his own orgasm from him. He kept moving, keeping Rig shivering and shuddering through aftershocks.

Slowly Rig relaxed under him, eyes blinking slow, soft little moans sweet in the air. He pulled out slowly and then collapsed next to his skinny cowboy, one arm and leg over Rig. Rig snuggled in without a word, hand soft on his belly, cheek on his shoulder.

He grunted, pulled Rig a little closer.

Yeah. That was it.

He waited until Rig's breathing evened out, slowed as his Rabbit fell asleep and then he let go, snoring almost before he was asleep himself.

Rig was hotter than a two-dollar pistol, stretched out on the bed, one hand working his cock, the other pushing three fingers deep into his ass. It wasn't working as good as it would with Rock, but it would do.

For now.

Just to make his nerves stop buzzing.

Take the edge off.

"Hey now, I'm not sure whether to be pleased you're all ready for the main event or pissed you started without me."

Oh, he knew that growl, knew those blue eyes that were burning into him, Rock's focus clear.

"I need, Blue. So fucking much." Just the sound of that voice ratcheted him up higher, his heels digging into the mattress.

"I'm here and I've got what you need, Rig." Rock was working off his clothes, shirt stripped away just like that, pants opening up to reveal that fine, fine prick.

He licked his lips, nodding. "Yes. Fuck, yes. Please."

"Funny you should say fuck." Rock winked, kicked off his socks and his jeans and his shorts and then all those muscles were coming at him, Rock climbing the bed.

"Hey. So, so good to see you." He spread, offering Rock everything.

And Rock took it all, sinking into him with a groan, just like that. "Rabbit..."

"Yours. Oh, sweet fuck." His body just burned.

"Sweet? I was thinking more hard and deep." Rock was as good as his words, too, pulling out and thrusting back in nice and hard, fat prick going deep. His eyes rolled, hips bucking up, taking all Rock could give. Rock purred, hands landing on either side of his head as Rock leaned forward, finding a nice, hard rhythm.

Just what he needed. Just like that. So fucking *good* to him. Rig nodded, hips rocking furiously. Those blue eyes looked down into his, Rock's gaze never wavering as he moved harder and faster, driving into Rig.

Rig groaned, spunk just pouring out of him. "Yeah..."

A low rumble came from Rock's chest and that cock drove into him even harder, Rock's hips snapping. Then, with a roar, his Blue came, filling him with heat.

"Mmm... hell yes. So fucking good to see you."

Rock purred. "Nice to see you, too, Rig." Rock took a nice, hard kiss, tongue pushing deep into his mouth. "Good to feel you, too."

He nodded, rocking now, easy in his skin. Those low rumbles continued to sound in Rock's chest as Rock met Rig's movements, rocking slowly with him, cock just sliding nice and easy.

"Yeah, that's it. Oh, we can do this for days."

Rock tilted his head. "Will there be chocolate pie at the end of these days?"

"Two of 'em, Blue. With real whipped cream."

"Oh, then count me in." Rock nodded and shifted, cock dragging across his gland.

His eyes rolled, body going tight. "Oh. Good. Good."

"Right there," murmured Rock, sliding into him again, pushing that same spot.

He nodded, beginning to pant. "Yes."

Rock nodded and brought their mouths together, tongue sliding along his lips. Rig moaned, opening up, drawing Rock's tongue in. The sweet, slow fucking was echoed in the invasion of Rock's tongue, whole body just taking his, slowly, surely.

He melted, lost in the sensations, in the heat. In his Blue.

"Fuck, a man could die happy..." Rock sure wasn't dead though, body hot and hard and pushing into him.

"Live happy. Sweet fuck, I needed you."

Rock chuckled and shifted, finding that spot again. "Oh yeah, right fucking there."

"Yes!" His whole body went tight-tight, knees drawing up.

Rock's chuckles turned to purrs. "Love the way you love fucking."

"Love the way you fuck me." He did. Every fucking bit of it.

"Good. I'm not planning to stop anytime soon." No, his Blue could go all night, a fucking machine.

They moved together, rocking and sliding, the bed just creaking away. The noises were familiar, necessary as breathing. And those blue eyes... they just saw right though him. Rig smiled, hands sliding on his Blue, on the hot, strong shoulders. Rock rumbled, the sound vibrating against him, surrounding him.

That fat cock just kept pushing into him, over and over. Arching, he bucked, hips jerking, getting closer and closer. One of Rock's hands slid over his chest, tugging on his nipple before moving down to wrap around his prick. It moved up his spine, the heat just sliding through him, making him moan.

"That's it, Rabbit. Give it up. Let me feel it. Come on my cock."

"Blue." He nodded, spunk pouring from him.

"Yes!" Rock roared, jerking into him and then filling him with more heat.

Rig hummed, just melting, snuggling into the sheets. Rock let his weight down slowly, still buried deep, heavy and right on top of him. Oh, fuck yes. He snuggled right in.

Rock purred softly. "I don't know what got into you, Rabbit, but it can get into you again."

"Just needed. Bad." He hummed, so settled. "Needed you."

"You got me." No hesitation, just sure, solid words.

Rig nodded. "Thank you."

"My pleasure," He was kissed, Rock's mouth warm on his lips.

Oh.

Oh, hell yes.

Their pleasure.

He wandered in around three am, smoky and half-drunk, tired from dancing all night. There was lipstick on the collar of his good shirt and he smelled of cheap perfume and cigarettes and whiskey and his own sweat and sawdust and the coffee from that sweet little bartender that he got after closing time.

Damn, it had been a fun night.

He shushed Grimmy and let the big lug out to pee, humming low as he pottered in the kitchen, waiting to let the pup in. Then? Shower, shave, bed until tomorrow. Hell, maybe he wouldn't wake up until Rock did.

He heard steps in the hall and then the sound of pissing, the toilet flushing. Rig grinned, shaking his head. As much as that marine liked to sleep, God forbid someone open that front door and try to get past him.

Then the footsteps came down toward the kitchen and Rock grunted at him, his Blue naked as a jaybird.

"Hey, Blue Eyes." He wandered over, hands sliding right around Rock's waist as he snuggled into that heat with a happy sound.

Rock grunted again, arms coming around him, holding him close. "Fuck, you stink."

"Sorry. I was fixin' to jump in the tub after Grimmy does his business." Ah, romance, thy name was Rock. He grinned against Rock's shoulder, kissing the hot skin.

Rock nodded. "I could fuck you against the tiles."

"Mmm... You have the best plans." He reached out and let Grim in, then locked the back door. "Come on, Rocketman. Let's head that way."

"Yep." Rock let him go and headed down the hall, bare ass leading him to the bathroom.

He didn't even bother with that whole resist-touching thing, hands running over the most perfect body on earth as they moved, his cock filling enthusiastically. Rock rumbled for him, bending over and shoving that ass into his hands as the water was turned on.

Oh, man, what a quandary.

Love on the finest ass in history or get naked?

Ass.

Naked.

Naked.

Ass.

Mmm... Rock's naked ass.

He leaned down, nuzzling the small of Rock's back, hands rubbing. Rock's rumbles got loud enough to hear over the running water and the muscled legs spread for him, giving him access to the heavy balls and hard cock.

"Mmm..." He took a deep breath, moaning low at the scent of his Blue. His hands slid between Rock's legs, wrapping around cock and balls, exploring and petting.

Rock moaned and the water was shut off, his Blue's legs spreading wider, hands braced on the lip of the tub. He licked and nuzzled, humming low at the flavor of need and salt and Blue on his tongue. Rock just growled, rocking back into his touch. He knelt down, managing to work his shirt open as his tongue slid over Rock's hole, teasing.

"Oh fuck, Rig." A ripple went through Rock.

"Yeah, Blue." He pressed against that tight little hole, fingers trailing over Rock's inner thighs.

"That fucking mouth is something else, Rig."

He hummed and pushed harder, pressing his tongue into Rock, slowly fucking his Blue. A shudder went through Rock's body, his Blue moaning low. It made him hard as nails, made him fucking burn inside, knowing what he did to this man, knowing that Rock wanted him.

"Fucking magic." Rock grunted, pushing back against him.

His fingers wrapped around Rock's prick, pumping in time, hand sliding over the tip.

"Fuck! Yes!" Rock set to moving, back and forth, moaning and letting him know how good it was.

He groaned, tongue pushing deeper, faster, cock fucking throbbing against his zipper.

"Fuck. Fuck." Rock kept repeating it, over and over and finally shouting it as he shot.

Rig groaned, fighting to get his cock free from the tight denim, needing to come.

Now.

Rock was still moving, groaning as ripples went through him.

"Want you, Blue. Fuck." He stood up and tore his jeans open, prick rubbing against Rock's balls and thigh.

Growling, Rock turned and went to his knees, mouth sliding over Rig's prick.

"Oh, fuck! Rock!" He damned near screamed, head snapping back at the heat.

The sounds Rock was making vibrated along his cock, his Blue's tongue sliding against him. He didn't last any time at all -- not with Rock's flavor on his tongue, Rock's mouth on him. His entire body shuddered as he came, jerking into Rock's lips. "Sweet fuck..."

Rock pulled off him slowly and then smacked him in the ass. "Shower. You still smell like fucking shit."

"I do not. I smell like Teresa's cheap-assed perfume."

"Like I said..." Rock stood and gave him a wink, fingers pulling his buttons open.

He chuckled and nodded, helping in the getting naked business. "Going to sleep in with you tomorrow, I'm thinking. Spend the day lazing about."

One of Rock's eyebrows went up, but there was a grin pulling his Blue's lips up. "You feeling all right, Rabbit?"

He nodded, grinned back. "Yes, sir. I'm feeling just fine."

Just fine.

CHAPTER NINETEEN

Rock was flipping channels, feeling more fucking nervous than he had in a long time. Maybe since he'd first joined up and was getting his first verbal reaming from Sergeant Muldunk.

He just wished Rig's folks would get here already and then he could relax and Rig would stop fucking scrubbing anything that didn't move.

Rigger'd been at it for weeks -- ever since he'd found out his folks were coming to check out his new home and the man he'd left Texas for.

He'd never met anyone's parents before. Hell, he'd never known any parents that accepted the old swing the other way thing. Rig's parents not only accepted it, they wanted to meet him. He knew that because he'd offered to stay at the barracks while Rigger's folks came to visit and check out his new house.

But no, they wanted to meet him.

So he'd put on his best shirt and a nice pair of pants and was ready for inspection.

The damned dog started barking, tail going like crazy, as a truck pulled into the driveway. Rig appeared in the kitchen door, looking half-panicked, half-excited. "Is that them?"

He stood and stretched, flicking the television off and tossing the remote onto the lounge chair. "Either that or someone's using our driveway for a u-turn."

"Smart-ass." Those grey eyes roamed over him and he got a wide grin. "You look fine, Blue Eyes."

"You wanna fuck me fine, or impressing the parents fine?" He moved over to Rig, taking the tea towel from Rig's hands and tossing it back toward the kitchen sink.

"That shirt makes your eyes look gigantic and you're giving me wood fine." Rig's hips nudged up against his, proving Rig's words.

He snorted and bent, giving Rig a soft kiss. "You want me to let them in while you get that under control? Or should I send them away and we can take care of it properly?"

"Don't tempt me, Rocketman." Rig grinned, eyes hot and happy. "Let them in, I'll be right back."

The knock came to the door about the time Rig's fine ass disappeared into the bathroom. He rolled his eyes and squared his shoulders. Just pretend it's your old drill sergeant, Rocketman.

He opened the door and held out his hand. "Hello there, you must be Mr. and Mrs. Roberts. I'm Rock- Jim. Jim South."

He got a good look at exactly what his cowboy was going to look like in forty years -- grey eyes, high cheekbones, scarecrow thin, white curls kept short-short -- there was no question who Rig belonged to as

Mr. Roberts held out one tanned hand. "Jeremy'll do, I reckon. Pleased to meetcha, Jim."

As soon as his hand was released, he was met by a little, round woman in a t-shirt and jeans, short hair dyed a deep, dark red. "So, you're the one he left Texas for."

He stood a little straighter, thinking he'd never felt scrutinized this hard by any drill sergeant. "I guess I am, ma'am."

"He speaks highly of you. It's good to finally meet you." He was given a hug, his back patted. "Now, where's my baby?"

"Charlene, the boy's full grown."

"Tut... He's still my baby and I didn't drive for a weekend to miss out on a minute."

"Momma!" Rig's voice echoed, Grim giving a sharp bark. "How was the drive? Y'all have any trouble finding me?"

He grinned and stepped to the side. "You need help with your bags, sir?" he asked Rig's father.

"Bags? Nah, but the shit that my wife insisted on bringing y'all so Alexander's house was set up?" Jeremy rolled his eyes.

He chuckled. "That sounds familiar."

"Yeah, he's the apple of her eye. I reckon we'll keep him." He got a wink and then Jeremy was heading out to the truck.

And trailer.

There was a washing machine. A dryer. The ugliest sofa in the world. A doghouse. Boxes and bags and plastic containers full of God knew what.

He gave Jeremy a wry grin. "You folks moving in?"

"Hell, no. Lots of this is kitchen stuff and Alexander's tools. A lawn mower. Stuff he'd been collecting and hadn't had a place for. I found the washer and dryer at a place that was going out of business. Reckoned y'all might use 'em."

Rock nodded. "We appreciate it, sir, thank you. I can call a couple of guys from my unit over, get them to give us a hand."

"Damn, Daddy! You brought the farm!" Rig's laugh was low, happy, shaking his head as he wandered over. "Oh, man. My lawnmower. My lathe. Oh, is my skil-saw in here? I've been thinking on making more shelves for the front room."

To his amusement, Jeremy nodded, wandering over to the truck, pulling out some long pieces of pine. "Found these extra for you. Reckoned I could help get you set up and all. Your momma brought a cooler worth of food, too. Heard y'all couldn't get a decent brisket here."

Rock just shook his head and went to the back, started to haul stuff out to put in the garage. If they couldn't manage the heavier stuff on their own, he'd call the boys in tomorrow. It didn't take as long as he'd imagined, especially once Rig's Momma came outside to help and both her husband and her son busted their asses to make sure she didn't have too much to do.

He and Rig got the washer and the dryer settled in where Rig wanted them and then he offered Rig's father a beer. "And what about you, ma'am?" He peered into the fridge. "There's lemonade here if you don't drink."

"I'll take a beer, thanks, son, and quit with the ma'am shit. Call me momma." Charlene took the bottle he offered, drinking deep. "Unloading's thirsty work."

Rig was chuckling, shaking his head.

"Yes, ma-- Momma." He took a swig of his own. "Rig gonna give you the five cent tour?"

"Oh, now. I'm the mom. I get the quarter-show and tell and you get to pretend to enjoy doing it." She stood, slid her hand in his arm. "Lead on, son."

Both Rig and Rig's dad were chuckling now.

He shot Rig a help me look, but he wasn't getting any help at all. "You sure you don't want Rig to show you? He's better at this kind of thing."

"I'm sure. Alexander can answer any questions, after." She patted his arm. "I'm a little old lady, Jim, I don't bite."

"No ma'am, I didn't think you would." Much.

"Well this is the kitchen." He led her down the hall. "Bathroom here on the right. One bedroom on the left, another one up here on the right and the last one on the left here."

"What are y'all doing with the two spare rooms?"

Well, there. No question that they knew him and Rig were sharing a bed, was there? "Storage?"

Blue eyes twinkled up at him. "You've never even been in the rooms, have you?"

"Well, ma'am... no, I haven't." At least not after the initial fuck to make them part of home. Come on Rig, save me here.

"Rock's busy, Momma. He works hard." Rig sounded tickled, happy.

"Leave us alone, baby. Jim and I are touring."

He cleared his throat, unable to shake the feeling she was having a good old time at his expense. He supposed he should be grateful she didn't hate him because he was a man. "You want to see in the rooms, ma'am or go see the front room?"

"Oh, let's go see. I reckon my Jeremy and me will have to sleep in one or the other of them." Sure as shit, one of the rooms was set up with Rig's little old bed and a bedside table from somewhere. "Oh, baby, those curtains I sent worked perfect in here!"

Wow, it looked almost like a hotel room. "Yeah, not bad."

Rig's head poked in, Momma's cheek getting a kiss.

"Thanks for the curtains. The other room is Rock's. It's nowhere near as finished."

He gave Rig a surprised look. His?

Rig blushed a little, heading down the hall. "You kinda have to use your imagination."

The door opened to a decent sized room with an old weight bench and a heavy bag leaning against one wall, chains waiting to hang it. There was a stereo and an old chair, two big fans on the floor and one wall about half mirrored, the rest of the tiles in boxes. Three big old antique Marine posters were framed and hung, too.

Whoa. "It's like a home gym... this is pretty cool, Rig."

"Man needs a place that's just his, yeah?" Rig shrugged. "I'm putting the ceiling fans in next, thinking about a skylight. What do you think, Daddy?"

"Y'all get a lot of rain, son. You'd best seal it good."

"Thanks," he told Rig, silently promising a proper thank you later.

Rig nodded, gave him a grin, then went back to talking construction. Charlene nodded and urged him back down the hall, a soft, almost wistful look on her face. "So, Jim, what's your favorite thing for supper?"

"Well, I guess it's a cross between steak and pizza. Well and Rig's fried chicken's pretty good. And his Chili. Roast." He gave her a grin. "I guess you could say I like food ma-momma."

"Pizza makes Jeremy sick to his stomach, which is a damned shame, 'cause I love it. I vote we all go out and eat tonight and I'll put the brisket in the oven in the morning." They sat, Charlene settling with a soft sigh, stroking Grimmy's ears idly. "So, what all do you do in the service? Alexander says you work with explosives?"

"Yes, ma'am. Damn, I'm sorry -- 's natural as

breathing, that. I'm a Gunnery Sergeant. I shoot the big guns."

She chuckled, nodded. "Jeremy was a mechanic in the Army, lost his brother in an accident and mustered out. And now, look at my baby boy, almost military himself."

"That's right. Patches us up. Those medical flight crews are lifesavers."

"That suits him, then. That boy is stunning in an emergency. Goes all auto-pilot and practical." She tilted her head. "Course, you know that he sort of crumbles a little after, I guess?"

"I suppose I do." Not that he shared that kind of information. It was between him and his Rabbit.

She nodded, seeming to be satisfied. "Now tell me all about you, son. I know your birthday's in May, that you're a Yankee and you don't like vegetables except doctored up green beans."

"I'm not sure I even like doctored up green beans, unless Rig's been slipping them past me." He wasn't sure what to tell her, what she wanted to know. "Joined up when I was eighteen. I'm a lifer. I like football and beer and your son."

"It's a special kind of man, who can serve his country his whole life. I bet your momma worries on you."

"I don't know about that, ma'am." He got up. "Can I get you another beer?"

"No, one'll do me. Y'all have any iced tea?"

"I'll have to ask Rig."

Her chuckle sounded. "What does he have to ask you about, son?"

Rig's voice sounded. "Rock's not a tea drinker, Momma. He takes care of a whole different set of things."

"Like what?"

"Like me."

There was a long pause, then a "Well, I can't ask for more than that, baby boy. Did you make me tea?"

"Yes, ma'am. It's in the fridge. You need anything, Daddy?"

"I'll get you another beer, too, sir, while I get some tea for Rig's momma." He gave them a nod and hoped he wasn't bee-lining to the kitchen as bad as he wanted to. Rig's folks were nice, but it was weird, having them here, asking questions, sizing him up.

He'd gotten the fridge open, the tea pulled out, when hands slid up his spine, rubbing. "Hey, Blue Eyes."

"Hey." He put the tea on the counter along with three longnecks and closed the fridge door, turning to give Rig a squeeze. "You think they like the place?"

"I do. 's weird, having them here. Steakhouse for dinner, you think?" Rig's hand rubbed circles on his belly, slow and easy.

He nodded. "Your mom mentioned eating out. Said she liked pizza but your father can't eat it. They got decent pizza at the Steakhouse. Well, decent for a steakhouse." Though why anyone would want pizza when they could have steak at a place where they knew how to really do it right, he didn't know.

"Yeah, he's not much for tomato sauce and they have a great coconut cream pie. We'll have chocolate tomorrow." Rig was rambling, but those hands kept moving, kept touching.

He growled a little in warning. "Making me want, Rig."

Those grey eyes went wide, the touches stopping for a second. "Wasn't even thinking about it. Just wanted to touch."

"Yeah, well your momma's in the other room wondering where her tea is and I don't know if they like me well enough for us to play hide the salami in the kitchen."

Rig's laughter was warm, made him feel good. "No shit, Blue Eyes. Besides, Daddy's got a jammed up pistol he's trying to figure out how to ask you to look at."

"He should just ask. Though I suppose he had to wait for your momma to finish her interrogation." He gave Rig a wink and a hard kiss, then grabbed two of the beers and a glass of tea and headed back into the front room.

Rig's dad had settled on the sofa and was flipping channels, Charlene leaning against him, eyes closed. "It's hell when baseball's not well started and football's over."

"Amen to that, sir." He handed over Jeremy's beer and put Charlene's tea on the coffee table before settling in his chair. "Rig tells me you've got a pistol needs looking at?"

"Yeah, if you have a chance while we're here. My little Saturday night special is all gummed up and I can't see where the trouble lies."

Rock leaned forward, elbows on his knees. "You've broken her down and cleaned her? Oiled her up?"

He got a nod. "Replaced the firing pin, even. Damned thing's as twitchy as a virgin in a whorehouse."

"I'd be happy to take a look at her for you, sir."

"I'd be mighty grateful. Wouldn't mind seeing your collection either, get some advice from an expert."

"Well I hear you were in the Army yourself and you've a whole lifetime of caring for your weapons, but I'd be happy to help if I can." He nodded at Rig. "You want to go eat now, or can Jeremy and I go talk shop?"

Rig looked over at his momma. "You gonna wake her when you move or is she really napping?"

Jeremy grinned. "She's tired, son. Didn't sleep,

figuring it'd get her here faster.

Rig chuckled. "Well, then, y'all go on and talk. I'm going to arrange stuff in the garage. We'll have a late dinner."

"Cool. We'll try not to get in your way in the garage, Rig." He got up and led the way, already feeling more comfortable now that they had something in common and the topic was turning to it.

He just might survive his first meet the parents visit.

Dinner had been good -- easy and peaceful, Momma laughing over having pizza at a steakhouse, Daddy still crowing about how Rock had fixed his pistol, Rock rumbling and pleased over the praise.

They'd stopped at the video store on the way and picked up a couple of movies for the next few days, given that there wasn't shit on worth watching. Momma tried to get him to stop at the grocery, but Rig talked her into going in the morning, when she wasn't dragging so hard.

Rock was driving the Jeep, Daddy up front while he sat in back with Momma, the two of them talking away like they were old friends already.

"I like him, son. He's good people."

He nodded. "I told you he was, Momma. Didn't I say him and Daddy would get on like a house afire?"

Momma nodded, grinned. "Like your house, too. Nice and solid. A good place."

All of a sudden Daddy burst out laughing, Rock's lower chuckle sounding with it. He was proud enough to bust. He knew Momma'd come around to liking his marine, it was Momma's way. But Daddy? Was a tougher customer.

"Did I tell you Julia's expecting?"

He blinked, "Really? A baby? When?"

"October. So y'all will have a baby to hold when you're home at Christmas."

He grinned, nodded. He'd been waiting for the 'home for Christmas' lecture.

They pulled up next to the house, Rock parking the jeep in the street. "You always make plans this far in advance?" Rock asked as they made their way to the door.

"Son, you'd best just plan to spend Christmas at the farm. She's a barracuda that way." Daddy grinned, slipped out of the Jeep before Momma could pinch him.

Rock chuckled and let them all in. "Beer, Jeremy? Or something a little stronger?"

"I'll have whatever you're having, Jim." Daddy met Momma's eyes and she shook her head.

"Not after the pizza, Jeremy. I'll make a pot of coffee for me and Alexander."

Rock followed him to grab a couple of lowball glasses, dropping a kiss on the back of his neck while his Momma's back was turned, rubbing up against him a bit before heading back to the front room. He grinned, shaking his head and relaxing. Man, even Rock was doing okay. Life was good. He started the coffee, answering Momma's questions of 'where's this' and 'where do you keep that' while she got the brisket in to marinade. He could hear Rock and his Daddy talking, every now and then the murmurs turning to chuckles and laughter.

"I think you hit a winner, so far as your daddy's concerned." Momma salted the meat, then grabbed the garlic powder. "Is he good to you?"

He hid his smile, nodded. Good to him? Did bears shit in the woods? "You know it, Momma. I'm happy."

"Who's happy?" Rock asked, coming in. "We want munchies. Told Jeremy I was pretty sure we had chips and salsa."

Rig nodded. "There's some guacamole and sour cream, too, if y'all want it, or stuff for queso."

"Mmm, sounds great." Rock helped himself to the bag of chips and the sauces, balancing them all in his arms.

Momma laughed and grabbed the Velveeta and the Ro-tel. "I'll be out with the queso in a minute. Y'all don't start that movie without us, son."

"Yes, ma'am. I'll set it up though -- which one do you want?"

Rig laughed. "The Stallone one, Rock. She likes his butt."

"Jeremy Alexander Roberts! The things you say!" Momma blushed bright red, kept grinning though.

Rock looked shocked, nearly dropping his sauces. "O-kay." The man left in a hurry.

They started laughing, Momma giggling so hard tears started flowing. "Damn, Momma. I think we broke him."

"Hell, son, that would be a shame. He's a fine looking man."

"Yes, ma'am." Fine as fuck.

"We're about ready out here," Rock called.

"Fine-looking and pushy." She popped the queso in the microwave, wiping her eyes.

"He's a marine, Momma. That's how they come."

"Oh, right."

Rock appeared again, grabbing a couple more beers out of the fridge. "So we don't have to come back for them after the movie's started."

The brisket got shoved in the fridge, the queso pulled from the nuker and two Irish coffees made. "Come on, Momma. They're waiting on us."

Rock was sitting in his chair, leaning forward and talking with Daddy, who was at the near end of the couch.

The two of them had already made a dent in the chips, and their beer.

Rig took a chance, sitting on the floor near the coffee table, close enough to feel Rock's heat, but not too close, letting Momma have the sofa. Rock's hand dropped to his shoulder, solid and warm.

Oh. Yeah. He relaxed back as the movie started, grinning like a fool. Rock relaxed too, leg sliding against him.

It was... Good.

Home.

Pretty fucking cool.

Rock was half asleep by the time the movie was over. He might have been snoring, though he wouldn't admit it. He turned the TV off as the credits rolled, snorting when he realized the snores hadn't come from him but from Jeremy.

He wondered how many times Charlene'd made the man sit through this one. He knew he'd already seen some of Rig's old black and whites more times than he cared to remember.

"Bedtime?"

Rig nodded, hopping up and gathering up the dishes.

"Leave those, Rig. They'll be there in the morning."

"I'll just..."

"Son. Bed. It's late." Jeremy's voice was sure, firm, and Rock hid his grin as Rig nodded.

"Yes, sir."

"G'night, Jeremy, Charlene." Rock gave them nods and went and locked up. Front door, then back. Rig was heading into the bedroom as he walked down the hall, his cowboy yawning, stretching up tall.

He growled, keeping the sound nice and low. "Someone's looking fine."

Rig shivered, giving him a grin. "Love that sound, Blue Eyes."

"I've noticed that." He walked up behind Rig and nestled against that fine ass, pushing Rig into their room and closing the door. Rig leaned back against him, ass rubbing, rocking.

He growled again. "We gotta be quiet."

"Promise. I will. Want you." Rig's hands slid down his thighs.

"Yeah. Me, too." He tilted Rig's head and licked that spot on Rig's neck that made his Rabbit nuts.

"Oh..." Rig leaned forward, ass pushing harder against his cock.

"Slut," he murmured.

"Yours." The whisper was sweet, needy.

"That's right." He turned Rig's head, taking that sweet as fuck mouth, plundering it.

Rig turned the rest of the way, pushing close, hands working his shirt open. Not to be outdone, he went to work on Rig's clothes, pulling open the shirt, working his hands into those pants. The kiss got harder, sharper, Rig's tongue pressing deep. He redoubled his efforts in getting Rig naked, pushing the shirt right off, pulling down his Rabbit's pants. Once their clothes were gone, he pushed Rig onto the bed.

Rig groaned, legs sprawling, bouncing a little. He went for Rig's neck again, fingers sliding over those sensitive little titties.

"Drive me mad, Blue Eyes..." Those fingers were wrapped around his cock, pulling, pumping.

He jerked, hips pushing into that hand. "Ditto."

His hand slid under the pillows, finding the lube. So he slicked himself up and teased a finger around Rig's hole. Rig spread wider, nodding, sweet ass rocking, trying to take him in. He kept teasing, grinning down at Rig.

"Beautiful bastard." Rig was wriggling, panting, fingers fucking everywhere.

He chuckled and the sound was husky, wanton. Leaning down, he licked one nipple and then slid his finger right into Rig.

"Yes..." Rig arched, then started riding his finger.

Fucking sexy.

The sexiest fucking man ever, that was his Rig.

He slid another finger alongside the first, letting Rig feel it, giving him something a little thicker to ride. That got him a groan, Rig's whole body rippling, a low moan splitting the air.

"Shh," he warned, free hand sliding over Rig's mouth.

Rig nodded, mouth opening, taking two of his fingers in and sucking.

So fucking sexy.

He swallowed his own moan, angling the fingers inside Rig, searching for that little gland that would make Rig fly. When he found it, Rig's eyes went wide, the suction of that mouth getting stronger, almost fierce. He stroked it again and again and then pulled his fingers from Rig's mouth and slid those in next to the other two. Rig's teeth sank into that bottom lip, hands wrapping around the headboard as his Rabbit rode him, cock slapping against that flat belly.

His own prick was hard as nails. The need to plow into the tight heat that gripped his fingers was strong, but he waited, letting Rig ride his fingers.

Rig moved, eyes watching him, fastened on him. "Fuck me. Need your cock."

He nodded; he wasn't going to make Rig ask him twice. His fingers slid away, hands moving to grab Rig's hips as he pushed his cock into the tight heat. Rig leaned up, hid the low cry in their kiss, hips moving furiously, riding him. Growling into Rig's mouth, he thrust, meeting that skinny body with his own need.

No one needed like his Rabbit, his cowboy, his own personal slut. That body gripped him like a fist, squeezing and working his cock. He slid one hand from Rig's hip to wrap around Rig's swollen prick, making a tight tunnel for that heat to pass through. Rig pushed a whimper into his lips, those eyes fastened on him, bright and needy. He moved harder, faster, giving his Rabbit everything.

When Rig came, he felt it all around his cock, tight and sure and hotter than anything. His roar filled Rig's mouth as he pushed in hard one last time and came. Rig's arm circled him, holding him close as they rode out the aftershocks. He stayed buried deep, letting Rig hold his weight for awhile, just resting in the sweet, sated sensations.

Rig relaxed, holding on, octopussing and snuggling close. He shifted slightly, enough to be supporting most of his own weight and then let his eyes close, his body relax completely.

"Night, Blue." Rig reached out, turned off the lights.

He purred, nuzzled. "Night."

Rig kissed his chin, the sensation chasing him down into sleep.

Rig watched Momma and Daddy drive off, the old pickup rattling as they backed out of the driveway. The housewarming visit had been productive – besides the used washer and dryer, there was a lawnmower and a weedwhacker. Momma'd brought a bunch of plants and some of the old furniture from Pappy's house, along with eight huge boxes of kitchen stuff. Daddy'd brought some old tools. Sissy'd sent along a bunch of linens and towels.

It was sort of like heading off to college the first time, but cooler, because there was a handmade gun case for Rock and Momma'd clucked over the state of Rock's civvies and taken Rock shopping.

At Wal-Mart.

While him and Daddy sat at home and *laughed*.

The screen door opened. "You gonna watch until the sun goes down?"

He grinned, shook his head. "Nope. Just watching 'em go."

Rock squinted. "Well either I need my eyes checked or they're gone. Come on in."

The smell of pot roast floated out, Momma insisting on starting it before they left. He came in the house, moving right into Rock's space. As soon as the door closed Rock's arms came around him and he was given a long kiss. Oh. Oh, that felt just about perfect.

He pushed closer, moaning into Rock's lips, hands sliding around Rock's neck. "Hey."

"I like your folks well enough, Rig, but I fucking missed your ass while they were here."

Oh. Now that felt even better. His belly felt hot and good and he put that pleasure into his kiss, tongue sliding into Rock's mouth, taking a deep, slow taste. Rock's big hands slid right down to his ass, tugging him in against that hot, hard body.

"Oh... Yeah." He just sort of melted, eyes closing halfway. "Damn."

"See what I mean?" muttered Rock, mouth sliding over the skin of his neck.

"Uh-huh. Don't stop." He slid his hand down Rock's belly to cup that fat prick.

"I won't if you won't," growled Rock, hands kneading his ass, tongue licking every bit of bared skin.

"Deal." Rig worked the button open on Rock's jeans, hunting cock.

Rock's fingers were busy insinuating themselves into the back of his jeans, so fucking hot against his skin. His fingers found Rock's prick, dancing over the tip and gathering the drops there. Whimpering, Rig brought his hand up, licking his fingers before sliding back down.

"Fuck." Rock slammed him up against the wall, mouth taking his in a no holds barred kiss.

The fucking room started spinning, his hands shoving Rock's pants down so he could grab hot flesh. Rock was humping against him, rubbing their bodies together hard. Fuck, Rock blew his fucking mind like this, hungry and hard and hot against him, fucking devouring his mouth and driving him insane.

Rock roared, spunk spraying all over his hand. He brought his hand up, licking at it, moaning and jerking as he shot, toes fucking curling.

Rock growled, hoisting him up as soon as he'd come and carting him back toward the bedroom. He held on, tongue sliding along Rock's jaw, legs wrapping around Rock's waist.

"Gonna fuck you into the fucking mattress," muttered Rock.

"Yeah. Please. Want you, Blue Eyes." He nipped Rock's ear, moaning. "Need it."

"You're gonna get what you need." Rock got them to the bed and got them stripped before pushing him down with that big, hot, hard body.

"Always." He tilted Rock's head and took a kiss, tongue pushing deep. "Fucking *always*."

"You know it."

Rock's fingers slid into his body, two wide, slick

fingers, stretching him. They rubbed together, shoulder to hip, rocking and sliding, his pleasure intense, sweet.

"Can't fucking wait," muttered Rock, fingers sliding away, his Blue shifting until that thick prick waited at his hole.

He nodded, arching until his hole stretched over that fat cockhead, sucking Rock right in.

"Fucking Christ." The words were little more than a moan, pleasure painting his Blue's face.

"Good." He held on, watching as he fucked himself on Rock's prick, sliding sure and steady, filling himself.

Rock let him do it, watched, arms starting to tremble with the effort not to take over. He whimpered, pushing harder, riding that sweet cock, crying out. With a growl Rock started to thrust, fucking him hard and fast, fucking him right through the mattress. He cried out, fingers digging into Rock's shoulders, hips slamming against his Blue's.

"That's it, Rabbit, that's it." Rock kept on thrusting, looking like he wasn't ever going to stop.

He would have warned Rock he was going to shoot, going to fucking explode, but he couldn't speak, couldn't catch his breath, couldn't do a fucking thing more than ride his lover, his orgasm starting at the base of his neck and sliding down.

"Fucking perfect," murmured Rock, nailing his gland.

The world fucking stilled when he came, body convulsing with pleasure that just slammed through him like a fucking freight train. Rock kept moving into him, pulling shudder after shudder out of him before Rock roared, filling him with awesome heat. He just sort of collapsed, gasping, entire fucking body dissolved.

Rock came down on top of him, breathing heavily. "Needed that."

"Uh-huh." He held on, petting and humming softly.

Rock slid out and shifted to lie next to him, one solid leg thrown over his. Snuggling close, Rig's cheek found its place on Rock's shoulder, hand petting Rock slow and easy. Rock rumbled, the sound happy and good, right.

It wasn't long after that the familiar snores started.

Rig settled in, eyes falling closed. It'd been good to see Momma and Daddy, right enough, but damn, it was nice to just be them at home again.

CHAPTER TWENTY

Rock growled as he pulled into the driveway beside Rig's Jeep. His skin fucking ached. Twelve straight hours in the fucking sun wearing nothing but his skivvies. The baby-greens were fucking lucky tomorrow was the start of a three-day pass for him or he'd be taking their heads off. As it was, he was pretty pissed off he had three free days and couldn't move without wincing.

He manhandled his pack into the house, letting it thump in the hallway and started to strip, his fucking uniform chafing the hell out of his red skin.

"Oh, man... Blue Eyes... Damn..." Rig's voice was sympathetic, floating from down the hall. "Go hop in the tub and I'll grab the vinegar and the aloe. Shit, that looks like it hurts."

"I've felt better." He actually felt better just getting home, knowing Rig was gonna take care of him. Rig was good for that.

"I bet. We'll fix you up." By the time he'd made it into the bathroom, Rig was there with a huge glass of ice water and the bottle of white vinegar and big assed tube of aloe vera gel. Rig handed him the glass, then bent to start the water, giving him a sweet look at that barely covered ass.

He made an appreciative noise, reminding his cock he was in no shape for anything other than sitting still. The water was cold and refreshing in his throat, better than the beer he'd been wanting all day.

"Finish that glass up and I'll get you another and an aspirin for your head." A generous plop of vinegar poured into the bath and he eased into it, the tepid water almost too cold to his skin.

"You pickling me?" he asked.

"Drawing the heat out." There was something about his Rabbit in full nurse-mode -- focused and sure and fucking sexy as hell. "You ready for another glass of water?"

"Sure." He handed over the glass, watching Rig. "This'd be more fun if you were naked, too."

Rig filled his glass up and handed over two aspirin before shimmying out of those short shorts. "Better?"

"Yep." He took the aspirin and then reached out, hand sliding along one warm thigh.

"Mmm..." Rig spread for him, grey eyes shining down at him. "Love your hands."

He grinned, sliding his hand between Rig's legs and cupping his Rabbit's balls. "Yeah?"

"Yeah." Rig grinned, that cock starting to fill, curving just slightly.

"Well that's a good thing, as my hands might just be all you're going to get tonight."

"I'll live. You just soak and let that heat go." Rig

tsked over him, stroking his hand. "What were y'all doing?"

"Fucking 'teambuilding' games." He growled. He hated them under the best of circumstances. "Split into fucking groups -- half of us wearing shirts, half not. CO didn't fucking end it until Banting had fucking blisters."

"They ought to know better. Who was your field medic and why the hell didn't he say something?" Rig rumbled and fussed. Nothing pissed Nurse Roberts off like medical stupidity.

"He did. CO told him to fuck off." He settled back against the cool ceramic, enjoying being pampered.

"Sorry motherfucker." Rig growled and knelt near the tub, slowly pouring handfuls of water over him, the soft splash feeling so good.

"Yeah, he is." He groaned. "Fuck that's nice."

"Mm... good. Just relax. When you're done soaking I'll lube you up and order something for supper." Rig's ministrations never stopped, the water always moving, always cooling his skin.

He chuckled. "I like it when you lube me up."

Rig chuckled, "And I'll never turn down an excuse to get at your bod, so we're even."

"I'm all yours. Especially if you work your magic." He was already feeling better, in fact.

"That's my job, Blue Eyes." Rig leaned over, licked his lips. "Beautiful son of a bitch."

He took a kiss. "Boiled lobster's more like it today."

"Mmm... you're already looking better." Rig gave him another kiss, slow and sultry.

"Feeling better too," he murmured.

Rig purred, one hand sliding down to circle his cock. "Feel fucking great, Rock."

"Fucking A." He groaned, hips pushing his prick up into Rig's hand.

"Be still, let me take care of you." Rig's lips were soft on his cheek, his ear. "Mmm... such a sweet, fat cock."

He settled back down with a happy moan. "All for you."

"Oh, yeah." Rig's tongue slid over the edge of his ear, hot and wet. "So fucking good."

Oh, fuck, this was almost worth the sunburn. Another pump of his cock had him changing his mind -- it was definitely worth the fucking sunburn. Rig kept moaning and pumping and licking, whispering perversions into his ear, eyelashes tickling his skin. Fucking awesome. He was a lucky fucking man.

"Gonna get the edge off, then I'm going to slick you up, feed you and suck you until your balls are dry. Nurse Roberts' guaranteed sunburn remedy."

He groaned, prick jerking in Rig's hand.

"That's it, Blue Eyes. So fucking hot, my fucking studly old man."

"Fuck! Rig!" He came hard, spunk spraying over Rig's hand.

Rig took his mouth in a long, hungry kiss, making a load of promises that made the shitty team-building and sunburn so fucking worth it.

He was almost breathless by the time Rig was done. "About time you lubed me up, isn't it?"

"Oh, yeah. Let's get you up and lubed and settled with another glass of water." Rig took one last kiss.

He let Rig help him up and dry him off, hands groping and feeling his Rabbit up.

Rig chuckled, wriggling those hips and teasing. "Come on, marine. Let's get you nice and slick. If you're a very good jarhead I'll make you a steak for supper."

"I can be good." He gave Rig a wink as he pinched that fine ass. "Of course it depends on your definition of good."

"Well, last I checked, my definition had a lot to do with access to that fine cock of yours, so I reckon we'll be okay there."

"You reckon so?" Rock asked, drawling the word like Rig had, teasing his cowboy.

"I do, Yankee. I surely do." Those grey eyes shone over at him and Rig grabbed the aloe.

"Where do you want me?" He knew it was a leading question, he asked it anyway.

"Everyplace I can have you, Rocketman. But right now? Bed so I can slather your studly fucking self with green goo."

He chuckled, following that sweet fucking ass. "That's the latest sex craze with you nurses, is it? Green goo?"

"Oh, yeah, baby!" Rig laughed, sashaying down the hall. "Goo me, lover!"

He sped up just enough to catch Rig as he reached the door to the bedroom, goosing that smartass.

Rig squeaked and jumped, hand squeezing the tube, aloe gel pouring over Rig's fingers. Rig started laughing, eyes just dancing. "You made the goo spooge, Rock!"

"That's because I'm a Class A Stud." He grabbed Rig around the waist, ignoring the tightness in his skin and pulling Rig close.

Rig nodded, lifting his face for a kiss as cool, slick hands rubbed over his skin. Oh, fuck that felt good. He groaned, eyes closing as he lost himself in the fucking heat and cool of Rig's mouth and gooey hands. Rig moaned into his lips, cock sliding against his own, hot and hard, wet at the tip.

"Fucking sexy motherfucker," he murmured.

"Yours. Fuck, you taste good. Make it hard to remember I'm supposed to be rubbing stuff *in*, not rubbing off *on*."

He chuckled, moaned. "I'm more interested in the latter than the former myself."

"Oh, thank God." Rig bit his bottom lip, pushing closer, hips rubbing a little harder, a little faster. "Need you. So fucking hot."

"Yeah, I'm on fire." He laughed as he said it, horny and wanting. He pushed Rig back onto the bed, following that sweet body down.

Rig arched beneath him, all long neck and legs separated by lean belly.

"This stuff good for more than just sunburn?" he asked, holding Rig's slick hand up.

"Oh, yeah. All slick. All natural." Rig's eyes were hot, hungry.

"Then get yourself ready to ride, cowboy."

"Oh, fuck. Yes." Rig's teeth sank into that full bottom lip as that long hand pushed between them, sliding behind Rig's balls.

"Fuck yes."

Shit, his Rabbit was the sexiest motherfucker... His cock twitched hard and he groaned, sunburn forgotten.

"Uh-huh. Oh. Oh, Blue..." Rig's eyes closed, eyelids drooping.

"Take all the time you need, but hurry," he instructed, eyes on Rig's fingers and they disappeared into that fine, fine ass.

"Need you. Fuck, Blue. In me. Now." Rig's balls tightened, muscles in that flat belly rippling.

He bent and took a kiss and then settled between Rig's legs, nudging Rig's fingers with his cock. Rig's fingers wrapped around his prick, sliding his tip over that tight little hole.

"Fuck." He groaned, pushing in, sliding in deep.

"Yes!" Rig's hands wrapped around his hips, pulling him hard, holding on tight. He loved that, loved that Rig never made you wonder if he really wanted it.

He grinned down at his lover and started fucking. His Rabbit moved with him, not holding a fucking thing back, all about the sensation and the heat they were making between them. It was hotter than any sun, burning away everything but those grey eyes and the fucking tightest heat. Rig planted his feet on the bed, pushing up hard into him, eyes fastened on him like he was the center of the fucking universe.

Harder and harder he thrust, the need settling in his balls, making him ache.

"Oh..." Rig's shoulders left the mattress, ass grinding down against him. "Yeah... There, Blue."

"Yeah, I know what you need." He thrust again and again, nailing Rig's gland.

"Always. Oh, fucking hell. Always."

Rig's mouth crashed against his, his Rabbit crying out as spunk sprayed between them. That sweet ass fucking squeezed him tight and he shot deep, groaning into Rig's mouth as he let Rig have it all.

Rig's fingers stroked his ass, careful not to touch his back. "Mm... 's good."

"Yep." He pulled out and lay down carefully next to his Rabbit, grunting at little at the sheet against his skin.

"Roll over on your belly, Rock. Let me get this aloe on you. It'll feel good."

"You just want to have your wicked way with me," he teased, rolling easily enough.

"Yep." Rig didn't sound the littlest bit sorry, either, straddling his ass and squirting the cold gel on his burning skin.

"It's yours," he groaned.

"Lock, stock and barrel." Those hands started sliding, spreading the cold and the relief over his back.

"Among other things," he murmured, eyes starting

to drift shut.

"Mmhmm." Rig's voice was soft, gentle as those hands.

"You still owe me a blow job and a pizza." He wasn't sure he said it out loud though, finally succumbing to the fucking heat and falling asleep.

He'd danced all damned night -- two-stepped and waltzed and three-stepped and schottisched and even did some of those line dances. He was happy and three-quarters drunk and sweaty and a little bit hungry and more than ready to park the Jeep and be home.

Damn, sometimes it was fun to be a redneck.

Rig headed out of the club and toward the car, humming along with the song in his head, thinking about getting home and getting some from the big, muscled, sexy, blue-eyed, not dancing stick-in-the-mud he lived with. He made his way home - after stopping at Jack in the Box for a bite to eat and a coke, the gas station for a pack of smokes for the glove compartment and five dollars in gas, the twenty-four-hour grocery for dog food and donuts and another Coke.

Hell, by the time he got home? He was damned near sober. He grabbed Grimmy's food and the donuts, whistling as he let himself in. Grimmy met him at the door, tail wagging like mad, making soft whining, happy sounds. Over that he could hear the quiet murmur of the television and Rock's low snores.

"Hey, sweet baby. I got you some kibbles at the store. You been a good pup?" He nudged Grimmy back and locked the door, Grimmy's tail beating him half to death. Poor baby. Stuck in the house with Rock.

"Come on, pretty boy. I'll give you some."

Rock's growl called out to him, low and sexy. "That

better be me you're propositioning and not that spoiled mutt."

"He's not spoiled..." He chuckled, and put his stuff on the kitchen table. "I brought you donuts."

"A midnight snack, cool." The sound of the TV went off. "Shit, Rig, it's dammed near morning."

"Yeah. We closed the club down and I was feeling my beers, so I ate, then I needed ci...gas and then I remembered Grimmy needed food." He poured Grimmy some kibbles and Rock some milk to go with the donuts. "Had a good time. Danced my ass off plumb off."

Rock grunted. "Better come here and let me check on the state of it, then."

Rig grabbed the donuts and headed into the front room, handing them over before settling close. "Hey, Blue Eyes. Have a good evening?"

"I'm feeling very rested." Rock bit into a jelly doughnut and made one of those fuck it's good, but my mouth is full noises, lips covered in powdered sugar. "Now that you're home I can get unrested."

"Mmm..." Rig leaned in to lick the sugar off Rock's lips, making sure he got every single bit. "Taste good."

"Of course I do." Those blue-blue eyes were wicked.

It made him shiver and he leaned in for another taste. "Always." Sexy bastard.

Rock gave him a grin and pushed grey sweats down over that fat prick. "There's the real flavor."

"Mmm... Is that all for me?" He grinned and leaned down, lips sliding along the filling shaft. Hot, beautiful, pushy, sexy bastard.

"You know it. Been saving it up special." Rock groaned for him, fingers sliding through his hair.

"Yummy." He purred the word, tongue sliding over one throbbing vein, then up to flick over the ridge at the tip.

"Oh Fuck, yes." Rock pushed up for a moment and then spread his legs, shifting and settling until his Blue was right where he wanted to be.

He toed off his boots and got comfortable, stretched out and happy. He took his own sweet time, licking at those heavy balls, rubbing the shaft with his cheek, loving that prick with all he had. Rock didn't try to hurry him, just rumbled and growled and petted him.

God, he was happy.

He fucking loved this -- loved the long, slow touches, loved the salt on his tongue. Loved the scent and heat of Rock all around, and those growls?

Damn.

"Love your fucking mouth." Rock's thumbs slid along the edges of his mouth, played with his bottom lip.

He grinned and slid those fingers in alongside Rock's prick, sucking with a slow, easy rhythm. Rock rumbled and kept the motion of those fingers going on his prick, meeting his lips again and again. His cheek was sliding against Rock's belly, fingers moving to roll and cup those balls. So fucking sweet. Rock's legs spread wider, giving him more room, better access.

The sun was thinking about coming up, filling the front room with that weird pre-morning light and he closed his eyes, focusing only on how Rock tasted and sliding his finger back to play with that tight little hole. Rock started moving, hips just barely pushing up to slide that prick a little further into his mouth and then back down against the pressure of his finger.

Pleasure moved right on through him and he purred, pulling a little harder, adding another finger in that tight hole. Rock jerked and those big hands went to his head again, holding him in place as Rock started to fuck his mouth. His own cock was hard as nails, rubbing against the denim of his jeans, throbbing with every push of Rock's hips.

Rock was grunting, rumbling and growling, pushing harder now, rocking up and down, cock getting even harder in his mouth. He relaxed his throat, letting Rock in all the way, fingers curling to peg Rock's gland, wanting to make his lover fly.

Faster and faster Rock fucked his face. "Rig!" The sound of his name was a moan and then heat poured down his throat, Rock's body gripping his fingers tight.

Bitter salt and hot and pure fucking Rock. He drank his Blue down, easing his fingers free, tongue drawing out each little aftershock. Rock purred for him, the sound happy, sated, as the fingers in his hair gentled. He slowly let Rock slide free, cheek resting on that warm, soft skin.

"Fucking love that mouth, Rig." Rock's fingers slid over his swollen lips again, sweet rumbles coming from his Blue.

He nibbled and sucked the tips of those fingers, blinks coming slow as his body noted it had been dancing for seven hours and up all night and damn, it was tired.

"You needing, Rabbit?" Rock asked, tugging him up.

He went easy, moaning and pushing against the broad chest. "You? Always."

Rock purred, and one big hand wrapped around his prick. "Let's just take care of this and go to bed -- I'll fuck you when we wake up."

"Mmm... Yeah..." He nuzzled into Rock's neck, moaning low, hips just barely moving. It felt like swimming in warm water -- felt so good.

Rock's free hand was on his butt, hot and holding him close while the other worked his prick, thumb sliding across the tip. Oh, fuck. Just what he needed. He licked and nuzzled, toes curling.

He was almost asleep as he came, spunk pouring over Rock's fingers. He felt like he was floating, lying on a cloud and traveling through the sky and then he was in bed, jeans tugged the rest of the way off and Rock's body warm against him.

Rig snuggled right in, hand curled on Rock's belly, head on Rock's shoulder. Before he knew it, he was dreaming and dancing with his Rocketman and laughing.

There'd been a spot of trouble on base and the CO had kept them late, dressing them all down but good. It didn't matter that it hadn't been their unit that screwed up, everyone got to stink of shit with this one. At least they'd been spared making that literal with fucking latrine duty.

It put him in a hell of a mood though and he pulled into the drive beside Rig's Jeep with a deep need to work off some of his frustration. A few thousand or so push-ups would do it. And if they didn't, there were always sit-ups, running and a case or two of beer.

He jogged up the stairs, ready to growl at Grim to keep the dog from being too friendly.

He slammed open the door and Rig looked up from cleaning a pistol, brushes and oil and parts on the coffee table. "Hey, stranger. How's it hanging?"

His reply was a growl. He didn't feel like making fucking small talk.

One white eyebrow raised and Rig went back to work. "There's hamburgers and chips in the kitchen for when you want them."

He grunted and headed for the backyard to do some pushups. He'd done four reps of twenty when Rig came out, two longnecks in those long fingers. Nothing was said, two tops were popped, one set down close enough for him to reach. He did another two reps and then sat up and took a long haul, draining over half the bottle.

"Thanks."

"Anytime." Rig nodded to him, eyes quiet. "A nice long fuck and a massage might cure your ills. When you're ready, I'm here."

His prick perked up. "That's the best damn thing I've heard all fucking day."

"You want to start in the shower or the bed?"

He gave it a half a second's thought. "Shower so I can get the stink of shit hitting the fan off me."

He got a quick nod and Rig stood up. "I'll get the water started."

He watched that fine ass go as he finished his beer, feeling about one hundred and ten percent better already. He followed slowly, shedding clothes as he went. Rig was naked, steam filling the air by the time he got to the bathroom, a bottle of massage oil heating in the sink. Make that two hundred and ten percent better.

He stepped in with Rig, moving up behind his cowboy, pressing his hard prick along that fine, fine ass.

"Mmm..." That tight little butt rubbed against him, eager.

He nibbled at Rig's neck, sucking the water off warm skin. His Jackrabbit spread for him, hips canting, offering him that tight little hole, that hard little body. He reached over and got the soap, slicking up his fingers and pressing one into Rig.

"Mmm... Good." Rig started moving, humming, body moving in and out of the steam.

Always so fucking eager, no matter the flavor of their loving. He growled happily, the day's irritations fading completely as one finger became two. Rig opened for him, took him in and then that long body begged for more. He slid his fingers out and his cock in, groaning at the tight, grasping heat. Rig reached up, grabbed the showerhead, body tightening, fucking rippling around his cock like mad.

He wrapped his own hands around Rig's hips and started to fuck, pulling Rig back onto each thrust. Rig's ass worked him, the long back muscles rolling as Rig gave as good as he got. He kept it going for a good long while, letting it build and build and build. Then he wrapped his hand around Rig's prick, pulling in time.

"Mmm... Fuck, yes. Rig's hips sped the rhythm, head falling back on thin shoulders.

He nuzzled Rig's neck, pushing hard, pulling harder. A flush traveled down Rig's spine, the heat and tightness of the orgasm beginning deep inside his Rabbit, around his cock.

"Yeah, that's it -- come on my cock." He pushed in hard, prick sliding over Rig's gland.

"Oh... oh, fuck. Blue!" Rig jerked, entire body fucking rippling for him as spunk filled his hand.

He groaned, pushing in again and filling Rig with heat as he came. He stayed buried deep, head on Rig's shoulder, hand petting Rig's belly. Rigger hummed, not saying a word, just letting him lean a minute.

They stood together until the hot started running out and then he grunted, sliding from Rig's body, leaving a kiss on his Cowboy's neck and getting out of the shower. The water ran for a second longer and then Rig got out, wrapping a towel around slim hips. The oil was grabbed, along with his hand, and he was led to the bedroom.

"Best mouth in the Americas, fucking awesome hands, you cook, you clean. Is there anything you can't do, Rig?"

Grey eyes met his, dead serious. "Yeah, Blue. Tons. But that's what I've got you for, yeah? Get in the bed and let me at those sweet fucking muscles."

"My pleasure." He climbed into the bed with a groan. Oh, this was going to be good. Maybe almost as good as the fucking.

A warm weight settled on his ass right before the heated oil trickled along his spine. Those hands started working him, Rig distractedly humming whatever tune was playing through that cowboy brain. He just closed his eyes and floated there, caught between the bed and warm skin, Rig working his muscles.

Rig's quiet meaningless chatter started up after a while. Nothing he had to focus on, really, or even listen to -- it was just random comments about Rig's day, what came in the mail, a new truck that was coming out. Rig didn't expect him to answer. Hell, with those fingers finding spots of tension he didn't even know he had? Rig better not expect anything but the occasional rumble.

He was almost asleep by the time Rig asked him to turn over and he flopped over with a smile. "Good to me."

"Yep." Rig started with his feet, thumbs pushing deep into his arches, finding pressure points and working at them.

He groaned, absolutely fucking melting. Rig's lips preceded those fingers, soft, little brushes of kisses before the hard, rubbing touches. Okay, so maybe he wasn't *entirely* melted.

His legs, his hips, his chest -- everything was touched. Hell, his Rabbit massaged his fucking *hands* and it was sheer fucking magic. Then those hot fingers touched his jaw, his temples, his face. Damn. He was practically fucking purring, torn between utterly boneless and perfectly horny. Then Rig shifted, ass sliding back down on his prick, rocking slow and sweet, all tight heat and perfect fucking pressure clasped around him.

He moaned, the sound coming from deep inside him. This had to be what heaven was like or he just wasn't fucking interested in it. Those hands never stopped touching, just slid and stroked, drawing the pleasure out between them. "So fucking sexy, Blue Eyes. Fucking made to touch you."

He purred and rumbled, too fucking gone to speak.

A slow, deep, mind-blowing kiss stole his breath, those grey eyes focused on him, smiling for him. He nodded, licking at Rig's lips, silently begging another kiss, mind about blown, body a half step behind. He got one. Then another and another and then he was flying, this whole thing so much more than fucking.

At some point it slid into coming and he was filling Rig with heat, the feeling starting in his toes and his fingers and just taking him over. Rig settled against him, humming low, fingers curled against his belly. He wrapped one arm around Rig, the other slid with his Rabbit's fingers. Fucking perfect.

Who needed a workout -- he had Rig.

CHAPTER TWENTY ONE

Rig pulled into the driveway, singing with the radio. Thank God for Fridays. They'd had a long fucking week, lots of training and brass on post, but now it was three nights and two days of relaxing and fucking and beer and maybe a bit of Frisbee with Grimmy.

He grabbed his shit and the beer. Not only that -- it was Rock's night to cook. Hallelujah.

Grimmy was barking as he got to the door. "Evening, marine. Happy Friday!"

"Hey, Rigger." Rock came to meet him, gave him a kiss, opening his lips, but not making it deep. "Got company."

He arched an eyebrow, giving Rock a curious look. "Must be damned friendly company. Anyone I know?"

"You remember I told you about the new kids we got in on Monday?" Rock asked, hand sliding around his waist and drawing him into the front room.

He leaned into Rock's body and nodded. "Yeah, Rocketman. I seem to recollect that y'all had some baby greens."

"Well this one's also cherry red." Rock's hand squeezed gently. "Rig this is Nute Wilson. Nute, this is here is Rig Roberts. I invited Nute for supper."

"Pleased to meet you." Rig smiled, nodded his head. "You're more than welcome. Now, tell me. What sort of name is Nute? That's a new one on me." He moved around to the sofa, sitting easy, giving his Blue a grin. There was something almost endearing about how serious the big guy took this, easing the wee baby queer marines in, showing them the ropes.

"My mom's Swedish. What about... what about Rig?" The kid was cute. A little on the short side, hair was probably blond, though it was hard to tell with that brand new baby green haircut. The shy eyes were blue. Oh, not like his Blue's, just a nice simple blue.

"I'm a flight medic. I run around rigging y'all groundpounders up when the shit hits the fan. Name sorta stuck." He chuckled, let himself grin. "The old man running your ass ragged yet?"

"Hell, yes, he is."

Rock growled a little.

"Or not," the kid quickly added.

Oh, *that* was funny as fuck. Rig laughed long and happy. "Oh shit, kid. You better need more than a little growl to scare you. You want a beer?"

Nute looked to Rock.

"You don't need my permission," snorted Rock.

"You're not going to card me?"

"Does this look like a fucking bar?" Rig grinned, shook his head. "Ain't nobody looking to get anybody in trouble. You want a beer or don't you?"

"I do."

"I'll get 'em. Call for pizza at the same time. Meat lovers, double cheese'll do by you, won't it, Nute?" It wasn't a question, but Rock waited for the kid to nod before heading to the kitchen.

"Get a Supreme, too, Rock. I've fucking forgotten what vegetables *taste* like." Rig pulled off his shoes, got himself comfortable, gave Grimmy a nice long loving-on. "Where're you from, kid?"

"Minnesota. Hated school and didn't want to do college so I figured I'd sign up." He got a shy smile. "I didn't like school but I'm no dummy -- the Marines are the best."

"Oh, you keep saying that, Nute. That's a song near and dear to the Rocketman's heart." Oh, the kid was sweet one. So shy. So... military. Cute as fuck. "Minnesota, huh? I reckon it's cold there."

The kid laughed. "You could say that."

"Oh, now, I'm not one to think kindly of the cold. Give me the summer any damned day."

"You get used to it. Anytime we complained my mom threatened to send us to Sweden to live with my grandparents. She said then we'd know cold."

"Fuck that. Course... there are supposed to be some good looking men in Sweden, so there's a plus for you."

Rig wondered if Rock had gotten lost in the fucking kitchen. Ordering pizza was the culinary skill the man had *down*.

On cue in came his Blue. "Fucking busy signal over and over again. Then they tell me it's going to be a fucking hour."

"Yeah, it's Friday." He murmured his thanks over the beer, scooted over to give Rock some room. "Baby green says he's from fucking Minnesota."

"No shit. I bet it's cold there."

Nute laughed, giving a little snort.

Rigger grinned over, winking at the kid. "Yeah, you damned Yankees, living in the friggin' cold like it's a natural thing."

"Well we can't all live in Texas," Rock told him, hand sliding on his thigh.

"Mmm... this is true. Heaven calls her special few." Rig let his legs part a little, eyes drooping at the touch of that hand.

Rock snorted, hand working slowly up. "Well we've got an hour to kill."

"That we do." Rig relaxed, shifted under that touch. "You got a suggestion about spending the time wisely?"

"I do. Nute? Just how much of a cherry are you?" Poor Nute went about the right shade for a cherry.

"I'm thinking that's pretty cherry, Rocketman." He smiled, letting his eyes wander over that trim body.

Nute nodded. "Bit of necking in the basement."

"Oh, now that won't do," Rock said, shifted over, leaving a space between them. "Come sit."

Nute went to move, but looked at him first, waiting.

Rig gave the kid a grin. "I don't bite. Promise."

"Not unless you want him to." Rock winked and the kid was laughing as he came to sit between them.

He met his Blue's eyes, loving the heat there, the familiar twinkle. "Are you telling my secrets?"

"Did I say a thing about your foot and a half schlong?"

Nute's mouth dropped open.

Rigger blinked and then started cackling, holding his belly he was laughing so hard. "Oh! Oh, shit, Rock! I *knew* it was time to get your eyes checked, old man!"

Rock gave Nute a wink and then leaned past the kid to give him a kiss. He met those lips eagerly, laughter fading, pushing into the kiss with a happy, hungry moan.

Yeah, Friday nights were all about this.

Rock didn't skimp on the kiss for one moment, but when it was over, his Blue turned to the kid. "I'm going to kiss you first because once you've had one from Rig, I'm in second place."

"Oh, that's no fair, Rock." He leaned in, brushed his lips against Nute's jaw. "Don't let him bullshit you, kid. The Rock can kiss."

"It sure looked nice when you guys were doing it."

Rock chuckled. "You've got good instincts, kid." Then Rock was kissing the cherry, just a full on take your mouth Rocketman kiss.

He hummed softly, watching, cock getting hard and hot in his scrubs. "Oh fuck, that's pretty."

Nute whimpered, hands coming up to hold onto Rock's shoulders.

Pressing close, Rig snuggled in, whispering soft into the cherry's ear. "So fucking hot, the way that tongue pushes deep, the way he fucking takes what he needs."

A tremor went through Nute and Rock shot him a glance, bluer than blue eyes twinkling.

He winked, giving his Blue a warm grin. Nothing like stroking that ego from afar. "You should touch him, Nute. They don't call him Rock for nothing. He's fucking *magic* -- hot and hard and sheer fucking sex."

Nute whimpered again, hands tightening on Rock's shoulders and then sliding down over the muscled chest.

"Mmm... That's it." He licked Nute's ear, blowing soft. "Feels so fucking hot, doesn't he? Gonna let me touch you, baby green? Gonna let me know how you feel?"

Nute nodded as best the kid could with Rock's tongue halfway down his throat.

Rig reached between them, sliding his hand over the kid's belly, then up. "Come on, Rock, gimme a turn."

Rock broke the kiss, turning to grin at him. "Impatient."

"You were hogging him." He gave Rock a teasing look, leaned in to lick those hot lips before turning to brush his lips against Nute's. "My turn, yeah?"

"Yeah, okay," said Nute, both blushing and smiling wide at him.

"Cool." Rig leaned in, taking those sweet, soft, open lips like he meant it, using his tongue and lips to drive the kid absolutely fucking insane.

He was treated to a whole symphony of whimpers, Rock chuckling in harmony. "Best fucking mouth on the continent."

"I'm going for hemisphere, next." He licked the kid's lips and dove back in, tilting Nute's head so the kiss could deepen. Rock's laughter was sweet like the cherry taste of the kid's mouth.

One of Nute's hands slid over his shoulder, stuttering a little. Then Rock started working on their clothes, pulling his scrub top off first. Oh, yeah. Shit, he loved fucking -- all of it. The tastes and sounds and scents and heat. The rubbing and sucking and kissing and touching -- all of it.

The kid's hands found his chest, sliding over it like they had Rock's. That sweet cherry tongue slid tentatively into his mouth.

"Mmm..." He pushed into the touches, moaning low, letting the kid know how good it felt.

Rock's mouth closed over his neck and then his Blue guided Nute's hands to his nipples. The kid wasn't a dummy; he got the hint right quick and started stroking. Yeah. Damn. He deepened the kiss, damned near purring into the cherry's mouth. Fucking sweet. Rig cupped the kid's cock, stroking along the hard shaft.

The kid's body rippled, making Rock chuckle against

his skin. "Nothing like a cherry to make you feel like a fucking god." Like he needed a cherry.

Rig broke the kiss, panting. "Too many fucking clothes, cherry."

"Oh. Yeah, okay. I can do less clothes."

"'Atta boy, Nute!" Rock gave the kid a quick hard kiss and backed off, pulling his own clothes off, revealing all those sexy as fuck muscles.

Rig let himself admire, let himself reach for that hot, strong belly. "Rocketman..."

Nute made a little noise. "Shit, Sarge... that's some body."

Rock grinned and flexed, happy as a pig in mud.

"Oh, he's better than some body. Rock's a pure-D stud." He leaned forward, licking Rock's abs.

"D? I'm only a D?" complained Rock.

"Quit fishing, you sexy motherfucker." Rig nipped a little, grinning to beat the band.

Rock chuckled, hand sliding over his head. "I'll have you know I'm Grade A Prime American meat."

Nute was chuckling at them and started to pull his shirt off. He caught Rock's eyes as the kid was busy, smiling up at the sexy bastard he left Texas for. Those Blue eyes gazed down at him, full of every reason why it had turned out to be a good idea.

Rig dropped a soft kiss above Rock's bellybutton and then turned his focus back to the cherry. "Let's see what we've got here, hmm?"

Nute wasn't badly built -- the kid had gone through basic and that left its mark on them. The kid was somewhere between trying to flex like Rock and being shy about it.

"Mmm..." Rig started touching, leaning in to smell and nuzzle and lick. No reason a man couldn't appreciate a sweet little thing like this, now was there.

"Oh, God." The kid gasped, cock twitching hard.

"You smell sweet, kid. Taste pretty fucking good, too." He licked his way to a tight little nipple, teeth teasing.

"Oh... oh, I'm gonna...I."

Rock's hands slid around Nute cock and the kid shouted, come spraying up his chest.

"There you go... take the edge off, yeah?" Rigger chuckled, rubbing the spunk into Nute's belly. "Might even make it 'til the pizza comes, now."

Rock grumbled. "'s not going to be here for another forty-five minutes, Rig. I don't want to wait."

"Not going to hurry this sweet thing along, are you?" The tease was fond, warm.

Rock reached out and stroked his lips. "No, that wasn't my plan. But I can hurry you along."

"Yeah?" He chuckled and fastened his lips around Rock's thumb, head bobbing as he sucked nice and slow.

Nute's groan was a little higher than Rock's, the sounds in concert. Oh, yeah. He moaned soft, gave them both a show, moving sure and steady.

"Fucking sexy."

"Oh yeah, he is. You are. God."

Rig gave the kid a grin before turning his eyes up to Rock, so fucking hungry for it. Always.

"You watch this, Nute. Watch and learn."

"Okay, Sarge," murmured the kid, voice husky.

He ran his hands up Rock's thighs, fingers moving to frame that fat, heavy cock, teasing the warm, soft balls.

"You're going to suck him?" Nute asked.

Rigger chuckled, tickled. Only every fucking day. "I don't know, Rocketman. Am I going to suck you?"

"I'm counting on it," Rock told him, giving the kid a wink.

"Mmm... I suppose it wouldn't do to disappoint,

then." He grinned, moving to kneel in front of his Blue, tongue sliding along the shaft.

"Oh fuck, yeah."

Rock groaned for him and Nute made a little squeaking noise. Rig took his time, pulling one heavy nut into his mouth, then the other, sucking slow and careful. Nute sighed and shifted, hand starting to stroke his cock. Humming at the pretty sight, Rig worked his way up Rock's prick, tongue sliding over the slit as his lips worked the head.

"Oh God. That's... wow."

"Yeah, you got it, kid," muttered Rock, hands sliding through his hair.

He gave Rock all he had, keeping the pace steady, driving his lover higher and higher. Rock let the kid hear how good it was, groaning and moaning, hips moving, fucking his mouth. Nute's breath came faster and faster, the sound of flesh hitting flesh louder and louder. He started deep-throating, thighs parting wide, cock so fucking hard it was killing him. Fuck, Rock tasted good. Strong, male, necessary.

"Oh my god!" The scent of the kid's come filled the air, Rock's groaning following a moment later, seed pouring down his throat.

He swallowed hard, moaning, drinking that hot, bitter spunk and need and... Oh, fuck, it was good.

This was good.

"Oh God. Shit. Cool." Nute seemed confined to monosyllabic words and it set Rock chuckling.

His Blue pulled out gently and turned his face up, thumb stroking his lips. "Gets better every fucking time."

"Mmm..." He licked at Rock's fingers, lips tingling and swollen. "Oh, yeah."

Rock smiled down at him. "Wanting, Cowboy?"

"Every fucking minute of every fucking day -- twice that on Fridays."

"What do you think, Nute? What can we do to help out here?"

"Um... I... a blow job?"

Rig leaned in, hiding his grin from both of them. Rock was *not* a cocksucker, not at heart.

"You're an eager one," Rock said with a grin. "Come on, Nute. Up and at him."

"Oh, I... okay. I uh... don't have any condoms."

"Now, now. A marine should always be prepared." Rig stood with a grin, adjusting his cock in his scrubs before heading to the drawer in the telephone table. "Or is that a boy scout?"

"Goes double for marines," growled Rock. "You never ever put your dick anywhere without a glove, kid. That's rule number one for the straight guys and it's rule number one for us fags as well. No condom, no fucking, no sucking. You got that?"

Nute was looking up at Rock who was just looming over the kid, eyes huge, nodding quickly. "Yes, Sarge. I got it."

"Now before you go thinking me and Rock don't play by the rules?" Rig dug out the package of Trojans. "We got tested, played it safe 'til then."

"So I could suck you without-"

"No, kid, you can't. You never take the other guy's word for it. Ever."

Nute looked chastised. "Okay."

"If you don't learn anything else this weekend, kid, you learn that. Gay boys that think they're exempt from the condom rule the corps so firmly espouses get sick. Period."

Rig nodded. "You find yourself a long-term partner, you get tested. You're both clean, you bareback. Fucking's great kid, but it's not worth dying for." He handed the cherry the box. "Okay, lecture's over. Let's play!"

Nute laughed, fingers fumbling with the box while Rock tugged at his scrubs.

It didn't take long for Blue to have him naked, big hands stroking his ass, his back, his thighs. "Mmm... 's good, Rock."

The kid got into the box and opened a condom, trying to slip it on upside down.

"Other way, sweet thing." Rig moved closer, took the kid's hands in his own and helped.

Those soft blue eyes looked up at him. "Sorry."

"We all learned at the beginning, kid," Rock told him, hand sliding over Nute's cheek.

"Mmm... don't you worry. You're doing just fine." His voice was rumbly, drawl pronounced now.

Nute stroked him a couple of times. "Hopefully I'll do better with the sucking part -- I was watching you do the Sarge."

"Just take it slow and easy and no biting." Rigger winked, moving in the kid's hands. "All the rules you need."

"That no biting one is the most important," Rock noted. His Blue nudged him. "Up on the couch, Rig, straddle the kid."

"That cool with you?" At the kid's nod, he moved up, settling close enough to feel the kid's heat. Damn.

Those blue eyes looked at him again and then the kid's tongue came out, licking at the tip of his cock.

"Oh..." He shivered, nodded. "'s fucking sweet, cherry. Do it again."

"What's it taste like without the condom?" Nute asked, tongue coming out to swipe at his cock again.

"Salty, rich. All fucking male." He caught Rock's eyes. "'s damned addictive."

Rock kissed him hard and then snuggled up behind him again, hands on his skin, mouth on his neck.

Nute licked all the way down to his pubes and then back up to the tip again. "You really got Sarge's whole prick in? I mean, I saw it, but it still seems... really big."

"Takes practice. That, and trust. You gotta relax to take it all the way in, down in your throat." Rig leaned into Rock, gasping a little.

Nute glanced up with a shy grin. "You get lots of practice then."

"Every fucking morning, kid. The Rock likes his wake up call."

"Wow." Nute frowned suddenly, mouth fucking close, but not doing anything yet. "Every morning? So how come you're always so grumpy, Sarge?"

Rig chuckled, looking up at Rock, eyebrow arched.

"Baby greens make me grumpy, kid. Shut up and suck the nice man off."

Nute prudently bit back a smile and then leaned forward, taking the head of his cock into the warm, tentative mouth.

"Who're you calling nice? Oh... Oh, lick right there. Harder. Yeah. Nice. Good."

Rock just chuckled, the sound sending air along the back of his neck.

The kid used his tongue and lips, licking and sucking. There wasn't that much of his cock in the kid's mouth, but Nute was warming up to the task. He kept from moving as long as he could, then Rock's fingers started playing his nipples, heating him up. The kid pulled off and took a deep breath and then took him in again, taking more this time and proving had had been paying attention as warm fingers slid over his balls.

"Oh. Oh, yeah, kid. That's good." He started moving a bit, thighs parting, stomach tight as he swayed.

Rock was fucking cheating, fingers working his nipples, mouth over the sweet spot on his neck. He reached up with one hand, down with the other, moaning to beat the band. Fuck, yeah. Fucking *sweet*. Nute glanced up at him and then went back to what he was doing with renewed enthusiasm.

"Oh, yeah. 's good, kid. Gonna make me come." He moaned, lips parting as Rock took his mouth, fucked his lips with that tongue.

One of Rock's fingers slid down to his crease, the tip pushing inside him. Oh! His eyes popped open, ass pushing against that finger, body begging for more.

"Slut," whispered Rock, pushing the rest of that fat finger in deep.

"Yours." He mouthed the word against Rock's lips, knowing his Blue heard, his ass clenched tight around that finger.

Nute's head bobbed slowly, suction even, tongue stumbling a little, but managing some licks. It built slow, steady, as he rocked between that hot tongue and that thick finger inside him. "Oh... God. More."

Rock carefully worked another finger into him, taking it slow. The kid moved faster, head bobbing quicker on his cock. That was what he needed, hips moving faster, eyes closing as he soared. Fucking sweet.

"That's it, kid. Keep it up, he's almost there."

Nute made a sound around his cock and bobbed faster, harder.

Rigger raised up on his toes, shaking as the pleasure spiked. "Fuck! Now. Now."

Rock's finger caught his gland and the kid's lip caught the tip of his cock and he fucking lost it, shooting hard. Even with the condom on, the kid jerked back, surprise in the blue eyes. He would have said something comforting, but *fuck*, he was busy.

"There you go, kid. You caused your first orgasm."

Nute chuckled, looking shy and pleased all in one.

"Mmm... congrats, sweet thing. One more cherry popped." Oh, he felt nice, all loose and goofy.

Nute and Rock laughed and Rock helped them all flop together onto the couch. "That pizza shouldn't be long now."

Rig nodded, grabbing his scrubs with his toes. "'s cash in my wallet, if you need it."

"'S my night, I've got it." Rock pulled on his jeans and checked the back pocket. "Yeah, I've got it."

"Cool." He leaned into the pillows, snuggling in. "Gotta fucking *love* Fridays, yeah kid?"

Nute nodded. "More than ever."

"Smart boy." Rig grinned, reaching out for Grimmy and just melting into the cushions.

The doorbell rang, making Grimmy head for the door, barking, Rock following behind.

"You do this kind of thing often?" Nute asked.

He shook his head. "The Rocketman's picky about who he brings home."

"Well I'm glad he brought me home. Thanks."

"He's a good man. You're more than welcome." Rig smiled, watched his Blue move. Oh, yeah. A good man. His good man.

Rock came back with two boxes and dumped 'em on the table. "You ladies talking about me?"

"Of course, don't you know you're my every waking thought, Rocketman?"

Rock winked at Nute. "As it should be, Cowboy."

The cherry laughed. Sweet kid.

Rig grabbed a slice of pizza, grinning, feeling good. Felt pretty damned philanthropic, too. Him and Rock, popping cherries, one queer baby green at a time.

Hallelujah.

CHAPTER TWENTY TWO

His plans had been to repack the ball bearings on Rock's truck and change the oil on his Jeep, but when the ice had started falling at noon and the temperature plummeted, Rig decided to retreat into the house, glad that he hadn't gotten the tires off before the weather hit.

He started a pot of coffee and then started washing his hands at the sink, shivering. He grinned at the sound of explosions and gunfire from the front room TV. His Blue must have found the way out of bed. "Fuck, man. It's plumb *nasty* out there. I was freezing my ass off."

"Better stay inside then," called Rock. "I'm mighty fond of that ass."

Rig chuckled, hanging his jacket by the washer and drying his hands on his jeans. "You eaten yet? There's some hamburger patties left over from last night and some chips."

"I'm hungry. But not for food."

He grinned and sauntered into the front room, body responding to that low voice. "Yeah?"

Rock was slouching on the couch, arms out along the back of it, legs spread wide. His sweats did nothing to hide exactly how hungry he was. Rock turned to give him a slow grin that warmed him right down to his toes. "Yeah."

Oh, yeah. Fucking A. Rig headed for the sofa, moving straight up to straddle those fine fucking thighs and leaning down to lick Rock's lips. "Mmm..."

Rock chuckled. "Taste good?"

"Always." He licked again, tasting Rock's smile, teasing those hungry lips with his tongue.

Rock's tongue slid along his. "Yeah, so do you."

He rubbed against Rock, letting their tongues slide and play, the kiss warm and easy, sort of like the feeling of being in Rock's arms.

Rock's hands slid down to his ass, grabbing at each cheek like it was a melon. "Just checking it's still all there," Rock said with a wink.

"Just barely. I managed to avoid the ice by the skin of my teeth." He wiggled, rubbing himself against those big fucking hands.

One of Rock's eyebrows rose. "You've got skin on your teeth?"

He groaned dramatically and winked. "Damn Yankee."

Rock threw his head back and laughed. "We use that expression north of the Mason-Dixon line, you know." Rock kneaded his ass, fingers pushing the seam of his jeans against his crack.

"Really? Go figure. Didn't think y'all were that clever, as a rule." The tease was easy, toothless, just fucking around with his man. God, he was lucky redneck.

"Most of us aren't." Fuck, but those blue eyes could twinkle.

"Guess I lucked out finding the good apple." He pretended to think. "'course you *were* in Texas, which gave me a clue, straight off."

Rock nodded. "I understand you Texans need a lot of clues."

"Oh..." Nice one, Blue. You're getting good at this game. "Well, Rock, when you're having to deal with the lost, the impoverished, the Northerners -- it takes practice. I admit it, sometimes we forget just how lucky we are."

"If you need luck..." He was given another wink.

"Then you must be a Yankee. If you *have* luck, you hail from the Lone Star State." He wasn't going to be able to keep from giggling for long.

"What is it with that one lonely star anyway?" Rock asked, hands still massaging his ass. "Couldn't y'all afford another?" The drawl was slow and deliberate, a passing fair imitation.

"Rock. You dear, sweet, deluded soul." He grinned, let the come back build. "Don't they *teach* y'all that stars aren't for sale up north?"

Rock snorted. "Everything's for sale, you just gotta know the right price."

"Not true!" He leaned forward, kissing Rock hard. "That's not for sale."

Rock licked his lips. "No? How about this?" The big hands squeezed his ass again.

"We'd have to be pretty fucking hungry before I'd go for selling that, I'm thinkin'." He took another kiss. "And I don't see you renting it out, either."

"Fuck no. You're a slut, sure as I'm sitting here with a fucking boner, but you're my slut any day of the week."

"Lock, stock and barrel." No reason debating that

fact at all. He knew where he belonged.

"Now I do like a man who knows his guns." Rock was grinning wide now, all but chuckling.

"Is that what that's from?" He gave Rock his best innocent, wide-eyed civilian look, cackling happily as Rock started tickling. "Stop! Stop! Uncle!"

"Rig, I'm not your Uncle."

"Don't make my break my foot off in your ass, butthead."

Rock snorted. "Like you could."

"Hey! I'm damned near as big as you." He hid his grin in Rock's neck, laughing hard. Well, okay big and tall weren't *exactly* the same thing, but still...

That earned him another snort. "I can hold you in one hand."

"No fucking way."

One of Rock's hands fell onto the couch beside them, the other flat in the centre of his ass. "Yes, fucking way."

He rubbed back, humming just a little, lips vibrating against Rock's throat. "Nope. Not chance. Wouldn't work."

Rock chuckled. "What exactly wouldn't work, Rig?"

"Your hand, there, holding me." He started licking the salt from Rock's skin, hips moving against that hand.

Rock froze. "No, I meant..." The words trailed off, those blue eyes suddenly hot and intent on his own.

Rig swallowed hard, not sure exactly what they were talking about. His cock sure seemed to know, hard as nails, throbbing against Rock's belly.

Rock growled. "Jesus, Rig, that's a hell of a thing to suggest."

"I..." He wasn't suggesting anything, was he? His cheeks were burning, but he didn't look away, didn't back down.

"You really want that?" Rock asked. "I've never done it before, kind of a serious thing. A serious trust thing."

"Me either." That hand felt huge where it was sitting. Fucking *huge*. Still. "I'd trust you with everything, Blue. Anything."

Rock's hand moved over his ass, slow and solid. "I bet I could make you fly."

"Oh..." He rested his forehead against Rock's, looking into those amazing eyes. "Yeah. I'd feel so *full*."

"Touch you so deep, Rabbit. Deeper than anything ever." There was a hint of a growl in Rock's voice.

He shuddered, so hot he thought he'd bust. "Have me in the palm of your hand."

"God fucking damn, Rig." Rock growled this time, hand pulling him tight against that hard body, mouth taking his, tongue invading, pushing deep.

Rig wrapped around Rock, arms and thighs, hips pushing hard against that rock hard belly. He opened to that sweet fucking tongue, pulling it into his mouth and sucking fiercely.

"I want to do it," murmured Rock, hand tight on his ass.

"Yes." He nodded, rocking back into that hand. He trusted his Blue more than he trusted himself. He was made for those fucking hands. "Yes."

Rock growled, hands going between them, opening his jeans and pulling down the grey sweats. "This first." One of those big hands wrapped around both their pricks, working them together.

"Fuck, yeah." He dove into Rock's mouth, kissing his Blue hard, fucking those sweet lips with his tongue.

Rock grabbed hold of his tongue and sucked, hand moving tight and fast and right. He cried out, sharp and sweet, bowing his back as he came hard, shooting over Rock's fingers. Rock growled, low and sexy as fuck, the scent of his spunk strong.

Relaxing, he rested against Rock's strength, listening to that heartbeat slow.

Wow.

Rock's hand stayed warm and solid around their pricks, the other one sliding over his ass in small circles, not letting him forget it was there.

Oh. Yeah. Wow.

He took a deep breath, nuzzling against Rock's throat, relaxing as he exhaled. Rock purred. "We gonna do this, Rabbit? Gonna let me hold you like that?"

"Yeah, Blue. We're gonna do this." He kissed Rock's throat. "Want to feel you deep inside me."

"All right then. How do you want to do this? You want to clean up first?"

Rig thought and then nodded. "Yeah. I think I'd better. That way we won't have to worry about it."

"You gonna handle that yourself? Or you want a hand?" Rock gave him a wink at that, though those blue eyes were as serious as he'd ever seen them.

"I can handle it, but I want you there. We can shower together after." He wanted this to be theirs, to be something beyond a kinky experiment.

Rock brought their mouths together, barely a kiss, more a breathing of the same air. "Then let's go."

"Yeah." He nodded. "I'll get my gear set up. You probably ought to get some towels for the bedroom and check our lube supply."

"You picked up some yesterday -- it was on your list. But I'll make sure it's easily accessible." He got another kiss and then, without a backward glance, his marine was headed for the bedroom.

Rig blinked for a second, then stood and headed for

the bathroom, cock hard and hands trembling. He wasn't sure how they'd gotten here, but he wasn't backing away. Not a fucking chance.

He started the water running, let it heat up while he pulled his bag and tubing out from the top of the linen closet, grabbing a handful of good towels as he went. A squirt of liquid soap and an adjustment of the water's temperature -- just a little too hot now so it would be warm enough later -- and he was ready.

Rock came up behind him, already naked, and worked his open jeans off for him. Quiet, but most definitely *there*. He leaned into Rock's strength, soaking up that heat, then he handed over the KY and leaned over the sink. "Get me ready?"

Rock made a low, rumbling sound of confirmation and those big hands were back on his ass, hot and wide and solid, kneading his skin. Rock kept massaging his ass, fingers teasing along his crack, down against his inner thighs and balls. His Blue was taking his sweet time. Fucking foreplay. Who'd'a thought.

He dropped his head on his arms, humming low, thighs parting as he moved toward Rock's touch. Rock's mouth slid over his neck, finding the sweet spot on the left side and working it hard.

"Oh... fucking sweet. Blue..." He groaned, body rocking slow and easy. So good. *So* good.

He got a rumble in reply and one of Rock's fingers slid into his body, warm and slick and perfect. He just melted, letting Rock touch him, feel him, dissolve his tension and just leave need. By the time Rock had three fingers in him, he could feel that thick cock, hot and hard and wet, leaving trails against the back of his thigh.

"Oh... Fuck, Blue. Making me hot." He whimpered and arched, prick heavy and hard, tight.

"That's the idea, isn't it?" Rock shifted, fingers sliding

out of him. "Ready?"

He nodded, trying to catch his breath. "Yeah." He wasn't even sure which question he was answering.

Rock stood back, blue eyes hot on him.

He greased up the nozzle with trembling fingers, tempted as fuck to reach down and pull himself off again. He grabbed a towel and settled on the floor so that gravity would help the water flow, thanking God that he'd just mopped. Then he looked up at Rock. "You want to do the honors or watch?"

Rock had his hand on his cock and was pulling it slowly. "I'm enjoying myself right here. You are one sexy motherfucker, Rig."

His cheeks heated and he focused on getting the nozzle in, focused on relaxing. By the time he had the tubing in and got the water flowing, tremors were rocking his body.

Rock settled down next to him, warm hand sliding over his belly. "Shh, it's all right, Rig. I'm here."

He rested his hot cheek against Rock's thigh, panting quietly as the water filled him, making him feel swollen and crampy.

"Who'd have thought something like this could be so fucking sexy."

"S...sexy?" He moaned softly, dropping an open-mouthed kiss on those hard muscles. Oh, fuck. So full.

"Oh yeah, I'm ready to shoot just watching you."

Turning off the flow of water, Rig leaned forward, rubbed his cheek along that sweet fucking cock, dropped a kiss on those heavy balls.

"Fuck, Rig," Rock growled a warning.

Rig hummed and repeated the motion, incredibly turned on by the thought that he was drawing those sounds out of his Blue.

"Fuck, Rig." The words repeated, but this time Rock

jerked, his Blue's spunk spraying him in the face.

He moaned, shivering hard now. "Blue..."

"Rabbit..." One warm hand slid along his spine. "You're something else."

He started to stand, the pressure unbearable, letting Rock help him over to the toilet. He listened to Rock start the shower, the hot steam billowing by the time he'd cleaned himself up and stood.

Rock was already in the shower, hand held out to him. He moved into those arms like he was made for them, moaning happily as the hot water and hot skin touched him simultaneously. Rock held him, supported him, drugged him with soft, slow kisses that stole his breath. By the time the water was turned off, he didn't even know his own fucking name.

Rock got him out and dried off and then, one strong arm under his knees, the other under his shoulders, he was carried out to the bedroom. Rig buried his face in Rock's throat, licking slowly, boneless and loose. His entire universe was collapsed to just them, just now. Warm and safe and wanting while the ice rained outside the windows.

The sheets were cool against his back as he was spread out on their bed, Rock kneeling down between his legs.

He smiled up, shifting slightly, loving the touch of those eyes on his body. "Sex on a stick, Rocketman."

Rock chuckled, the sound low, sexy as fuck. "That would be you in a few minutes here, Rig."

He snorted, laughing softly as he shook his head, warm all through. "You think so, asshole?"

"I do." Bending over him, Rock's mouth met his, hot and intoxicating. Reaching up, he wrapped his arms around those strong shoulders, body turning to twine around that heat.

Rock kissed him until he was breathless before pulling back, blue eyes warm and serious as they gazed down at him. "You're sure?"

He met that gaze, unflinching. "I'm sure, Jim. You'll make it good."

"I will." No hesitation, no doubt. That was his Blue.

He brought their lips together again, moaning softly as his tongue slid into the warm, wet mouth. Rock rumbled happily into his mouth, making him tingle. Almost without his noticing it, one of Rock's fingers slid into his body. He rode that finger with shifts of his hips, rocking slow and easy.

Rock took his time, but at the same time wasn't lingering and a second finger soon joined the first. He moaned, pushing a little harder, cock filling, balls drawing up a bit. Rock's mouth left his, moving down to explore his neck and shoulders as a third finger was pushed inside.

Humming, the sensation full, hot, and familiar, Rig stretched out, then bent his knees, spreading wide. "Mm... 's good. Makes me fucking hot."

"So far just like always," murmured Rock, tongue moving to tease at one of his nipples. "But now's where things get different."

He lifted his head, gasping at the shock of electricity flaring from tit to cock. "Shit!"

Rock murmured something indistinct and took the nipple he was teasing between his lips, tugging on it. Oh. Oh, fuck. Oh, yeah. His hips moved faster, riding those slick fingers, moaning steadily.

"I'm going to do it now," Rock warned him, shifting slightly.

Biting the tip of his nipple before sucking it into that hot mouth again, Rock was suddenly pushing that whole huge hand into him, letting his own motions pull in that wide girth.

"Oh... Blue..." His motions slowed, thighs parting farther as he tried to ease the pressure, the amazing fucking pressure that just kept coming. He shuddered, gasping.

Rock's lips nuzzled their way down along his belly, licking at his navel, at the tip of his cock, even as that hand just kept pushing, slowly, deeper and deeper.

"Oh. Oh, God. Blue. So much. So fucking much." He whimpered, head falling back, body so fucking *tight*.

Rock's mouth continued to wander over his body, giving him something to focus on aside from the hand pushing into him.

"Almost there, Rabbit," Rock whispered against his hip. Rig nodded, hands fisting into the sheets. Almost there. Almost. Oh, God. So *huge*.

All of a sudden the widest part of Rock's hand was through and he could feel his body snap shut around Rock's wrist. A harsh groan was pushed from him, Rock's hand -- oh fuck, oh fuck, Rock's *hand*, Rock's fucking *hand* -- leaving no room for the sound.

"God fucking damn, Rig. My whole fucking hand."

"You... You've got me. Oh, fuck, Blue." His breath pushed from him, quick, shallow pants all he could manage.

"Yeah, Rig. I've got you."

Rock's mouth moved slowly up his body, warm and making him shiver. When their lips met, Rock started to move his hand. He blinked up into those blue eyes, pleasure so vast it hurt. He took a deep breath, *Rock's* breath, crying out as that hand shifted inside him.

"Ready to fly, Rig?"

"Yes. God, Blue. Please. I need..." He bit his bottom lip and arched. He didn't even *know* what he needed, he just knew Rock would give it to him.

Rock growled, the sound low, wrapping around him. That so fucking huge hand moved inside him.

"Blue! Oh, God!" His head and shoulders lifted, body curling up toward Rock, wrapping around that solid heat within him.

"Good?" rumbled Rock, growl going through him.

"So fucking huge. Oh God, I can feel you *everywhere*." He shifted, body sliding on that huge hand. He looked into Rock's eyes. "Bigger than good, yeah?"

"Yeah, Rabbit. Bigger than pretty much anything."

Rig nodded, breath starting to even out. His body relaxed, head settling back into the pillows, prick hard as diamonds. Oh, he was burning, full and flying and so fucking high on sensation. "Please. I need you."

Rock never left him wanting and this was no different. Those blue eyes held his as Rock fucked him with that hand, each motion drawing long shudders through his body.

It didn't take long before everything was so big, so huge, the pleasure and pressure unbearable. "Please... Please, Blue... Oh, fuck. Please."

"Anytime, Rig. All you have to do is let go and come on my hand. My *hand*, Rig."

He shuddered, slowly reaching out and following that muscled arm down and down and down to where it disappeared inside his body. Where Rock was holding him inside. Oh. Oh, fuck.

He sobbed as he came, seeing nothing but blue on blue. He flew and he flew into that blue and when he started to come down, Rock had him. Rock was holding him in the palm of that big, capable, reliable, beautiful hand. He was never going to breathe again.

And then Rock's mouth was over his again, pushing air into his lungs. With each breath that big hand moved out a little bit, slowly working it's way in reverse. He whimpered into those lips as Rock stretched him wide again, then left him empty. Rock held him close, fat prick burning along his thigh as Rock moved against him.

"Mmm... so hot, Blue." He purred softly, hand sliding down Rock's belly, face lifting for another kiss.

Rock rumbled, pushing the thick cock up into his hand even as his breath was stolen by another long kiss. His hand felt clumsy, but he kept pumping, searching for his Blue's pleasure, stroking that heat.

"Fuck, you're something else," Rock told him, eyes locked to his as heat poured over his hand.

"Y...yours." He lifted his hand for a taste, entire body slowly trembling with aftershocks and overwhelmed by sensation.

Rock growled and pulled him close and safe into those wide arms. "Mine."

He nodded, eyes falling closed. Yeah. Rock's. Lock, stock and barrel.

He was vaguely aware of Rock getting up and cleaning him and the bed, covering him with the blankets and then Rock was back, holding him close.

He felt empty inside, but outside he was warm and home, the ice pattering against the windows. He needed a nap, needed things just like they were for a little while, until he felt like he was in his own skin again. Rig curled in close. He needed and Rock would know. His Blue always did.

CHAPTER TWENTY THREE

Rig was hiding.

He wasn't ashamed to admit it.

Hell, any man with half a brain wouldn't blame him.

It hadn't *started* out being a hiding offense. Momma'd called, chatted, talked about Thanksgiving, about the weather, about Christmas and Sissy's little girl.

Then she'd asked to talk to Rock to find out what he wanted them to get him for Christmas.

Still not bad.

Then, Sissy'd got on the phone with Rock and, from the look on Rock's face, either started telling about how the current pregnancy was going or discussing how the kids were going to call him "Uncle Jimmy".

That's when he'd bailed.

After all, he was Southern, not stupid.

It was quite a while before Rock started looking for him. If you could call shouting from the front room 'looking'. "Rig? You get that cowboy ass out here, because if I have to come looking for it, I'll... I'll call your fucking family back and make *you* talk to them for a fucking hour."

He snorted, like that was a threat. He idly considered sneaking out the bathroom window, but he figured Rock would catch him before he rounded the corner of the house. Besides, it was more fun to get caught *inside*.

"If I ever hear about 'spotting' again, Roberts -- it's gonna be too soon." That growl was growing closer, Rock coming down the hall.

Rig swallowed his laugh and climbed onto the lip of the tub, quietly pushing the screen out of the tall window. Spotting? Shit, Sissy, Rock was gonna kill him. He should have just given the curious little bitch details about Rock's... endowments. She'd warned him paybacks were a bitch.

"Oh, I don't think so."

The words echoed along the tiles, a thick, warm arm wrapping around his waist and pulling him up sharp against that solid body. For a big guy, Rock sure could move quietly when he wanted to.

He shuddered, cock going from zero to sixty in nothing. Did Rock *know* how fucking sexy that was? "Hey, Blue."

"Next time you hand me the phone, you sure as fuck better stick around so I can hand it back."

"They just want you to feel like family..." He leaned into Rock's muscles, fucking vibrating at the heat.

"I haven't talked to *my* family in ten years, Rig." Rock didn't move or loosen his hold at all, but those blue eyes had started to burn.

"Yeah, but they're mean. My kin like you." He

wrapped his arms around Rock's shoulders, hips shifting.

"Well I'd hate to hear what they said to me if they didn't!" Rock shuddered and his hold shifted, hands coming down to land on Rig's ass. "I mean it, Roberts -- you abandon me to Sissy and her spotting and her labor pains again and it will end in not fucking."

"Not fucking? Now that's just a mean thing to say." He bent his head, offering a lick to those warm lips. "No more pregnancy stories if I can help it."

After all, Sissy was due in four frigging days.

Rock tilted his head back. "Or labor stories or fucking breastfeeding stories -- if I wanted to know about sucking on tits, I'd turn straight."

Rig nodded, meeting Rock's eyes. "They do think of you as their own, you know? That baby will be fighting over your lap come next Christmas, 'long with the others."

"God help me." There was no heat in the words though -- he knew damn well that Rock would enjoy playing Uncle Jimmy. Or at least he would for the first day or two. Or until the sticky fingers came out.

"Now I'm going to collect my reward for not hanging up on them."

"Yeah?" He leaned in for another teasing kiss, tongue sliding along Rock's teeth.

"That's right." Rock's lips closed over his tongue, sucking it in.

He hummed, wrapping his legs around Rock's waist, lips open wide as Rock pulled. Fucking *hot*. Rock growled, the sound vibrating along his tongue and his lips. Those big hands pulled him tighter against the solid body and Rock started walking them toward the bedroom. Rig just held on, diving into their kisses, determined to make up for the last hour and make his Blue need.

He was tossed onto the bed, Rock following him down and grinding their hips together, pushing him into the mattress. Tugging away clothes, Rig searched for skin, moaning into Rock's lips when he found it, licking and nibbling and tasting. Rock gave him one of those rumbling purrs, his own clothes melting beneath Rock's fingers. He gave Rock a low cry when they were naked, when his prick was licked by the long, thick heat of his Blue's.

Rock's hands slid over his skin, tickling and teasing. He started laughing, chuckling into those lips, wriggling enough to make it good, make them hot. Eventually Rock started to growl, rubbing against him, sliding that fat prick along his hip.

"Mm... So fucking hot. Want my mouth or my ass?" He reached down, cupped Rock's ass and squeezed.

"I fucking want both."

"Everything." He took another hard kiss before tugging Rock up, encouraging him to bring that amazing cock toward his mouth.

Rock rumbled, all but purring, and then that thick prick was nudging against his lips, painting them with the first few drops of fluid need. Some men were great politicians, artists, runners. Him? He was made for this -- to blow Rock's fucking mind.

"Fucking sweet," muttered Rock, pushing his cock deep.

Yours. He closed his eyes and gave Rock everything he had, hands and lips and tongue working hard. Growls and rumbles filled the air, Rock's hips working, pushing and pulling that fine prick in and out of his mouth. Blunt fingers slid over his scalp. Rig started humming, purring and happy and hard and... Fuck, yeah. Yeah, Blue. The hands on his head tightened, Rock pushing harder, faster.

A single word -- his name -- was bit out and then salty heat flooded the back of his throat. Drinking Rock down, Rig pulled and sucked until the last shudders and aftershocks had faded, Rock panting above him.

"Fucking sweet," Rock growled again. hands gentling in his hair, sliding over his head in a caress.

He hummed in response, nuzzling Rock's pubes with his nose.

"Slut," Rock murmured, voice fond.

"Mmm... Yours." He licked the tip of that fat cock, hard and happy all at once.

"And don't you forget it." Rock's hands slid under his arms, tugging. "Now get up here and let me fuck you through the mattress."

"You think you'll get it up again, Rocketman?" he teased as he moved, that sweet cock already at three-quarter full.

"With this ass as inspiration?" Rock squeezed his ass, rubbing against him.

"Mmm... You like that, do you?" He wiggled, arching up into heat, back into the touch.

"You know it." Rock reached under the pillow and handed him the lube before taking one last squeeze. His Blue settled on his side, head propped up in one hand. "Get yourself ready. I want to watch that sweet ass in action."

"Perv." He leaned over for a quick kiss before slicking his fingers up and sliding them down to circle around his hole.

Rock's chuckle turned into a heartfelt groan. He answered that moan with one of his own, two fingers pushing deep inside, slick and stretching.

"Fuck." Rock's fingers slid against his own, against his stretched skin.

"Mmm... yeah. Fuck." He parted his thighs, chin

touching his chest as his pleasure spiked.

"Enough," growled Rock, tugging his fingers away and rolling over him.

That hot prick slid along his crease as Rock put his legs over the broad shoulders.

"Fuck, yeah. Want you." He reached up for the headboard, bracing himself for his Blue.

Smooth as honey, that fat cock slid into him, Rock setting up a rhythm right away, in and out like a fucking well-oiled piston. He moved into each thrust, the two of them finding the perfect spot just like that, natural as fucking breathing. One of Rock's hands found his prick, wrapping around him tight and tugging in time with the hard thrusts. Those blue-blue eyes never left his.

"Blue... Just what I need..." He reached up and pulled Rock down for a kiss as he came, shuddering and moaning low.

Rock went with the kiss, tongue fucking him as deep as that cock. He just fucking floated, rocking and purring and happy, caught inside his own personal Rock. The kiss went on and on, that fat prick impaling him over and over and then Rock groaned, thrusting hard and filling him with heat.

He held on, letting the kiss ease and become soft. Then they settled, Rock's weight welcome, warm. Solid as fuck.

No need to fucking hide from this.

No need at all.

He sang at the top of his lungs, lap full of Christmas lights he'd found at a garage sale. Three huge boxes and almost all of them worked, even if they were tangled as fuck. His favorite radio station was playing carols all month long and there were fresh brownies on the stove and coffee brewing. It was cold outside, but Grimmy was sleeping on his feet, so all was good.

Real good.

He was getting ready to decorate his house. His *own* house.

Rig grinned and started untangling another strand, singing "Mary, Did You Know" along with Kenny Rogers.

"Fucking shit. What a mess." Rock's still sleep heavy voice came from the hall. "Is there coffee?"

"Yep. Just made some. Got some cinnamon rolls at the bakery, too. They're on the table." Poor Blue. The man wasn't meant for mornings.

Rock disappeared and came back a minute later with a cup of coffee and a plate with four cinnamon rolls. He supposed he should be happy the man was using a plate and hadn't brought out the box.

Rock sank into the big armchair with a grunt. "What the fuck is all that?"

"Christmas lights." He gave Rock a look. "They did have these in Yankee-land when you were a kid, right?"

Rock's eyes narrowed. "Of course they did. It's just the fucking tangled mess I'm talking about. They didn't come out of the box like that. And is it even December yet?"

"It's after Thanksgiving and that's what counts. I bought them at a garage sale. Three bucks for all three boxes. Got a light up snowman for the front yard too and a spare tire for your truck." It had been a good find, all-in-all.

"A light up fucking snowman?" Rock shook his head. "Christ."

Well, didn't that just take the wind out of his sails. Rig chewed on his bottom lip to keep from snapping and went back to untangling. Maybe he'd just take the snowman up to work. The guys would get a huge kick out of it.

Rock drank his coffee and downed the cinnamon rolls, glowering and growling the whole time. "What time is it anyway? Feels like the fucking crack of dawn."

He counted to ten. Slowly. Then looked at his watch. "It's quarter to noon. What woke you up?"

Rock shrugged. "Who knows."

He just nodded and finished a string, rolling it up when he was done and grabbing another. He had a little tester he'd gotten from wallyworld and a few dozen extra bulbs. Was the perfect excuse to get them the staple gun and new extension cords, too.

Oh, he did love when Alan Jackson sang carols.

"You gonna be doing that all day?" Rock asked him after watching without saying a work for nearly fifteen minutes.

"No." He took a deep breath and let it out. "I take it you're not a Christmas light fan."

It hadn't really occurred to him -- their first Christmas together they'd been in little apartments.

"I like Christmas lights just fine. It's all the fucking fuss with the tangled cords and the broken lights and I haven't even gotten so much as a good morning asshole kiss."

Okay, Alex. You just keep your mouth shut and don't you say a fucking word about how you didn't even get a fucking good morning or a thank you about the spare or breakfast or coffee. Or about how you didn't get a fucking kiss or an offer of coffee even though you are piled under about ten tons of lights. Just put the mother fucking lights in the mother fucking box and take them out to the mother fucking garage.

He put the untangled lights in the near-empty box, the bundles of the others on top. Then he turned off the radio and muscled the boxes to the garage and loaded them into the Jeep along with the snowman. There were lots of guys on post hurting for money with kids who could use them.

Fuck, he was aggravated.

"What the fuck are you doing now?" growled Rock.

He slammed his hand down on the bumper of his Jeep, just fucking vibrating. "I'm putting the fucking lights in my fucking Jeep. Do you have a problem with that?"

"Fine. I'm going back to fucking bed."

"Fine." Rig whistled up Grimmy and got them both loaded in the Jeep and headed over to Reed's. Man had a new baby girl and enough Christmas spirit for anyone and had mentioned wanting help decorating over the weekend.

Merry Fucking Christmas and all that shit.

Rock wasn't sure what he'd done, but he knew he was in the fucking doghouse and he knew it was over the goddamned Christmas lights.

When a couple of hours had passed and it became pretty fucking clear his stubborn-assed redneck was not coming back anytime soon he headed down to the mall -- the fucking goddamned mall on a fucking Saturday afternoon, Rig has sure as fuck better appreciate this -- and bought two hundred fucking dollars worth of goddamned fucking outdoor lights and doodads and light up Santas.

He then proceeded to turn the house into a fucking first contact signal for life on Pluto.

Of course after the nosy old bat from next door had come out while he'd been on the ladder putting them up, looking more or less horrified, he started to have a little fun with it.

He'd managed to spell out semper fi on the roof.

He'd played with the lights until the two netting sheets of lights draped over the garage door in a pretty fucking good rendition of the Stars and Stripes.

Santa and at least eight reindeer were lit up on the lawn. In fact they were going to run Frosty the fucking Snowman and his wife over.

The old bat had come out twice more and shit bricks.

Fucking A.

Of course it was a colossal fucking waste of time if his redneck never fucking came back. Two fucking thirty in the morning.

He saw the Jeep's lights flash and then heard the Jeep door shut. Then the clapping and laughter started. It looked like Grimmy was going to get his doghouse back.

He stayed on the couch, casually flipping channels.

Rig came in, hands full of two paper sacks from his favorite fast food joint. When their eyes met, he got a tentative grin. "It looks like a Marine Christmas exploded all over the house. I love it."

He held a fist up in the air. "Semper Fi." He nodded at the bags. "Something smells good."

"I thought you might be hungry. Double burgers with fries and fried apple pies." That grin got wider, Rig moving over to the sofa.

"I'm hungry." He looked Rig in the eyes. "I could eat, too."

"Yeah?" Those grey eyes danced for him, shining. "You think?" Rig scooted a little closer, setting the bags on the coffee table.

He wrapped a hand around one of Rig's hips and tugged his redneck in close. "Well now, thinking's never been my strong suit."

Rig reached up, wrapped those long arms around his neck. "What is your strong suit, Blue Eyes?"

"Fucking a certain cowboy into the floor." All it took was a tug and Rig was straddling his lap.

"Oh, thank God." Rig leaned down and brought their lips together, tongue sliding deep into his mouth.

No one had a mouth as talented as his Rabbit and Rock let Rig have control of the kiss for a long time before taking it, taking that mouth like it was his to own. Rig moaned and opened wide, hands tugging open his shirt and looking for skin. He groaned as Rig found what he was looking for, hands sliding, fingers pinching, stroking. His own hands wrapped around Rig's ass, rocking their groins together.

"Yes. Fuck, Blue. Please." Rig rubbed against him, sighing into his mouth.

"That's the idea, Rig. Gonna fuck you." He wrapped his hand around either side of Rig's shirt and pulled it open, buttons losing their hold on material. Cheap crap.

Rig shrugged the shirt the rest of the way off, skin flushed and warm. "Good. Need you. Didn't even get my taste of cock this morning. Got all day to make up for."

His prick jerked at the thought of Rig's mouth around his cock. He growled low and started undoing his jeans. "Then why don't we start right there?"

Rig slid down his lap, ending between his legs, lips nuzzling his belly.

"Yeah. Fuck." He growled, fingers tangling in Rig's hair, guiding that lovely fucking mouth to his cock, feeling Rig's breath through his jeans.

"Make me hungry." Rig worked his jeans down and off, mouth moving over his pubes.

"I know." He rubbed his cock along Rig's cheek.

Rig hummed, eyes closing and lips parting. Slut.

Beautiful fucking slut. "Oh... Fuck yeah..."

He rubbed the tip against Rig's lips, painting them with the drops that were beading on his cock. Rig's tongue slid out, lapping at his slit, hands parting his thighs. He moaned, legs spreading easily. Fuck, his redneck was fucking special.

Those lips wrapped around his cockhead, leaving one sucking kiss after another. He could feel each pull all the way through to his balls, up into his belly, making his skin flush with color. That was talent.

Then Rig started taking him down to the root, deep throating him with a sweet hunger. Now, that? That was fucking amazing. His fingers found Rig's cheeks, caressing and stroking as moans were drawn from him. So hungry and so needy and focused on him -- his cock, his taste.

Moans and groans came from him, his balls tightening. "Soon," he growled, letting Rig know.

Rig groaned, pulling harder, those pretty eyes looking up at him. He stroked his fingers gently across the top of Rig's cheek and then he was coming, roaring as his hips jerked. His Rabbit took it all in, drank him down, licking and sucking even as the orgasm faded.

He rested back against the couch, hands sliding over Rig's face, growling softly. It was good. Rig was good. Rig nuzzled into his touch, humming softly, happy.

"Feeling better?"

Rig nodded and crawled up into his lap. "Thank you for the light show, Blue Eyes. It's great."

He grunted and nodded. "You can take 'em down after Christmas."

Rig nodded. "It's a deal."

"Good. Now. Greasy hamburgers or round two next?"

Rock hated paperwork, but they were shipping out in four days and his will needed updating. He was planning on coming back, but he wasn't going to leave Rig high and dry if something happened.

It was done now and all he needed was to get it notarized and file a copy with the Corps. That way no one could accuse Rig of falsifying it later. Sarge had taught him that, taught him that a gay marine had to take care to make sure his worldly goods went exactly where he wanted them to. Of course it was a good lesson for any marine, but if a man had a wife, it was less urgent.

It was funny though, how a man changed. He'd had a will since he was twenty, but the prospect of it being needed felt more real now that he was over thirty than it had then. He wasn't old, but he wasn't a kid anymore.

He grunted.

He needed a fucking beer before he got morbid.

Rig wandered through with another load of laundry, ass covered in a pair of tissue-paper thin jeans, empty longneck dangling between two fingers.

A beer or a good long fuck.

He reached out a hand and grabbed hold of Rig's arm. "Slow up a minute, Cowboy."

"Hmm?" Warm grey eyes met his. "You needin' something, Blue Eyes?"

"Yeah, I am." He took the basket from Rig's arms and put it on the floor, tugging his Rabbit in between his legs.

One white-blond eyebrow went up, a happy little sound echoing in Rig's chest. "Mmm... Hey."

He wrapped one arm around Rig's waist and the other around Rig's neck, tugging that smiling mouth down for a kiss."

Rig gave it up without a fight, diving right into his mouth like a starving man. Oh yeah, there was nothing like his Rabbit to make a man feel like a stud. He let Rig into his mouth, sucking on the eager tongue as his fingers pushed up under Rig's t-shirt and drew circles on Rig's skin. Rig's hands were holding his head, muscles rippling and dancing, moans pushing into his lips.

It was fucking sweet.

He stood, bending Rig back over the desk. Now this was a legacy he wanted to leave. One leg curled over his hip, Rig bending nice and easy. He broke the kiss in favor of licking along Rig's jaw and down to that sensitive neck. He knew just the spot he was looking for.

"Oh!" Rig jerked, head falling back. Sweet slut.

He rubbed their pricks together and pushed Rig's t-shirt right up and over his head, moving in on those sweet little titties once it was off.

"Fuck..." Rig's hands grabbed his shoulders, holding on, rubbing against him. So fucking responsive.

His hands slid down to tease Rig's abdomen, the long body stretched, skin warm and smooth under his fingertips. Rig's belly jumped and rippled for him, those long thighs parting. Oh yeah, that was his slut.

His mouth followed his fingers and he licked at Rig's navel as he undid the top button on the sinfully tight jeans. They were worn enough he could have just ripped them off Rig's body, but damned if the man didn't have objections to him doing things like that. And besides, this way he got to see them, cupping the heavy cock, that sweet tight cowboy butt.

He carefully pulled down Rig's zipper and grinned against Rig's belly as that hot prick bumped against his chin.

"Oh, fuck..." Rig's voice was all about wanting. "Need you."

He rumbled happily, head turning to take the tip of Rig's prick into his mouth. Salty and rich, but somehow sweet, Rig never tasted bad, never made this hard for him. He slid his mouth down about halfway, sucking, tongue playing over the head as his hands tugged Rig's jeans further down. He cupped those sweet balls as soon as they were freed.

So fucking soft, hot in the palm of his hand. "Rock..."

He rumbled around Rig's prick and then let it slide from his mouth. Grinning up at Rig, he slid his cheek along the silky hardness. "You want me to stop?"

"Hmmm?" Rig's head rolled, cock rubbing his face.

He chuckled, face turning so he could mouth the hot prick. He pulled Rig's jeans right off, spreading those legs and nosing Rig's balls.

Rig spread wide, the moan low and sweet as fuck. "Making me hotter than a two-dollar pistol."

He chuckled. "That's a good thing, right?" Before Rig answered, he slid his hands under that fine ass, thumbs spreading Rig open.

Rig's answer was a hissed 'yes', one of Rig's legs propping up on the desk chair. He nudged Rig's balls out of the way and licked at the small hole, tongue pushing in between his thumbs. Rig rippled, hips tilting, a sharp cry echoing. A steel cup full of pens and pencils hit the floor with a clatter.

He ignored it, driving his tongue into Rig over and over again. Rig rode him, low noises sounding over and over, hips bucking. He opened Rig up, slicked that little hole with his saliva and then stood and tugged Rig until that ass hung over the edge of the table. Then just like that he was pushing in, Rig's body gripping his prick.

"Yes!" Rig's head fell back, throat working. "Fuck, yes."

"Yeah, Rabbit. Fucking A."

With a grunt, Rock started to work Rig's ass,

thrusting in hard and fast. Rig's legs wrapped around his waist, adding that lean strength to his. He wrapped his hands around Rig's hips, pulling him into each thrust. Yeah. He could do this all fucking day. Panting, nodding, Rig rode him, eyes fastened to his, making him feel like a fucking god.

He slid one hand around Rig's prick, tugging in counterpoint to his thrusts, keeping Rig on the edge. The low moans slid down his spine, Rig squeezing him, riding him. Yeah, fucking good. He shifted Rig just enough that his prick slid across that sweet little gland with every push in.

"Fuck! Blue! Right fucking there!" Rig's eyes rolled, a flush traveling along the thin body.

He knew it. He increased the pace of his thrusts, fucking Rig hard, riding him like a madman. That fine ass squeezed him, Rig's spunk shooting, splashing on that flat belly. He roared, pushing in one last time and coming hard. Rig panted, ass squeezing him with each breath.

He leaned over Rig to give his Rabbit a long, hard kiss and then pulled out and helped Rig up.

He put his arm around Rig. "Come on. We're getting a couple more long necks and then I'm going to stick something else to your ass again."

"Oooh. You have the best plans!" Rig pressed close, eyes laughing for him. "Then I can start reminding you of all the reasons you need to come home safe."

He growled, wrapping both arms around Rig and grabbing that sweet ass. "If this isn't reason enough I'm already dead where it counts."

"Amen, Jim." Rig kissed him good and hard. "Beer and then more fucking."

"Amen indeed."

He might not be a kid anymore, but he had a hell of a lot to come home for and that was exactly what he was going to do.

CHAPTER TWENTY FOUR

Rig polished the bumper of the truck until he could see his face in it. Then he started detailing the paint, every scratch lightly sanded and repaired before the entire body was washed and dried and waxed to a mirror polish. The interior was dusted, vacuumed, Armor-All-ed. The tires were washed, the carburetor removed and cleaned, the fluids checked.

It took hours of work, the unseasonable sun burning through what was left of his tan, leaving him blistered and lobstered. When he was done, that little blue truck shone, looked brand new. Fucking perfect. He stumbled inside to take his shower and cool off before he sat down and watched the news.

Watched to see when the owner of that spotless fucking truck could be coming home.

***

The rumor on base was that the unit that shipped out a couple weeks before Christmas was fixing to come home Thursday.

Thursday.

Monday, Rig washed Rock's truck, gave it a tune-up, changed the oil and then dropped it off Tuesday morning in the unit parking lot so Rock didn't have to call a cab. After work he grabbed a ride home and did his errands - bills and the beer store and the Home Depot for some wood - Grimmy'd outgrown another doghouse. Dropped a few of their uniforms at the cleaners.

Wednesday night he hit the pharmacy for the toothpaste Rock used and a new toothbrush, some KY, massage oil and some Tiger Balm, because six weeks playing with the sand fleas was hell on a man. Then to the grocery store for steaks and fixings for chocolate pie and black-eyed peas because damn it they'd not had their New Years dinner and corn meal and milk and real butter and bacon, 'cause Rock didn't like sausage and...

Thursday. Yeah.

The mission had been rough.

Really rough.

They'd taken hits.

They'd done what they had to do.

Then when they'd gotten back, there was the debriefing.

Fuck.

He was numb.

Running on autopilot.

Rock got home and toed off his boots, dumping his duffle somewhere near the washing machine.

Grimmy was out in the back, barking, which probably meant Rig was out there, too, but he headed straight for the shower. Sometimes you just had to wash it off before you could really be home. He set the water to fucking hot and got under the spray, palms flat on the cold tile as the water pounded on him.

Slick hands slid up his legs, over his ass, cleaning him.

He let his head drop without a sound, eyes closed as he spread his legs some more, giving Rig access to all of him. Rig didn't say a word, just touched him, fingers massaging deep, mouth pressing on his shoulder. He started growling, fingers curling, trying to dig into the tile. Another kiss brushed his shoulder, slick fingers trailing down his spine, around his waist, to wrap around his prick.

He roared as Rig started stroking him, shudders moving through him as the sensation slammed through him. Rig slid around him, that hot fucking mouth moving over his belly, sinking down over his cock, suction drawing his balls down.

"Fuck." He couldn't have stopped his hips for all the world, couldn't have stopped the fucking sobs that ripped out of his chest.

His Rabbit took him deep, hands pulling him in and holding him, letting him take what he needed. He pumped hard and fast, letting it all out. Those long fingers spread over his belly, throat squeezing his cock.

He roared again, coming hard.

Rig stood before the aftershocks faded, hands washing again, sliding over his head and holding him. He wrapped his arms around his Rabbit, bringing their foreheads together and just breathed. Just fucking breathed. Those grey eyes watched him, sure and still and not asking for a goddamned thing, not needing anything but this.

Fuck, he could hardly believe he was home, but those grey eyes, they made him believe it.

Rig tilted his face, lips slowly pressing together, kiss deepening until he couldn't remember how to breathe. He leaned back against the wall, letting the kiss swallow him up. Rig's fingers stroked his temples, his jaw, that tongue fucking his lips. He purred, one hand sliding down Rig's spine, finding that sweet ass and cupping it. Rig cuddled right in, rubbing against him, smiling into their kiss.

"You needing some, Rabbit?"

"Every fucking minute of every fucking day, Blue Eyes."

He growled softly, Rig bringing him down like nothing else ever had, ever could.

"Come to bed. Clean sheets. Hot oil. Your cock. My ass. A great meeting of the minds."

He chuckled. "It's not your mind I want to meet."

That warm cowboy laugh tickled his skin. "No? What all are you lookin' to meet?"

"Oh, I have been gone too long."

"Yeah. Too fucking long." Rig kissed him again, rubbing against his belly.

He bent Rig back, leaning down to turn off the water, refusing to break the kiss. Rig groaned, fucking melting for him, cock hard and hot against him. He pulled one of Rig's legs up over his hip and then grabbed that sweet ass.

"Blue..." Rig's hands were hard on his head, those eyes dark, hungry.

"Come on, Rabbit. Lets go fuck."

He hoisted Rig by his ass and headed for the bedroom, not giving a shit if they were dripping.

"Hell, yes, Blue. Welcome the fuck home."

Yeah. Home.

The autopilot was off. The Rocketman was home.

Rig was puttering through their CDs, alphabetizing them or something, muttering about the unseasonably cold winter. Or was that unreasonably cold winter? At any rate, the man was clearly not impressed with the snow that was falling and trying to stick.

Rock didn't mind it so much. It was Saturday and they had nowhere to be, the white stuff would be gone by Monday.

Still, maybe it was the right time.

He pulled the ring box out of his pocket and set it on the coffee table before settling down on the couch, beer in one hand, remote in the other.

It didn't take long for his curious-as-a-damned-cat redneck to scoot over so Rig was organizing with those bony shoulders leaning against his legs. "What's in the box, Blue?"

"I got you something," Rock answered, voice low.

"Yeah?" Rig dropped a kiss on his knee and then reached out and picked up the box. "You gonna let me open it now?"

"That's why it's there, isn't it?"

Rig nodded. "It's just a weird thing, yeah? Somebody gives you something and it feels weird to just open it, but it's weird to ask, too." Those long fingers lifted the lid and Rig's words dried up.

He nudged Rig with his knee. "I can take it back if you don't like it."

He couldn't actually. He'd had it custom made, but if he told Rig that it would be a big deal and it wasn't. It was just a ring. It didn't mean anything. Nothing more than a thank you for coming and for staying when you hate the weather here and there's nothing but asshole marines and groundpounders for company.

It was just a ring.

"The fuck you will! I'll kick your ass first. You gave

it to me." The ring was pulled out and closely inspected and then slid onto Rig's finger just like it belonged there. "It's fucking perfect."

Grey eyes that were glowing met his and then his arms were full of redneck, a kiss making his head spin. "Thanks, Blue."

"I thought you might like it," he growled, arms sliding around Rig to grab that fine ass.

"I do." Rig straddled his waist, taking another kiss and another, making sure they didn't have to worry about stupid shit like talking or thinking or anything that wasn't fucking.

Which suited him just fine. He pulled Rig close and then shifted them, lying Rig on the couch and following him down. Rig wrapped around him, those eyes focused and bright and fuck, it felt good to be looked at like that -- made him feel like the center of the goddamned universe. He slid his hand under two fucking sweaters and a t-shirt before he found skin, fingers teasing the muscles of Rig's belly as he took short, sucking kisses.

Rig chuckled, sound tickling his lips even as it turned into a moan. "How do you stay so fucking warm?"

He shrugged. "I just do."

"Feels fabulous. Think I'll keep you."

He chuckled. "And I'm going to keep your skinny ass, even if you are cold all the time."

He closed his mouth over Rig's, hips grinding Rig into the couch.

Rig's hands slid into his sweats, cupping his ass, pulling him in closer. Rig was hard, cock pushing up against his, making him groan into those open lips.

Cold or not, they were both wearing too many fucking clothes.

Growling, he broke the kiss long enough to push Rig's layers off over his head.

"Pushy bastard." The insult was offered with a wild grin, Rig tugging at his own sweatshirt, mouth fastening over one of his nipples and pulling hard.

"Slut," he shot back with a groan as he got the sweatshirt over his head. Fuck he was hard.

"Yours." His nipple was given a sharp bite, then Rig started wriggling downward. "Want you to fuck my mouth, Blue."

He growled, tugging his sweats down. Fuck yeah, he could do that. "Anything you want, Rig."

"Want that sweet fucking cock. Want *you*." The words ended as Rig's lips covered his cock, sliding down his shaft.

Any answer he might have given was lost in his moan. Fuck, Rig had a talented mouth. A fucking treasure. Slow and steady, Rig took him in deep, swallowing around the tip of his prick before leaning back and fucking the slit with his tongue. Fucking hell! He growled and held himself still for a count of ten before he started fucking that hot mouth.

So fucking good.

Rig's hands were wrapped around his hips, taking him in deep. Oh, fuck... he could feel himself sliding into that tight throat, Rig so fucking *hungry*. He started slowly, pushing with long, even strokes into Rig's mouth. A man couldn't be expected not to go fucking nuts with his prick in that mouth though and he was soon fucking deep and hard, speeding to his finish.

Rig hummed, the suction enough for him to feel it in his balls, Rig's fingers sliding down to tease his hole.

"Fuck!" He shouted out, thrusting deep as he came, shooting down Rig's throat.

Those lips stayed wrapped around him, pulling soft and easy, cleaning his prick and finding each and every aftershock. He reached down, petting Rig's head, his face, murmuring as a last shudder moved through his body. Slowly, Rig worked his way up, stopping now and again to kiss and bite.

When they were face to face again, he let himself drop onto the thin body, pressing a deep kiss into Rig's mouth. He could taste himself there, along with Rig. Rig wrapped around him, arms and legs twining as his Rabbit snuggled close, grey eyes happy.

He pushed his hand into Rig's jeans, teasing the head of the hard cock he found there, middle finger pushing against the slit.

"Mmm... Blue. Yeah. Fuck." Each little cry came with a thrust of those hips and a kiss.

He undid the top button and then the zipper, moving slowly, thumb teasing the tip of that sweet cock.

Rig's face was buried in his neck, entire body moving with each motion of his thumb. "Oh... Oh, Christ. Blue..."

He growled low in the back of his throat and inched the zipper down the rest of the way, wrapping his hand around the hot prick. Rig's hands grabbed his ass, hips humping up into his hand, Rig giving him everything, not holding a bit of need back. He pressed their mouths together, taking a long, deep kiss as he jacked Rig off.

Those grey eyes were wide, completely focused on him, on his touch, on what he was making that long body feel. He kept on pumping, every now and then stroking his thumb across the tip of Rig's cock, spreading the leaking liquid, making his strokes smoother. Rig keened, the motions of that long body growing jerky and rough, lips parted and tongue sliding over the edge of those white teeth. Rig's breath was hot, still rich with his own spunk.

He touched Rig's tongue with his own, hand tightening around hot flesh. That touch did it, Rig coming hard, wet heat pouring over his hand. He growled happily as the deep scent of Rig's pleasure filled the air. Rig's response was a soft hum as the long body relaxed, eased into the sofa.

He pressed against Rig, taking a soft, deep kiss. Rig's hands were stroking his lower back, his ass. Every so often he could feel the metal of the ring, made warm by their body heat.

It felt good. Right.

Not a big deal at all.

CHAPTER TWENTY FIVE

They'd been in the house a good while, not a year, but they were all settled in and squared away when Rig realized it was fixin' to be Valentine's Day.

Of course, he wasn't doing the roses and chocolate thing, 'cause that was stupid. And he wasn't buying a card, 'cause Rock would bitch. There was no fucking way he was cooking up a big dinner, because he was busy as hell and because Rock would tease and end up wanting hamburgers later anyway.

Still... it had been two whole years since they'd met and he wanted to do *something*.

Fortunately Reed was selling his old pool table and was willing to help him haul it downstairs while Rock was in the field. Then with a little money and a little luck, he'd hung a bar light over the table, hung a holder for the cues, put a little stereo and a tiny little bar in.

Then, the night of Valentine's day, after a pizza and a couple of beers, Rig put on a loose pair of scrubs and went down without a word, waiting for Rock to get curious and follow him.

It didn't take long before the stairs creaked. "Rig? What're you up to?"

He dropped the seven ball and walked around the table, eyeing the six. "Chilling out. Having a beer. There's one down here for you." Come on Blue. Come see and play.

"Beer in the basement." Rock chuckled and came down the rest of the way. "Fuck, Rig. When did the basement turn into a pool hall?"

There was admiration in Blue's voice.

"I woke up one morning and it was like this, Blue Eyes." He motioned over to the bar, grinning wide as anything. Oh, yeah. He did good. "Beer's in the little fridge behind there."

Rock chuckled and one of those large hands slid over his ass as Blue went by him to the fridge.

The six went in after a few tries, Rig distracted by the sight of his Blue, body tingling. It had that first night, too.

Rock leaned against the wall, eyes bright as they watched him, slowly drinking his beer. "You're a little off your game there tonight, Cowboy."

"Yeah?" He let his eyes trail along Rock, slow and hungry. "Distracted by some mighty fine scenery, Marine."

Rock nodded, winking. "Yep, it's a pretty nice little set-up."

He let his grin widen. "Ain't nothing little 'bout you, Rocketman."

"Oh you meant me." He got another wink and Rock put his beer down, stepping away from the wall, eyeing him.

"I did." He set the cue down, remembering these dance steps just fine, thank you. "You look like you could handle a cue just fine, even if you are a Yankee."

"I do know my way around one, thank you." Rock took another step toward him. "I'm thinking you're after a demonstration."

"I think I can handle you... that just fine, thanks." He finished his beer, lips wrapping around the bottle as he drained it dry.

Rock rumbled, fingers stroking his cheek. "Fucking love that mouth, Rigger."

He put the bottle down, turned his head and took those wide fingers in, sucking slow and easy. Making promises he intended to keep. Those blue eyes dropped to half-mast, the low rumble getting louder.

He moaned, took a step closer. Oh, fuck, there was nothing like Rock when the man wanted. Made him fucking ache, made him need. Brought him halfway across the country into this God-forsaken state where you couldn't get decent chicken-fried steak or iced tea.

Rock pulled his hand away, fingers leaving his mouth with a wet pop. They were replaced by Blue's tongue, the kiss hard, deep. Rig's mind shorted out, pushing up hard against Rock's strength, arms wrapping around the thick neck as his mouth was fucking *taken*. Rock's hands slid around him, slow and easy, at odds with the kiss, before wrapping around his ass and pulling him even closer.

He started pulling at Rock's t-shirt, humming into the kiss as his hands met skin. "Sexy motherfucker."

Rock chuckled, nipping at his lips. "You're not so bad yourself."

Then he was being kissed again, Rock walking him back until his ass hit the pool table. Pushing forward, Rig rubbed into the cradle of Rock's hips, fingers finding the hard little nipples and teasing. Growling now, Rock bent him back over the table. Rig went easily, one leg curling up around Rock's hip, holding tight. One hand slid up under his top, thick fingers finding one of his nipples, sliding across it, tugging, pulling.

Electricity shot right up his spine and he jerked, crying out into Rock's mouth. Oh, shit. Sweet. Fucking *sweet*.

A pleased rumbled filled his mouth and Rock's other hand slid up along his other side, fingers working the same magic on his other nipple. His hips were pushing hard now, steady as his rubbed his cock against that heat. He wasn't fucking going to last, not like this, not with Rock sending him to the fucking moon. Rock gave him no quarter, tongue fucking his mouth, fingers playing his titties like a violin, hips pushing that fucking hard as diamonds denim wrapped cock against him.

Oh, sweet Jesus, this is why he left Texas. There was nothing else like this man in the entire world. Rig cried out, eyes catching on pure blue as he shot, coming hard enough that his spine fucking melted.

The kiss gentled just a bit, the hands on his chest stroking down to slide over his belly and then Rock pulled him up. "Pool table works."

"Yeah. Made sure of it." He sucked at Rock's bottom lip, humming and melted.

Rock chuckled, the sound husky and sexy as fuck. "I suppose you think I didn't get you anything."

"Didn't really worry on it, Blue. I got what I need." He'd known Rock had been working that fine ass off in the field and wasn't even sure that Rock would remember the date they'd met. After all, he'd been the one who followed, who needed.

Rock grunted, looking pleased. Still, he stepped back and reached into his shirt pocket, pulling out a folded envelope.

"Open it."

He arched an eyebrow and grinned, letting go of Rock long enough to tear it open. There was a single piece of paper inside, official looking, signed and notarized. Bold letters across the top declared it to be Jim South's last will and testament.

"Blue?" He pulled it out, unfolded the paper. A will?

"You make sure your name's spelled right there and then tuck it away somewhere safe. There's a copy on file at the lawyers and with the Corps. Had it done just before I shipped out."

He swallowed hard, then nodded, meeting those blue-blue eyes. "It's all right."

Folding the paper carefully, he put in back into the envelope and set it beside him. Yeah, it was all right. He reached up for Rock, holding their gaze, brought their lips together without another word. Those big hands were back on his ass, pulling him in close, Rock's body hard and hot.

Rig worked at getting to skin, tugging at buttons and fabric and zippers. He was done playing, now he wanted to touch his man. Rock started working just as hard at getting his clothes off, using the scrubs to wipe away the come on him.

"Bent over the pool table or on the floor?"

"Over the table, the floor's fucking *cold*, Blue."

Rock chuckled, blue eyes twinkling. He was kissed again and then turned, bent over the table with his legs spread. The finger that slid into him was slick, thick and warm.

Rig hummed, arching his back and tilting his hips. "Mmm... is good. More."

Rock was chuckling again, pushing a second finger

in along with the first.

Skin warmed his back as Rock leaned over him, lips soft against his neck. "You really are a slut, aren't you?" whispered against his ear.

"Yep, through and through." He rubbed against all that skin, letting Rock know how good it was, how hot he was. "Good thing I'm yours."

"Good thing," Rock agreed, fingers disappearing, that fat, hot prick pushing against his hole.

"Oh... Yeah." He pushed back, feeling his body stretch, focusing on the sensations sliding over his fucking skin. He was made for this, made for fucking.

Rock started to fuck him with long, slow strokes that he could feel up along his spine and all the way down to his toes. He rocked into each thrust, groaning and humming, fingers twining with Rock's against the felt of the table. His eyes were closed, toes curled, cock stiff and hard sliding against cool, smooth wood.

Rock fucked him long and hard; he knew Blue could keep this up until he was screaming, but Rock always seemed to know just exactly when the pleasure became too much. One of those big hands wrapped around his cock, pulling in time with Rock's thrusts.

"Oh, fuck! Rock! Yes!" Just what he needed, always just what he fucking needed. He clenched around Rock's prick, wanting to bring Blue with him.

Rock roared, pushing hard into him as heat shot up his ass. He groaned as he came, cock sliding against the rough heat of Rock's palm.

They stayed that way for awhile, Rock's breath slowing, that wide chest rising up and down against his back. Then Rock kissed his neck before slipping out of his body and pulling him up against that solid chest. He turned, wrapped his arms around his Blue and held on tight.

Rock's lips found his, the kiss soft and endless. He didn't let go, just keep tasting and touching. He'd followed Rock here and not regretted it once -- he reckoned he'd found himself a home in those arms.

End.

Don't Ask, Don't Tell

Don't Ask, Don't Tell

Made in the USA
Lexington, KY
23 July 2010